THE GOLDEN CITY

Catherine Nicolson was born on the Equator on the hottest day of the year. Her father was a Skyeman who grew up with Gaelic, her mother one of the team at Bletchley Park who worked on breaking the Enigma codes during the Second World War. Inspired by this example, Catherine Nicolson learned to read before she could speak. She grew up between Bristol, Manchester, the Fen Country and the White Man's Grave, going on to study French and Latin at Oxford University, where she gained a First. Before becoming a full-time writer she worked in publishing, audio recording, photojournalism and interior design. *The Golden City* is her fourth novel, following *Miss Nobody, Chase the Moon,* and *Silk.*

Catherine Nicolson lives in London with her artist husband, their two sons and a breeding colony of musical instruments. She follows the Hay diet and writes in a cupboard.

CATHERINE NICOLSON

THE GOLDEN CITY

VISTA

A Vista paperback
First published in Great Britain by Victor Gollancz in 1998
This paperback edition published in 1999 by Vista,
an imprint of Orion Books Ltd,
Wellington House, 125 Strand, London WC2R 0BB

Copyright © Catherine Nicolson 1998

The right of Catherine Nicolson to be identified as author
of this work has been asserted by her in accordance with
the Copyright, Designs and Patents Act, 1988.

All rights reserved. No part of this publication may be
reproduced, stored in a retrieval system, or transmitted
in any form or by any means, electronic, mechanical,
photocopying, recording or otherwise, without the
prior permission of the copyright owner.

A CIP catalogue record for this book is available
from the British Library.

ISBN 0 575 60386 0

Printed and bound in Great Britain by
Guernsey Press Co. Ltd, Guernsey, Channel Isles

For 2000

Contents

PART ONE

Vilis vilissimus, in via eiectus

1 *The Black Seed*

'Oi, miss! Not up there!'

Mary Mizen didn't wait to argue. Quick as an eel she dodged past the conductor and up the narrow steps. On the rainswept upper deck rows of male faces, each sandwiched between an identical dark hatbrim and wedge of beard, swung round in shock. Mary halted for a second, then the omnibus lurched into sudden motion and pitchforked her straight down the aisle between the boarded seats.

Luckily, because it faced against the weather, the seat right at the front was empty. Mary dived under its wet tarpaulin with a shiver of delight. Rain, slanting in almost level from the east, needled her face but she was too excited to feel it. As the icy drops hit her cheeks and slithered down her neck she half expected to hear them sizzle off like water from a flat-iron.

With eyes half-closed she could almost taste the rich brimstone smell of coaldust and dung and horse sweat that swam up from the dark street below. The clang of steel-studded wheels and hooves was deafening; it was like being in a smithy. Underneath it she seemed to hear a deeper, blurred roar, like rushing water, as if behind the cliff-faces of the buildings a flood was building up that might break through at any moment and tumble everyone away.

Not that the people in the street below seemed to care a green gooseberry pip about that possibility. They walked and talked and

11

laughed in their finery, while under their feet the gaslight conjured every rainy pavement into gold.

Mary tugged the wet tarpaulin up to her chin, enjoying its toady coldness as if it were the finest ermine. Into her mind came spinning, in a glittering jumble, all the treasures she had ever coveted. A magic lantern. A kaleidoscope. The painted monkey from the apothecary's window.

This place was all of those things and their master. The golden city. At the back of her mind, where the tin monkey still banged its gilt-fringed drum, she had always believed it existed somewhere. Now, swaying above the rain-black carriageway, she advanced towards it like a warrior queen in her chariot. Before her the gaslights trembled, the pavement shimmered in amazement, and all the world stood still.

'The devil!' A hansom cab halfway down Piccadilly halted with a jerk that left it quivering on its excellent springs.

'Very sorry, sir. Trouble in the road, sir.'

Quintin Lavery gestured the driver back with irritation. Leaning forward over the glossy wooden apron that enclosed his knees, he observed he had reached the junction with St James's. The road ahead, black with rain, gleamed like dowager's jet. Piccadilly was packed with vehicles, as befitted a rainy October evening in the richest quarter of the richest city in the world. Parliament was in session again after the summer recess; the Little Season of 1909 had just begun. Everyone who mattered had come streaming back from Scottish grousemoors and German spas into the single sooty crucible of Mayfair's square mile.

A scavenger boy, profiting from the sudden halt in the traffic, darted between Quintin's hansom and the old-fashioned victoria ahead to scoop up a steaming parcel of droppings. Beyond the boy, through a mist of rain, Quintin saw that an omnibus had come to grief across the corner. One horse had fallen in its traces and the others were fighting their harness.

Quintin frowned. The conductor of the omnibus should have known better than to permit his vehicle to be overloaded in these conditions. Whatever the weather, St James's was never sanded, and it had been known for a carelessly driven hansom to overturn completely.

Already a crowd had gathered, blocking the way even more. One by one, disconsolately, passengers began to leave the stranded omnibus. Out of habit, Quintin studied the ankles of the females as they stepped off the lower platform. His attention was caught by one young woman in particular. She came down from the top deck, which in itself was unusual. No respectable female would choose to display her lower limbs to the eyes of strange men by mounting or descending a staircase in public view.

Yet this young woman swung down the narrow stairs with aplomb. Then, instead of hurrying away as fast as she could to find another omnibus, she joined the bystanders round the stricken horse. The sight of the beast upended, with its animal parts exposed, did not appear to discompose her.

Intrigued, Quintin studied the girl more closely. She wore no coat and, at a time and a season when no woman would have dreamed of appearing in public without a hat, she was bare-headed.

The girl stepped forward. The crowd, sensing drama, fell back a pace. The girl pulled the back hem of her skirt between her calves and tucked it into the waistband of her skirt. A ripple of shock ran round the onlookers. Used as they were to the activities of single women in St James's, such boldness was unheard of.

The girl ignored the sensation she had caused. Quintin observed smooth naked skin above her heavy ankle-boots and his eyebrows rose. Even the poorest Whitechapel streetwoman prided herself on the possession of at least three petticoats, but this girl appeared to wear no undergarments at all, not even stockings.

The girl paused for a moment looking down at the horse. The animal lay silent, its eyes rolling. Its team-mates jostled uneasily in their harness. Quintin recognized the situation as one of considerable danger. At any moment one or other of the standing horses could lash out at random, injuring anyone within reach.

Suddenly, with a movement almost too quick to see, the girl reached down and seized the fallen horse's bound tail with both hands. For a giddying moment her heavy boots slid on the greasy cobbles, then all the strength of her braced body snapped into a single, efficient, double-handed wrench.

Cartilage cracked like a pistol-shot, and then, with a high-pitched protest of pain and outrage and a clattering, skidding convulsion, the horse heaved to its feet. It stood, legs splayed and quivering, clearly amazed to find itself once more upright. Its team-mates teetered and bridled at the shock, shaking their heads reproachfully over the tangled harness.

The girl stepped back, as meek as a book returned to its place on the library shelf. Her face showed no change of expression. She loosed her bunched-up skirt, turned on her heel and strode back into the crowd. From the swing of her body Quintin could tell she was uncorseted.

Stockingless, uncorseted, and alone.

Quintin struck the partition with the flat of his hand and swung down from the hansom. A nod was enough to make sure the man would follow him; a cabbie would go through hellfire for an unpaid fare.

And there was no time to lose. A girl of that type would not last long in London.

Quintin kept his eyes pinned to the girl's wiry black head all the way down Piccadilly. She travelled quicker than a cock pheasant in his second season. At Piccadilly Circus she turned sharply north. A few paces into Regent Street she stopped dead, her attention caught by a brilliantly lit shop window. As she stared, stock-still, the gaslight outlining the edge of her face with an orange glow, she seemed for a moment lime-lit, like a pantomime devil.

Hers was a sharp profile, with a pointed jaw and knife-blade of a nose. Her mouth was wide and muscular, a purposeful orifice quite unlike the currently fashionable rosebud. Quintin took in a stone-pale eye, set in black spikes of lashes, a thick, unplucked brow, a single blue vein snaking down her neck to disappear inside the unbleached linen shift she wore under her wool. He was somewhat disappointed. The girl was plainer than she had seemed from a distance. Still, she was young; fourteen, maybe fifteen.

And there was something impressive about the way she stood so still, completely ignoring the passers-by who jostled her. She seemed to quiver with energy like a cat about to pounce, her stare fierce and unwinking, as if she could somehow pierce the windowglass to what lay inside by pure will alone.

Quintin took a step closer. The girl seemed unaware of his presence. All her attention was fixed on the shop window. It was a milliner's, with a selection of the new season's hats displayed on wooden forms. One in particular seemed to fascinate his quarry. It was of rose-coloured velvet, its brim a cloud of ostrich plumes tinted a lighter shade of pink and anchored by a spray of deep violet orchids.

'That hat takes your fancy, I gather?'

The girl glanced up at him sidelong. The raindrops caught in her hair glowed like embers.

Quintin studied her carefully. Her face was expressionless, with a perfection of blankness that was almost royal. Nothing in her eyes, colourless as neat gin, showed that she had even heard what he said. She stared at him, appearing to assess him in her turn, her eyes moving slowly from his slightly lifted hat to his wing collar and the silk-faceted lapels of his coat. Finally she gave a single brief nod.

'In that case,' Quintin continued smoothly, 'I would consider it an honour if you would permit me to purchase it on your behalf.'

Now the girl's eyes widened in a look which Quintin had no difficulty interpreting. Quintin offered her his arm. She hesitated only a moment before placing her hand upon it. Her ungloved fingers were calloused. Quintin remembered that hand twisting

15

up a hundredweight of horseflesh unaided, and smiled to himself. Just so, in his turn, he had needed no more than a moment for mastery.

The devil's door. As Mary passed under the lintel into the shop, colour and light flamed up around her, taking her breath away. She'd never seen anything so beautiful. Even the air smelled sweet.

And it was so warm. She'd never been anywhere so completely, carelessly warm. She could feel the rain on her face prickling as it dried. Her fingers tightened on the man's arm. Such clothes he had. They looked as if no one had ever worn them before. Even his beard looked as if it were laundered every day.

'*Bonsoir, Mathilde.*'

The black-dressed woman behind the mahogany counter bobbed and rustled. 'Ah, *Monsieur* Lavery. What a great pleasure to serve *monsieur* once again.'

Mary shot a quick glance at the hat again. Desire for it hit her like a lead weight in the pit of her stomach.

The man spoke softly. Mary held her breath as the woman released the hat from the window and lifted it up to the light. The stuff it was made of rippled as if it were alive. The woman settled the hat on Mary's head, adjusted the angle, then skewered it firmly into her hair. The six-inch long hatpin, with its chestnut-sized cork protector, slid in as smoothly as a grocer's wire through butter.

Mary studied herself in the mirror. Under the wide brim her eyes were in shadow. She sat very still. She almost expected to hear some kind of voice, warning or welcome, but none came. She lifted one hand and rubbed a mudsplash off her cheek.

Yes. This was what she wanted.

Mary rose from her chair. Already she could feel the hat changing her. From under the shade of the brim the world looked different, smaller, far away.

As if it curtseyed.

'Enchanting, quite enchanting.'

Mary had forgotten the man. Now she studied him carefully. He seemed quite old to her, but it was hard to tell behind the beard. She'd never seen such a man before today. He seemed lifeless to her, like a huge doll, crimped and gloved. His eyes were very dark and deepset, but his skin was dull and white, as if he spent most of his time indoors or in the dark.

The man smiled at her. A small smile, carefully measured, like a dose of medicine. His mouth became no wider, but the beard moved around it.

At his signal the woman reached up to remove Mary's hat.

'No!' Mary ducked her head and stepped back smartly.

'But *madame!*' The woman was taken aback. 'I was merely going to pack it for you.'

'No.' Mary clamped both hands on the brim. 'I shall wear it.'

'Oh, *madame!*' The woman wrung her hands. 'But the rain – the hat will be ruined!'

Smoothly the man intervened. 'No need to distress yourself, Mathilde. I have a hansom waiting.'

He held out his arm to Mary once more.

Mary gazed from one face to the other. What about the hat? No price had been fixed, no money had changed hands. Which meant that who owned the hat hadn't been decided. As she took the man's arm Mary determined not to let it out of her sight, just in case.

Quintin hid a smile of satisfaction as he helped the girl up the high, swaying step of the waiting hansom. It was impossible, on a hansom's single narrow seat, for a man and a woman to sit side by side without impropriety.

His companion, however, seemed quite unmoved by the implications. All she appeared to care about, as she mounted into the two-wheeler, was her damned hat. In which, if the truth be told, she looked utterly ridiculous. To wear such a hat successfully required height, elegance – and above all, breeding.

'Mind my feathers.' The girl's tone was accusing as Quintin

leaned back against the padded seat. Her voice had a flat, grating accent which he now recognized as that of the Fen country, that windswept, marshy region in the east so isolated from the rest of civilized England that it produced little but waterfowl and village idiots.

Which might explain the blankness of the girl's stare, Quintin supposed. But neither accent nor stony gaze mattered when he could feel the warm resilience of her thigh pressed close to his, smell the scent of damp wool and young skin. The girl's matter-of-fact acceptance of her compromised situation, so unlike the usual mock protestations, invigorated him. He felt younger than he had done for months.

There remained, however, the slight problem of where to take his new acquisition. His usual haunts, the Cavour or the Savoy, were out of the question. He had no intention of being remarked by anyone who mattered in the company of a girl like this. Nor, tonight, did the thought of one of the tawdry rented rooms in nearby Soho appeal to him. The hat at least deserved something better.

Outside number 68 Regent Street the cabbie paused suggestively. Quintin considered a moment, then nodded. No one was a keener judge of social standing than a cabbie. The Café Royal, legendary haunt of penniless artists, drunken bohemians and fading cocottes, opened its doors to everyone and remembered no one. And it was impressive in its over-gilded, decadent way, to those who knew no better.

The girl stared about her open-mouthed as Quintin ushered her swiftly through the public rooms. The garishly lit Domino Room, with its tall pillars, vast mirrors and incongruous hatstands slung with dripping coats, was thick with tobacco smoke. Half-naked caryatids smiled vaguely down on scuffed marble tables and faded red velvet benches which, in better days, had seated Whistler and Oscar Wilde.

Such noise and glare were of course the essence of vulgarity.

Perhaps the Café Royal's clientele needed it to shock their jaded senses into some kind of life. One young man of the worst type, yellow-skinned as a Kaffir, was actually asleep in the midst of all the clatter and activity, half-propped against a pillar, his hand still clutching a glass of absinthe.

Quintin's lip curled a little. The Domino Room had always been a home for degenerates.

But fortunately the *cabinets particuliers*, special private rooms hidden away in the recesses of the Café, had been designed for a different clientele. In the eight years since his Coronation, King Edward VII had had to give up entertaining his mistresses in London. But the cafés, hotels and restaurants he had frequented as Prince of Wales were still full of these secluded meeting-places, Edward's legacy to the nightlife of the capital.

The private room that met Quintin's eyes was therefore a tiny diorama of royal taste: crimson draperies and panelled walls, velvet-covered couch, tiny gas stove and hothouse flowers placed in readiness on the white-covered table for two.

'Will madam be requiring the services of a maid?' the waiter inquired discreetly. The girl stared mutely back at him. Quintin intervened.

'That will not be necessary.' The man was a fool. It should have been obvious to the least skilled observer that in this case there were no stays to unlace.

Quintin ordered at once, choosing dishes that could be eaten quickly and easily digested. But his companion seemed far more interested in her surroundings than in his choice of food. Quintin watched in faint amusement as she ran her grubby fingertips along the panelled walls, prodded the red plush on the couch, investigated the tap which controlled the gas jets and the lit candle under the chafing dish.

As Quintin watched her eat, however, his amusement faded. The girl had no manners at all. She spat the custard shapes from the clear soup into her hand and left them on the cloth, poked the ham mousse for bones before scooping it up and swallowing it whole. He was relieved when the last *petit four* was crunched between those strong white teeth and he could summon the waiter to clear away the debris.

It was hot in the tiny room now. The smell of gas from both lights and stove combined with fumes from the champagne to thicken the air. Quintin had drunk very little, but the girl's face was flushed. Small beads of sweat stood out on her upper lip. Despite the heat, she still had not removed her hat.

Quintin rose from the table and crossed to the door as if to check that it was closed. While his back was turned he twisted the key silently in the lock and slipped it dextrously into his waistcoat pocket. He enjoyed such moments.

'Well, my dear.' He looked down at his quarry. She seemed almost pretty in the gaslight. Her gaze was a little unfocused, the pupils of her eyes dilated. Quintin noticed that one corner of her mouth was chapped. He could already taste its saltiness on his tongue.

He had waited long enough.

'Permit me to relieve you of your hat.'

The girl recoiled. 'It's mine!'

'But of course.' Quintin spoke lightly and pleasantly. 'Yours – but not yet paid for.' He reached up above the couch and pressed the button in the oak panelling which let down the concealed bed. It slid down noiselessly on its counterweighted hinges, releasing a faint smell of lavender mixed with camphor.

Quintin turned to observe the girl's reaction. It was not quite what he had expected. She seemed almost disappointed.

'Is there anything the matter?'

'Yes.' The girl gestured at the bed. 'I thought you was going to take me home.'

Quintin was shocked into a moment's silence. He had hardly furnished Ainsley House, the largest and most splendid of Park Lane's mansions, with a brand-new sprung maple dancing floor, hung his frescoed ceiling with the latest crystal gasoliers and installed a new staircase that cost more than an entire estate in Derbyshire, for a cheap little streetgirl to queen it up the marble steps to his bed. The idea was laughable.

And yet there was something about the girl's expression, the angle of her head, that stung him. He'd seen that look before, in ruffled drawing-rooms, in gilded ballrooms. Women were all the same, whether they wore wool or satin. Whatever a man offered, they would hold out for more, upping their demands at the slightest sign of indulgence. No price was ever enough, no bargain sacred. They were cheats and deceivers all.

The girl, as if she had read his thoughts, darted to the door. Quintin watched her rattle the handle uselessly. He placed one hand over his waistcoat pocket. The key was there, warm now with his body heat.

The girl's eyes flicked quickly round the tiny room. Quintin smiled. There was no other exit, not even a window. Once again he was master of himself and the situation.

Slowly, he advanced towards his quarry. Cornered, the girl flattened herself against the door as if she thought by making herself smaller she might become invisible. Quintin reached forward and gripped both her arms just below the shoulder. She stood quite still and silent, looking up at him with her colourless eyes. Her arms were thin. Quintin tightened his grip, letting her feel his strength. Her eyes watered, but she did not wince.

Using his full weight, Quintin leaned against her, trapping her body between himself and the door. He enjoyed the small involuntary noise she made as the breath left her lungs. He smelled champagne, sweat, fear. Triumph swelled at the pit of his stomach. Slowly, deliberately, he bent his head and fastened his mouth over hers.

The girl made a sound at last, small and high, quite different from her speaking voice, and twisted under him, kicking at his shins with her heavy boots. He pinned her legs effortlessly between his

21

knees, feeling the braced strength of her body with a swell of satisfaction. She was strong, but he was stronger. He moved his hand down to explore her body through the rough cloth. She was his now, trapped, absolutely in his power.

Even as Quintin savoured that thought he felt a white-hot pain lance through his left hand. He whipped round to see, placed dead centre through skin and sinew and still quivering with the force with which it had been planted, the six-inch-long steel hatpin.

Dazed, breathless, the sound of her own blood thundering in her ears, Mary was conscious only of the sudden release of pressure against her chest. She'd struck out at random, and now, unexpectedly released, she fell to the floor. She crouched there for a moment, her bruised ribs aching with the effort to take in air. Unable to move or think, she looked up to see the man close his right fist round the hatpin embedded in his hand and wrench with all his strength.

The pin refused to shift.

Stumbling, the breath rattling in her chest, Mary rose to her feet. She'd been lucky. Now she must get away. She had no idea what the punishment would be for pinning a gentleman to the doorjamb of his dining-room might be, but she didn't want to find out.

Out of the corner of his eye, through a red haze of pain, Quintin was vaguely aware of the girl slipping away. She held something in her hand.

The key. Quintin's pain intensified with the furious pounding of his pulse. While he struggled to remove the pin, she must have hooked the key out of his waistcoat pocket. Sweat poured down his forehead and seared his eyes. He braced his foot against the doorjamb, and heaved again. A blue ring of blood began to well up round the puncture in the back of his hand. Still the pin refused to move.

Behind him, Quintin heard the door of the *cabinet* swing open, letting in the hubbub of the restaurant outside. He was skewered instantly by a second realization. Not under any circumstances could Quintin Lavery permit himself to be discovered nailed to the doorjamb of a *cabinet particulier* in the Café Royal.

His choice was simple. There was no other alternative.

With a strangled curse Quintin hurled his whole weight backwards.

He heard the sickening sound of ripping flesh; blood spurted high in violation. Staggering, he snatched up a lace antimacassar from the couch and forced it into the open wound.

As pain ballooned to take in the universe, the girl's face seemed to hang before him like a carnival mask. Quintin fixed his mind and soul upon that image. It was the only one strong enough to penetrate the pain.

Slowly, with tiny, Herculean applications of pure will, he inserted his bundled hand into his frock coat. Pain throbbed inside it like a giant drum, making it seem enormous. But he would hide it, he must. Before he passed under the door into the purgatory of the crowded Domino Room Quintin scoured every vestige of expression from his face. No one must ever know what had happened here tonight.

No one would ever know. He would make sure of that.

'Wake up! It's time to go home.'

Leo blinked as a blaze of light met his eyes. For a moment he thought he was back in Morocco, sleeping on the roof of the baked earth house till the dawn sun woke him. Then, as his vision cleared, he became aware of a face only inches from his own. Two pale eyes, fierce and humourless as those of a bird of prey, stared into his own. Between them dangled a rose-pink ostrich feather.

Leo struggled to right himself. His neck felt stiff and cold from leaning against the marble pillar. He hadn't intended to fall asleep, but while he'd been away he'd learned to snatch sleep where he could.

'Hurry!' The owner of the eyes took hold of his arm and tugged it. 'There isn't much time!'

'Really?' Leo couldn't help but smile at her. She was such a strange-looking girl. Her nose particularly intrigued him. It looked as if half of it had been omitted by mistake. Perhaps the missing portion was wandering around attached to someone else's face, like that plaster maquette covered in half a dozen mouths that he'd seen last summer at the Salon des Indépendants. In fact, with her big boots and incongruous velvet hat, the girl could have stepped straight out of an opium dream.

'Come on!' The girl practically wrenched him to his feet, spilling his glass of absinthe in the process. Leo felt both flattered and mildly taken aback. He was used to women's interest, but this was something out of the ordinary. He felt a twinge of sympathy. The city was full of girls in her position, though they didn't usually demonstrate such urgency. But if she wanted money, she'd chosen the wrong man.

Leo began to explain her mistake, but the girl cut him short.

'Help me.' She didn't beg or whine. It was almost as if she were addressing him man to man. 'There's someone after me. I have to get away.'

Probably for good reason, Leo thought, but he didn't hold that against her. These were hard streets for a woman, even a pretty one – which she was not.

It was the girl's lack of physical appeal, finally, that decided him. Quickly he retrieved his precious parcel from beneath the table, tucked it under one arm and then, hoping with all his heart that this chivalrous gesture would not lead him into too much trouble, offered the girl the other.

Mary took a deep breath to steady herself. She'd never drunk champagne before; it had made her muddled. She could see now that the other man had been a mistake from the beginning. She didn't like to think of the expression in his eyes back there in the hot red room.

She took advantage of the bright café lights to study the young man beside her carefully before they entered the street outside. He'd been the first one she saw who was on his own. Him being asleep against the pillar had made him seem more approachable; a man just woken from sleep was easier to manage. When he'd uncoiled himself from behind the table she'd been taken aback by his size and height, but that too might turn out useful.

Now, however, she could tell that there was something strange about him. His clothes, for instance. All the other city men she'd seen today had been braced into stiff close-fitting coats and narrow trousers, with high wing collars and tall hats. Their hands had been gloved, their faces half covered by beards, as if to show an inch of bare flesh would be to risk death from cold.

This man, however, was clean-shaven, and his clothes were a mixture of colours and fabrics, all of them crumpled and loose, so they moved as he walked. He wore a strange shapeless hat like a bag, a faded green velveteen jacket and a soft-collared shirt barely held together at the throat by a green scarf. His face was brown, as if he'd worked in a field all summer, and yet his hands had no calluses. His eyes were the same golden brown as his skin and hair, in fact he was all over one colour, like an animal.

He was a mystery. He spoke slow, like a countryman, but clear, like a man of the cloth. He walked slow, like a man who worked land, but kept his head up, like one who owned it.

On the other side of Regent Street, under the bright lamps, the young man turned and smiled down at her.

'My name is Leo de Morgan. Remember it. One day it will be famous.' His tone wasn't boasting, just matter-of-fact. Mary said nothing. The distant future held no interest for her. Tonight and tomorrow morning were quite enough for her to deal with.

Now they'd left the brightly lit crescent of shops and arcades behind them. Ahead were much smaller, meaner houses, and a maze of dark, narrow lanes.

'That's a fine hat you have,' said Mr de Morgan. With a thrill of dismay Mary realized he must have been studying her with the same kind of attention. 'Is it new?'

Mary hesitated, sensing danger. Before she'd decided how best not to answer him a shout from behind them stopped her companion in his tracks.

'Wait!'

Mary froze to the spot. There was no need to look round. Every hair on the back of her neck recognized that voice, hoarse now, with an accusing edge which sent ice down her spine.

She heard steps, measured, precise as the ticking of a clock, then the raised voice again, with a bite like lye.

'Do you know whom you have there, sir?'

Mary ducked her head down, ready to run, but her companion turned, and she, anchored to his arm, was tugged round in his wake. Forced to face her pursuer, Mary's heart stopped dead. The glossy figure from the champagne-smudged dinner had vanished. Above the beard his face looked as if it had been bleached in a lime-pit. The skin over his cheeks was stretched and grey, his eyes blank holes. Hatred flickered out of him like St Elmo's fire.

'I say again, sir, do you know?' The man struck his cane hard on the cobbles, making each word a flung stone.

'I cannot say that I do, sir.' Mr de Morgan seemed unaware of any danger. 'Perhaps you would care to perform the introduction?'

There was a long pause. Mary saw the older man take in Mr de Morgan's appearance for the first time. Something he saw seemed to give him a strange sort of satisfaction.

'No, sir, I do not think I should care to do that.' The man drew himself up a little, as if stepping carefully across a gutter so as not to soil his spats. The effect, given the expression on his face, was terrifying. His voice rose. 'I might have suspected that no true

26

gentleman would choose to be seen walking in public with such a female.'

Mary felt the muscles in the arm on which her hand rested go suddenly stiff. She looked questioningly from one man to the other. They seemed to have taken a dislike to each other on sight. That was lucky. With them muscling up to each other like a couple of barnyard dogs, she might be able to slip away unnoticed.

'I see.' Now Mr de Morgan's voice held an edge. 'In that case, I presume you have no further interest in this lady.'

'That is none of your business, my good man.' The contempt in the older man's voice was plain as day this time. 'But you need have no fear.' He paused, a small wet smile curling the lips in his beard, and patted his coat. Metal jingled. 'I shall make it worth your while to – ah – terminate your acquaintance with this lady. I know how much you people appreciate the value of silver. I trust you understand me?'

Alarmed at the mention of money, Mary looked up at the young man beside her. His eyes were narrowed and a muscle jerked in his cheek, but he was still smiling. Remembering the shabbiness of his clothes, the ambition she'd heard in his voice, she realized at once that she was lost. Once money entered the balance, it changed everything. She let go of his arm, but even as she did so she felt his other hand clamp around her wrist. Twist and turn as she might, she couldn't break free.

'I understand you perfectly.' Mr de Morgan held Mary at arm's length, out of reach of her kicks, without even looking at her. He was as strong as a carthorse. Mary felt the nip of pure despair. One man she could outwit, but two? The injustice of it!

'But before we discuss terms,' Mr de Morgan continued mildly, 'I must know what it is exactly that she has taken from you.'

'Of course.' The other man gave a small bow. 'You understand the strength of your position and you wish to bargain. Very well. Ask her how she came by that hat.'

Silence smouldered. Mary felt two pairs of eyes fixed on her, the woman in the case, the prisoner in the dock. When it came to brass tacks and property, the two men, even though they'd disliked each other on sight, were on the same side. Whatever Mary said, whatever she did, they would pronounce judgement on it, and find her wanting, because this was their world and they made the rules.

Fear, exhaustion, and worst of all, the thought of losing the hat, finally split the shell of self-control Mary had kept round herself all day.

'I paid for it!' She flung back her head and hurled the words out like flints. 'And it wasn't worth it, neither!' Her voice echoed piercingly down the alley. Somewhere a window went up. Mary didn't care. She had nothing to lose, except the hat.

There was a moment's silence. Then, without warning, the older man rushed forward. Mary heard his heavy-topped cane whistle through the air above her head and dropped instinctively to her knees. The hat, no longer anchored by its pin, fell forward over her eyes, blinding her. She heard the cane crack like a whiplash onto the cobbles inches from her body and threw herself desperately to the side. Sprawled full length on the cobbles, her hair in her face, her legs trapped inside the heavy folds of her skirt, she sensed rather than saw the cane upraised once more, heard its highpitched flight through the air and instinctively pulled the hat hard down over her head, as if its padding of velvet and feathers could protect her.

A lifetime went by, then another, but nothing happened. It was as if time itself had stopped, suspended with the cane. Gradually, Mary became aware of scuffling sounds; heavy breathing, grunts, the creak of boot leather. Peering cautiously out from under the brim of the hat, she stared out, amazed, at two pairs of feet moving to and fro in a clumsy, aimless pattern, like farmworkers at a barndance. On the ground between them sat Mr de Morgan's green brocade parcel.

Suddenly, right in front of Mary's nose, the cane dropped, bouncing and twanging off the stones. Even before it stopped moving it was snatched up by a pair of hands. Mary peered anxiously into the dimness to see Mr de Morgan, his face distorted with anger, lift the cane over his upraised knee and snap it clean in half.

Mary gasped. Cautiously, she turned and saw the other man spread out like a piece of darkness. His hat had come off and she could see that his hair was shiny with oil. One of his coat-sleeves, torn from its moorings in the struggle, trailed linen like split bone. Somehow, on the ground, he seemed more terrible than before. Slowly he gathered himself together, like a thundercloud building. Mary watched him carefully.

'You say you have paid.' Mr Lavery's voice was so quiet now that it seemed to speak inside her head, a dead man's voice. 'But you have not. Not yet. Not enough.' He made a small movement towards her and she shrank back, automatically rubbing her bruised knees. The insides of his lips, drawn back over his teeth, glistened. 'But you will. Oh yes. You will pay For this.'

Slowly now, his eyes on her face, he took out from inside his coat a shapeless white bundle. As he held it out towards Mary the wrappings curled away to reveal his left hand.

Mary was shocked. Blood, black as ink in the half-dark, coursed from the ripped flesh of his palm. She couldn't understand how her small weapon could have caused so much damage. It was as if she'd made a tiny hole in a doll and now no one could stop the sawdust pouring out.

Sinew glinted white in the torn flesh inches from Mary's eyes and she turned her head away. In that moment, taking her completely unawares, the man lashed out with his injured hand and hit her full across the mouth. Knocked sideways as much in surprise as by the force of the blow, Mary tasted blood and couldn't be sure whether it was his or her own.

'Enough!' Mary heard Mr de Morgan take a threatening step forward. The other man halted. The sound of his breathing seemed to fill the narrow alley. His eyes were fixed unblinkingly on Mary. One-handed, with an eerie, clumsy determination, he bent and gathered up from the gutter the two halves of his broken cane. Muddy water dripped like blood down his white-gloved right hand.

'No,' he said calmly. He smiled then. It was a smile Mary had never seen on any human face. 'Not enough. Not yet.' He tipped the brim of his hat to her with dreadful politeness, and slowly, supporting himself with one hand against the wall, backed away, still fixing her with that terrible, staring, dog-like grin. Only twenty yards away did he finally turn away and begin to stride with swift, jerky movements in the direction of Regent Street.

As the sound of his footsteps died away silence closed down on the alley once more. Mary was aware of Mr de Morgan's eyes on her but she didn't bother to meet them. She'd lost her chance of a night's safe harbour for herself and the hat, that much was certain. She rose carefully to her feet. Her knees ached, but there were no bones broken. Her mouth felt hot and was already swelling. She touched her lower lip cautiously, feeling a stir of admiration. No one had managed to hit her in the face for years.

Luckily the hat too had survived. Even without its pin, it had stayed where it belonged, and now only the brim needed righting. But her skirt was soaked, cold and sticky with mud from its dip in the gutter. Now it tugged at her bare calves like a drowning sailor. Mary held the heavy fabric away from her, frowning. Flesh healed, but she had only the one skirt.

Still, there was no help for it. She let the muddy fabric drop and stamped her boots to shake off the wet. To stay dry shod, that was what counted.

'Any damage?' Taken up with her inventory, she'd almost forgotten Mr de Morgan. His green brocade parcel was once again safely tucked under his arm.

She shrugged. 'I can look after myself.'

'Yes, I believe you can.' Mary searched for disapproval in his tone but found none. Perhaps she still had a chance. She waited, neither explaining nor complaining. Silence often worked better than words.

The pause stretched. Then, abruptly, without looking behind to see if she were following, Mr de Morgan turned away.

'Come with me. I can dry you out at least.'

He turned down an alley on the right and stopped outside a rickety door set deep in the sooty brick. Here, where the houses leaned in overhead, the darkness was thick as lampblack. Mary didn't mind. She felt more alive at night, like any other small, sharp-toothed creature going about its business under the moon. Darkness balanced out the differences.

The door opened into a narrow hall, bare-boarded and smelling of boiled beef and onions. Mary realized suddenly how hungry she was. That food at the restaurant had been all bits and pieces, not a real meal at all. The potatoes had been hardly bigger than halfpennies, the bread just air and water.

Ahead, a coffin's breadth of corridor led to a dusty stair with treads that mewed underfoot. The steps were deeply bowed in the middle and barely wide enough for one person to go up at a time. Mary had to duck her head as she rounded the dogleg corner. She wondered why such a tall man had chosen to live in such a poky house.

At the top of the stairs there was another door, even smaller than the first, hardly more than a hatch. But it opened into what seemed to Mary like a huge cave. Against the far wall she could just make out three pale grey rectangles of windows, uncurtained, but there all resemblance to a room ended. Above, the roofspace had been hollowed out so that the rafters showed. High up, gaps between the slates showed small and spidery.

2   *A Secret Fire*

Inside the room the air smelled of cold, and dust, and silence, as if no one had ever lived there. But Mr de Morgan seemed quite at home. He strode to the back of the room. Phosphorus flared, and a single tongue of flame licked up, outlining the big belly of an iron woodstove. Now Mary saw that the whole end wall where the chimney-breast stood was bare of plaster, the boards under her feet unvarnished and floured with dust. The only piece of familiar furniture was a palliasse in one corner, with poking springs and escaping horsehair.

But the room wasn't empty by any means. It was full, with a ghostly, mysterious fullness, of things: strange shapes sulking in corners, propped against walls, hanging from the bare rafters. Mary couldn't tell what things they were or what purpose they served, but the room was alive with them, as if they were servants waiting silently for their master's orders.

Mr de Morgan disappeared beyond the shadows and Mary heard rustling. A few minutes later he came back holding a length of green brocade. Mary felt a moment's disappointment. She'd wanted to find out what was inside that package he'd carried so carefully all evening. And why, now, was he offering up to her the cloth he'd used to wrap it?

Mr de Morgan pointed at the stove, now glowing brightly. 'Your skirt.'

'Oh.'

Taken up with the room, Mary had forgotten her excuse for being there in the first place. Mr de Morgan fetched from the shadows a wooden screen covered with battered dragons. He unfolded it round her with swift, impersonal skill, as if this was something he'd done many times before.

When Mary came out from behind the screen with the heavy green brocade bundled round her waist she found that he'd dragged the palliasse in front of the fire. Her muddied skirt was hanging on some wooden contraption beside it, but Mr de Morgan himself was nowhere in sight. Mary sat down on the palliasse and spread the brocade carefully around her. It was fine stuff, silky and furry both at once, like the hat. She kept the hat on, to stop it drying out of shape, but shook her head from time to time, to fluff out the feathers.

Behind her as she sat, Mr de Morgan moved about in the half-darkness, as if he knew his way about blindfold. Yet to Mary's eyes there was nothing homelike about this place, nowhere to cook or store food, no cupboards or chests for clothes. It was as if the two of them were camping in the desert.

In the tents of ungodliness, Mary thought suddenly. Where the wicked flourish like the green bay tree.

At last, his mysterious chores completed, Mr de Morgan came and sat beside her on the palliasse.

'Is this where you live?'

'Sometimes.'

'Then where's your real home?'

He shrugged. 'More to the point, where is yours?'

Mary knew better than to answer that question. Mr de Morgan might appear different from other men, with his strange clothes and even stranger room, but there was no telling when the iron gate might come thumping down. A man's world had no place for unlabelled women.

She thought hard. Out of the corner of her eye she could see her skirt steaming away like a kettle on the boil. After it was dry she'd have no more excuse for staying.

In the light from the fire Mary studied her host sidelong. His face was a challenge. At first glance it had seemed open, even innocent, but now Mary could tell there was something hidden. He was young, only a few years older than herself, but there were deep lines scored from his mouth to his nose by thoughts that weren't young.

There was something else surprising about Mr de Morgan, Mary realized slowly. He wasn't vain in himself, she'd noticed that straight off from the state of his clothes, but now she could tell that he didn't mind being looked at either, at least not in the way most men minded. He didn't shift or frown under her eyes, or send her black looks to make her stop. He stayed quite still, staring calmly into the fire, aware of her, yet not troubled by her, as if for a woman to look at a man was the most natural thing in the world.

Suddenly, with a creak of horsehair and bedsprings, Mr de Morgan leaned back. Mary watched his wide chest rise and fall as he crossed his arms under his head and half closed his eyes. She was fascinated. Was he going to fall asleep again, as he had before in the noise and bustle of the Café Royal? She'd never seen a man give himself up so completely to bodily ease. Most men were guarded, afraid that if a woman saw too much she would steal the secret of their power. But this one seemed to be saying, with his body, that the secret he had would be given back to him a hundredfold when it was known.

Mary frowned. She wasn't sure what to do next. Mr de Morgan seemed too easy altogether. Where the grass grew greenest there was often a cunningly laid trap.

But with every passing second her skirt became a little drier, and the chance of a bed for the night tiptoed a little further away. She must act, no matter what.

Taking a deep breath, she reached forward her hand, and placed it carefully just below the line of Mr de Morgan's loose jacket.

34

Under her palm, through the soft cloth of his tweed trousering, she could feel the muscle of his leg, warm and hard and solid. That reassured her. There was no mystery about a leg, at least, it was simple human flesh and blood.

Mr de Morgan turned to look at her. His expression was neither encouraging nor disapproving, just curious.

Mary bit her lip. She took back her hand, feeling vexed. Anger would have been more of a compliment than nothing at all. With an inward sigh of regret, because both fire and palliasse had been very comfortable, she rose awkwardly in her green brocade and reached for her skirt on its wooden gibbet.

But before she could take hold of it Mr de Morgan reached out one long arm and whisked it out of range.

'It's not dry yet. Better wait till morning.'

Mary stared down at him, taken aback. He smiled at her.

'You mean I can stay?'

'If you want.'

Mary watched him carefully as he rose to his feet and stretched wide, making the seams of his jacket creak. Did he mean what he said, or was he just pretending, like the other man?

Mr de Morgan smiled at her again, a kind smile which deepened her puzzlement. He stood for a moment, staring at her. Then, from his great height, he reached leisurely down and took off her hat.

Mary started backwards. For a moment she thought he was going to take it away from her. 'What are you doing?'

He shrugged. 'You look better with it off.'

Mary felt a sharp jolt of anger. If he knew how much that hat had cost her! Then, looking from the hat to his face and back again, she saw the truth reflected in his eyes. Her anger deepened, narrowed down to a glowing point. Now she understood. The other man had lied to her from the beginning.

Mr de Morgan handed the hat back to her.

'Thank you.' Mary meant it. He hadn't lied to her. He'd paid her that compliment at least.

She stared down at the hat with dislike. Now it meant nothing. It had broken all its pretty promises. The whole contraption, with its mock flowers and dead bird's feathers, had been a cheat. She swivelled round abruptly and with a swift sure movement poked the hat into the open jaws of the wood stove. The flames gave a grateful hiss.

Mary watched the hat burn with satisfaction, the man forgotten. It was always best to put the past behind, move on.

She turned to find Mr de Morgan watching her. The expression on his face surprised her. His eyes were narrowed, his mouth set. He looked almost angry. Mary recognized that expression, the look of a man discommoded by his own desires. He wants me now, she thought, mystified, and wondered why. It must be because of the hat. She'd looked wrong in it, that was why he'd turned her down before.

The relief of understanding made Mary feel much better.

But one problem remained. She no longer needed him to want her.

'Goodnight.' Suddenly, Mr de Morgan turned and walked away. Wide-eyed, Mary watched as he pulled out a couple of half-filled hessian sacks, kicked off his boots, then dropped fully clothed into the makeshift bed. It was only when his breathing slowed that she could feel sure he wasn't coming back.

Hardly able to believe her good luck, Mary lay back carefully on the palliasse and tucked the green brocade folds tight around her body. Muscle by muscle she let herself relax against the ticking. Now, with Mr de Morgan asleep and the room so big, she felt almost as peaceful as if she was on her own.

As always, before allowing herself to fall sleep, she sifted through the happenings of the day. Already she'd learned a lot, though not all of it made sense. City men were strange, that much was certain. The first one, with his cold eyes and small red mouth like a cat's arse in his beard, had wanted her from the first minute he'd seen her. She understood that, and his anger when she escaped him. She'd felt the same way about the hat.

But this Mr de Morgan was different. He'd wanted her too, in the end. But he'd turned her down.

And yet, he'd let her stay all the same. Why? If she hadn't put her hand on him, he'd have turned her out for sure. But because he'd refused her, he'd allowed her to stay. It was a mystery.

Mary stored the observation away carefully in her mind. She didn't understand it, but it might come in useful one day.

It was cold as church under the brocade. She pulled the fabric closer round her mouth and chin, blocking out the acrid smell of burned feathers. She was glad the hat was gone; it had disappointed her.

The secret ingredient must lie elsewhere. She would find it. Whatever it might be, it could be bought or begged or stolen. And here, in the golden city, the paradise of earthly pleasures, was where it would be found.

Mayfair. Mary rolled the sound of it on her tongue, testing it, tasting it. In her mind's eye she could see the dark city streets radiating out from where she lay like a spider's web full of brilliants. She was here at last, one step further along the path, one step nearer the hot, smoky heart of what she wanted. And this was only the beginning.

Leo lay still, breathing deeply and steadily, but he couldn't sleep. Not a sound came from under the green mound of curtain on the other side of the room, but the girl's presence troubled him like a piece of grit in his sacking. He'd be glad when it was morning and he could send her away with a clear conscience.

The fire spat and Leo couldn't help smiling into the darkness. She'd looked extraordinary in that hat, like an organ-grinder's monkey. There was something about her, he had to admit, a sort of attraction, like a mongrel dog's, half impudence, half sharp white teeth. No, he had it. The little robber girl in the fairytale, the one with the tangled hair and the dagger. Brave and bad and loyal to the death.

He could still feel the heat of her hand on his thigh. A predictable move, easily resisted; but then, when she'd thrust her precious hat into the stove, without so much as a by your leave or a backward glance, he'd been stirred despite himself. He'd felt a sort of recognition, half pleasure, half pain, like catching sight of himself reflected in a mirror he hadn't known was there.

A moment's foolishness only, it meant nothing.

Leo sighed, stretched, and closed his eyes at last. Another girl's image, golden, invincible, swam up to greet him, as if she had been waiting. Somewhere in the city, enfolded by the same darkness as himself, she was sleeping. But he would find her, of that he was certain. All that separated them was time.

'I shall be ruined, Lucette, ruined!'

Lucette Bailey dimpled at him coquettishly. It was so amusing of dear Robert, on this her fortieth birthday, to bring her to the new Selfridge's to view the actual aeroplane in which gallant M. Blériot had just flown across the Channel.

'Death duties, Lucette! On top of land taxes! What can Lloyd George be thinking of?'

'Of the poor, I expect, dear.'

Lucette could not help thinking that a small pension of her own would not go amiss. Like Blériot, she'd come a long way on mere paper and string, but all she possessed as security for her future was a fine bosom, some minor jewellery and the unexpired portion of a lease.

'But what about Tom?' Robert went on, his face purpling. 'If Lloyd George has his way there won't be a Gifford's Oak left for him to inherit! The Oak's been in our family for eighteen generations – if Lloyd George gets his hands on it—'

'The King will stop him,' Lucette spoke with absolute authority.

Robert nodded. 'That's true.' His face cleared. Solemnly he raised his glass. 'To the King!'

'To the King,' Lucette echoed devoutly, toasting in memory a certain decisive encounter over the Poet Laureate's black-draped coffin in Westminster Abbey seventeen years ago. She owed everything to the Prince of Wales. Not directly, of course; as princes went, Edward had been shockingly poor. But other, wealthier men had been keen to follow a prince's choice. Without Edward, Lucette would never have become the occupant of 7 Derby Street, nor her mother the proprietor of her very own millinery shop in Regent Street.

As for Robert — Lucette had never been able to understand why it was that she had found attractive in him things she would have found unbearably irritating in anyone else — his worried spaniel's expression, his physical clumsiness, his pompous but always courageous insistence on what was right.

It was that last trait, of course, which had brought their two-year affair to an end. Robert had hated assignations, and coded letters, and anonymous roses. So one night, outside his club in St James's, with the doorman hawking and spitting ostentatiously behind them, he had asked Lucette to marry him.

Lucette had hesitated only an instant before saying no. If Robert divorced his wife he would destroy in one stroke his reputation, his career and his future. She couldn't bring herself to be poor for the rest of her life, not even with Robert.

'Will you, Lucette?' Lucette surfaced from memory to find Robert gazing at her intently. His eyes were only a little blurred with drink.

'Now, Robert.' Lucette smiled at him, her own eyes a little blurred too. He still had such charm for her, and probably always would. 'You know all that is over.'

Sadness struggled momentarily with relief in Robert's expression.

'Birdcage Walk?' Some spirit of devilment inspired Lucette to suggest it. The Walk had been the setting for their first assignation.

To this day she doubted if she would have managed to persuade Robert to kiss her if it had not been for the merciful shade of the over-arching trees.

Robert pulled out his hunter and made a great business of tapping and squinting, for all the world like a guilty husband racking his brains for an excuse to slope off and visit his mistress.

'It's S-S-Sibell, you see,' he managed finally. 'I promised to collect her from her Aunt's. She has been away at Brighton with her cousins. For almost a week,' he added on a note of surprise and what seemed to Lucette quite unwarranted paternal pride.

'I see.' Lucette allowed her voice to tremble just a little. She was unprepared for Robert's daughter to come between them. Clearly, there was more than one kind of younger woman. 'In that case, would you be so kind as to escort me home first? I am not so strong as I was, you know. Perhaps I am getting old.'

'You, Lucette?' Robert's voice cracked with astonishment. 'Never!'

Lucette stared into his eyes, the sort of grey that never changed or faded, reliable as chips of granite in the worn red brick of his face, and knew that he spoke the truth. She forgave him instantly for his refusal of Birdcage Walk. The leaves would have been turning anyway.

'Is this her house, then?'

'Yes.' Leo glanced up from his copy of *Nash's* magazine. Mary Mizen had trotted after him all day as gamely as a Shetland pony. Now, he was looking forward to the coming meeting. It would be a collision of continents.

'All of it?'

Leo nodded.

Mary felt dizzy, as if she were floating in the middle of a cloud. Around her was a haze of silky pastels, lilac, mauve, duck egg blue, tea rose fading into honeysuckle. There was nothing in the room that the eye could get hold of, not a straight line anywhere, just

40

fluff and vaguery. Even the walls, covered in mirrors, seemed to curve in on themselves like the inside of a shell.

Mary was mystified. She'd never seen a room less suited to masculine tastes. What man wouldn't be unsettled, straight off, by the sight of so many breakables, such a clutter of tiny china figures and glass bowls which, now she looked closer, seemed to hold little brown messes of part-rotted flower petals? Men needed space, somewhere to knock out a pipe, put their feet up, spit if they wanted. Nothing in this room seemed good for anything except the marble fireplace with its two fat bellpulls.

One for down, Mary thought, and one for up. Suddenly, as the firelight danced off velvet, glass, silk, ivory, mother-of-pearl, she was aware of her muddy boots and tangled hair, her rough clothes and the smell of her body inside them. For the first time in her life she felt at a loss. Perhaps that, in the end, was the purpose of the room?

Behind her, someone swept in on a tide of perfume and a rustle of skirts. Mary turned to see a woman who matched the room so exactly she might have stepped straight off the wallpaper. She was dressed from head to foot in mauve lace, with three silk roses fastened by a pale pink satin bow at her waist. She was only of medium height but she seemed much taller because of her hair, piled up soft and plump on top of her head like an unbaked loaf. The skin of her face too was soft and floury. In it her moist eyes and lips were beguiling as currants in a bun.

Mary drew in her breath and held it. Without a word said, the lady made sense of the room, filled it, brought it to life. Mary stared, drinking in every detail, from the seaweed trail of drapery at her feet to the rouged lobes of her tiny, close-set ears.

'Well, my dear Leo, who have we here?' Now, Lucette was glad that Robert had seen fit to bring her home disgracefully early from her birthday luncheon. She let her eyes brush Leo's for the merest split second. As she did so she was aware of the girl's scrutiny, but it did not trouble her. No fault could be found with her own appearance, and clearly this girl, whatever her connection with Leo, was no competition, no competition at all. She was shabbily dressed, completely uncoiffed and barely grown.

'Mary.' The girl spoke up for herself, in a rough little voice like a fledgeling bird. 'Mary Mizen.' Meeting her eyes for the first time, Lucette was confounded and a little touched. She had never seen such naked admiration in another woman's eyes. Few would have felt it, let alone been fool enough to reveal it.

'How kind of you to come and see me, my dear.' Lucette leaned forward, and with superb grace kissed Mary on each cheek, hoping that Leo would be surprised and impressed. 'Any friend of Leo's is always welcome in my house.'

Gracefully, giving Leo the full benefit of the semi-transparent gusset running from the nape of her neck to the base of her spine, she crossed to the fireplace and tugged the bellpull summoning Violette. As she swung round she was glad to see that Leo had stopped pretending to read his copy of *Nash's* magazine. She kept a good stock of society papers, but his sudden interest in the gossip columns did not deceive her for a minute.

'And what have you brought for me, my dear Leo, from your travels?' Leo smiled and lifted up a cloth-covered package propped against the sofa.

When she saw what was inside the green brocade wrapping, Lucette caught her breath. Absurdly, she found she had tears in her eyes. She had wanted Leo to make her look younger, of course – what else were portraits for? – but she had not expected him to read her inner wishes with such uncanny accuracy. It was truly her self, the essence of her, her soul and will, that smiled out of the painting. To capture that, Leo must have read more than her mind.

'My dear Leo, you are a genius!' Lucette turned to him, once more poised and serene. He must never know just how much he had pleased her. Too much gratitude made young men feel uncomfortable. But praise – ah, that was different.

'I know.' Leo captured her hands and bent to kiss them. The

brief contact flustered her once more. Fortunately, Violette entered almost immediately with the tea. Dear Violette. How clever it had been to engage a maid whose hair, though natural, was a far less becoming shade of red than her own.

'Thank you, Violette.' As the girl set down the loaded tray, Lucette saw that she looked flushed. There was a black smudge down her cheek, and several more on her apron.

'Why Violette, what on earth have you been doing to yourself?' Looking more closely, Lucette perceived that her sandy eyelashes were singed.

'Not me, madam.' Violette's lips tightened. 'The range. It's been out ever since Elsie left this morning. I was just trying to light it again, when the b—' She checked herself just in time. 'I'm sorry, madam – but one riddle, and a flame three foot high!' Her green eyes were indignant. 'I mean, it's not what you expect, is it?'

'Not dangerous, I hope?' Lucette was anxious. A basement fire was the worst kind. If it took hold it could lick through four storeys in minutes.

'Not any more, madam.' Violet shook her head. 'It's gone out again.' Her voice took on a meaning tone. 'I heated water for the tea on the breakfast-room fire.'

'Oh dear.' Lucette's heart sank. Usually she restricted the fire in the breakfast room to a couple of hours every morning. Kept going all day, it would cost a fortune.

'It's no good. Violette. I cannot wait for Elsie to return. For all I know her mother may be ill all winter. You must find another kitchen maid at once. Ask the butcher's boy. He always knows.'

'Yes, madam.' Violet's voice took on a doubtful tone. Lucette felt a pang of anxiety. Upstairs servants hated to deal with tradesmen. Between that, and the recalcitrant range, she might run the risk of losing Violette too.

'I could do it.'

Lucette swung round. In her preoccupation she had almost

forgotten her other guest. The girl was standing very still, her pale eyes bright.

'You could find a new kitchen maid?' Lucette took a step towards her. It was just possible, after all, that Miss Mizen might have a friend she could recommend. 'Do you think so?'

The girl shook her head. 'No.' Her expression was grave. 'But I could light the fire.'

'Could you?' Lucette clasped her hands in front of her. The girl simply nodded.

'What do you think, Violette?' Lucette turned back to her parlourmaid. Violet's face was a study in conflicting emotions. Clearly she felt trapped between two evils, the big black monster downstairs and this smaller one in her employer's drawing-room. But just as clearly, she had no choice in the matter.

'Follow me, miss.'

Leo waited until the two sets of footsteps had faded away down the stairs then turned abruptly to Lucette.

'You're not thinking of engaging her?'

It was almost as if he'd read her mind.

'Your friend Miss Mizen, do you mean?' Leo nodded.

'Do you think she might be willing?' Lucette tried hard to keep the hopeful note from her voice. It was so difficult to find belowstairs servants, particularly when the complement of staff in a household was not large, and the situation not entirely regular.

Leo hesitated a moment, then shrugged. 'Oh, she would be willing enough, I expect.'

Lucette felt a touch of irritation. It was all very well for Leo, living his Bohemian life, to rise above domestic considerations. He had no idea that a willing kitchen maid was a pearl beyond price; more valuable even to a woman in her position than his charming portrait.

'What about references?'

Leo shrugged. 'I doubt if she has any.'

Lucette hesitated. She knew it was risky to take on a new girl without references, but her need was extreme – and no one but Leo need ever know. It also occurred to her that a girl without references might be prepared to work for considerably smaller wages.

'Well, of course, she is young.' Now Lucette's mind moved busily, her irritation already forgotten. Whichever way she looked at it, the girl's arrival was providential. If she employed a protégée of Leo's, it would give him a good excuse for calling on her more often.

'I shall put it to her, I think, despite your reservations. It's unlike you, *chéri*, to be so cautious.' She smiled at him sweetly. It was unwise to let a silence drag on too long. A man might begin to notice things – lines at the corner of an eye, the slightest plumpness developing under the line of a jaw. 'I am so sorry about this – domestic intrusion.'

'I am not.' Leo's honey-brown eyes rested on her quizzically. Lucette found them hard to meet. The situation, to her eyes at least, was not entirely satisfactory. She and Leo were alone together, and yet not alone, because at any moment Violette and Miss Mizen might return. Lucette could hardly suggest that Leo and herself adjourn to the bedroom and leave Miss Mizen, her kitchen-maid-to-be but as yet her guest, to serve herself tea.

As always when she was a little flustered, Lucette dipped back for consolation into her room. She picked up a velvet case with two paste buckles in it, flipped back the lid, then snapped it back down again. The usual comfort she felt when touching one of her familiar treasures was not forthcoming. She felt oddly restless, her skin under the beige lace of her teagown prickling with awareness of Leo's presence.

He is too young for me, she thought. I knew it the first moment I saw him. He is a child, a baby. Young enough to be my son.

Out of the corner of her eye she studied Leo. He looked brown, and thin, and even a little older than his nineteen years. But his skin had the even burnish of perfect health, his movements the ease and vigour of youth. He will never catch up with me, she thought, no matter how far he travels or how long he stays away.

To her dismay, as she set down the velvet-covered box, Lucette realized she was filled with an inner trembling, a breathlessness, like a very young girl. She felt incensed. What was the point of being forty if one could not have a little presence of mind?

Abruptly, Lucette crossed to the chaise-longue, settled herself upon it and reached purposefully for the silver samovar, warming over its tiny spirit lamp. But even the familiar silver and fluted porcelain fought her touch today. She fumbled and clattered, nearly scalded her wrist on the hot water jug, and finally, unforgivably, dripped cream into the sugar bowl. Three silky yellow globules sat quivering on the spotless white surface, obstinately refusing to sink in and disappear.

'Zut!'

If that were not enough, as Lucette handed up a full cup of tea to Leo the saucer slipped in her hand and she looked down to see a spreading pale brown stain on her lace lap.

'Let me help.' Leo knelt before her with a white napkin, studying the stain with what seemed to Lucette quite unnecessary interest. He was near enough for her to hear and feel his breathing. She brushed uselessly at the lace with the back of her hand.

'*Ce n'est rien*. I shall change, later.' Lucette sensed rather than saw Leo's smile. He loved to watch her change her clothes. He had once told her that it was like watching a flight of swans settling on a lake. He also liked her spine, he had said, and the bone just at the base of her neck. He had a habit of brushing that bone with a kiss, then walking away.

Lucette shivered. Suddenly she was overwhelmingly conscious of the embrace of her stays inside her teagown. She could hardly catch her breath.

Leo's eyes met hers. There was no misinterpreting their expression. Lucette relaxed a little. Leo might be young, but he was still a man, with the same predictable needs and desires as any other.

She gathered herself to rise. Let Miss Mizen return to an empty drawing-room; what did it matter, after all? There were some moments when good manners had to give way to good sense.

'No.' Leo pushed her gently back down onto the chaise-longue.

As Leo's hands, big and brown on the delicate lace, closed over her knees and slid upwards possessively, Lucette felt a flare of purely social anxiety. Suddenly, between one moment and the next, she had ceased to be mistress of the situation. Under that warm, gentle, remorseless pressure, she felt her sense of herself waver and dissolve.

'Leo!' Lucette bit her lip as she realized she had forgotten another of her self-imposed resolutions, a lifetime's discipline in never calling any lover by his name. She swallowed hard as she caught his warm hands in her own. 'This is impossible, *chéri*. What about Miss Mizen?'

'I never heard of her.' Gently but remorselessly Leo disengaged her fingers, then applied his mouth gently just above her knee, blowing warm air through the lace to reach the tender skin beneath.

'But she might come back at any moment.' Lucette heard her own voice, hoarse and unconvincing, wholly at odds with the sense of her words. 'Whatever would she think?'

Leo laughed suddenly, deep in his throat. He buried his face in her lap, worrying the fabric of her gown and growling like a terrier. Lucette was instantly transfixed by the smell of his hair. Leo did not wear pomade. His mop of glossy brown hair smelled of nothing but himself, sweet and sinful and irresistible as hot biscuits. Lucette was torn between a longing to bury her face in it, and the equally pressing need to grab it with both hands and wrench his head away. Both courses of action were impossible. For the first, she was too old, for the second, not old enough.

Leo spoke into her lap, indistinct, a bumblebee murmur of words and moist air against her skin. 'How long does it take to light a fire?'

Not long, Lucette thought, helplessly. Warmth rose up through her body. Now, as Leo caressed her through the lace, she was swiftly becoming incapable of speech or thought. Despite herself, her eyes closed.

Now Leo's hands slipped under her skirt, sliding up through the layers of silken camisole before she could think to prevent them. She felt his fingers unknotting, releasing, shifting inside her lace like two small animals. Lucette's face flushed. She felt her breath coming in quick little gasps, and wished she had not instructed Violette to lace her in so tight. Trapped between her stays, Leo and the tea-table, she could hardly move.

Now Leo had found the vulnerable point between garter and corsetière. Lucette felt her breath flutter in her chest. His hands moved upwards under her gown. Her body rose towards him as if magnetized.

'None of your tricks, Lucette.' Leo's voice growled into her ear. She shivered to hear it.

'Let me, please. I know the way.'

Leo shook his head. His hands moved down, with a steady, relentless pressure.

Lucette gasped. For an eternity she remained stiff, agonizingly poised on a knife-point. And then, as he touched her again and again, sensation exploded inside her. Liquid fire raced to her fingers' ends, devouring every nerve.

It was at that exact moment that Lucette heard footsteps returning up the stairs. She pressed herself against Leo, as if somehow she could disappear out of sight beneath him, but it was too late. Cooler air rushed between their bodies as he withdrew.

There was just time before the door swung open for Lucette to tug her lace skirts back to ankle level. Flushed and dazed, she looked up to confront Miss Mizen's inscrutable grey gaze.

'The fire's lit.' The girl's eyes flicked from Lucette to Leo and back again. 'I thought you'd like to know.'

Lucette moistened her lips desperately. Her mind was a blank. With every nerve of her body she was aware of Leo, standing with his back against the blaze. The swelling at his groin had not subsided. It rebuked her, that swelling, a mute witness to her professional misconduct.

To make matters worse, she was also aware that her hair was coming down at the back.

'I am so glad, Miss Mizen.' Lucette cleared her throat. 'Sit down, my dear.' She swallowed. 'I have a suggestion I would like to put to you.'

'In that case . . .' Leo detached himself from the mantelpiece and picked up the discarded length of green brocade from the sofa where he had left it.

'Surely you are not leaving so soon?'

'I shall see myself out.' Leo bent to kiss her lightly on each cheek, his casual tone completely at variance with the appearance of his groin, directly level with her gaze.

'But you must not!' Lucette felt suddenly outraged. How could he leave, in his condition? It made no sense; why – she groped for a word to express the sense of shock she felt – it was disgraceful.

'Why not?' Leo smiled lazily down at her from his great height. 'I have given you what I came for.'

Lucette felt her cheeks go crimson. 'And what was that, may I ask?' she inquired with as much dignity as she could muster.

'Your portrait, of course.' His tone was utterly serious. 'Had you forgotten?'

'No.' Lucette's blush intensified. 'Of course not.' Every thought of the portrait had completely fled her mind, but now she seized on it with relief. 'That is why you cannot leave. I have not yet paid you.'

Leo's smile broadened for an instant, lifting foxily at the edges. His eyes rested momentarily on the chaise-longue with a meditative expression. 'Oh yes you have, my dear Lucette. Payment in full. Gratefully received.'

With that he was gone. Suddenly Lucette felt exhausted. It took a superhuman effort for her to turn and smile at her maid-to-be.

'Tea, Miss Mizen?' Lucette reached for the samovar. Dimly, she wondered if she would ever again be able to occupy the chaise-longue with a quiet mind. 'I'm afraid it may be a little cold.'

'That's all right, Mrs Bailey.' The brilliant eyes blinked once. 'I like cold tea.'

Forty-five minutes later Vi ushered Mary reluctantly into what had been Elsie's cubicle in the basement.

Mary barely glanced at the interior.

'I can't sleep here,' she stated bluntly.

Vi was taken aback. 'But this is where the kitchen girl sleeps.' She sent a puzzled look round the kitchen. 'I mean, there is nowhere else.'

'But I can't, I just can't.' Mary's voice quivered. She clasped her hands dramatically to her breast. 'You see, once I was buried alive.' She leaned forward confidentially. Her eyes narrowed to vanishing grey slits, her voice dropped to a whisper. 'I couldn't sleep down here, I just couldn't. I think – why – ' she paused to shudder. 'I think I'd wake up dead with fear.'

Vi was impressed. Looking round Elsie's cubicle she saw it with new eyes. The power of Mary's performance made her feel the suffocating weight of brickwork and masonry above, almost as if she were lying on the bed with it resting on her chest. Suddenly the air seemed too thick and clammy to breathe.

'You do see, don't you, Vi?' Now there was the hint of a break in Mary's voice. 'And I need this work, I really do.'

Vi thought hard. Madam's house became more pinched for space as it neared the top, but there was a tiny boxroom across the landing from her own room in the attic. It had no windows, only a skylight, but with a bit of a clear-out it could be made to do.

'Look.' Vi made up her mind. 'I'll do what I can. I can't promise anything, mind – but, well, you did light the range.' Despite her relief at having the kitchen warm again, Vi was glad Madam had not witnessed exactly how the miracle had been achieved. Mary had soaked a pair of Madam's old drawers in best Napoleon brandy, then stuffed them into the range's cold black heart and set them alight. They had burned furiously.

'I'll sleep anywhere. On the floor, in a cupboard, anywhere.' Mary's voice was earnest. 'Just so long as it's not down here.'

'You'd have to be up early, mind, back down in the kitchen by half-past five at the latest. Madam's an early riser and – well, sometimes she has gentlemen callers. There's no back stairs in this house, and it would never do for them to meet you halfway down.'

'I promise.' Mary laid a grubby hand over her chest. 'I'll be good as gold and quiet as a mouse. You won't even know I'm there.' She smiled then, for the first time since Vi had met her. Her teeth were very white and small, except for the two dog teeth, larger than the rest and a little long. They gave her smile a raffish, terrier-like quality which was curiously attractive. Vi found herself smiling back, with relief and pleasure and, she hoped, the beginning of friendship. It looked as if Elsie's replacement might work out all right after all.

Outside, Leo launched himself into the cold dark street with a sense of wild exhilaration. Above him, the indigo sky was full of stars. The beauty of that sky behind the yellow gas lamps made the hair lift on the back of his head with delight.

He strode away down Derby Street, barely feeling the cobbles beneath his feet. He felt winged, all-powerful. For on Lucette's chenille-covered table, amongst the artful disorder of society back-numbers, between the covers of *Nash's* magazine, he had found exactly what he wanted. The photographic portrait had jumped up in front of his eyes as if it had called his name. There, captured in *profil perdu*, with a cluster of primroses and a single black aigrette plume in the smooth sweep of honey-blonde hair, was the girl. Her face, the only one, her smile. A hard choice the photographer must have had to make, between her profile, with its delicate upper lip and lovely line of jaw, and the perfect symmetry of her full face.

But he had chosen well, keeping three-quarters of her beauty hidden, only guessed at.

A string of pearls in a black silk case. The dark side of the moon.

Quietly, while Lucette's delectable back had been turned for his admiration, Leo had removed the page from *Nash's* magazine, folded it, and placed it inside his jacket, next to his heart. Already, although he had never spoken to her, had only glimpsed her once for a few seconds on a crowded station platform, she had changed his life. Since yesterday every step, every breath, had been taken with her in mind. The thought of her had been with him as he slept and ate, endowing the most mundane action with a halo of light, like the one which outlined her golden head in the portrait he carried. It was she who had given him patience with Mary Mizen and kindness with Lucette, because a little of her was in all women, and all women were in her.

And now, at last, Leo had a name to put to the image he had been carrying with him in his bones and blood since yesterday. He whispered it to himself like an incantation. It suited her. He had never seen a face that spoke so clearly without words, reached straight into his dreams.

Leo dwelled for a moment, with a tinge of regret, on Lucette. There would be no more visits to the house in Derby Street. From tonight, there was no room in his life for any woman except one. He would find her soon, he knew it. It was inevitable. Everyone came to Mayfair sooner or later. It was simply a question of where, and when.

3   *The Single Vessel*

'You look very pretty, my dear.'

'Thank you, Lady Celia.'

Sibell Gifford curtseyed, as she had been taught, and hoped that when she was old she would never be as thin and dry and shrivelled-looking as Lady Celia, and driven to 'run' débutantes for the Season, in order to make ends meet in a dark, gloomy house off Rutland Gate.

But there, Sibell had to admit, was a mystery. She herself would not be presented at Court until next April, and yet here she was, in the middle of November, in town with Papa, instead of at home with Mama and Fräulein Ritter, massacring German verbs and swapping curses with the stable lads, and longing for her twin brother Tom to return from Eton to bring her news from the great outside world.

And tonight, a bare six months after her seventeenth birthday, she would make her entrance into the great adult world. She felt at once excited and afraid. It seemed almost sacrilegious to have her hair up, coiled into a Greek chignon of pinwheel curls, with the added height of a wired pompadour. She hesitated to turn her head in case the whole edifice collapsed. The smell of singeing still lingered, for the *friseur*, in his haste, had overheated his tongs in the dressing-room gas jets.

The colour of her gown, palest blue mousseline-de-soie embroidered in blue and hand-painted with forget-me-nots, from Lucile in

Hanover Square, was something of a compromise, because though Sibell might have escaped schoolgirl drab, she had not yet reached the exalted white of débutante. But her elbow-length gloves were the very best white kid, and over her left wrist she carried a small square gold mesh bag with a gold pencil and a lace handkerchief.

Secretly, upstairs in the dressing-room, when Lady Celia's maid had gone down to announce that her charge was finally ready, Sibell had darkened her eyebrows with a hairpin blackened in the gas jet, and applied a little powder to her flushed cheeks. She couldn't help wishing her exquisitely shod feet were not quite so large, and her hair such an unfortunate shade of yellow, instead of the soft nut-brown that all the actresses favoured. Then there was the Gifford nose, which might have looked well on eighteen generations of Saxon ancestors but which Sibell would really rather have done without. If it had not been for these faults, and the elderly chinchilla stole which Lady Celia had insisted she wear over her mousseline, Sibell would have been supremely happy.

'Your father will be meeting us at Ainsley House.'

Sibell followed her chaperone's upright back, braced into its mulberry-coloured brocade, to the waiting victoria. What seemed only moments later, the carriage swept into the courtyard of a high-walled mansion in Park Lane. On either side of the porticoed entrance stood two gold-and-cream-liveried footmen, while between them wide red carpet spilled extravagantly over the steps and onto the gravelled drive.

Breathless with excitement, Sibell alighted from the carriage into the bitter November air to find a footman instantly at her elbow proffering an enormous umbrella.

'This way, miss, and madam.'

The footman was very tall, in his knee breeches and white stockings, and held the umbrella so respectfully high that Sibell felt like a queen. She let her chinchilla slip a little from her silk-clad shoulders. Behind her, Lady Celia twitched it back into place. Sibell blushed.

The entrance hall was ablaze with light. Above, a huge chandelier illuminated the serpentine curve of a wide marble staircase between pillars of gold and lapis lazuli, up to an arched gallery. Sibell was momentarily dazzled. It was like entering upon a stage, after a lifetime in the wings.

'Now remember, my dear. You may not refuse to dance with anyone who asks you, for to do so would be to cast aspersions on your host's choice of guests. Rest assured, however, that anyone whom you find uncongenial may quite civilly be ignored if you meet again elsewhere.'

'Yes, Lady Celia.'

At last, there was Papa, looking as always red-faced and hot in his tight-fitting dress clothes. He bowed to Lady Celia, then tucked Sibell's arm in his own before they were carried bodily upwards in the glittering tide of people ascending the marble stairs. Sibell was glad of his support as their names were announced in ringing tones and they were ushered into an enormous first-floor ballroom whose triple-height windows, uncurtained, overlooked the Park. The glass, reflecting back the light of the massed crystal chandeliers, shone like black diamonds.

'Well, my little sphinx.' Papa's voice sounded a little hoarse. Sibell saw by the faint sheen on his face that he had been drinking more heavily than usual, and felt a tinge of disappointment. This was her first ball, and she was so proud of her fair, burly father that she wanted everyone else to see him at his best. But she loved him all the same.

'How do I look, Papa?'

'Beautiful.' He sighed, one of the heavy sighs she had heard him give in his study at home, faced with a mound of papers to read before an all-night sitting at the House.

'What is the matter, Papa?'

'Seeing you grown up – it makes me feel old, I'm afraid.' His face twisted in a comical grimace of regret. 'You are not my 'cello any more.'

Sibell smiled. It was a game he had played with her when she was small, drawing an imaginary bow across her midriff till she had screamed with delight. Then, she had never noticed the brandy on his breath, thinking that all Papas smelled the same.

But this was too special a moment to be spoiled by sadness.

'Come, Papa.' She slid out her arm from his to clasp both his hands. 'I have saved my first dance for you!'

'Have you indeed, you forward hussy?'

He opened his arms to her, and she slid into them as neatly as a billiard ball into its pocket, inhaling the warm familiar smell of leather and shaving soap and Rothschild Havana which was and always would be Papa. Then the music caught her and lifted her and she forgot everything else but the fact that this was her first ball and she was the happiest and most fortunate girl in the world.

Outside in the darkness a young man, uncloaked and hatless but wearing full evening dress, dropped lightly from the branches of the ilex tree which bordered the high garden wall. Methodically he dusted off his hands, smoothed back his hair, then withdrew from the inside pocket of his dress coat a large cigar. For a moment, in the flame of a wax vesta, his face was clearly illumined. It was set in an expression of absolute concentration.

Slowly, his cigar glowing red in the darkness, the young man advanced towards the pillared portico. The shadow he cast behind him was very long. Floodlit by the yellow light from the windows and in full view of the two waiting footmen, he paused, frowned, sucked vigorously on his cigar, shook his head, then slowly, without looking to left or right, mounted the steps.

The footmen exchanged a doubtful glance. They were both tall men, chosen for their stature, but this man was a full head taller than either; how could they possibly have failed to notice him arriving? One thing was certain: it was a hanging offence to interrupt a gentleman in the consumption of a cigar, especially one that was not drawing as it should.

The first footman, the elder of the two, thought quickly. It was never permissible to question a gentleman directly, but some action must be taken.

'Fine night, sir,' he hazarded, a little lamely. It had stopped raining, it was true, but a greasy November fog was beginning to roll in from the river to the east, slipping over the high wall to wreath itself sluggishly round the bases of the trees.

To his relief, there was no reply but a grunt. The young man, still sucking noisily at his cigar, passed between the two footmen without glancing at either and strolled back into the lighted interior. The footmen exchanged a brief, satisfied nod. The grunt, the walk, the refusal to meet their eyes or engage in conversation – he was a gentleman, for sure.

Inside, in the ballroom, Quintin Lavery noted the arrival of Lord Gifford's party with a sense of triumph all the more exquisite for the need to disguise it absolutely. The Giffords might be land-poor, but their ancestry went back before the Norman Conquest. Lord Gifford spent most of his time buried in the country, and the rest in the dusty precincts of his club or that other cemetery, the House of Lords. For him to be seen at an evening entertainment was almost unheard of.

Now, Quintin's task was to prevent the Giffords leaving as early as they had arrived. This was his chance at last to be accepted into the inner circle, to dissolve at a touch the invisible bramble hedge of prejudice that closed out all those, like himself, considered too recently, shinily rich.

Slowly, nodding and bowing to left and right, Quintin threaded his way through the crush of guests until he found Mrs Bailey, his hostess for the evening, resplendent in Nile-green orion satin. With a nod of his head he summoned her into the dance. Crowded though it might be, the dance floor was the only possible place for private conversation.

*

Sibell, revolving in her father's arms, noticed that he was staring at a lady in green who had just taken the floor.

'Who is that woman, Papa?'

'Hmm?' Papa looked vague, as if he had not heard.

'She is very beautiful.' Even as she spoke, Sibell realized that was not quite the right term. What the woman in green possessed was not beauty but a sort of sureness, the sleeked-down, perfectly satisfied look of a cat that had just washed itself and was now stretching its limbs in the sun. Sibell envied the woman her composure. She must be aware of Papa's staring, but she showed no sign of it. Sibell sighed.

'I would like to look like that, one day.'

Abruptly, Papa released her. For a moment, as the pair of them stood there like statues in the midst of the swirling dancers, his face, shiny and tight, looked like a stranger's.

'I must go, little sphinx.'

'Oh, Papa!' Sibell heard her voice rise in a childish wail and bit her lip. She was grown up now, she must learn how to control herself.

'Duty, my dear.' Papa spoke shortly. His mind was clearly elsewhere. 'A late session at the House. But Lady Celia will look after you. It's all for the best,' he went on heavily, half to himself. 'Nothing else to be done.'

Sibell was not sure how to reply. She squeezed his arm encouragingly.

'You must not worry, Papa. I shall be all right, I promise.'

'Yes.' Papa spoke with astonishing vehemence. 'You will be all right.' He patted her hand clumsily. 'Girls need things.' He paused, searching for words. 'All sorts of things. And you shall have them. I shall make sure of it. Remember that, my dear.'

'Yes, Papa.' Sibell was not sure what it was that he meant her to remember, but she wanted to please him. He looked so worried. She felt glad that she was not a man, with mysterious responsibilities.

Papa led her back to the chaperone's bench.

'See that the girl has ice cream, Lady Celia. As much as she wants.' He took both Sibell's gloved hands in his. 'Goodbye, my dear.'

He did not kiss her, just stared at her for a long moment, his moustache twitching, as if he were saying goodbye for a year, not a few hours.

As she watched his broad back recede through the crowd Sibell felt suddenly lost and more than a little lonely. The only other male face she knew in the crowd was the Duke of Shelburne's, and that was only because he had come to Gifford's Oak the Christmas before last. Papa had invited the young man, the year after his father's death, thinking he might be lonely. The Duke had no brothers or sisters, and his mother had died when he was a boy.

But Sibell had never met anyone who seemed less vulnerable than the Fifth Duke. The Shelburnes were rich, richer even than Mr Lavery, the host of this party, whose father had made a fortune quite recently out of South African mines. The Shelburne fortune, built on leasing London land then vast tracts in the colonies, was two centuries older; now it was a law unto itself, beyond the interference of monarch or man. Papa said that Oliver, the Fifth Duke, was the nearest Sibell would ever see to a free man.

Quintin, on the other side of the dance floor, accepted Lord Gifford's excuses with a smiling face and gritted teeth. He could not imagine what fault could have been found with his arrangements. Now, to make matters worse, every time he revolved with Mrs Bailey in the decorous pattern of the dance his eyes were caught by Gifford's daughter, marooned with her old trout of a chaperone. The girl wasn't yet out, so no one was likely to ask her onto the floor. As host, he could not risk asking for the first dance himself; if she left soon after, it would give the worst impression. Infuriatingly, he was helpless.

'You shall and you will,' he hissed into the scented shell of Mrs Bailey's ear. 'It is for that that I am paying you!'

'My dear Quintin, what on earth can I do? I doubt if she would appreciate me as a partner!' Lucette brushed an imaginary speck of fluff off the gleaming stuff of her skirt. Inside she was seething with offended pride. How dared Robert Gifford stare at her in that reproachful, accusing way, as if she were nothing better than a woman of the street, not fit to tread the same parquet dance floor as himself and his precious daughter? It was unforgivable. Just how did he think she spent the three hundred and sixty-four days of the year that she did not happen to be lunching with him – tatting in the chimney corner?

'Find Miss Gifford a partner. Immediately.'

'Mr Lavery!' Lucette drew herself up with dignity behind her fan. 'I am not a procuress!'

'Of course not, Mrs Bailey.' Quintin curbed his impatience with an effort. 'But I assure you, Miss Gifford's enjoyment of this ball is of the greatest importance to me. If you would be so good as to find her a partner, I would be most grateful.' He paused, significantly. 'Most.'

Lucette eyed him consideringly for a moment, then nodded. She knew exactly what form his gratitude would take. Quintin had always been, in that respect, entirely reliable. 'Very well then, I will do my best.' She sailed away, regally, indignation lending an added brightness to her eye and determination to her smile.

As she scanned the assembled guests a young man standing alone underneath one of Quintin's Gainsboroughs caught her eye. He was unusually tall, broad-shouldered and clean-shaven, and wore his thick black hair swept back from his forehead. A second later Lucette realized with a shock of recognition that she was face to face with Leo. The hair, smoothed back and darkened with macassar, had almost fooled her, but there was no mistaking those bold brown eyes with their golden lights. He wore evening dress superbly, with a careless grace which thirty years of training could not have bettered – but under the close-fitting cloth Lucette could see that all the muscles of his arms and shoulders were bunched and tense. From head to toe he was one line of force, silent, motionless, but radiating energy as if at any moment he might explode.

'My dear Leo. What on earth brings you here?'

'I was invited, my dear Lucette.' Leo's golden-brown eyes narrowed, inviting her to contradict him.

'I beg to differ.' Lucette tapped him lightly on the arm with her folded fan. 'I was responsible for the guest list.'

Leo smiled at her at last, but there was a reckless edge to his expression that only increased Lucette's disquiet.

'Then you desire me to leave?'

'I did not say so.' Lucette unfolded her fan again.

'Then you desire me to stay?' Leo leaned closer to her. He smelled of cologne and the heavier musk of hair oil, which only seemed to intensify the well-remembered scent of his skin, the irresistible sweet, spicy smell of hot bread and baking biscuits that emanated from Leo's body like incense from a censer.

'Leo, you are impossible.' Glancing round, Lucette saw that her gesture and tone of voice had attracted a certain amount of attention. That would never do. Ejecting an uninvited guest, no matter how tactfully, always blighted a party – and she, as the female in charge, would undoubtedly be held responsible.

'Listen. Since you are here, you might as well sing for your supper.'

Leo raised an eyebrow, placed one hand on his heart, and made to drop on one knee. Lucette, aware of the curious eyes around them, was forced to tug him upright with both hands. 'Listen, I said! Do you see that girl over there, the one in pale blue, sitting down? I want you to ask her to dance.'

Mercifully, Leo went suddenly quiet. He stared at her fiercely, the yellow lights in his eyes glinting.

'Why?' His tone was light but the expression in his eyes was dangerous. Lucette hastened to explain.

'Because Mr Lavery – your host, for heaven's sake, and please remember that in case his name arises in conversation – wants her to be happy.'

Leo said nothing, simply smiled, a wide, wild smile that sent a momentary ripple of foreboding down Lucette's spine.

'Why not?' His eyes were shining, as if he were in possession of some secret too exhilarating to share with anyone else. 'Just this once. As a favour to you.' He bent suddenly and kissed her, his lips hot against the skin of her bare neck just below her ear. Lucette shivered. Her mind went dark as she remembered the chaise-longue.

'Well then?'

'What?' Lucette blinked.

'Have you not forgotten something?' Leo's eyes burned. Lucette wondered for a moment if he was drunk. He looked exalted, almost crazed. 'Miss Gifford. The girl in blue. Her chaperone will never permit her to dance with me unless you introduce me first.'

Sibell was astonished when the beautiful lady in green stopped to address her chaperone.

'I do so hope you are enjoying the ball, Lady Celia. Mr Lavery is very much looking forward to escorting you in for a little supper presently, but in the meantime perhaps I might introduce a young friend of mine, Mr Leo de Morgan?' For the first time Sibell realized that behind the green vision's opalescent skirts loomed the tall figure of a young man. She felt a thrill of nervousness.

Lady Celia looked the young man up and down through narrowed eyes, hesitated for what seemed to Sibell an age, then finally extended her hand. 'Delighted, I am sure.' Sibell wished her chaperone had not stared quite so closely. In her seated position she too could see that the young man's boots were rather scuffed. But then, men did not have to be so careful about dress and reputation. Papa said that any young man with a modicum of manners and eighteen pence for a hansom could dine abroad every day of the week, if the fancy took him.

'May I present my ward for the evening, Miss Sibell Gifford?'
Sibell looked up to see a pair of smoky golden eyes staring straight
into hers and felt herself shrink with shyness inside her blue
silk.

'I would be honoured if you would dance with me, Miss Gifford.'
Mr de Morgan spoke directly to Sibell, with a clarity and intentness
that was nothing like the light, neutral, unexpressive tones to which
she was accustomed.

Tongue-tied, Sibell felt very conscious of the rustle of her dress
as she rose to her feet. She hoped very much that the fabric had not
become overly creased from sitting so long. She listened anxiously
to the orchestra, sighing a little with relief as it struck up a rhythm
she recognized. Her partner must not be allowed to suspect that
this was the first time she had ever danced with a man who was not
a relation.

But dancing with Mr de Morgan was very different from dancing
with Papa, or even Tom. He was much taller, for a start, and wider,
and he had a springy strength to his arms and shoulders which
made Sibell feel both nervous and strangely protected all at once.
For the first few steps she hardly dared breathe, for though the
dance was a familiar waltz, it was nothing like the waltzes she had
practised in Miss Pritchard's class, where she and Tom had lined up
with ten other little boys and girls in sailor suits and frilly muslin
dresses.

'We have met before, you know.' Sibell could feel the movement
of Mr de Morgan's lips against her carefully curled hair. It was an
odd sensation, yet pleasurable too. She hoped very much that there
remained no telltale scent of singeing.

'I hardly think so, Mr de Morgan.' She hastened to provide the
correct response. 'I am quite sure I should have remembered.'

He executed a turn so swiftly, with such reckless ease and dash,
that Sibell gasped for breath. She wished Miss Pritchard could have
seen it. Tom and she, especially in their sixth year, when she had
been a full two inches taller than her twin brother, had always

fought at the turns over who should lead. 'Not like a wheelbarrow, Thomas!' Miss Pritchard had called despairingly, and then – 'Sibell, do stop moving your lips! If you must count, please do so *silently*.'

'You will remember, one day.' Mr de Morgan's voice, deeper than Papa's, with a young man's resonance, throbbed with absolute conviction. 'We have always known each other, you and I.'

Astonished, Sibell missed a beat, but he scooped her up in mid-step and set her down exactly back in time. Sibell, dazzled by the chandeliers, revolving like planets above his shoulder as they danced, began to feel a little dizzy. Surely she could not have heard aright?

'I think you must be mistaken, Mr de Morgan.'

'No.' Sibell had not been contradicted so forcefully since Tom had left for Eton. A tremor went down her spine. 'And I am not lying, either. I will never lie to you.'

'Why are you saying these things to me?' Sibell whispered.

Mr de Morgan's arms tightened around her. His voice too was a whisper, yet Sibell seemed to hear the crash of walls falling. 'Because I fell in love with you the first moment I saw you. On the station platform. Three weeks ago today.'

Sibell caught her breath. She became aware that her heart was thudding, with a hollow drumming which seemed to shake her entire body. Everything in the ballroom faded away. The other guests vanished and there were only the two of them left, dancing alone on an acre-wide floor.

The music ended, on a sweet prolonged note that seemed to Sibell to echo right inside her bones. Abruptly her partner halted. The movement of the dance carried her close against him, so that the diaphanous tissue of her dress swirled up against his legs and caught there for a moment before falling back again. Her head flung back, her whole body from midriff to ankle pressed against his, Sibell looked up to face him fully for the first time.

The shock of his face took her breath away. It was the most real, the most alive face she had ever seen. His brilliant golden eyes blazed with an awareness of her that was almost violent, as if he were trying to get underneath her skin, to become her, to break down all her boundaries so that they could flow into each other like two cells merging under Tom's microscope.

'Please.' Sibell realized she was breathing in short gasps, as if she had run a mile uphill instead of dancing for five minutes. 'I must go back to Lady Celia.'

He pulled her to him, almost roughly. Sibell felt the heat of him scorching her through her clothes. He was so strong – and yet he was shaking, echoing her own deep internal trembling, as if they were sharing their own private earthquake, after which nothing would ever be the same. Somehow that terrified her more than anything.

Suddenly panicked, Sibell twisted herself away. Lady Celia's mouth tightened into an almost invisible line of disapproval when she saw her returning from the floor without her partner. As Sibell followed her into the refreshment room she was glad that the presence of their host prevented her from being reprimanded for her breach of etiquette.

She accepted a burnt almond ice prettily spiked with caramel wafers, but it tasted of ashes. All too soon it was time to return to the ballroom. Any hope Sibell had of hiding behind Mr Lavery and Lady Celia as they re-entered the huge brightly-lit chamber was dispelled by Mr Lavery's good manners, as he ushered the two women determinedly before him.

'If I might have the pleasure of this dance, Miss Gifford?'

Sibell did not hesitate. On the dance floor, in conversation with her host, she would be protected from further encounters with Mr de Morgan.

After a decorous interval, Mr Lavery, ushering her expertly into territory she would find familiar, began a conversation about life at Gifford's Oak. As she described the practical jokes the family played on each other, the time she had decoyed Papa with soapsuds instead of whipped cream on his favourite rum trifle, and the occasion her younger brother William had placed a live toad in the tea caddy, Sibell was able almost to forget her anxiety about Mr de Morgan.

'The King must enjoy it,' said Mr Lavery.

Sibell fumbled a turn, surprised. Was it possible that Mr Lavery, coming as close to a direct question as was socially permissible, was seeking personal information about His Majesty? Surely he must know that those country friends with whom the King stayed would never reveal any detail of his activities? It was a matter of loyalty. Now, for the first time with her host, Sibell felt uncomfortable.

Fortunately, the music ended before she had to reply. Even so, as she curtseyed to her partner Sibell's relief was mingled with real gratitude. Her safety was now assured. After two waltzes, one of them with her host, even Lady Celia would feel they could now return home.

But as they neared the chaperone's bench Sibell realized to her astonishment that Lady Celia's chair was empty.

For a moment, Sibell and Mr Lavery stared at each other. Clearly there was no cause for concern about Lady Celia, for if she had been taken ill she would never have left her bag, with its store of smelling salts and liquorice water, lying on her chair. Doubtless she had been called away, and would be back presently.

Sibell realized instantly that she had now become an imposition. Her host could not possibly leave an unchaperoned young female guest alone, but for the two of them to remain in public talking together could only lead to unwanted speculation. She felt herself begin to blush with embarrassment. As the orchestra struck up music for yet another waltz, Mr Lavery lifted his hand to summon a servant.

It was then that Sibell glimpsed, over her host's shoulder, a tall figure advancing towards her through the crowd. Her whole body went hollow with apprehension. Mr de Morgan was going to ask her to dance again.

'Mr Lavery.' She found herself, in a passion of urgency, clutching Mr Lavery's sleeve. If the situation had not been so desperate she could never have brought herself to be so forward. 'Would you be so kind as to dance with me again? I would so much enjoy it.'

Mr Lavery's eyelids widened infinitesimally. 'My dear Miss Gifford.' He hesitated diplomatically. 'Believe me, I am flattered, but – two waltzes in succession?'

Sibell felt a tide of heat rise to her face. In her haste she had forgotten that no girl must ever dance two consecutive waltzes unless with her betrothed.

'These tiresome shibboleths.' She shrugged and smiled, aware all the time of the tall figure advancing steadily towards her. There was no word for what she felt but terror, the sort of terror she had not experienced since she was a child and Tom had told her if she left her mouth open in the dark moths would fly in to choke her.

'Perhaps . . .' Driven beyond all caution, Sibell increased the brilliance of her smile. 'Perhaps we could continue our conversation elsewhere?' She calculated feverishly. 'The conservatory, perhaps?' She pressed one gloved hand against her flushed cheek. 'This heat, I declare, is making me quite faint.'

Quintin studied the Gifford girl, frowning a little. Her suggestion placed him in a quandary. It was ill-bred to refuse a guest, and yet the conservatory, with a young, unchaperoned girl, could be more dangerous for a single man of means than a jungle.

'There is so much I would like to tell you, Mr Lavery.'

'About what, Miss Gifford?'

The girl lowered her voice. 'The King, you know.'

'I see.' Quintin smiled. Now he understood perfectly the need for privacy. If Miss Gifford wanted to impress him with her insider's knowledge of the King, he could not pass up such a golden opportunity. Hesitating no longer, he summoned a footman to go in search of Lady Celia and inform her that Miss Gifford was awaiting her in the winter-garden.

*

After the dry heat of the ballroom, the conservatory seemed a haven of green, sweet-scented coolness. Its glazed wrought-iron roof was curtained with vines and creepers. Beneath, water trickled from small fountains set here and there in the tessellated pavement.

Sibell felt herself relax as soon as she entered. Mr de Morgan would never be able to follow her here. She watched Mr Lavery remove a Lucana Turkish cigarette from a gold-trimmed shagreen case and felt the last tremor of tension ease itself from her bones. A man who smoked was a man at peace, good-tempered, amiable. To her, Mr Lavery seemed almost as old as Papa.

'So – tell me about your friend the King, Miss Gifford.' Obediently, Sibell recounted what little she knew – that the King hated to be beaten at croquet, especially by a lady; that when he came to visit there must be no reading, but lots of hearty jokes and plain food and pretty women; that he loved to gamble on the least thing, the fall of a leaf or a slice of buttered toast; that he liked children, and poached pears.

Then, to change the subject, because her small store of information was exhausted, Sibell touched the edge of a waterlily floating in a tiny pool beside her. The black water dipped and rippled, slow as oil, and for a moment Sibell did not recognize it as water at all. She began to feel a little uneasy. The air that had seemed so refreshing when she had entered the conservatory now seemed thick and damp and difficult to breathe.

But it would never do to show even the slightest sign of her discomfort, for that would cast aspersions on her host's hospitality. Clearly, Mr Lavery had taken a deal of trouble with his winter-garden. Sibell felt a touch of pride as in her turn she drew him out on the subject. Mama would have been pleased with her efforts. She listened, a little bemused, as he described how for one orchid, a dark, waxy creature clinging onto a decaying log beside the bench on which they sat, two men had died. To her horror, Mr Lavery plucked the creature from its host and bestowed it on her. Sibell thanked him as prettily as she could, which was only fitting, and held the blossom gingerly. The bench was narrow, and in such close proximity she could not help noticing that the growth of Mr Lavery's beard was of a different quality from the hair on his head, as if either or both were false.

Now Sibell could feel the damp air beginning to drag at the light stuff of her dress. The fumes of Mr Lavery's cigarette seemed to hang in a cloud about her head and she longed for fresh air. Adding to her discomfort was her growing realization that by now Lady Celia must have received her message – and the fact that she had not come to fetch her meant that she must approve of this tête-à-tête with Mr Lavery.

But just how long, Sibell wondered a little wildly, could she maintain a conversation on the subject of cross-pollination?

A faint smell of scorching proved a welcome distraction. The lighted end of Mr Lavery's cigarette had fallen onto her silk skirt and lay there, pulsing redly. Automatically Sibell reached to brush it away. But Mr Lavery grasped her wrist, preventing her; with the tip of one very well-manicured finger he flicked away the offending ash. Glancing down at his restraining hand on her wrist, Sibell noticed for the first time that across the back of it, ridged and gaping like an unsightly second smile, was a scar. Repelled by the sight, Sibell flinched, recognized her breach of good manners in the same instant and quickly, hardly knowing what she must do to make up for her ineptitude but knowing she must act at once, willed herself to smile brightly and lay her own gloved hand over the scarred one on her lap.

'Good evening, Lavery.' It was with relief that Sibell heard a cool, hard voice cut across the warm green dimness. The substantial figure of the Duke of Shelburne filled the doorway of the conservatory. There was a long pause in which no one spoke or moved. Faint strains of music from the ballroom drifted in like smoke.

'Miss Gifford?' At last the Duke spoke, not to Sibell, not even at her, but somewhere above her head, as if he were doing her the greatest favour possible by pretending she were not there at all.

Sibell drew in her breath in a silent gasp. The change in his behaviour towards her cut deeper than any accusation. It demonstrated with a clarity beyond words just what it was that she had done. She had committed the worst crime a young girl in her position could commit, that of public indiscretion. No excuse could be made, no explanation offered, because the damage was already done, and could never be repaired. The presence of the footman at the double doors, motionless but quivering with suppressed curiosity, ensured it.

Awkwardly, a hundred years too late, Sibell withdrew her hand from Mr Lavery's. Head down, her cheeks burning but her heart like lead, she curtseyed hurriedly, then fled beneath the Duke of Shelburne's impersonal gaze, the crimson orchid still clasped in her left hand.

There was silence in the conservatory after she had gone, a silence broken only by the plashing of water over the brilliantly coloured pincushions of moss between the stones. The two men stood motionless, facing each other.

'She came with me willingly, Shelburne.' Quintin's tone was neutral. A listener might have thought he was discussing the weather.

'But of course, my dear boy.' The Duke's tone gave the impression not so much that he did not believe his host, but that it was not worth his while to make the effort to believe or disbelieve.

Quintin felt anger twist inside him. He was not to be permitted to explain, he could see that. He could even understand it. It was his duty as host to ensure the welfare of his guests.

If only it had been someone else who entered so inopportunely; anyone but Shelburne. Shelburne was unshakeable – too sure of himself to be persuaded, too rich to be bribed, not clever enough to be deceived.

Now Shelburne promenaded his vague blue gaze around the

winter-garden as if trying to make sense of an abstruse mathematical problem.

'Won't do, y'know,' he said at last. 'Take my advice.'

'And what precisely might that be?' inquired Quintin savagely. Shelburne swung round, surprised, as if everything had been quite clearly explained, as if not to have understood him was in some way a fault of character or breeding for which he found it in himself to be genuinely sorry.

He paused for a moment and then, for the first time since he had entered the conservatory, he looked Quintin straight in the face. Fleetingly his gaze was hard and clear.

'The proper thing, my dear boy,' he answered quietly. 'The proper thing.'

Lady Celia, her eyes fixed on the glazed doors of the conservatory, saw Sibell emerge, looking dazed and flushed, and breathed a sigh of relief. Her little stratagem had worked better than even she had dared to hope. The Duke's intervention had been quite providential. Now her thousand pounds from Robert Gifford was well and truly earned. The girl would be set up for life – which was not such an easy matter to arrange in these modern times.

Yes, Robert Gifford had made the right decision for his daughter. Sibell was far too pretty to risk on the Season proper, which was always packed out with penniless younger sons. Anything could have happened – but now, her chaperone could retire to her bed with a glass of gin and hot water in the satisfaction of a task well done.

'Fancy a bite?'

Mary started. It was the footman, winking at her as he knocked his umbrella to shake off the drops, then furled it. She hadn't noticed him before. Her eyes had been fixed on the girl with pale upswept hair as the carriage closed on her drift of blue tissue like the wingcases of a big black beetle and swept her off through the

71

gates and out into Park Lane, so close to Mary that gravel from the great wheels had spun up to sting her cheeks. Now all that could be seen was the tail-lamps, glowing dimly through the fog.

'The rest of 'em won't be out for hours yet. Hungry work, waiting.' The footman stooped to reach behind the gate and came back up with a packet wrapped in a white cloth, and a bottle. Mary studied him, fascinated, as he unwrapped it. He was wearing powder on his face, like a girl. Little drops of November fog clung to his rows of fat little curls. She was glad now that she'd stayed. The other onlookers had left long ago, because of the cold.

'Well, what do you say?' The footman held out something to her, a wedge of whiteish cake stacked with berries, looking almost black in the yellow light.

'Maybe.' Mary knew better than to say no immediately, but she didn't feel hungry. She pointed to a trumpet-shaped flower poised on top of the cake. 'What's that?'

'Spun sugar.' The footman lifted it between thumb and forefinger and held it up to the light for her to see. It was as transparent as glass. Mary wished more than ever that she could see right inside the great house. If so much trouble had been taken with a cake, inside must be marvels beyond telling.

'Do you want it?' The footman held the spun sugar flower temptingly in front of her. Mary looked at it, then shook her head. The emptiness inside her wasn't for something that could be touched or tasted.

The footman looked surprised and a little disappointed. He uncorked the bottle, took a swig, then offered it to her. Without pausing to wipe the rim, Mary drank.

The footman watched her.

'That's enough.' He took the bottle back from her, his voice gruff. He shifted a little uneasily from foot to foot.

'Fancy a walk?' The footman glanced quickly back towards the lighted mansion. 'I've got ten minutes.'

Mary hesitated. The emptiness inside her hadn't gone; she could feel it gnawing away inside her. It needed something.

The footman gave her an intent look. His eyes glistened now, like his gold braid. He led the way into Park Lane, moving purposefully. Mary followed him, admiring his legs in their white silk.

Round the first corner, she stopped.

'Here,' she said. She wanted to stay near the great house, near the light and the music.

'Are you sure?' The footman looked uncertainly right and left. They were in Mount Street, between one lamp and the next.

Mary put her hands on her hips to rally him. Having come this far there was no point in going back.

'What's the matter? You changed your mind?'

He laughed and pulled her towards him. Mary reached up her hands, and ran them over the studs at his collar, his powdered wig, the hard gold stuff of his epaulettes. His uniform was so tightly fitted that it was hot to the touch.

Around them the fog rolled and eddied. Mary could smell the powder on his curls.

He pushed her against the wall. She held on tight. He was strong. She felt him butt against her, warm and cold at once, soft and hard. Wide-eyed, she stared over his shoulder at the golden gas lamp, looking like the sun through its halo of fog. The rough brick of the wall scraped against her back and she braced herself against it. He gasped. His body began to shake and Mary gripped harder onto his gold epaulettes. Close to, she could see they weren't really gold at all; underneath the top layer they were black with tarnish. She closed her eyes then. He moaned and shuddered, his face buried in her neck. It didn't take long for him to finish. After her feet touched the pavement Mary had to prop him up for a minute.

'Where do you live?' He leaned back towards her, his voice hoarse. Mary looked at him. His wig was crooked. He seemed younger all of a sudden. She wondered what he would look like out of his uniform.

But there had been no lights, no music. The emptiness inside her was as dark and silent as it had been before.

'No.' Mary shook her head as she brushed down her skirt. She'd grazed her back on the brick wall. The warmth was comforting.

'Please.' He fumbled for her hand. Through the tight white silk Mary could feel he was hard again. He grabbed her by the shoulders. She looked up at him levelly.

'Tell me where you live. At least tell me your name.'

'Better not.'

She twisted neatly out of his grasp and walked away down Mount Street, head high, without looking back. The footman took one step to follow her, glanced behind him at the lighted gateway, cursed, then turned back, heavily, to take up his post once more.

Half a mile away, in Rutland Gate, total darkness pressed in on Sibell like a heavy, dusty-smelling curtain. In the high Victorian bed, under layers of thin old blankets, topped by a shiny counter-pane whose starched ruffles bit into her neck, she felt as if she'd been trapped inside a suit of armour. The room was very cold after the greenhouse heat of the Ainsley House ballroom, and yet, despite the chill, the air seemed stifling. Sibell was not used to sleeping so far above the ground.

Nor was she accustomed to being surrounded by so much disapproval.

Despite herself, Sibell gave a small moan. This was the worst thing that had ever happened to her. Nothing would ever be the same. Even if she devoted the rest of her life to good works, she could never succeed in wiping her slate clean. Overnight, she had become the sort of girl whom men avoided, except when they were drunk, and women looked at coldly from the corners of their eyes. No one would ever marry her now.

I cannot bear it, Sibell thought suddenly. I shall run away. I shall go to the South of France and become a femme fatale. I might as well, since I am halfway there already. I shall win a fortune at the casino and become the mistress of a Russian Grand Duke. Then one day, far in the future, I shall return to Gifford's Oak covered in sables, and stun them all.

But even as the image danced enticingly before her mind's eye, Sibell knew it was a fantasy. She could not go chasing off to the South of France or anywhere else. She was a Gifford, and Giffords never ran away. 'To the Death' was the family motto – and anyway, she did not have enough money for the boat train.

Abruptly, Sibell threw back the covers. If she stayed in bed a moment longer she felt that she would suffocate. She swung her feet round, searching blindly for her robe in the musty darkness. The boards under her bare feet were freezing, but somehow preferable to the damp chill of the bed. Her teeth chattering, she crept to the window. Lady Celia's thick, old-fashioned curtains provided a complete seal against the light. She pulled them aside. The window was tight shut, the catch wedged fast. Sibell struggled with it futilely, her nails scraping and sliding, but she could not shift it.

Panting, she rested her forehead against the glass. Her head ached and her eyelids burned. Four floors below she could see the formal garden, a bleak geometrical pattern of dwarf shrubs and narrow paths, with a sundial in the middle. In the darkness it looked unreal, as if it were made of paper. In the street beyond fog wreathed itself, catlike, round the lampposts. It was utterly quiet. Every leaf on every tree was still. To Sibell, standing cold and motionless at the window, it seemed as if time itself had stopped.

Then, from behind the high front wall which separated the garden from the street, a shadow, fractionally darker than the blackness that surrounded it, moved. Sibell, startled out of her immobility, drew back instantly from the window, but the shadow remained still. Inch by inch, she leaned forward. Now she could make out the pale blur of a face. It was a man, staring up at her window.

Slowly, as if aware of her gaze, the man reached up and removed his top hat. Sibell watched, fascinated, as he placed it neatly on top of the garden wall, then lifted himself athletically after it. He stood there for a moment, his head thrown back, his eyes never leaving her window, and then, moving swiftly and confidently, placing one foot in front of the other as skilfully as a tightrope walker, he began to make his way along the wall towards the house.

Sibell could only watch, her heart in her mouth. She was afraid for him, not for herself. If he were discovered, if a policeman rounded the corner and saw him, he would be arrested immediately.

Sibell could not be sure at what point it was in his steady progress along the wall towards her that she recognized Mr de Morgan. The knowledge seemed to grow in her gradually, as if she had suspected who he was as soon as she saw him. She felt no surprise, only a curious sense of relief. Now, as she watched him, she held her breath, like a child riveted by a conjuror, someone who could turn buttons into silver, handkerchieves into parakeets.

Soon he was close enough for her to see his face clearly. It was white in the darkness, and intent, and determined. Behind the glass, Sibell shivered, but could not turn away. To do so seemed, somehow, hardly civil, after he had come so far in search of her.

And he had found her. For a long, breathless moment, they looked at each other, from darkness to darkness, through the glass that separated them. He could go no further towards her. There was no more wall.

As she looked down at his upturned face, Sibell became aware that the fog, swelling up from the street behind him, had begun to ripple over the high wall and down into the garden. It poured across the ground, rolling and tumbling, playfully erasing every line, blurring every contour, like water running down a child's painting. First the stone paths were swallowed up, and then the sundial, its hard edges melting into the milky haze. Soon only the dark shapes of the evergreens remained, bouquets of holly and privet and myrtle leaves floating on a pearly sea.

Sibell felt something rise inside her, a slow tide of longing, for the night and all it contained, the freedom of the black paper garden. She wanted to taste the fog, feel the grass under her bare feet, crush between her fingers the inky myrtle leaves. She wanted to be there, with him, to become him, to dissolve into the darkness and disappear.

But she did not. Instead, when she could look no longer, she turned back to her bed. The sheets as she slid her cold body between them crackled like autumn leaves. But she left the curtains undrawn, open to the sky, and far above, a blue-ringed, frosty moon.

'You are a very lucky girl, my dear.'

Sibell blinked in amazement at her mother's words. Since her return from Lady Celia's yesterday everyone at Gifford's Oak, from Mama right down to Alfie the boot boy, had treated her with an elaborate kindness that made her feel perfectly wretched – but surely this was going too far?

'Lucky, Mama?'

'Yes, my dear.' Beatrice Gifford took a deep breath and wished that Robert, so forthright in other matters, was not such a coward where his only daughter was concerned. 'Your father heard this morning from Mr Lavery.'

'Oh.' Sibell bit her lip. Preoccupied with her own disgrace, she had almost forgotten Mr Lavery. Only not riding straight to hounds or cheating at cards could ruin a man's reputation. Still, she knew how men hated to be made conspicuous.

'Well, child?' There was a trace of impatience in Beatrice Gifford's tone. 'What have you to say to Mr Lavery?'

'Well, I—' Sibell thought hard. 'I would like to tell him—' she knew it sounded weak, but could think of nothing else – 'I would like to tell him I am very sorry.'

'You mean that you are refusing his proposal?'

Sibell stared at her.

'Proposal, Mama?'

'Of course.' Beatrice Gifford's voice mingled relief and reproof. 'Mr Lavery is—' she hesitated an instant – 'has conducted himself like a gentleman.'

'But Mama . . .' Sibell was completely taken aback. 'I mean, I hardly know him.'

'Really, Sibell.' Lady Gifford's tone was dry. 'And this is the man with whom you retired, unchaperoned, to the conservatory, and remained closeted in private conversation for a full half hour? I find that hard to believe. Surely you must have experienced some feelings towards him?'

Sibell shook her head mutely.

'Not even gratitude, Sibell?' Lady Gifford's expression was stern. 'After all, in the circumstances, Mr Lavery's conduct has been everything that one would wish.'

'Yes, Mama.' All of a sudden, Sibell felt a sort of burning in the base of her throat, as if she were about to burst into tears like the child her mother appeared to think she still was, despite Mr Lavery's proposal of marriage. Her mother looked at her sympathetically. 'Mr Lavery is very rich, my dear. Oh, there is no need to shake your head at me like that. Money is important, you know. Especially for a woman.'

'Would you like me to marry Mr Lavery for his money, mother?' Trained all her life in the Gifford way, to travel third class in railway carriages and wear shoes with the toes cut out for growth, Sibell could not believe what she was hearing.

'I would not suggest it for a minute, my dear, except – these new taxes, my dear. I know that financial affairs are hard for we women to understand, but believe me when I say that recently life has been very difficult for your father. Lately, he has been unlucky with his investments – bad advice, I'm afraid – and now he and I have been forced to consider the possibility that sometime in the near future, unless something is done, we shall be quite poor.'

'Oh.' Sibell was relieved. 'But I will not mind being poor, mother, truly. I would far rather be poor, here at Gifford's Oak, than married to Mr Lavery.'

'Yes, my dear, I appreciate your sentiments.' Lady Gifford's voice hardened. 'But I am afraid you have not quite taken my point. You see, if you do not marry Mr Lavery, it is more than likely that there will be no Gifford's Oak at which to be poor at all.'

Lady Gifford watched her daughter's face carefully. Then, quietly, as she turned to pick up her needlepoint, she played her last card.

'Tom's future, my dear. It rests in your hands.'

Silently, Sibell left the room, tucking her merino wrap around her shoulders because although her mother's boudoir was warm the corridor was not. She felt very strange. It seemed extraordinary that the fate of Gifford's Oak, which had existed centuries before her birth and would continue to exist for centuries after, should rest in her seventeen-year-old hands. That was a real honour, and something which a fragile female branch of the family tree, undistinguished by red underlining, could never have expected. Sibell felt awed by the thought of it.

Sibell Lavery. The name bubbled up onto her tongue, unbidden. Tentatively, she rehearsed the syllables. They sounded well, and summoned up an entrancing image, a tall elegant creature in a fetching hat, carrying one of the new parasols. Mrs Lavery. Mrs Quintin Lavery. Surely no one could crush such a being? She would be too poised, too sure of herself and her place in the world, ever to feel a moment's dismay.

But living with Mr Lavery, in Mr Lavery's Park Lane mansion, that was another question altogether. How could Sibell know in advance what it would be like, how could she possibly judge?

As always, when she was confused, Sibell went in search of Tom. Tom knew so much more about the ways of adult life than she did that he was always able to make her problems feel quite small.

She found him in the library, his blond head outlined against the caramel-coloured panelling by a single attentive ray of winter sunlight. Every time Sibell saw Tom she was struck by his beauty, so much more impressive than a girl's because it was unnecessary, and because he himself paid no attention to it at all. Today, as usual, his wavy hair, which shone even without being brushed a hundred times every evening, had been mercilessly suppressed with cold water, and his even features were screwed up into a manly frown. Tom had planned out his life in every detail. He was going to become Prime Minister, and sit on the Bench, and publish an anthology of poetry to celebrate the birth of his first son.

Seeing her brother amongst the polished wood and leather bindings Sibell knew that everything was going to happen exactly as he had planned. Wherever Tom found himself – at Gifford's Oak, in the House of Lords, on the Bench, or in some learned publisher's offices off the Strand – he would fit in perfectly. It was herself and William, with his unboyish interest in watching nestlings hatch instead of shinning up the tree to capture the eggs, who were out of place; mere appendages, as females and younger sons must always be.

'Tom.' He looked up with a frown from the book he was reading.

'Yes, Sibling?'

'I want to ask your advice about something.' Sibell knew she would get his attention that way. Tom loved to give advice.

'Speak, Sibling. You have my best attention.'

'Do you think I should get married?'

Tom's eyebrows went up. 'Do I know the fellow?'

'No.'

'Does Father?'

'Yes.'

'Does he approve?'

'Yes.'

'Well, then.' Tom went back to his book. 'I think you should.'

'Why?'

'Well—' Tom shrugged. 'It's what women do, isn't it? You might as well get it over with.'

Sibell felt rather deflated. What was the point of her supreme sacrifice if it was going to pass almost unnoticed by its main benefactor? She regretted the thought almost instantly. Seeing Tom's head, bent over his book in a passion of attention, she felt a rush of love and loyalty and tenderness for him. She would have liked to stroke his head, where there was one tuft of hair that had rebelled against the water, but of course that was out of the question.

In the corridor Sibell met William, skulking as he always did. Even Sibell had to admit that her younger brother was a most irritating child. The family was always waiting for William to grow out of some unsuitable habit, like picking scabs off his knees, or whistling under his breath, or rubbing the red patches of eczema in his elbows against his sides, like an old pony on a scratching post. At school he suffered from the trail of glory blazed by his brilliant brother. Tom said he had been made to eat flies.

But Sibell was nothing if not fair. William was her brother too, and he should be consulted.

'William, do you think I should get married?'

'No,' William replied instantly. 'Kissing's boring.' With that, and a fierce, squinting look from his pebble-coloured eyes, he disappeared in the direction of the broom cupboard, where he kept his ant farm.

Sibell gazed after him thoughtfully. Until this moment, she had not thought of kissing Mr Lavery. Of course, if she married him, and if she wanted children, she would have to – but perhaps not so very often.

And as soon as she had children, she would bring them to Gifford's Oak. They would grow up knowing the old house as well as she did. They would learn every old yellow Cotswold stone of it, every silver patch of lichen, every whisper in the eaves. In the tithe barn mentioned in the Domesday Book Tom would teach her children cricket, and in the low-beamed bedrooms she would show them how to chase out the bats with billiard cues, and in winter, when they came in from church, they would tumble into the echoing Great Hall and lift their faces to the blaze of the huge oriel window, a furnace of golden light on the coldest day.

And if, to keep Gifford's Oak safe for her children, she had to kiss Mr Lavery a hundred, a thousand times, that would be a small price to pay.

4 *The Temper of Leaven*

Leo de Morgan entered the eating house in Golden Square on a gust of January air that made his coat tails blow. He threw himself down into his usual chair by the window, wedged his long legs uncomfortably under the matchwood table, and rubbed his eyes. He felt light-headed, slightly crazed. For two days and nights he had been painting like a demon. Covering glazed cloth with oil was the only way to dissolve the hours.

It was exactly seven weeks, three days and twenty-two hours since he had last seen Sibell Gifford. If not for her, he would have been long gone. Staying in London during the winter, without light, warmth, colour, was for him a sort of suicide.

But he could no more have left London now than cut off his own hand. He had to be here, where he had spoken to her and held her in his arms. There was so much he had to say which only she, being the root and cause of it, could understand. That was all he could think of. The moment when she would return.

Leo's reverie was interrupted by the waiter, bringing his usual order. Leo stared for a moment at the chipped plate. He was extremely hungry, yet reluctant to begin. Eating paved the way for other, more troublesome appetites. He was better off when he was painting and half-starved.

But though he could survive almost indefinitely without sleep, he had to eat. Leo pulled his loaded plate towards him and began to devour lamb chops, bread and beer, propping his newspaper between himself and the other clientele because the sight of any human face which was not hers caused him to feel her absence like an actual physical pain. His eye fell on the society pages. They were almost empty, echoing the lull between the Little Season, which finished just before Christmas, and the beginning of the summer Season in April.

Next year, Leo resolved, he would rescue Sibell from that meaningless migration. It did not take wealth or breeding or luck to escape the English winter. The Roman sky, even in January, would be purest Alexandra blue. He would take Sibell there. He wanted to see her on the Corso, with the wind in her hair.

Automatically, Leo scanned the pages, barely paying attention to what he read. How could he, when her image glowed in front of his eyes like a candle in a smoky church? Here were the announcements of births, deaths and marriages, cold and small in black and white, leading on inexorably one from the other like stations on one of the new commuter lines. No mention of love, or joy or sorrow, the pulse that beat under a child's scalp, the heat and weight of a woman's breast, the fearsome beauty of corpses. Just the impersonal, ritual words, 'An engagement is announced.'

Leo's eyes moved on. And then, he stiffened. His heart seemed to stop beating, every vein in his body to fill with ice.

'Rape, Lucette. You might as well admit it.'

'Impossible. A woman cannot rape a man.' Lucette Bailey cleared her throat of its cobwebs and pulled the sheet defensively up to her chin. After last night's exertions they had both of them slept till long past midday, Violette leaving them undisturbed with a tact that Lucette was not sure she altogether appreciated. Now she felt woolly-headed, heavy-eyed, and distinctly sore in private places. What she craved was hot coffee and a bath, not an interrogation. 'You must have been dreaming.'

'Perhaps.' Leo frowned 'But I don't think so. I clearly heard someone laughing. Was that you, Lucette?'

'It might have been.' Lucette felt an uncomfortable blush rise to her cheeks. In the light of day she hardly felt inclined to go into details. Leo had arrived at her house at three o'clock in the morning, swaying like a tree in a storm and bidding fair to wake every neighbour for miles around. It had taken the full effort of Lucette, Violette and Marie to propel him up the stairs to Lucette's bedroom, and Marie had seemed to find the procedure thoroughly amusing.

'I thought as much.' Leo lay back against the pillows and propped his arms behind his head. The contrast between the white lace and the brown of his skin was delicious; Lucette had to look away. She was not used to thinking of herself as a rapacious woman.

There was a long pause. At last Leo turned to her.

'How much would you charge, Lucette?'

'Really, Leo.' Lucette's discomfort deepened. 'We are friends and always have been. There is no need for us to discuss payment.'

Leo shook his head. 'You misunderstand me. I meant, if a man took advantage of you in similar circumstances, what would you demand of him in recompense? An apology? Dinner at the Savoy? A new hat?'

'Certainly not.' Lucette was scandalized. 'I would not set my price so low. A new hat, indeed! It should be emeralds, at least.'

'I see.' Leo's mouth lifted in a contemplative smile. His eyes glinted as he looked at her. 'Shall I ask for emeralds, then?'

Lucette shifted uncomfortably on the crumpled sheet. She hoped very much that she had not become one of those middle-aged women who fell over themselves to pay for young men's favours. Apart from anything else, she could not afford it.

'Hardly, my dear Leo. Emeralds are quite beyond me, I'm afraid.' She gave him a flirtatious glance. 'Could you not settle for something a little more within my reach?'

'Anything?' Leo eyed her quizzically.

'Of course.' Lucette smiled bravely, but inside she felt a qualm. After last night, she was no longer sure she could accommodate all of Leo's desires.

I am getting old, she thought. I am not as elastic as I was, even in that department.

'Is that a promise?'

'A promise, my dear Leo. That is,' she added hurriedly, 'if what you desire lies within my power.'

'Oh yes.' Abruptly Leo rose from the bed. He stood for a moment stark naked, yawned widely and stretched himself. Then, completely untroubled by her gaze, he picked up his clothes and began to dress. As he buckled his belt he turned and faced her. His expression was intent, almost severe.

'Well, my dear?' Lucette lifted herself on the pillows and leaned her head on one side coquettishly. 'Have you decided what it is you want of me?'

Leo looked at her for a long moment. When he spoke it seemed almost at random.

'Sibell Gifford is to be married in the first week of the Season.'

Lucette blinked.

'Yes, I know. She is betrothed to my old friend Mr Lavery.' She eyed Leo curiously, trying to follow his train of thought. 'No doubt, in due course, I shall be receiving an invitation to the wedding. Perhaps you would care to accompany me?'

Leo's mouth twisted.

'No.' His voice was harsh. 'The ceremony does not interest me.'

'Well then?' Lucette was puzzled. Fully clothed, Leo seemed once more to have become a stranger, the fierce, unpredictable man who had planted himself foursquare in her parlour last night and refused to let her soothe him. 'What *do* you want?'

'Sibell Gifford.' His voice was flat. A second after she registered the name Lucette realized with a crashing sense of dismay that last night, in this very bed, she had volunteered herself as a substitute for another woman.

'Impossible.' Lucette's voice shook a little with repressed anger.

'Why?' Leo's voice was icy calm.

Lucette sighed. Suddenly she felt very old. It was hard to explain the structure of English society to someone like Leo, who had no vested interest in it. 'For the simple reason that Miss Gifford is betrothed. I am afraid, Leo, that you have not realized what that means. A wedding has been arranged. And not just any wedding, but a wedding between one of the oldest families in England and one of the richest. It will be the event of the Season. Therefore it will take place as planned. Nothing in the world can prevent it.'

Leo picked up his jacket.

'I shall,' he said simply.

Lucette shook her head, half in irritation and half in admiration. 'I really believe you might, given the opportunity. But you will have none. Miss Gifford has not even come out. Before the wedding she will be locked up at home at Gifford's Oak as tight as a pickled cucumber. No man will be allowed within six feet of her, except her fiancé, and even then she will be chaperoned every minute.'

Leo looked at her thoughtfully. He appeared to have taken no notice at all of what she had said.

'Then what would prevent this wedding?'

Lucette smiled unwillingly. Her heart was bruised, but she could still appreciate a hopeless passion when she saw one. 'An earthquake, I suppose. Or a revolution. I am afraid that nothing less would do.'

Right up to the last minute, no one believed it would ever really happen. There had been countless alarms before, all of which had come to nothing. This was England, after all, where there had been neither earthquake or revolution in four hundred years.

On the mild Friday evening of the 6th of May, 1910, the usual rumours and counter-rumours raced round the streets like greyhounds casting for a hare. He had rallied. He was on the mend. He was failing. He had called for brandy and a cigar. His cough was worse. He was signing papers as usual.

Fifteen minutes before midnight the news spread over London

like a black wing. The people in the streets felt stunned. They had no words to express their sense of outrage. He had been the phrasemaker, the master of condolence, the healer of breaches. Without him, there was nothing to say, no gossip worth relaying. Now, the long sunlit garden party was over. The guest of honour had left, and would not be returning. Edward the Peacemaker was dead.

At midnight, in the silent house, Lucette dressed in the same mourning black she had worn when she first met the Prince of Wales at Tennyson's funeral. It fitted her as easily as if it had been made yesterday. That pleased her. Edward had always liked a trim waist on a woman, perhaps as a contrast to his own, celebratory girth.

As she went slowly downstairs Lucette felt the years between slip away. In the area cellar she found what she was looking for: Edward's last remaining bottle of vintage port. The Prince's first task on the induction of a new mistress had always been to instruct her in the keeping of a good cellar.

Back in her bedroom Lucette lay down fully dressed. She had no intention of sleeping tonight, but she might as well be comfortable.

The cork squeaked out as cleanly as if the wine had just been bottled. Lucette filled her glass to the brim and lifted it in a toast. '*À toi, chéri.*' The wine, cold, seemed to taste of the grave. That was only fitting. She drank deeply.

'May the nights in heaven be long, and the angels hospitable.'

She drank again. Past and present began to blend in her mind. Edward had been a man, that much was certain. All over London and half Europe women would be remembering him tonight. Truly he had been a King for all the people.

Lucette reached for the copy of Tennyson's poems she kept on her bedside table to impress new lovers. It had been the Prince of Wales's first gift to her, dedicated in his own hand, 'To Lucette, the Dream in Black'. The volume fell open where he had marked it, at

88

the only poem in the whole collection that Lucette had ever read. She knew it by heart.

> When the dumb hour, clothed in black,
> Brings the Dreams about my bed,
> Call me not so often back,
> Silent voices of the dead,
> Towards the lowland ways behind me,
> And the sunlight that is gone.
> Call me rather, silent Voices,
> Forward to the starry track
> Glimmering up the heights beyond me,
> On, and always on.

'On, and always on.' Lucette smiled to herself, for that phrase had become their private code. 'On and on,' she and Edward had whispered to each other in the warm nest of afternoon bedclothes, on rugs, on couches, in windowseats, laughing like children, a secret society of two. 'On and on,' they had shouted from the royal enclosure as they cheered on the Prince of Wales's colours. 'On and on,' he had sighed to her at country house prayers, or musical recitals which persisted beyond endurance. 'On and on,' she had teased him, in admiration for his stamina, the joyous appetite that matched her own.

But now Edward was gone. There was no one left to remember those summer afternoons behind drawn curtains; no one whose eyes would glisten in anticipation of delights to come as she whispered into his ear at dinner, somewhere between the anchovy fritters and the caramelized pears, 'On, and always on.'

Lucette slipped off the bed and went to the fireplace. She bent the book of poetry backwards, splitting it ruthlessly down its leather-clad spine. The pages clung to her hands as one by one she stuffed them into the embers.

But even as the paper flared blue Lucette knew it was not enough.

There was one more honour she must do him, one more pledge she must make. He had always known the right word, the right gesture, to end without tears.

So would she. It was time.

There, on her knees, with the empty bottle of port beside her and the coverlet wrapped round her shoulders, Mary found her mistress at six o'clock the next morning. Luckily Vi had taken the day off to visit her mother, poorly with her seventh, because she would have hated the look of the grate, alive with fine ash that flew like the devil. Mary didn't mind at all. Clearing it up gave her the chance to prove what a good upstairs servant she'd make, given half an opportunity. She was fed up to the back teeth with the kitchen, from which she saw nothing but feet.

'The King is dead, Marie.'

'Yes, madam.' To Mary, the King's death was hardly a surprise. He had been enormously old, almost seventy. She couldn't imagine what it must be like to be so old.

And fat, too.

'Shall I run your bath, madam?' Having studied Vi's routines for months, Mary was sure she could do them better. She'd already polished the silver-lined bath with a silk cloth. Vi didn't know what really mattered to a woman like Lucette.

'Not yet, Marie.' Lucette stared contemplatively into the grate. 'Do you know what the King said, just before he died?'

'No, madam.'

'I will tell you. He said, "No, I shall not give in; I shall go on."' She paused and looked up. '"I shall go on." What do you suppose that meant, Marie?'

'That he didn't like the thought of dying, madam,' Mary answered, more sharply than she'd meant. She couldn't see the point of this conversation. 'People don't, as a rule. Not even royalty.'

'Perhaps.' Lucette looked into the grate, then back up at Mary.

90

There was a strange expression on her face. 'But all the same, it is over, Marie.' She rose stiffly to her feet. 'One must go on, of course. But everything will be different now.'

Mary felt a chill of unease. Carefully, she began to let up the outer blind.

'No!' The crisp authority of her mistress's voice took Mary aback. Glancing over her shoulder she realized with a shock that even though Lucette was fully dressed, she had put on neither rouge nor powder. In the old-fashioned black dress, with its high neck and tight sleeves, she looked as old and quaint as the late Queen Victoria.

Mary's unease deepened into dismay. One way or another, it looked as if she too was going to regret that the King was dead.

That morning, as the news percolated outwards like a stain, every blind in every house throughout the land came down and stayed down. The King was dead, and not to display grief was treason.

The entire summer calendar of balls and soirées and entertainments collapsed like a concertina. The town houses of the rich, newly painted, polished and spring-cleaned from attic to cellar, were locked up once more. The society families, with their retinues of cooks and nursery maids and grooms and servingmen, trailed back to the country, their hatboxes still packed and their Noah's Arks of trunks still layered with pastel chiffons never to be worn.

Amongst the dressmakers and pieceworkers of the East End, dismay at the King's death was a little softened at the thought of so much mourning black. This summer, at least, there would be enough work for everyone. Nevertheless, they were concerned for the future. Edward the sensualist had loved finery in his women. Each season had brought a wider hat, a more luxurious quantity of ostrich plumes, a longer train. But Edward's successor, George, was a country man of simple tastes, while his wife, Mary, with her perpetual toques and high pearl chokers, had chosen one style of dress which suited her and stuck to it for years, neglecting her royal duty as an arbiter of change. The future looked grim.

All London, that sunny Saturday, was fearful of what the future would bring. Like children caught out at a midnight feast, gorged sick with currant cake and sugar plums, they could hear Nanny, armed with harsh words and castor oil, crackling up the stairs.

Only one man, as he strode across the deserted Park under a sky of kingfisher blue, was totally, passionately happy. Leo wore no black and felt no guilt, He felt sure that the King, a great lover of other men's women, would have smiled on him today.

For now, at last, he had his chance. The battle was on, the race begun. He had been passed the baton by a royal hand and he intended to run with it till he dropped.

'There is being betrothed, and there is being seen to be betrothed, my dear. I am afraid that one is no good without the other.'

Beatrice, Lady Gifford, trying her best to appear calm despite the jouncing of the carriage, knew that she had taken a great risk in accepting the Duke of Shelburne's invitation to his annual Ascot house party, mere weeks after the King's death. Anyone less comfortably cushioned by wealth and position than the Duke would not have dared to entertain at all during a period of national mourning, but Shelburne was Shelburne.

Beatrice sighed. Despite the Fifth Duke's enormous wealth, she still could not feel entirely happy about him. The Abbey, with its turrets and gables and ridiculous mullioned windows, was an unashamedly vulgar dwelling, and though the Fifth Duke could hardly be blamed for his father's taste in architecture, the idea of installing a colony of baboons in the ornamental Grecian temple had been his alone.

But it was astonishing how much the possession of a marriageable daughter changed one's point of view. It was absolutely vital for Sibell and her new fiancé to be seen together in public as a betrothed couple, to make up for the unfortunate postponement of their wedding brought about by the King's death. Thankfully, Mr Lavery had sent down one of his own carriages to Gifford's Oak, complete with coachman, page and two upstanding footmen. It would have been most embarrassing for Sibell and herself to arrive in the dogcart, which smelled so terribly of straw.

There was one other problem, however, which would not be so easily resolved – the attendance of Sibell's younger brother William. He was recuperating from the chickenpox, and Fräulein Ritter had been almost prostrated at the thought of caring for him single-handed. Last time William had been left in her charge he had removed all the whalebones from the poor woman's best corset, to see if they would dissolve in nitric acid – which of course they had.

'Best behaviour now, William.' Her son gave her an oblique look. Beatrice felt helpless. She hoped the adult company would do him good, though so far, he seemed most interested in the baboons.

William stared out of the window and tried, by thinking very hard of the baboons, not to cry. He spent almost all of his waking hours in this effort. He lived in a state of ferocious unhappiness, dreading, like Captain Hook, every tick of the clock.

School had been a torment from the very first day. Fleetingly, last year, with Papa's financial trouble, he had hoped he would have to be taken away, but now, with Sibell engaged to marry the rich Mr Lavery, even that hope had faded.

But five more years of Eton were more than William could bring himself to contemplate. If his present plan failed, he knew exactly what he was going to do. He had already collected, from the exposed copper piping in the dormitory, a matchbox full of luminous green verdigris. Cook had told him years ago, when he asked her why she checked her tin-lined copper saucepans so carefully, that even a little verdigris was poisonous.

So Sibell was his last hope. He was glad she was looking so beautiful nowadays. Even a brother could see it. At home, a stable-boy had had to be dismissed for staring up at her window with a pair of racing-glasses.

Somehow, William had to make Sibell's magic work for him, not against him. He had no choice. It was, quite simply, a matter of life and death.

That evening Oliver, Fifth Duke of Shelburne, known to his intimates as Nollie, surveyed his long liver-red dining-table with satisfaction. Opposite him his wife and former cousin Augusta looked pale, as she had done for the past four months, but tolerably animated. Even so, he intended to take no chances with his unborn son and heir. Since the third month he had made it clear that he would not be visiting her suite in the East Rooms for any other reason than to inquire about her health.

But Nollie was fond of his wife, and knew that it was unhealthy for a breeding woman to mope alone with nothing to occupy her mind, so this spring he had commissioned a young painter to carry out Augusta's portrait in oils. One dabbler was much like another, but this one came highly recommended by Mrs Bailey, who knew about such things.

What was more important, he was a well set up, good-looking fellow, handsome enough to take no interest in Augusta, but wise enough in the ways of the world to understand that bread was all the better for a lavish application of butter. The flattery of having her portrait painted would take Augusta's mind off her husband's frequent absences in Town. The quality of the finished portrait mattered very little. If it turned out a frightful daub it could always be consigned to an uninhabited suite in the West Wing.

That was one of the advantages of having a large house – somewhere to put things.

Nollie's eye fell on Lucette. Any other year the change in her would not have mattered particularly, but this Season, with London as cheerless as a graveyard, he had hoped to find her available. After all, the Duke of Shelburne could hardly go shopping for company down Regent Street like any Tom, Dick or Harry.

But Lucette had taken the King's death very hard. Now, even decked out in full fig for dinner, she was a poor shadow of her former self. No scent, no rouge, and, more important, none of that flirtatious charm and dazzle which set a man so much at ease. Her famous décolleté was obscured by a net of scratchy black lace and her hair hardly dressed at all, simply dragged back into a prickly-looking bun which sent quite the wrong kind of shiver down Nollie's spine.

Still, Lucette had promised to keep an eye open on his behalf, and that was comforting. Lucette's taste was always reliable.

Lucette, catching Nollie's eye, smiled. The vow she had made to the dead King's memory was proving to have unexpected advantages. Sitting here, at the Duke's dinner-table, she felt more relaxed, more genuinely herself, than ever before. It was so much more comfortable to be a spectator in the grandstand than one of the contenders. And she had a talent for picking winners. The Duke would have no cause for regret.

Glancing down the table she caught sight of Leo, leaning back in his chair and frowning slightly, with that disgraceful air of being totally at his ease which she had always found so attractive. He was the only element of her sacrifice which she truly regretted.

But at least she was still important to Leo, still implicated in his life. If it had not been for her influence, Leo would not have been invited to the Abbey at all. That thought gave Lucette great pleasure, a satisfaction that was almost maternal. She was glad that she had been able to give Leo his chance at last.

Leo, placed between an elderly, stone-deaf dowager and a middle-aged spinster so shy that she blushed if he so much as glanced in her direction, was left free to study Sibell to his heart's content. She was seated exactly opposite him, so he was able to observe the graceful column of her neck as, after each course, she turned her attention obediently from the grey-haired man on her right to the young Guardsman on her left. Her hair was dressed in a new style which added a touch of lightness to her fair seriousness. One thick buff blond curl descended from her chignon to lie against the white skin of her neck. From time to time, as if troubled by its touch, she lifted one hand to tuck it back, then, remembering just in time, lowered her hand once more.

Each time Sibell made that small, tentative gesture, Leo felt his heart rise into his mouth and his blood beat in his temples. He wanted to take that nervous, straying hand and imprison it in his own. He wanted to reassure her, to prove to her that her anxiety was without foundation, that she was perfection itself, the most beautiful woman in the room. He wanted to lift that springy, heavy curl and coil it round his finger, inhale its scent, warm from her skin. He wanted to kiss the nape of her neck where it lay, then brush his lips down the white satiny slopes of her back, till she shivered at his touch.

And yet, he had no idea if Sibell was even aware of his presence. So far she hadn't so much as glanced in his direction. But that didn't matter. He was there, within four feet of her, close enough to see the movement of her mouth and the glistening of her black silk bodice as she breathed. He had eaten, but tasted nothing, barely touched his glass of wine. His hunger for her was absolute, a passion that ruled out every other appetite. The emptiness inside him was something only she could fill. They were made for each other, his darkness to her light.

Sibell, as she listened patiently to the young Guardsman's long description of the correct way to polish a pair of cavalry boots, was achingly conscious of the man across the table. At first she had thought he was staring at her because there was something wrong with her new hairstyle, concocted perhaps a little too quickly by that clever little maid Mrs Bailey had insisted on lending her for the evening. Then, between one heartbeat and the next, as if she had always known, deep down, that one day she would meet him again, she had recognized Mr de Morgan.

From that moment, despite her best efforts, Sibell had felt her attention disengage itself, the subdued hum of civilized conversation recede, the brilliantly lit table fade into dimness. She had to pinch herself under the table from time to time to continue to function at all. There seemed to be a sort of hypnotic music emanating out of Mr de Morgan's silence, a melody only she could hear. He was the only one at the table to sit so still, neither talking nor eating. From where she sat she could feel the warmth of his gaze on her face. She had no idea how he came to be there, or who had invited him. Perhaps he was a ghost or a mirage, a figment of her imagination, summoned up from some dark part of herself she had not known existed. She dared not look at him, dared not challenge the spell. Ghost or not, he was more real than she was. If their eyes met, it would be she who dissolved into mist and disappeared.

William Gifford, as the two females either side of him talked busily over his head, stared glumly at his gold-rimmed plate and mourned the loss of his salmon trout. It had taken him a full ten minutes to remove every scrap of flesh from the spine without dislodging a single vertebra. He had already planned out in his head what he would do with the skeleton. He would wrap it in muslin, boil it carefully, air dry the bones, then thread them up with gut, so he could study the way they moved.

But good manners, in the end, had been his downfall. Mindful of his borrowed dinner coat, he had been digging for his handkerchief to wrap up the skeleton when his whole plate had been whisked away under his nose, to be replaced by another, bearing a sullen little mess of cod's roes without a bone to its name. Not for the first time, it had occurred to William that being allowed down to grown-up dinner wasn't quite the privilege it was made out to be.

Now, the conflicting scents of the two ladies on either side of him made William feel quite ill. He sat between them like a prisoner, flanked by insurmountable walls of jet beads and black taffeta. To protect himself, jutting out his lower jaw and squinting, he made a face like a baboon.

Quintin Lavery caught sight of his fiancée's younger brother and averted his eyes. It seemed extraordinary that Sibell Gifford and that unattractive boy should be brother and sister. It would be just his luck to be forced into marriage with a beauty and then sire a monster.

In the months since the disastrous night of the November ball Quintin had reconciled himself to his forthcoming marriage as best he could. It had one advantage: automatic entrée into the closed world of the country gentry, the sort of English respectability which would take centuries to acquire in any other way.

But even so, Quintin felt trapped. He had wanted to enter the golden circle, but in his own time and under his own volition. Now he had been caught in the machine. That left a bitter taste in his mouth.

Quintin stared at his bride-to-be. He was aware that she was a beauty, but to him her beauty seemed glassily unreal. This empty-headed, unmade girl, who knew nothing of the world, possessed his future. She had stolen it from him. He would never forget that. How could he? Every time he saw her it would be like looking into the face of a gaoler.

Beatrice Gifford saw the laden dining-table through a haze. She was feeling very odd, almost light-headed, though she had drunk no more than half a glass of hock. She was finding it very difficult to concentrate on her neighbour's conversation, though she had noticed how often his gaze dropped to her cleavage. Glancing down herself in order to check his interest, she noticed to her horror that the skin over her upper chest had broken out into unsightly red blotches. Hastily, she picked up her fan to hide them. As a wave of heat passed over her body then receded she tried to force herself to think clearly. Was this the beginning of the change? If it were, it could not have come at a worse moment. With a wedding to plan for, she needed all her wits about her.

Mary Mizen skipped round a corner and cannoned straight into a waistcoat. For a moment, her heart in her mouth, she wondered if by ill luck she'd run into Mr Lavery. He'd think twice about trying anything in the Duke of Shelburne's house at ten o'clock in the morning, but all the same she wanted to steer well clear of him. She stepped back quickly and saw to her relief that the occupant of the waistcoat was the Duke himself.

'Careful, my dear.' He bent with the dignity of a much older man. 'And who might you be?'

'Mrs Bailey's maid, sir.' Mary dropped a quick curtsey. She wasn't yet used to her new position. After the King's death, it had been touch and go. Mrs Bailey had been going to dismiss her, until Mary offered to work as both parlour and personal maid at kitchen girl's wages. Madam hadn't been able to resist such a bargain. She'd sent Vi off to work for a friend of hers. Mary was sorry about that, but she would have paid to get out of that kitchen. Now, she felt as if she'd gone to heaven.

A light touch, that's what Mrs Bailey needed.

The Duke frowned a little.

'Mrs Bailey's maid . . .' He paused, giving Mary such a long time to study the pattern of his paisley that her eyes blurred with the strain. At last he spoke. 'Is it you that is responsible for your mistress's hair?'

'No, sir.' Mary bobbed another quick curtsey. It couldn't hurt. 'Madam dresses her own hair now, sir.'

'Ah.' There was a weight of understanding in the Duke's tone. He shook his head regretfully. Then, seeming to have forgotten Mary's existence altogether, he strolled away.

Mary frowned after him. It wasn't often that a man looked straight through her like that. It was a challenge. If she hadn't been busy she'd have tried at least to make him notice her a little.

But first things first.

She found Leo in the long west gallery, studying one of those brown-stained paintings which all looked the same to her. There were dark rings under his eyes and he didn't look at all pleased to see her.

But he would feel better when he found out what she had to tell him. Mary felt a pleasing sense of importance.

'Ever had the chickenpox?' she asked him, brightly.

Leo frowned. 'Why do you ask?'

'Lady Gifford hasn't. Not ever.' Mary smiled. 'Not till now.'

Leo stiffened. 'They're leaving?'

Mary shook her head. 'Not yet.'

'How long?'

Mary shrugged. 'A few days. Two, maybe three.'

'Three days.' For the first time, Leo smiled. His whole face lit up from inside like a lantern. Mary dropped her eyes. Happiness like that could damage your eyesight, like staring too long at the sun.

Leo turned to the window. Studying his face in profile, Mary noticed for the first time what a curly mouth he had. At the moment, it lifted at the corners as if drawn up by strings. He was thinking of Sibell Gifford, as blind to the world around him as he'd been that night in Lucette's drawing-room, drunk on cheap brandy.

Mary felt a tug of irritation. That made two young men this morning for whom she'd become invisible between one second and the next. It wasn't right.

But it wouldn't always be like that, she told herself silently. Everything changed. The secret was to catch the tide on the turn.

'Wait a moment.' Leo's voice halted her as she turned to go. Mary did as he asked, a little impatiently, as he walked towards her. His face still had that gilded, unreal look. He stared down at her for a moment. Then, taking her completely by surprise, he dropped a kiss on her cheek. 'Thank you.'

Mary was shaken, she had to admit it. Even though the kiss hadn't been meant for her. She opened her mouth to speak, but Leo was already gone, striding down the length of the gallery like a man going into battle. Mary could almost hear the jingle of spurs.

Feeling a bit flat, she went to the window and looked out. Down below, tiny as pegs on a cribbage board, she could see Sibell Gifford and her young brother making their way slowly towards the ornamental lake. It was early yet, but already the sky seemed dazzlingly bright. It was going to be a fine day.

As she walked, Sibell could feel the heat of the sun on her shoulders, beating through the thin fabric of her parasol. With one hand she held up her skirts to prevent the hem becoming too damp with dew. Despite the heat the grass was still wet, beading her ankle-boots with moisture. Her black dress was heavier than she would have liked for this weather, but perhaps by the lake the air would be cooler.

As she followed William sedately down the incline Sibell was aware of a new constraint between herself and her brother. Overnight, it seemed, their roles had been reversed. Yesterday, William had been at least partly her responsibility; now, with Mama ill, he had become her chaperone. Such a turnabout was unsettling.

William negotiated the ha-ha with a jump, then made off at an ungainly, bounding run. 'William!' Sibell hissed after him. 'Remember our bargain!'

Chastened, William returned to help her down the four-foot drop, designed to prevent deer from grazing the parterres near the house. There had been much argument at breakfast over the day's programme. William had wanted the baboons first thing, of course, but Sibell had drawn the line at apes before luncheon. Finally they had settled on the drainage arrangements of the ornamental lake, and the rose garden, in that order.

The lake, in its sculptured hollow, was much bigger than it had appeared from the house, and more irregular in shape. Insects twirled in the haze that clung to the water. The water itself was invisible, being covered over by a bright green mat of weed which seemed, from where Sibell now stood, almost solid, like a flat mossy stone.

The air was warm and still and scented. Its damp touch reminded Sibell of childhood visits to the laundry room at Gifford's Oak. On the lake's central island stood a newly-painted summerhouse, its pointed roof protruding from the willows like the neck and head of a nesting waterbird. In the clear morning sunlight the setting, with its lake and island and pagoda, had the deliberate delicacy of a watercolour painting. Yet there was some element in it which made Sibell feel uncomfortable; the weed, perhaps, too violent a green for England.

William knelt by the reed-fringed edge and fished out a big clump of the stuff. Instantly, as if offended, it drooped in his hand, all its colour and substance dribbling away to slime. But he seemed delighted.

'It's in flower,' he told Sibell excitedly, bringing the handful for her to examine. She stepped back as water dripped from it onto her boots. The clump exuded a milky greenish fluid and a sweetish smell.

'So is the rose garden,' she reminded him, taking a firmer grip on her parasol. 'Please, William, let us find the drains and be gone.'

'They must be here somewhere.' William began to ferret about in the reedy undergrowth. 'The lake is definitely man-made. Hey, Sibell!' He surfaced from the undergrowth with a rope in his hand. 'I've found something!'

'What?'

'Look!'

Following his eyes, Sibell caught sight of a diminutive rowing-boat, barely big enough for two, and painted the same shade of viridian as the weed.

'Just think! We could go to the island!' William's eyes sparkled.

Sibell shook her head. 'I do not think that is a good idea, William.'

'Why not?'

Sibell hesitated. She could not explain her own reluctance. Somehow, she felt that the Chinese pagoda was meant to be admired from afar, not entered. 'We're not supposed to.'

'Don't be such a wet blanket, Sibs,' William replied with a touch of scorn. 'If we weren't supposed to, why would there be a boat?' He tugged on the rope. The boat bobbed sluggishly. 'Oh do come, Sibs. I can't go if you don't.'

Sibell bit her lip. She did not need reminding that if it were not for her, William would be free to ramble wherever he chose. 'Very well then,' she agreed unwillingly. 'But let us go a little further to the side, out of sight of the house. Just in case.'

William was more expert with the oars than she had expected. Digging manfully into the sticky green soup, he soon had the boat turned and nudging towards the island. With each scoop of the oars he succeeded in carving out a small space in the weed, but within seconds, like an eye shutting, the hole he had made was silently, seamlessly closed. Even the empty space behind the boat sealed itself up as soon as they moved on. Sibell drew her skirts in around her ankles and kept her feet together in the dead centre of the boat. She cared not at all for the moist sucking sounds the weed made against the bows as the boat ploughed forward.

Halfway across the lake Sibell noticed that a small pool of blackish water was beginning to gather underneath her boots. She lifted them a little anxiously, for they were brand new, and braced them against the side of the boat.

'Don't unbalance the vessel,' William ordered importantly. Busy with the oars, he had noticed nothing. Staring downwards Sibell saw that the water beneath her feet had begun to deepen rapidly. Now it had developed a current of its own, spinning merrily like a miniature whirlpool. She let out a cry of dismay.

'Nearly there, Sibs,' William reassured her.

'William!' Sibell half rose to her feet. The boat rocked wildly under them. 'William, we're sinking!'

Under the mat of weed there was no telling how deep the water might be. Sibell felt a chill of fear. She could not swim. The thought of that green stuff touching her skin, getting in her hair, in her mouth, was terrifying. She and William stared at each other in horror. He flailed wildly with the oars, but the boat was too low in the water now to respond.

'Help!' To Sibell, her cry sounded desperately weak, the squeak of a mouse behind the wainscoting. The heavy air muffled it absolutely. She stared helplessly down. May sunshine reflected off the black moiré of her skirt in dazzling patterns, dragonfly green and blue. The beauty of it mocked her. Inside the boat soupy water mounted inexorably, starred with dancing bright medallions of weed. Already Sibell's new boots were soaked through, her skirts wet to knee level. And yet she dared not move, for fear of toppling the boat and ushering in the thick green tide which waited to engulf them.

'Keep still!'

The voice was calmly authoritative, echoing Sibell's own thoughts so exactly that she obeyed it without question. William too responded instantly. The oars dropped from his hands with a flat, wet sound and lay on top of the weed, neither quite in nor quite out of the water. Sibell had a sudden vision of herself borne away bodily on that lush green carpet, like Millais's drowned Ophelia. Paralysed with terror, she gripped the sides of the boat.

'The rope! Throw it to me, as hard as you can!'

William, his face flushed scarlet, fumbled in the inky water between his legs and fished up the rope. He hurled it with all his strength past Sibell, showering her with water in the process. Sibell did not dare to look behind her for the owner of the voice. She did not want to know how far away they were from the central island; hope would be too painful. At last the boat began to move, sluggishly at first, then with increasing speed. Sibell closed her eyes and prayed. The next moment she was lifted bodily from the boat, whisked through the air and set, teeth chattering and shaking in every limb, on dry ground.

'Thank you. Thank you.' She clutched at her rescuer blindly, hardly able to believe that she was saved.

'Wait there.' Gently but firmly the man prised away her hands and waded back into the lake for William, still marooned, ashen-faced, in what was no longer a boat but a mere outline, inches above the water. Even as Sibell and William clung to each other, sobbing with relief and guilt, the boat sank silently from view and disappeared.

'Come.' Sibell felt a strong hand at her elbow. Automatically, she responded to its pressure. 'You have had a shock. You had better sit down for a while.'

'Yes.' Sibell could barely hear herself speak for the chattering of her teeth. Still clutching William's hand, she stumbled towards the summerhouse, her wet skirts dragging at her feet like shackles. She almost fell towards the open door. Inside the pagoda it was dim and quiet and blessedly dry. Subsiding gratefully onto one of the dusty benches which lined the walls, Sibell inhaled with a tremor of pure relief the familiar summerhouse smell, a reassuring pot-pourri of old wood and potting compost, dried leaves and sun-stale air. She would be safe here. Through the latticed windows netted over with convolvulus and honeysuckle, no glimpse could be seen of the weed's virulent green. With a shiver of relief she peeled off her wet gloves, laid her head back against the boards and closed her eyes.

'Let me help you with those boots. They must be soaked through.' Sibell's eyes flew open in shock to see the man, whose presence she had temporarily forgotten, kneeling on the dusty boards in front of her. She found herself staring at a hatless head covered with glossy golden-brown hair. Her words of protest died on her lips as he looked up for an instant and she recognized Mr de Morgan.

105

'You too, William.' Mr de Morgan spoke over his shoulder.

'Yes, sir.' William sounded mortified. He sat down abruptly and began to tug at his boots.

'No. Thank you.' Sibell recovered herself just in time to thrust both her feet out of reach under the bench. 'I would rather keep them on.'

'Very well.' Mr de Morgan shrugged. 'But you will regret it, I'm afraid. If you let the leather dry out, those boots may have to be cut.'

Sibell suspected he was right. The boots were a size smaller than she really needed, and this morning it had taken the combined efforts of herself, Mrs Bailey's maid and a long-handled shoehorn to get them on at all. But under no circumstances could she bring herself to consider removing them in front of someone who was neither a servant nor a relative. No man she knew would ever even have suggested such a thing. Suddenly, Sibell found herself wondering how Mr de Morgan himself had arrived on the island. Perhaps he had swum? The thought made her feel violently uncomfortable.

A board cracked as William rose abruptly to his feet. Looking round, Sibell saw that he had removed not only his boots but his woollen socks as well. Against the dark wood his bare white feet, with red patches where the leather had rubbed, looked very young. But his face wore a curiously adult expression, at once guilty and determined. Refusing to meet his sister's eyes, he moved purposefully towards the door.

'Where are you going, William?' Sibell hoped very much her alarm did not show in her voice. It seemed churlish to be nervous of Mr de Morgan, who had saved both their lives, but the thought of being left alone with him for so much as a moment filled her with dread.

'The boat,' William announced gruffly. 'I must try to get it back.'

Sibell half rose to her feet to dissuade him, but he stepped quickly through the door and the sunlight severed him from her gaze as abruptly as a guillotine. Sibell sank back onto the bench, hardly knowing what to think. In her relief at not being drowned, she had completely forgotten about the boat, her host's personal property. William was quite right to want to retrieve it. And yet, with her brother gone, she felt curiously at a loss, unsure whether she had been abandoned by an ally or relieved of a potentially hostile critic. There were no witnesses now to what might take place between herself and Mr de Morgan.

Sibell searched for words to break the silence and found none. She felt very nervous, and could not understand why. After all, there was nothing to fear in the situation. It was morning still, barely eleven o'clock. Any other time of day – the afternoon, the evening, and most of all the night – could be dangerous, but she had never heard of anyone being compromised in the morning. Mornings meant lessons in the schoolroom, and church, and milk and biscuits.

But simply looking into Mr de Morgan's face seemed to deny every memory and every habit Sibell had ever had. It was as if he came from another world, where the significance of milk and biscuits was not understood and could not easily be explained. Sibell had always known that men ate and drank different things, visited different places, spoke a whole separate language, but until this moment that difference had never really touched her. She had known it without feeling it, just as she had known that males were taller and stronger than females, but had never felt it, close to, as she did now, confronted by the width of Mr de Morgan's shoulders, the curve of the powerful muscles in his thighs as he knelt before her, the sheer size and weight of him. He seemed like a member of a different species from her own, an animal featured in no known bestiary. If he chose to overpower me now, she thought a little wildly, I know no German verb that could prevent it.

Leo held his breath and willed his hands not to tremble as very gently he eased the pin from Sibell's black straw hat and laid it aside on the bench. He was aware with every fibre of his being that the slightest mistake on his part, any element of clumsiness or haste, would lose her. But he could hardly control himself. This was the moment he had waited for, prayed for, willed with every ounce of strength and passion in his body. Now, his desire for her smouldered inside him like a badly trimmed lamp. Everything about her touched him unbearably. Every tiny detail seemed enormously magnified, the white-blonde hairs on her averted cheek, the mysterious convolutions of her ear, the sound of her faint, rapid breathing. She was utterly strange to him, unlike any other woman he had ever known. And yet he felt that he had known her always, that she was a part of him, so close to him that there were no divisions between his body and hers, blood to blood, bone to bone. His longing for her throbbed inside him like a deep internal bruise, a desperate haemorrhage that only she could heal.

But he must act, he knew that. Slowly, with an infinite, agonizing slowness, he leaned towards her averted face and brushed his lips against her cheek. Her skin smelled of the nursery, a faint, innocent fragrance of sun-warmed skin and lavender-scented soap. Leo's heart thundered inside his chest. That elusive perfume aroused him more than any other woman's oils and potions could have done. Her stillness, her silence took his breath away.

Gently, he slid his lips across her cheek to her mouth, that soft, pink, unrouged mouth which had tormented him in dreams. He held his lips over hers, with a lightness that caused him physical pain. But he would not force her, he could not. She must come to him willingly or not at all.

He felt her lips quiver under his as if she were trying to speak, then she recoiled, and then, like a tide turning, inescapably pulled towards him over rock and gravel, sand and shingle, she came to him again, as he had dreamed she would, filling him with her scent, her taste, her sweet salt essence. Her lips parted, and she was his.

PART TWO

Fundamentum vero artis est corporum solutio

5 Atoms of the Sun

If only I weren't so frightened, thought William Gifford as he threaded his way through the back streets. His torch called up fleeting dim shapes in the blackout; a soldier, limping, his grey, stubbled face at odds with the neat white bandage that encircled it; a nurse, cloak flying, heels tapping, her face set. Nothing remained of the Mayfair William remembered, with flower-sellers on every corner.

Four years of war had made a different world.

Gripping his torch tight with both hands to stop the watery beam from shaking, William peered up to check the number of the house. Yes, this was the address that Nollie had recommended.

His heart sank.

If only I weren't so frightened, William thought for the hundredth time since that morning. Then I wouldn't have to be so brave.

On the first floor of the house above, Violet Briggs stared about her in amazement. She hadn't set foot inside Mrs Bailey's drawing-room in seven years, but she'd never have recognized it in a million. The room was painted black from top to bottom. Little lamps sprouted from the floor like toadstools, while the walls were hung with embroidered shawls and strings of beads and what looked very much to Vi like one of Mrs Bailey's corselettes, pinned out like a big pink moth.

Vi advanced cautiously into the garish dimness. It didn't seem right, even in wartime, for a front door to be left ajar at night and the hall all dark.

'Mary? Is that you?'

'But of course, my dear.' The extraordinary figure on the chaise-longue, reclining like a mermaid on a turquoise sea set off with lime green and purple cushions, gave a throaty chuckle. 'But it's Mara now. Ever since the Ballet Russe.'

That explained the silver-shot gauze over the blackout blinds. Vi didn't know whether to be scandalized or amused. 'What on earth have you done to your hair?'

Mary/Mara laughed and shook her head. Her outrageously frizzy hair flew out almost horizontally. It was cut shorter than Vi had ever seen on a grown woman, chopped level with Mara's pointed chin. The effect of this schoolgirl hairdo, combined with her made-up face and exotic beaded dress, was striking.

Vi shook her head. 'You're up to no good, Mara.' Young officers just back from the Front couldn't wait to spend their leave, and their money, on the nearest available female. Mara, here in the middle of the West End, was very conveniently placed.

Mara smiled and shrugged, sending an eddy down her shining green scales.

'I could say the same of you. There's only one place you'd come out looking like the Yellow Peril. I must say it goes a treat with your hair.'

Vi blushed with annoyance. The TNT at the Royal Oak munitions factory did have a yellowing effect on the skin, especially with masks and gloves in such short supply.

'The pay's good.' Even at half the men's wage, that was still true.

'So it should be. You could get blown up.'

'You're a one to talk! You want to be careful, Mara. You'll get yourself into trouble.'

'Not me.' Mara's eyes gleamed. 'I'm no fool.'

Vi fought a brief battle with curiosity and won. 'Please yourself. But where's Mrs Bailey?'

'Eastbourne. For three years now.'

'What did it, the zeppelins?'

Mara laughed. 'No, the Belgian refugee. She couldn't stand the way she chewed.'

Vi hesitated a moment. In a way, it was a relief that she didn't have to involve Mrs Bailey. With something like this, it was best not to be dealing with a jealous woman. But how far could she trust this new Mara?

'Go on, spit it out.' Mara disengaged herself from the divan and came towards Vi. She was still as skinny as ever but there was nothing childish in the way she moved, making all her green beads dance. Vi stared at her, trying very hard to see through the mask of powder and salve. 'Don't worry, I owe you a favour or two. Remember?'

'That's true.' Vi had almost forgotten her feeling of outrage when she'd had to leave this house seven years ago. Rightly or wrongly, she'd felt she'd been ousted by Mara.

But it was funny how things worked out. Mrs Bailey had found her a job in Lord Gifford's household, and when his daughter got married she'd become her personal maid. She'd really enjoyed that, until the war broke out and her mistress went back down to the country. Vi hadn't been able to bring herself to leave London and her family. She'd thought of becoming a VAD till she discovered she wouldn't be paid; then she'd signed up as a munitionette. The work was exhausting and dangerous, but she had lodgings of her own in Hammersmith and could go home to Whitechapel every Sunday.

'All right then. Bygones be bygones.' Vi reached into her large handbag, past the paste sandwiches she'd done up for herself before she left her lodgings, and drew out the letter. Mara took it from her.

'Leo de Morgan, Eggsquire . . .' Mara tapped the letter reflectively against her teeth, as if she were testing a gold coin.

Now she'd made her decision Vi felt a little doubtful. This morning, when she'd received a letter from her former mistress, with a sealed letter enclosed, she'd been amazed. It wasn't the proper distance to be kept between a lady and her maid.

But when Vi had read the letter addressed to herself she'd understood. It was the war, you see. It had turned everything upside down and sideways. And there wasn't much that Madam could do for herself, stuck there in the country with a small child and a widowed mother and no one to help her but her younger brother William, who'd never been much help to anyone, so far as Vi could gather. All she remembered about young William was that once, at Gifford's Oak before the war, he'd gone to some trouble to disentangle a spider from her hair – but Vi had known very well it was the spider he was rescuing, not her.

Funnily enough, it was thinking of that spider that had finally made up Vi's mind to come to Derby Street with her mistress's letter. Young William, despite his faults, hadn't liked to leave a fellow-creature trapped, and neither would she.

'You will make sure that he gets it?'

'I'll do my very best. Of course, with things being as they are . . .'

'Do you know where he's stationed?'

Mara laughed. 'Where they all are. Somewhere in France.' She paused. 'But I have my methods. Wherever he is, he'll get his letter.'

If he's still alive to read it, was the unspoken thought in both their minds. For a moment Vi saw her mistress's letter spinning off into a great black void, like a leaf in the wind. It was a strange world where people were held together only by bits of paper.

At that moment the front door bell pealed. Vi jumped.

'I must go.'

'Back to the fireworks factory?' suggested Mara with a trace of mischief.

'Rather that than what you're doing!' retorted Vi with spirit. 'At least I'm being useful!' She closed her handbag with a snap and hurried out, wishing that the new hobble skirts permitted a longer stride. As she rounded the stairs down to the ground floor entrance Mara's voice, with a mocking note, floated down to her.

'Are you so sure, Vi? Why don't you ask the men which they prefer, another round of ammunition or . . . ?' Despite the darkness of the hall, Vi took the last few steps in a gallop.

Forty-five minutes later a young man in a naval uniform several sizes too large for him shook Mara's hand punctiliously on the first floor landing.

'Goodbye.' He smoothed one hand self-consciously over his sandy-coloured hair. 'And thank you.' He blushed bright red. 'For everything.'

Mara smiled. 'And thank you, for telling me about the freedom of the sea.' She meant it. She wasn't altogether sure she'd understood what he was talking about, but she'd been pleased to listen anyway. She liked him. She liked the paler band round his hairline at the back of his neck where his new short cut let on that he was a raw recruit, and his freckles, and his pink cheeks, and the way he'd stammered over his false name. He was like a little new copper penny that she'd been the first to see.

But now it was time for him to leave.

When the door had closed behind her visitor Mara stood for a moment on the first floor landing, relishing the emptiness of the house. Now there was no one in the whole world who could see what she might or might not be doing.

Back in Lucette's bed, she pulled the counterpane up around her neck, making a tent of warmth around herself. Then she reached for the letter Vi had given her. It was faintly creased. Slowly Mara slid a fingernail between seal and envelope. She felt no guilt. She'd given her solemn word of honour that the letter would be delivered – but she'd never said she wouldn't read it first.

November 6th, 1917

My dear Leo,

Please forgive me. Something terrible has happened.
Tom is dead.

Even now I cannot believe it. Last month, for his birthday, I
sent him a collapsible periscope. Such a clever thing. It was
meant to keep him safe.

I should not be writing to you like this. But I can't sleep. My
mind keeps running round and round. I meant to keep my
promise, truly.

But Tom dying has changed everything. I can no longer bear
to have no news of you ever, never to know. To think that one
morning I may open the newspaper over breakfast, and—

I cannot write any more. I shall send this letter to Violet
Briggs in London, who was my personal maid before the war.
Maybe she will be able to find out where you are stationed.

Please, if this letter reaches you, please write just to tell me if
you are all right. It would mean so much.

November 7th, 1917

But why should anyone reply to such a dreadful, self-indulgent
letter? I have just read over what I wrote last night and I am
ashamed of myself. Tom would say that I am behaving just like
a girl, and he would be right.

Please excuse my fit of self-pity. Truly, I have nothing to
complain about. Mama, Hugo, William and I are warm, dry,
well-fed and perfectly safe.

I will now attempt to redeem this letter, and prove that I can
be a proper, sensible correspondent.

We are all well. Hugo has forgotten that he ever lived in
Town. At the moment his chief interest is the gardener's dog,

which he follows everywhere. I have shown him Buenos Aires on the library globe, and explained that his Papa has had to stay on there because of the war, but I do not think he understood, being only six years old.

Mama has made William promise not to join the Army before he is twenty-one. We hope and pray the war will be over by then.

Please, if you receive this letter and it is not too difficult to reply, will you tell me what I might usefully send? I am afraid I cannot knit. And please, if you can, tell me what the war is really like. We are sadly out of touch here at Gifford's Oak.

Ignorance can be such a torment. Do you remember, at our last meeting you asked me why I married Mr Lavery so soon after Black Ascot at Shelburne, instead of waiting till the Autumn, as had been planned? I did not feel able to tell you the truth then. I let you assume, like everyone else, that I wanted to make sure of the best offer of marriage I was ever likely to receive.

But that was not why I married, and now, when the war has changed so much for everyone, I can no longer bear that you should continue to think so. I think I would have told you at the time, if I had not been so ashamed of my ignorance. Tom always teased me for it, and I felt such a fool that I always pretended to know more than I did. Now, I wish he was still here to tease me. I would not mind at all.

But I knew nothing. I took for granted what went on in the stableyard, but never dreamed that it might have any bearing on the relation between man and wife. I was completely ignorant in that area of life.

That is why I married Mr Lavery so quickly after Shelburne. I was afraid that because I kissed you in the summerhouse I would have a child.

There, I have said it. I have never dared tell anyone else. It

117

hurts me still that if I had not been so foolish we might have had more time in which to know each other. I cannot say more without disloyalty. It was all so long ago, perhaps it no longer matters. But I wanted you to know.

I hope you will not think too badly of me for writing. I know it is wrong of me. This morning I almost decided to tear up this letter. Then I remembered the dream. It is one that has recurred from time to time ever since I can remember. I had it again last night.

It is always the same. In the dream I am a small girl, running through a field of wheat almost as tall as I am. The sun is hot on my back and the bees are humming and I know that if I run faster and faster I will either be falling or flying.

I always wake up before I know which it is to be. But falling or flying, I will remain

Your
Sibell

Slowly, Mara folded up the letter, slid it back into its envelope, warmed the seal lightly over her candle flame and stuck it down again. It was just an innocent sheet of paper, but she found herself handling it gingerly, as if it was one of those shellcases Vi spent her time stuffing with dynamite. There was no knowing what its effect might be. It might hit the target, or fall in no-man's-land, or maybe fail to go off at all, which happened more often than not, according to the men rather than the newspapers.

But Mara would launch the letter on its way all the same. When she could, she liked to keep her promises.

She wondered fleetingly if Leo and Mrs Lavery had been lovers before the war. She hoped they had, but somehow she doubted it. They wanted too much from each other for that.

But Mrs Lavery was still in love, that much was certain. The word wasn't even mentioned, but it was there all the way through, like a stick of rock.

Mara made a rueful face. Falling or flying, indeed. There was no need for such extremes. It was much better to make steady progress – with both feet firmly on the ground.

As she climbed the nursery stairs Sibell shivered in her stockinged feet. She was wearing two pairs of socks, the outer ones some of Papa's Argyle, that he used to wear for hunting, and two nightgowns, one silk, one flannel, over merino combinations, the whole ensemble topped by an old red woollen robe she'd had since she was fifteen.

But tonight, despite the cold and the dark and the need to take refuge under bedclothes before the old house cooled completely, Sibell was not ready for sleep. It had taken her less than a week to realize how much she'd failed to appreciate William's company while she still had it. Now thoughts tumbled in her brain: memories, wishes, fears so intertwined that she could not tell one from the other.

It was Christmas Eve.

Tonight there was a familiar snap in the air which meant frost. Before the war, frost would have had Papa stamping off to his study in a cloud of bad temper and cigar smoke, because the ground would be too hard for hunting. But now, whatever the weather, nobody hunted, or wore black for the dead, or coppiced woodland. Slowly, year by year, the war had eroded the habits of country generations.

Tomorrow, if there was a frost, she would tell Hugo that Father Christmas had put tinsel in the trees for him.

Slowly, Sibell opened the door she had left deliberately ajar at her son's bedtime. Under a mound of bedclothes topped by Mama's pre-war furs, Hugo, a small animal cocooned in his lair, was almost invisible. On top of the bed, looking like a shabby fur coat himself,

Kitchener gave her a beat of his tail and a sloping sideways look from under his whiskered eyebrows. He was not supposed to be on top of the bed, and he knew it as well as she did. Now Sibell comforted herself with the thought that at least on a frosty night the gardener's dog, used to sleeping in a shed by the greenhouses, would keep Hugo warm.

It was better, however, that Mama should not find out about Kitchener's intrusion. Mama, who never complained, who in the first years of the war had eaten some very peculiar dishes with no appearance of distaste – there had been a period when everything Sibell cooked, whether potatoes or eggs or rice pudding or stewed beef, had turned out the same, inexplicable shade of khaki – would not appreciate Kitchener's blurring of social distinctions. Mama accepted the war politely, just as she would have accepted the discomforts of a strange house she found herself obliged to visit, but made no further concessions.

Now, observed by Kitchener's slanting liquid eye, and listening carefully for any change in Hugo's breathing, Sibell reached into the bag she carried and took out the contents of Hugo's stocking. Walnuts, which he would not eat, but which she had made pretty with painted stars and goblin faces; hoarded raisins stuffed in an old lace handkerchief and tied with ribbon; a tiny musical box from the library which he had always coveted and which he might now have for his own, until it broke; a diamanté mask which Mama had worn at a ball in her youth; the best Worcester Pearmain from the garden store; and finally, for Kitchener, a black satin collar embroidered with his name.

For a moment the enormity of the task awaiting her – the huge pretence, for Mama and Hugo, that it was a charming novelty to eat lentil soup and sheeps' heads and toast and dripping in the kitchen – almost overwhelmed her. She could no longer even persuade herself that when the war was over everything at Gifford's Oak would go back to normal. When Papa had died two years before the war, sailing to America to check on his investments in that ship which everyone swore was unsinkable, his death had seemed the worst possible disaster which could befall the Giffords.

Now Sibell could see that Papa's death had merely foreshadowed a far greater shipwreck. For even when the war ended, as it must do eventually, Tom would never come back. William, if he survived, would inherit Gifford's Oak at the age of twenty-one, but two sets of death duties in quick succession had already devoured what remained of Sibell's marriage settlement from her husband. All she and Mama had to live on now was her pre-war allowance from Quintin, from whom she had had no communication in four years.

Hugo shifted in his sleep and sighed, a long-drawn-out breath of such comical world-weariness that despite herself Sibell smiled. Without acknowledging Kitchener's presence she dropped the lightest of kisses on Hugo's dark curls. He smelled of cinnamon, and autumn leaves, and dog. Closing the door behind her, she tiptoed out.

Moonlight from the uncurtained oriel window outlined a fragile coloured path down the stairs. On an impulse, Sibell followed it, past her own bedroom door and further, imagining as she padded down the familiar stairs that the hall below was filled with company, as it would have been before the war, a drift of chatter and women's scents, a glow of jewels and candlelight. Automatically, as she reached the lowest tread, she reached for her coat, slung across the banisters, and slipped her feet into her boots.

Her footsteps, slow and heavy in the empty hall, sounded like Papa's. She almost expected to see a line of light under the door of his study, hear him cough to clear his throat, his sign that he was working hard on government papers.

But everything was dark. Feeling strange and rather like a ghost in her own home, Sibell moved on past the study to the library. No Tom, looking officious as he studied the day's papers, but a smell of must, for the library was hardly used now. It was too large to heat and the tall windows too expensive of material to black out. Between two of those windows overlooking the South Lawn Sibell could make out the dim outline of the portrait that Leo had painted of her before the war. He had never meant to finish it, she knew that now. Like Penelope with her tapestry, he had spun out the sittings as long as he could, so that they might continue to meet.

How Sibell remembered those afternoons; the smell of paint and sunlight, the strangeness of her enforced stillness, the way time seemed to stop and yet dissolve away in an instant; the many seasons of his gaze. Often they had not been alone, but no matter who chanced to visit the studio, his eyes and his voice had been for her alone. His words seemed to summon up a world in which anything was possible, any choice or combination: Dutch white lead, the best and most brilliant, or fugitive verdigris, fermented with grape skins; Naples yellow gathered from the slopes of Mount Vesuvius, Egyptian cinnabar, vermilion; lapis lazuli, ultramarine.

Colours and words became Sibell's spells, her bastions against the world. During those sunlit dusty afternoons she learned how to protect a brush against moth by wrapping it in tobacco leaves, how to slake white pigment with safflower to preserve its perfect whiteness. Perfection of remembering, Leo told her, that was the impulse of art: the thirst for eternity of the temporary heart.

To Sibell it seemed that Leo, only a few years older than herself, had already amassed more experience than she would ever have in a lifetime. Now, as she studied the figure in the portrait Leo had painted, she saw a girl in a trance, drinking in the world with her wide, fascinated gaze: truly, Leo's creation. She wished she could have been that girl from the beginning. Everything would have been different then. But she had lacked the courage of Leo's convictions.

Now war had finished the portrait, for good or ill. As her eyes grew accustomed to the dimness Sibell could see reflected in the glass her own pale face and found it impossible to believe she had ever resembled the girl in the painting. Certainly she did so no longer. At this moment, in her many layers of underclothing, with her hair plaited for bed and suppertime potato cakes lying heavily on her stomach, she felt plain and leaden and at least a hundred years old. Not that it mattered. There was no one but herself to see.

Except that there was a man outside the window.

For a long, breathless moment every pulse in Sibell's body halted. The man stood motionless, tall and black against the already frosted whiteness of the gravelled drive. Sibell felt like a rabbit stopped in long grass by a bullet in the heart. Out there, poised, waited the hunter. He was all men, absent and present, dead and alive, intruder and rescuer, all the guests and relatives, friends and strangers.

The man moved fractionally, as if he were aware of her gaze. Sibell could not see his face. He lowered his head. He seemed about to turn away, to change his mind. Sibell almost wished he would turn away. She wanted no more, she could not bear it. But then he looked up, and the moonlight caught him, and the shape of his face, the set of his shoulders, brought memory flooding back, and with it, a rush of pain like blood returning to a frozen limb.

As Sibell ran to the door she heard her own heart pounding like a pursuer. The sound of her footsteps rang out across the hall. Her hands as she fumbled with the bolt on the oak door were clumsy with cold. The door swung wide, creaking back on its hinges with a noise like ice cracking. A rush of freezing air scissored Sibell's breath from her lungs. She tried to call out but no sound came. Her breath feathered silently out into the air.

And then, down the broad steps, utterly unfamiliar in the darkness, she felt herself fly towards him as if her feet touched no ground. The next moment the rough fabric of his coat was hard against her cheek. He was so tall, so big. Still far away, in the mind's eye of memory, but here. Now. Real. Sibell clung to that, to the convincing hardness of his coat, the size and solidity of him. He was solid, and real, and behind the rough cloth of his coat, he was warm, and she held onto him as if she was drowning, and her voice cracked as she said his name.

6 Operations of Nature

Mara, perched on the corporal's shoulders, swayed with the crowd. It was New Year's Eve, and Trafalgar Square, despite a salting of snow, was packed. Mara pulled the corporal's coat a little tighter round her neck and tugged his cap down over her curls against the cold. She was glad to be amongst so many people, sharing their frosty breath and the familiar wartime smells of damp wool and beer, disinfectant and tobacco.

A bottle, borne by the corporal's gloved hand, rose like Excalibur from the sea of heads beneath her. Mara shouted down her thanks and put her lips to the stone-cold mouth. Icy champagne misted her eyes. Up here on the corporal's shoulders she was taller than any man in the crowd, apart from Admiral Nelson on his column. What was it that young sandy-haired naval recruit had told her? The Battle of Trafalgar had been fought not to defeat an enemy but to defend the freedom of the seas.

At the time, Mara hadn't understood the difference. But now it came to her. This war, with its air raids, threatened to take away from ordinary people something they hadn't even known was theirs: the sky above their heads. Cocking her cap in the Admiral's rough direction, Mara lifted the champagne bottle and drank a toast which she felt he would appreciate; to the freedom of the air.

Only she must have drunk too deep, because the next moment the sky itself turned upside down and rained champagne as she lost her balance and lurched backwards into the faceless black sea beneath her. The corporal staggered, and the two of them would have toppled headlong if anonymous hands behind Mara hadn't pushed her back onto his shoulders.

'Steady, soldier.' As Mara righted herself, a small explosion of recognition forced its way through the champagne bubbles in her mind. She tried to turn, but a protest from the corporal halted such a risky manoeuvre.

Bending her mouth to his ear, Mara managed to make her wishes clear. Careful of her silk stockings on his tunic buttons, she slithered to the ground. Her view was abruptly cut off by the mass of bodies. She searched to left and right. In a small gap, faintly darker against the night sky, she caught sight of the silhouette of a man a full head taller than the rest, walking away.

Mara hesitated. Perhaps she'd imagined that voice? In any case, it was nearly midnight on New Year's Eve. A solitary soldier leaving the Square without waiting for Big Ben to chime twelve either wanted to be alone or was heading for a private rendezvous. What other reason could there possibly be?

Almost before Mara had framed the question in her mind the answer came to her. The man was walking head down, not fast, but steadily, with a doggedness that showed he knew exactly where he was going and why. In four years of war Mara had learned to recognize that gait.

He was nearly out of sight. Mara reached her arm hastily round the corporal and tucked the half-empty bottle of champagne into his belt. He tried to turn towards her but the crowd was too tightly packed. Standing on tiptoe, she shouted as close to his red-tipped ear as possible, 'Later!' He nodded, but there was no telling whether he'd heard her.

It was only fifteen feet away into the crowd, already buffeted and breathless, that Mara realized she was still wearing his coat and cap.

Leo had never known that happiness could be like a knife. He was impaled on it now. There was no escaping it. It was with him always, wherever he was, whatever he did, an ecstasy so acute that it was pain. He was aware of nothing else, neither breathing nor eating nor sleeping. He was run through with it, a silver sword.

It was possible, he realized, that after four years at the Front he had lost his reason. If that was so, if what he was experiencing now was madness, then he did not care. He had never felt so aware, so alive. He needed nothing else.

One week. Six days and seven nights.

In a garden hung with frost, a man and a woman walking, not touching, but between them an intensity of feeling so complete that neither of them felt the cold, or was aware of time passing, or who they were, or where. Behind them a small boy and a dog played, insubstantial as wraiths. Together, the man and the woman created a new world, crackling with danger, into which they plunged without glancing back, borne away in a spinning, frozen tide.

The world was theirs. They needed no words with which to create it. There was no other world but theirs.

But what happened? Leo's rational mind, not altogether silenced, inquired from time to time.

There was no answer from the realm of impoverished fact which could answer that question. We peeled potatoes together, Leo replied, and walked in the sunken garden on a frosty day. And these were visions from the beginning of time, always known, utterly new. Revelations. The robin came down, long-legged, with his bloodied breast, and looked at us from one eye and then the other, and we were the robin, and we were each other, and we were perfect knowledge. We walked like gods, we were trees walking, and the red of her fingers' ends against the white of the potatoes was the most beautiful thing I have ever seen.

But what else? his rational mind inquired. These are dreams and visions. What did you do?

We touched, Leo answered. Not with our bodies, but with our eyes, our hearts. We knew each other. Goodbye was implicit in everything we said and did. Just being was enough. We could have died, there, and it would still have been perfection.

That first night I lay with her on her bed, all night, and heard the creak of the bedsprings as she turned like the earth in my arms, and felt time tremble, shaken loose from its moorings. Yes, I lay with her, I held her. Into her I poured my self. That was all. That was everything. No one else could ever understand.

But you are parted, his rational mind insisted, and Leo looked up, and for a moment a wave of sickness passed over him. The world, her world, rushed away from him and he floated in a void. Not parted, no. It would not have been possible to part without dying.

By the time Mara reached Victoria Station midnight and its cheering had been and gone. The station was dark, the platforms thick with British and Dominion troops. Mara, faced with a wall of blue, grey and khaki, began to wonder quite why she'd run all the way from Trafalgar Square. Now the corporal's heavy coat seemed to have set like mortar across her shoulders and her feet ached. She should have realized that there would be very little chance, in the dim light, amongst all these men in uniform, of finding one particular soldier.

The long mournful yell of a leaving troop train rang out, followed by a machine-gun rattle of closing doors and an explosive puff of steam. The acridness of it made Mara's eyes water. Suddenly the scene, with its shadowed unknown faces and sulphur-yellow smoke, the great black wheels of the locomotive squealing and grinding, seemed like a glimpse into hell. The windows of the troop train compartment were already misted over; even if the man she was looking for was just on the other side of the glass, she would never know.

The guard's whistle shrilled and with a deep predatory cough the locomotive started up. High in the cab Mara could just make out the driver, a pale blur. Faceless, like the war itself; part of the machine.

Mara couldn't stand it a moment longer. She'd always hated being at the mercy of other people's timetables. Kicking and digging with her elbows like a terrier, she forced her way through to the platform edge. The train was gathering speed now; sparks shot up from the wheels to singe her stockinged legs. The carriages slid past her, snake-like on their invisible vertebrae. The rattle of their wheels told an ancient rosary. Mara glanced quickly over her shoulder at the end of the train. There were only three carriages remaining. She began to run.

With a lunge that almost wrenched her shoulder out of its socket Mara seized the nearest doorhandle and hung on tight. Half-dragged, half-running as the train gathered speed, she brought her other hand round to double her hold and then, between one breath and the next, the icy metal plucked itself from her fingers and flicked her away like a spent match. She fell back onto the platform with a bone-jarring shock. Bruised and half-blinded with smoke and steam, she was barely aware of the mocking rattle of the wheels as they pulled away, inches from her silk-clad ankles.

Then above her someone shouted and a door in the last carriage crashed open, nearly beheading her. Several pairs of burly arms reached down out of the smoky darkness, hooked her under the elbows and swung her bodily into the train.

'All right, mate?' Mara was set squarely on her feet, thumped on the head to right her cap, dug forcefully in the ribs. 'Left the goodbyes a bit late, didn't ya?' From the pitch darkness that surrounded her came a cackle of laughter.

Everything had happened so fast, in such a swirl of noise and fumes, that Mara could hardly breathe, let alone answer. Only the throbbing of the floor under her feet and her bruised knees convinced her that she was actually on board the train and in one piece. Muttering hasty thanks to her invisible helpers and keeping her face well down, she began to edge her way down the corridor.

Now the train was rocking and swaying from side to side as it gathered speed, reminding Mara of the crowd she'd left behind in Trafalgar Square. A very different crowd from these quiet trench-coated figures braced against the walls and windows of the corridor, knapsacks and kit piled up around their feet like sandbags round an empty building.

Slowly, Mara made her way down the train towards the engine. She felt strangely light-headed. With darkness inside and out the train could have been headed anywhere, into outer space or to the centre of the earth. One by one she checked the dark, crowded, silent compartments. One by one she crossed from carriage to carriage over the dim, glinting, rattling gap between the couplings. With each carriage that she searched the roaring of the engine ahead grew louder, the smell of smoke and burning coal stronger.

All too soon Mara arrived at the last compartment in the last carriage. The noise from the engine was deafening now, so loud she couldn't hear herself breathe.

He wasn't there.

Mara felt a stab of the most ridiculous disappointment. She stood in the roaring darkness and contemplated for a brief moment the full extent of her folly. She'd made off with a corporal's coat and cap, ruined a perfectly good pair of shoes and singed her best stockings beyond repair for absolutely nothing. It was hardly the time of year, or the time of day, for a spur-of-the-moment visit to the seaside.

'Happy New Year, Mara Mizen,' she wished herself sarcastically, as she rubbed her bruised shins. 'It serves you right.'

At least here, in the corridor at the head of the train, the soldiers weren't quite as close-packed as before, because of the noise and smell and vibration. They were mostly older men, with their arms folded and eyes closed. Asleep on their feet, Mara suspected, having chosen this spot with just that idea in mind.

One man, however, was neither old nor asleep. Propped in an uncomfortable position by the door, where the draughts would be keenest and the light from the dim blue unshaded bulb at its harshest, he was reading a letter. By the angle of his body he showed that what he was reading was both intensely important and absolutely private.

In that moment, for the first time, Mara truly wished she'd never left Trafalgar Square. Now that the champagne fumes had cleared a little from her brain she could see quite clearly that in front of her stood a man she hardly knew. The impulse which had driven her to follow him was out of date by more than four years. He was a stranger.

Mara's heart thudded. She was angry with herself for putting herself in this position. Behind her anger there was a sort of sadness she hadn't felt before. No one in the world would read any letter she might write with such attention, but that wasn't it. She'd never been one for letters. Letters were a kind of lie, and lying was better done face to face. Yet, as she watched his face in the hard light, she felt somehow in the dark, shut out of a world of signs which she'd never learned.

It was that, finally, which made up her mind. Slowly, her heart beating so loud it almost drowned the noise of the engine, Mara edged the final few yards down the corridor till she stood right in front of him, almost touching. He didn't move or look up.

Mara cleared her throat.

He didn't even blink. He was miles away.

Mara might have turned away then, but the train gave a sudden lurch as it went over points, and she was thrown off balance. She jerked towards him and the letter crackled between them. He looked up, his reverie broken, and as he did so, by pure force of will, Mara caught his eye.

All speech was impossible, because of the noise from the engine. There was a long pause in which Leo stared at her in the thunderous darkness as if she were a complete stranger. He looked very tired, as if he hadn't slept for days, and extremely fierce. Mara told herself that was just because he hadn't recognized her. She took off the cap. Then, with all the insouciance at her command, she reached up and kissed him on the lips.

She was astonished at his response. It was as if she'd released a giant spring. She found herself enveloped in his arms, hard and hot. His tongue filled her mouth; she felt his body vibrate as if he were groaning. The train swerved, throwing them bodily from side to side of the corridor. The din of the engine filled Mara's head, making it impossible to think. Leo's lips found her neck; she felt his stubble scrape there. She wondered, idiotically, where he'd put the letter.

Now his hands were roving over her body inside the corporal's coat. He seemed on fire, heat radiating off him like a furnace. Mara began to shiver. His hands were pushing and pulling at her as if he was trying to take her apart.

'This is very sudden, Leo,' she shouted at him, but it was like spitting into the sea; the noise of the engine drowned her voice completely. The humour of the situation overcame her suddenly. A naughty outing to the seaside was one thing – but this?

At least, she consoled herself, it wouldn't be possible for Leo to go much further in the corridor of a train, surrounded by fellow soldiers.

But she was wrong.

Mara sensed by the tension of Leo's body exactly when he reached the moment of no return. At that point, if she'd wanted, she could have slipped out of his grasp and fled. She'd never found a man disabled by desire impossible to escape.

But she did not. As she felt her narrow skirt ride up her thighs, Mara moved towards him instead of away. He was her train, her letter, the reason she had come so far; she would catch him, she would read him, she would accompany him as far as he was going.

At least, at last, she had his full attention.

'Lovely!' she shouted with amazement and delight as she opened to let him in, and it was as if she welcomed all the strange and lovely world.

7 Earth of Leaves

There was something about a train, thought Violet Briggs.

She risked another look at the young man opposite. Maybe it was the country light, maybe it was spring, but everything about that young man seemed interesting. He was so clean he sparkled, like properly polished silver. His blue and white uniform reminded Vi of the willow pattern plate Mum kept at home above the stove. His reddish hair sprang up beneath his cap as if it wanted to push it off.

From beneath her eyelashes Vi let her eyes dwell for a moment on the young man's empty sleeve, pinned neatly to the side of his jacket. She didn't know why, but she found the thought of this physical diminishment rather attractive. It made him, a man, a member of that master race, less of a threat. Vi had grown tired of the grabbers.

She wondered what it would be like to be held by one arm. His good hand lay perfectly relaxed against his thigh. It was a square, muscular, competent hand, with a curly thumb. On the back of it a few golden hairs caught the light.

Vi found herself glad that she was looking her best this morning. She wore overalls at the factory, so her long brown cord jacket, pre-war, with its little bit of dyed rabbit at the collar, gathered sleeves and matching full skirt, still looked good as new. Wartime had made Vi grateful for the brightness of her colouring; the obligatory duns and drabs which so disheartened the other girls rather suited her.

All in all, though it didn't do to brag about it, Vi had had a good war. While the men were away the women had made a good job of running the country, and notice had been taken. Now, at Park Royal, she and the other women workers had a cloakroom of their own, and a proper canteen, and steam-fed radiators instead of a few coke buckets that gave off more fumes than heat. Now even Lord Curzon had finally given in, and told the Lords to give women over thirty the vote.

Vi wouldn't get that opportunity for another three years, but just thinking of it made her feel important. She almost felt that if she wanted to, she could reach over to that golden-lashed sailor sitting opposite her and simply help herself to him, as a man might do.

Only of course she wouldn't do anything of the sort. Even now, as his quizzical gaze met hers, and Vi realized with a jolt that his eyes were almost exactly the same greeny-grey colour as her own, she felt her skin run hot and cold with embarrassment and looked away out of the window. The countryside outside was intensely, almost painfully green, spring ruthlessly shouldering away all the old growth of winter.

Vi felt breathless, as if something inside her was trying to expand. This year, they said, might be the last of the war.

The little train began to slow, making a meal of the process, juddering and groaning and sighing. Vi tried to keep her eyes fixed on the countryside but she was uncomfortably aware of the sailor opposite, who was being jolted from side to side in the same unpredictable rhythms as herself. She had the impression he might be smiling at her. With a flourish and a clang the train finally halted and to Vi's dismay her velvet bag, jerked forward by momentum, hurled itself bodily from the netting rack above her head into the sailor's crisp white lap.

'Well, bless my soul!'

'I am so sorry, sir.' Crimson-faced, Vi rose to her feet and reached to remove the bag, but there seemed something unnervingly personal about the action, like removing the fig-leaf from a statue, and she found herself frozen in mid-air.

'Please don't mention it.' The sailor smiled up at her, but made no attempt to remove her bag from his lap. Vi hardly liked to ask him for it; for all she knew, he was injured more than visibly. Perhaps he had difficulty standing?

'I'm afraid I have to get out now. This is my station.' Vi felt flustered. Why had she said 'I'm afraid'? It sounded so forward.

Suddenly, the sailor rose to his feet. Vi stepped back hurriedly. He wasn't a tall man, but he seemed much bigger standing. She tried very hard not to look at his empty sleeve. He stood over her, smiling, her bag swinging lightly in his hand.

'Allow me.' His voice was clear and musical; not deep, but with a sort of authority to which Vi found herself responding automatically. Quickly, because if she wasn't careful she was going to miss her stop, she ducked through the sliding door the sailor opened for her and down the corridor. Fresh spring air greeted her like a bouquet of flowers as she emerged from the train. Already the guard was advancing down the tiny platform to make sure that all doors were shut.

Vi turned to thank the young man for carrying her bag – but he was nowhere to be seen. 'Violet Briggs,' she said to herself, numb with realization, as the whistle blew and the train, with a shudder of pretended reluctance, began to move away. 'You've been fooled good and proper this time.' The entire contents of her bag, so carefully packed last night, flashed through her mind. The tin trumpet wrapped in newspaper. Her best nightgown, never worn. Two weeks' wages. Her blackcurrant pastilles.

'Excuse me.' A voice spoke behind her, so close that she almost jumped out of her skin. She whirled round and there he was, the sailor, crinkling his eyes and his curls at her. She could have hit him, or hugged him, or both. To her dismay the tears which had threatened at the back of her eyes chose that moment to pop out. She scrubbed them away with the side of her hand.

'What's the matter?' The concern on the sailor's face was almost comical.

'It's nothing.' Vi hardly recognized her own voice. 'It's just that I thought . . .' Her voice trailed away as she realized that to go on was as good as accusing him of thievery. Her face went scarlet again.

'Don't tell me, I've done it again. Should have known. Never separate a lady from her bag. Mother always said.' One-handed, the sailor held out her bag to her like a peace offering. 'All my fault. Please accept my apologies.' His eyes, so disturbingly like her own, were full of entreaty.

Vi took the bag. Through her glove she felt fleetingly the warmth of his hand. A bird called in the distance, a sudden, liquid sound, to be answered by one perched, it seemed, right above their heads. 'Pax?' he inquired, disarmingly.

Vi nodded. She didn't recognize the word he used, but there was no mistaking what he meant. He was as transparent as good aspic. Now, on the deserted platform, barely twenty yards long, feeling both conspicuous and insignificant in the spring limelight, Vi was suddenly, simply, glad that he was there.

'I am being met,' she said, taking a deep breath and remembering her manners. In wartime any form of transport was worth its weight in gold, and Mrs Lavery, when she'd begged Vi to come down to the country and help out while her mother was ill, had assured her there would be a vehicle waiting for her at the station. 'Perhaps if you live nearby . . . ?'

'I should be enormously grateful.' The sailor gave a smile of such radiance that Vi blinked. 'But first, we should introduce ourselves.' He bent towards her again with a look of deep concern. 'That is, if you would care to?'

'Of course.' Vi felt a bubble of pure, frivolous happiness welling up inside her. She hadn't felt like that for years, she'd forgotten what it was like.

The young man held out his hand, and with no more than a moment's hesitation Vi placed her own inside it.

'William Gifford,' he said.

With a sigh of relief Lucette peeled off the fine gauze mask she'd bought before leaving Eastbourne, to protect her against the dreadful flu about which she and Maman had heard so much. She'd forgotten how stifling London could be in July.

Now, summer sunshine picked out unmercifully the shabbiness of Derby Street after five years of war. In her dashing green travelling costume, just a little too tight across the midriff, Lucette felt as out of place as a Christmas goose. No one would think the Germans had just been turned back at the Marne.

The front door of number 7 had warped, and Lucette had to push it open, marking her lace gloves in the process. The air in the hall had a stale, sour smell. Lucette's eyes narrowed. She might have guessed as much. Mara's monthly reports had been too vague to be convincing.

But she was glad to observe, in the upstairs drawing-room, that the blinds were all drawn. July sunlight was quite strong enough to fade her favourite wallpaper. Perhaps Mara had not done too badly after all.

It must have been hard, in wartime, to keep up standards single-handed, and she had not been forewarned of her mistress's arrival.

Lucette raised a blind, letting in a shaft of yellow light, and turned, expecting to find her chaise-longue and larger pieces of drawing-room furniture chastely bridal under their dust-sheets, just as she had left them.

'Ça alors!' In the hot air of the room, disturbed by the sudden onslaught of light, five or six flies dropped like smuts from the ceiling and began to circle lazily. Lucette's eyes scurried from one side of the room to the other, searching for something familiar on which to rest, but found nothing.

Everything was black.

Gasping as if she had been buried underground, Lucette rushed to the other window. Light, she needed light. The blind flew up and tutted on its bracket.

'Who's that?'

Lucette gave a small scream.

There was a sound from the back of the room. Lucette, frozen, strained her eyes into the shadows. A dim shape advanced slowly towards her.

'*Madame*? Is that you?'

Slowly recognition seeped into Lucette's terror, releasing an inflammable mixture of fury and relief.

'*Salope!*' Lucette took two steps towards her maid, drew herself up to her full height, and with the full force of her right arm slapped her in the face. Mara, caught off balance, staggered sideways and sat down heavily on the floor.

The next minute, to Lucette's astonishment, the girl burst out laughing.

'*Mais qu'est-ce que vous faîtes là?* You should be ashamed of yourself!'

Mara nodded, apparently unable to speak, the corners of her eyes creased up in uncontrollable mirth.

'Your mistress returns, and this is how you greet her!' Lucette made a regal gesture towards the wreck of her drawing-room. As she did so she became aware of an ominous lack of constriction about her shoulders. She whipped round, alarmed, to discover that the force of her exertions had split her green costume neatly down the back seam; now she possessed not one jacket but two, drooping on her shoulders like the twin halves of a pea-pod. '*Aï!*' She rounded on Mara. 'Insufferable girl! Now look what you have made me do!'

'I'm sorry, *madame*.' Still gasping with laughter, Mara scrambled to her feet. She moved slowly and clumsily, and Lucette felt a pang of guilt.

'What is the matter? Are you ill?'

Mara shook her head. Lucette's eyes took in her standing figure and widened.

'What is this, Mara?'

Mara shrugged.

Lucette blinked. 'But surely . . . I thought . . .'

'So did I.' Mara took a step forward. 'It's your fault! You told me about the special days – you said it would be all right!'

Lucette felt flustered. Somehow, as so often with Mara, the tables had been turned. 'You must have made a mistake in your counting.' She was perplexed. Mara's condition was a complete surprise. According to the latest medical advice, the days in the middle of a woman's cycle were completely safe.

Mara glowered at her. In her crumpled ill-fitting dress she looked dreadfully plain. Lucette felt tears of annoyance and disappointment spring into her eyes. She had looked forward so much to returning to London, to life and gaiety, and this was what she found. For this she had braved the flu, and the heat, and the long, solitary, dusty journey. It was too much.

'You cannot stay here!' The words burst out of Lucette before she thought how they would sound. Mara looked at her once more, without expression. Against the dreary black walls her face was sallow, her hair dull. She looked used-up, a little old woman. It seemed impossible to Lucette that this could be the same Mara, vibrant with energy and promise, whom she had left in charge of Derby Street before the war.

I want to go home, Lucette thought, suddenly, with a child's poignant, absolute longing. Just as soon as this war is over I shall go home, with Maman.

'There's a friend of yours come to see you, Violet.'

Vi glanced up at her mother in surprise as she perched her hat on the top shelf of the dresser, out of harm's way – though with Vic and Jimmy away at the war, Bertie, Billie and Charlie almost grown and even Mack, the baby, a stolid eight years old, there was no longer any real need for such precautions.

She sensed something unusual in the air. When Ma called her Violet, it meant serious business.

'A friend? Who is it?'

Ma nodded importantly. Her eyes glittered with secrecy.

'That would be telling. All I can say is, it's a good job your father ain't here.'

With the suddenness of a bolting animal Vi's heart rushed up into her throat and lodged there, pulsing. William. Could it be, could it possibly be William? Just the thought of him made him immediately present to her imagination, as complete and vivid as if he were in the room beside her; the sound of his voice, his eyes, his smile. But surely, after everything she had said to him last month at Gifford's Oak, William would not call on her like this, at her parents' house, out of the blue?

And yet, William was William. He thought convention was a waste of time. He hadn't even seemed to notice the social gulf that separated him from herself, let alone mind about it. If, for whatever reason, William decided to come and visit her, he would stop at nothing till the deed was done.

Vi found herself blushing. The strength of her longing to have William think of her, even now, when she'd made it quite clear to him that they must never see each other again, was uncomfortable. Her last sight of him had been three weeks ago, at the station. He'd stood very upright on the platform and waved goodbye with enough energy for two men, let alone two arms. Watching him recede slowly out of sight Vi had felt a dull pain in the middle of her chest, a bit like indigestion. She had sat in her compartment and sucked a pastille to distract herself, but hadn't been able to taste it at all.

Of course, she had no one to blame for that but herself. She shouldn't have stayed on so long at Gifford's Oak, a full two weeks more than she'd meant.

'Don't go.' Vi could hear William's voice now. 'How am I going to manage here without you, poor cripple that I am?' He had rolled his eyes at her and made her laugh, as if it really didn't matter that she was East End and he was West End, as if spending time together was wholly natural and regular, as easy as breathing.

It was just like William to take himself off into the back room, thinking by so doing that he would not be making himself a nuisance. Suddenly Vi felt a panic of anxiety as to what he would think of his surroundings – the walls speckled with brown stains where the boys had cracked bugs, the grimy washstand, which had never been the same since Bertie and Charlie had tried to make ink in it, the rag rugs which had shrunk with boiling. The smells.

'I'm so cross with you, William,' she thought as she opened the back-room door, anxiety battling with an irrepressible upsurge of pure joy. 'I shall give you a piece of my mind.'

As footsteps and voices sounded in the next room, Mara swung her feet down from the upended chamber pot and prepared herself for battle. She and Mack were playing cards; so far, she'd won a half-eaten packet of tiger-nuts and a metal badge which Mack had been told by the gypsy who sold it to him was made of fragments from a zeppelin shot down over Potter's Bar. Neither of these trophies mattered to Mara much, but they would make good currency, and at the moment she needed all the leverage she could get. White-chapel was her last resort. Lucette had given her a month's wages in lieu of notice, but by the time Mara had got her clothes out of pawn there had been precious little left.

Mara hadn't expected much from Vi's parents' home in White-chapel, especially when she saw how small the place was, but the thin grey-haired woman who opened the door had been surprisingly welcoming. Mara had explained that she was an old friend of her daughter's, but the explanation had hardly been needed. Within half an hour Mrs Briggs had sorted out the arrangements.

'You and me'll sleep on the settle in the front room.'

Even the money Mara couldn't afford to pay hadn't seemed important to Mrs Briggs. She'd confessed that with her husband away fighting she and the three boys still left at home were better off than they'd ever been before, because of the wartime allowances. With Mr Briggs away, the money hadn't been washed away in drink.

But there were other kinds of reckoning. Now, as the door opened, Mara rose carefully to her feet. She'd been preparing herself all week for this. 'Hello, Vi.' She risked a cautious smile. 'Just like old times.'

'You.' Even in the dimness of the back room Mara could see that Vi's face had gone quite white, the freckles showing up on her skin like bug splatters. Sensing the development of an atmosphere, Mack edged out of the room behind his sister. 'What are you doing here?'

Mara shrugged. 'Nowhere else to go.'

Vi's eyes took in her figure and widened.

'It's not so bad.' Mara made a gesture at herself. 'Only two months left.'

Vi advanced into the room. Mara watched her warily. Vi's nostrils were pinched and greenish. Mara didn't blame her for being angry, only this didn't seem like anger, more a sort of disappointment.

'I don't want you here.' Vi's voice was flat and tired. 'Ma?'

Mrs Briggs poked her head round the door.

'Surprised to see your friend, Vi?'

'Very. Only she's not my friend.'

'Now, now.' Mrs Briggs's eyes flicked from one girl to the other. 'No need for that.'

'She can't stay here.'

'Why not? Just because she's got a baby on the way?' Mrs Briggs sounded almost belligerent.

'No, Ma.' Vi seemed surprised at the tone of her mother's voice. 'There's no room, anyone can see that.'

'Room enough, with your Pa away.' Mrs Briggs sniffed. 'Mara's good company, she is. It's nice to have another female in the house.'

'But you can't, Ma!' Vi sounded exasperated. 'You don't know her!'

'She's human, ain't she?' Mrs Briggs faced her daughter squarely. 'Anyone can make a mistake!'

'I know that, Ma! That's not the point. I don't want her here, that's all. This is my home!'

'Mine too, young lady. And you've no call to be so snooty, neither.' Two red spots had appeared in Mrs Briggs's cheeks. 'I always said I wouldn't tell you, so don't you tempt me!'

'What do you mean, Ma?' Vi looked astonished. Mara too could make no sense of this sudden attack. 'Tell me what?'

Mrs Briggs took a deep breath. 'It could have been me, standing right there!'

'I don't understand.' Now Vi's face was flushed.

'Well, maybe you should.' Mrs Briggs was breathless. She turned to Mara. 'You might as well know, an' all. It don't matter any more who knows.'

The man in the travel-stained white suit tipped back his Panama hat and squinted up against the blazing August sunshine at the house before him. At first sight, like England itself, it seemed intact, miraculously unchanged. Only a critical eye would notice that moss smeared the drive and ivy blurred the apple trees.

But the front door was ajar. That open door, sign of a servantless residence, was a silent statement of ruin. Gifford's Oak, where Dukes had danced, was now no more worth defending than a poor crofter's den in the Hebrides.

Inside, despite the August heat, there was a smell of damp. The hall was deserted. Grit squeaked under the man's feet on the unswept, unpolished floor.

They said that the war had cost England five million pounds a day.

Slowly, Quintin Lavery mounted the stairs. He had forwarded his luggage to the club, but the influenza epidemic raging in the capital had altered his plan to take a room there. After enduring five years of exile in Argentina in order to escape the war he intended to take no further risks with his health. But the delay was intensely frustrating; he had business to attend to.

At least, like every other man of sense and capital, he had done well out of the war. He had invested wisely in steel, wool, currency, chemicals. War was folly – and when folly ruled, money bred.

There was still no sound anywhere in the house. Quintin was offended by the shabbiness of the corridor. At his club in St James's, war or no war, there would have been an unlimited supply of hot water, good service and freshly laundered towels. Here everything was worn, threadbare, old. He had forgotten how old England was, how fond of her own decrepitude. Even the air smelled of mould.

Quintin opened a bedroom door. Here at least there were traces of occupation; silver-backed hairbrushes laid out neatly on the dresser, a sliver of multi-coloured soap by the washstand, a night-dress folded on top of the patched counterpane.

My wife, he thought with faint curiosity. After five years' absence he had almost forgotten what she looked like. That was not surprising. To his recollection, he had never seen her, in bed or out, other than fully clothed.

But he did have a son. Quintin felt a stir of pride and anticipation as he thought of the boy. Hugo must have changed a great deal in the past six years. All through the war the thought of his son had been at the forefront of Quintin's mind. The boy's existence meant more to him now than he could ever have imagined. He had spent hours planning how best to make up to Hugo for his five years' absence. He wanted to give his only son and heir the best of everything, make sure Hugo never had to struggle against prejudice as he himself had done. Quintin's father had been a boor, prone to mute rages and hard liquor. Quintin knew he could be a better father to his own boy.

The bedroom window was open. From it the disarray of the grounds below was even more clearly visible. Quintin surveyed the scene with a certain sense of vindication. Old England had finally driven back the Hun, but she had not succeeded in repelling more

144

insidious invaders. Ground elder had taken root in her lawns, dock and cow-parsley run riot in her parterres. From these intimate enemies there would be no America to rescue her.

Unless, of course, he himself chose to take up that Providential role. Quintin felt a quickening of interest. The idea had not occurred to him before, but he had the resources to rebuild this Purgatory, and with the addition of bathrooms, heating and a French cook, approximate it to Paradise. Later on, the place would make a fine wedding gift for Hugo. In the meantime the Giffords would be grateful, and there would be a certain satisfaction in playing the country gentleman here, at least in summer.

He could do it. It was within his power.

An incoming breeze ruffled some papers lying on the table in front of him. Quintin glanced down. Anchored beneath a copy of Swinburne's *Collected Verse* lay a partially completed letter.

In the kitchen garden behind the house two figures moved slowly among the overgrown raspberry canes.

'Look, I've found another one!'

'Yes, my darling.' Sibell held out her hand but Hugo shook his head.

'This one is for Grandmama.'

Sibell smiled. With his mouth stained with raspberry juice, his tanned cheeks and dark curls, Hugo looked like a miniature Bacchus. She marvelled at his skin; in summer he always looked as if he had been dusted over with pollen.

'Would you like to take it to her?'

Hugo nodded. Sibell's heart twisted. Before the war, there would have been enough raspberries to surfeit the whole household for three weeks running; now the few that nestled in her gardening basket constituted a bare half cupful, rare as rubies, and almost as hard. The raspberry canes had not been cut back for years, and the birds were quick to take the few fruit that ripened.

Hugo held his prize carefully in one grimy fist. From the bright, shiny look of it Sibell could tell that it too was unripe; she hoped Hugo would not insist that Mama ate it in his presence. Her illness in the spring had left her very frail.

'Come on, then.'

She offered Hugo her hand, but he preferred to concentrate his full attention on the raspberry. As they walked slowly back to the house, Kitchener trailing them, tongue lolling, Sibell half closed her eyes against the brightness. The afternoon sunshine flowed over her like honey. Around her were the sounds and smells of summer, always the same, war or no war; the mumble of bees, the scent of bay and honeysuckle, the rustle of greenery. Small dry sounds of a blackbird foraging beneath the lavender.

August ticks, Sibell thought drowsily, and behind that there's a sort of hum, like the grandfather clock in the library just before it's going to strike.

Hugo ran off immediately towards the drawing-room, where William was sitting with Mama. Kitchener, too hot for once to follow him, sloped off towards the kitchen, to the coolness of stone flags and his water bowl.

Sibell gave a silent sigh of relief. Hugo would be happy with Mama and William for at least half an hour.

Which meant that she would have time to finish her letter.

She opened her bedroom door with the sense of entering a different world. Here, last Christmas Eve, she and Leo had held each other all the icy night, too happy to speak, too happy almost to breathe. Now, he seemed to fill the room with his presence. Whenever she could, she liked to write to him here.

Sibell leant for a moment against the back of the door, closed her eyes and let the air from the open window cool her bare arms and hot forehead. The light in the room was dim. She must have drawn the curtains before she left.

The bedsprings creaked. Sibell's eyes flew open. In the dimness of the room, white as a sheet, white as a ghost, a dark hollow where

146

his face should be, a man's figure disengaged itself from the bed, rose and walked towards her.

Paralysed with disbelief, Sibell watched the figure approach. Behind it, her familiar flowered curtains, sun-faded rambler roses, fluttered in a mockery of normality. Two yards away from her, the obligatory distance for polite social intercourse between acquaintances, the figure stopped. Slowly, with nightmare delicacy, it removed its hat. Its face, though still in shadow, became visible for the first time.

'Quintin?' To Sibell her voice seemed to come from the bottom of a well. She pressed herself against the wood of the panelled door behind her. She felt as if she were falling. 'Is it really you?'

The man opposite her stood motionless, poised like a character in a play. 'But of course, my dear.' His voice shook a little with some repressed emotion she could not identify. 'Were you expecting someone else?'

Silence stretched untenably. Sibell knew she must speak, say something to express, if not joy, at least relief. But her mind was numb.

'Your beard.' Her voice scraped in her throat. 'You have shaved it off.'

'My beard?' Quintin ran his hand slowly over his chin. The skin of his face, which Sibell remembered as very pale, was burned ochre by the sun. It was hard for her to make out individual features, except the whites of his eyes, yellowish. More distinctive was the raised scar tissue, shiny and pale, on the back of his lifted hand. He wore no gloves.

Sibell shivered. The sight of him touching himself unnerved her.

'I had no idea you were so fond of it,' Quintin went on slowly. Was there an element of sarcasm in his voice? After five years, Sibell no longer knew him well enough to tell. 'That is easily remedied. For you, my dear, I will grow it back again.'

'No. Please don't.' Sibell spoke without thinking. 'I mean, not for my sake.' She felt herself flush. She had been abrupt, almost rude. Hurriedly, she attempted to retrieve herself. 'Please forgive me. It's just . . . this is such a surprise.'

'A happy one, I trust.' Quintin smiled at her, a cursory, meaningless movement of lips across teeth.

'Yes, but . . .' Sibell swallowed hard. She tried to smile in return, but the muscles of her face refused to obey her. She struggled to recover her composure, and her manners. 'What brings you to Gifford's Oak so suddenly?'

'Is that not obvious, my dear?' Quintin turned aside and laid his hat lightly, with what she now remembered as characteristic neatness, on her dresser. It looked alien there, an intruder. Sibell felt a chill of memory.

'You are my wife.'

He took a step towards her. Sibell recoiled.

'I see.' Quintin looked away. He seemed not surprised but somehow satisfied, as if she was confirming something he already knew. 'Very well, then. Let us divorce.'

'Divorce?' Sibell was taken aback. She had never understood her husband, but then at seventeen, when she married him, she had not expected to do so. He was a man, and men never explained themselves to their womenfolk. Now, his sudden suggestion of divorce was utterly confusing.

Divorce. Never in her wildest dreams had it occurred to her that her husband would ever permit her to divorce him. Now, just the sound of the word was like the opening of prison gates.

'Would you?' Sibell whispered.

'If you so desire.' Quintin met her eyes. His gaze was unreadable. 'I am not an unreasonable man.' He paused. 'You do realize what it would mean?'

Sibell nodded. Amongst people of their class, any man or woman who valued personal happiness more than the social fabric was considered worse than a Bolshevik. Divorce meant ostracism, and its stigma never faded.

'I see.' Quintin's face was expressionless. The look in his eyes

148

suddenly reminded Sibell of Black Ascot. All the pretty muslins, hurriedly dyed – they'd had just that matte, dead look. 'Very well. You have chosen. So be it.'

'Quintin, I am so grateful.' Relief and the beginnings of joy made Sibell tremble. 'I should never have accepted your proposal of marriage, I see that now.'

Quintin shook his head. 'It does not matter.' There was an edge of bitterness to his tone. 'It is no more nor less than what I thought.' When next he spoke, it was apparently at a tangent. 'Tell me, how old is the boy?'

'Hugo? Just seven.' Sudden anxiety struck Sibell. Hugo was almost old enough to go away to school. His name had been down since he was born. 'If we divorce . . . ?'

'Have no fear, I shall provide for him.'

'That is very generous of you, Quintin.' She had thought of Hugo's approaching departure for school with foreboding, knowing how much she would miss him. Now she realized how much better boarding school would be for Hugo, since Leo and herself, after the divorce, would have to live abroad.

The dizzying prospect of travelling with Leo filled Sibell with awe. She felt a pressure inside her heart, as if it were unfolding with a glory of places unvisited, all Europe's golden cities. In the holidays, Hugo would see Florence, and Vienna, and Rome.

To be free – it was like a miracle.

'No need for gratitude.' Quintin bowed lightly in her direction. 'There is, however, one condition on which I must insist.'

'Of course.' He had been so generous, so reasonable, that Sibell was willing to cede him anything.

'Only a small thing, but important to me. I am sure you will understand.' Quintin turned to her full face. His mouth tightened. 'I keep the boy.'

'Hugo?' An abyss of incomprehension seemed to open up in front of Sibell. The golden cities of Europe faded; instead, all she

149

could see was Hugo, radiant and tousled in the garden, his round head bent over the treasure in his palm.

Hugo. He was hers, part of her, her own flesh. During five years of war they had been everything to each other. For them to be separated was impossible, it could not be.

'But of course.' Quintin's tone was clipped. 'He is my heir. I have my own reputation to consider. But the choice, as I have pointed out to you, is yours. If you wish to be free of the marriage bond I will oblige you, on the condition that you leave the boy with me.'

'But Hugo . . . You hardly know him . . . You could not possibly . . .'

Quintin bent towards her with implacable politeness, only the rigidity of his body betraying the strength of feeling behind his words. 'I do not think you have understood what I am saying. The decision is yours to make, as you please. In the circumstances, I think I am being generous in the extreme. If you wish to remain my wife then I am willing to honour my responsibilities towards you both. But if – ' his face darkened momentarily ' – if at any point you give me cause to believe that you no longer wish to remain my wife, I shall have no hesitation in divorcing you myself. In which case, of course, I will still keep the boy. No court in the land would expect me to deliver up my son to an adulteress and her paramour. Do you understand me?'

Mutely Sibell nodded. She felt numb, as if this was a dream from which only time would rescue her. She had hoped that when Quintin came back they could simply agree to lead separate lives. Never in her worst nightmares could she have imagined anything as terrible as this.

'I am so glad,' said Quintin bleakly. He picked up his hat with a strange jerky movement, like an automaton. 'Under the circumstances I am sure you will agree it is better I should return immediately to Town. Please give my excuses to your mother. You may inform me of your decision at my club.'

*

All that week the furnace heat continued. Mara, in Whitechapel, barely put her nose out of doors. Saturday afternoon found her eyeing a tin of sardines on Mrs Briggs's kitchen table. She'd felt hungry enough when she opened it, but now she saw the fish in the flesh, so to speak, with their little fish faces and tails neatly interwoven and the oil in which they were embalmed oozing over the ragged edge of the lid, she wasn't so sure. Did she have room inside her for a sardine, or didn't she?

There were consequences to be considered. If there wasn't room, and sometimes nowadays Mara wondered if she had room left to breathe, let alone eat, then she was going to have the taste of fish repeating on her all afternoon.

The baby inside her, packed in its own tin as tight as the sardines had been, kicked.

Mara pushed away the meal untouched. She didn't feel like eating fish babies somehow, not in this heat. Mrs Briggs's tiny front room was stuffy and airless, even with all the family away. They'd gone down to Kent for the hop-picking, as they did every August. Mrs Briggs had suggested that she come too, but it had been clear to Mara that she'd be no good in the fields. She hadn't seen her feet since June.

Before she left for Kent, Mrs Briggs had made Vi promise to come in as usual from Hammersmith on her Sundays off, 'to keep an eye out, just in case'. Mara doubted very much if that was necessary; the baby she carried was as firmly lodged in her insides as a stone in the frog of a horse's hoof.

All the same, after almost a week of being on her own, stuck indoors because of the heat, Mara would be glad to see Vi tomorrow. Her body might be caged, but her mind needed exercise. She'd already read the labels on Mrs Briggs's tins of bully beef at least a hundred times. A bit of a battle with Vi would do her good.

Mara smiled to herself. Poor Vi, always so respectable. The news that all these years she hadn't been Mr Briggs's daughter after all, but the byblow of a darkie off an Indian boat, a lascar who didn't even speak the King's English, had knocked her clean off her perch. She'd been quite subdued ever since.

There was a rap at the door. Mara's eyes lit up. She struggled to her feet; it was like digging herself out of a ditch. Vi a day early, anyone, was better company than a tin of sardines.

After the dimness of the parlour the August light outside was bright enough to make Mara's eyes water. A man wearing a brand-new Homburg stood on the step; behind him waited a fine coach and pair, the two greys looking as out of place in the narrow street as pearls in a gutter. The coachman looked worried about scratching his paintwork. It's my Prince Charming, Mara thought, with a prickle of mirth, come to carry me off to a happy ending. Better late than never.

The man on the doorstep hardly glanced at Mara; once he saw her size, she might as well have been invisible. The lower half of his face was covered by one of the gauze masks people had taken to wearing in the hope of escaping the flu. Above the mask Mara could see that the man's face was a good few shades darker than the usual Englishman's. Why, she thought, her imagination spiralling even higher with delight, it's Vi's dad, the darkie, come back to claim her after all these years!

'Have I the pleasure of addressing Mrs Briggs?' the man asked. His voice was muffled by the gauze, but there was no mistaking the tones of an English gentleman.

'You have not,' Mara answered, a touch offended. She might not be looking her best but she was no mother of six. 'She's away in the country.' That sounded better than hop-picking, somehow.

'Ah.' The man glanced fleetingly up and down the street. 'Her daughter Violet is with her, I presume?'

'No, she ain't.' Mara bit her lip. Since living with the Briggs family her speech, which she'd improved so carefully while in Lucette's household, had taken a turn for the worse.

'In that case I would like to speak to her.'

'She's not here.'

'I see.' The man put his hand in his pocket. Mara marvelled at how he could seem so cool, wearing gloves in this heat. 'Perhaps you know where she could be found?'

'Maybe.' Mara was cautious. She knew better than to let on where anyone lodged without a good reason, though she didn't suppose debt collectors usually set out on a day's work in a coach and pair.

'It is a matter of some interest to me.' The man drew his hand slowly from his pocket. Between his gloved fingers appeared the glint of coinage. He glanced down the alley. 'But this is not the place to discuss business.'

Mara hesitated only a moment. She wasn't going to land Vi in the soup if she could help it, but gold was gold. If she was going to rebuild some sort of life after the baby she was going to need every penny she could lay her hands on.

The man preceded her into the dark parlour. He moved slowly, leisurely yet poised. In his glossy, smoothly fitting clothes, amongst Mrs Briggs's battered bits and bobs, he looked as out of place as a tiger in a farmyard. Mara saw his gaze fall on the opened tin of sardines.

'I hope I am not disturbing you?' His eyes flicked round the room, resting on nothing, noticing everything, then dropped to her ringless left hand. 'Or perhaps your husband?'

Mara knew she'd be in a better bargaining position if he didn't find out she had no man to support her. She improvised unblushingly. 'He's away at the Front. He'd kill me for not wearing his ring, but my fingers have swollen up something shocking. The heat, you know.'

The man said nothing, simply set down the gold coin centrally on the table, beside the sardine tin. Then, as if her mention of the heat had reminded him, he doffed his hat and peeled back his gloves. Something about the precise, delicate movement plucked at Mara's memory. She stepped forward automatically to take hat and gloves from him. As she did so, her eyes fell on the back of his left hand.

Despite the heat of the room, an icy trickle ran down Mara's spine. She looked up to see recognition, the mirror of her own, dawning in the eyes above the mask.

'Well, well, well. If it isn't the little Fen Witch.'

Mara's blood chilled. He'd never called her that before.

With terrifying slowness, as if he had all the time in the world, Quintin Lavery laid aside his hat and gloves. In one easy movement he reached forward and grasped the twist of hair at the back of Mara's neck. Caught off balance, unable to manoeuvre because of her heaviness, Mara found herself jerked towards him like a landed fish. The baby kicked protestingly inside her. A double assault: Mara knew that she was lost.

The first thing that struck Vi on opening the front door at eleven o'clock the next morning was the smell. It swam out to greet her in a rancid fog, making her eyes water and her stomach heave.

Holding her breath, her eyes half-closed, Vi cast about in the dimness for the source. It didn't take her long to find it. Trust that Mara to leave an open can of sardines lying about in this heat. What that girl didn't know about housekeeping would fill a book. The sardines were so far gone even the flies wouldn't touch them.

Using the coal tongs, Vi deposited the tin outside the door and covered it with a sheet of newspaper.

'Mara?' Irritation lent an edge to Vi's tone.

There was no reply. Vi wondered for moment if Mara might be out. Perhaps she'd taken herself off to church. The unlikeliness of that event struck Vi in the next second.

She strode to the back room and knocked sharply on the door.

'Mara, I know you're in there!'

There was the sound of movement and then a strange noise, a sort of grunt. Vi stepped back from the door a moment, alarmed. It hadn't occurred to her that Mara might not be alone. Perhaps she'd gone straight back to her old ways as soon as the coast was clear.

But it would be an odd sort of man to take an interest in a woman eight months pregnant.

'I'm coming in, Mara. Make yourself decent.'

Vi threw the door open.

'I can't.' The words were gasped out from the corner of the room. Vi's eyes widened in shock. Mara, in one of Mr Briggs's nightshirts, was on all fours in a corner of the room. She had dragged all the bedclothes off the iron bedstead onto the floor. Beneath the pin-striped cotton her body, rippling, convulsing, seemed to change shape before Vi's eyes.

'Jesus Christ, Mara, what's going on?'

'What do you think?' Mara's eyes flashed like a wild animal's behind her tangle of hair. She began to growl deep in her chest, an extraordinary, baritone noise that climbed upwards into a long wordless howl. Vi recoiled before the volume of noise.

'But it's too soon!'

Mara did not answer. Her back arched upwards, pulled by an immense invisible force. Vi stared, fascinated despite herself, as the other girl's body contracted as if it was trying to turn itself inside out.

'Do something!' Mara hissed out the words between clenched teeth. 'It's coming, it's coming!' Her hands reached out, seized Vi's forearm. Her skin was slippery with sweat and burning hot. Vi yelped with pain.

'It can't be!'

'Oh, b***.' Mara's grip tightened on Vi's arm. 'Please yourself.' Suddenly she let out an extraordinary high-pitched, shuddering, shivering cry. Her whole body began to shake as if she had a fever.

Vi had no idea what to do. Her job had always been to take the boys outside when the midwife called. Now, everything she had ever heard about childbirth churned uselessly around in her memory. Hot water. Clean sheets. Gentle reassurance of the anxious mother.

All completely useless. Why had no one told her birth was like this, so violent, more like a murder?

There was a moment's lull. Mara dropped her head onto the bedding and seized a fold of blanket in her jaws. Her body, propelled by gravity, slid heavily sideways. Vi gazed at her aghast. Mara's face was unrecognizable, her eyes staring and blank, the veins in her forehead swollen and blue. Under her, the sheets were soaking wet.

Tentatively, Vi reached out a hand to touch Mara's cheek. She seemed unaware of the touch, far away, so deeply concentrated that she had lost all contact with the outside world. Intermittent shudders racked her body.

And then, with a weary, deliberate effort that stirred Vi to admiration, Mara pulled herself once more onto all fours. Her thin arms trembled with the effort, the muscles in her back convulsed as if kneaded by enormous hands. There was a sudden rush of liquid, a waterfall, seemingly endless. And then, something long and pale and glistening shot forward in an arc between her thighs and spilled in a slick, wet, shining muddle onto the crumpled sheets.

It happened so suddenly, with such a flourish, that Vi was reminded of nothing so much as a draper's assistant shooting out a length of satin from its bale. She almost expected to hear a voice quote guineas per yard. For a long, astonished moment she did nothing but stare.

Mara subsided to the floor. On her face was an expression of beatific pleasure. She let out a long, luxurious sigh that seemed to come from the other side of the world. There was a minute's absolute silence.

Silence. As Vi emerged from her shocked trance she knew that there was something pressing that needed to be done. Silence was wrong. There was a third person in the room now.

The child lay quite motionless, white as the sheet on which it lay. Spurred into urgency by its silence, Vi picked it up. She had handled many babies, but this one was quite different. It was warm, but it had none of the solidity, the muscular resistance of her newborn brothers. Vi placed her hand squarely over the tiny chest. No rise and fall, not even a flutter. It wasn't breathing. What was it they said about an eight-month baby? Older than a seven-month, but less likely to survive.

Quickly Vi placed the baby face down on the soiled sheet. It lay there unresisting, a pathetic little object, perfect and pale.

Too pale. Vi massaged its back. A ripple ran down the small downy spine. Liquid trickled out of the child's mouth. It twitched, but still didn't breathe. Vi picked it up again. Was it her imagination, or was its skin a little colder?

There was no time to lose. Vi bent over Mara where she lay, grasped her father's nightshirt with both hands and ripped it from neck to hem.

Mara's eyes opened. 'What are you doing?' She sounded cross. 'You woke me up.'

Vi didn't answer. She lifted the child, still trailing its barley-twist of cord, and placed it on Mara's stomach. It lay there, unresponsive, its frail arms and legs spreadeagled. Poor little shrimp, Vi thought, and felt her eyes fill. It didn't want to be born. Maybe it's for the best.

'What's this?' said Mara. Her hands moved downwards, brushed against the baby's head.

'The baby,' said Vi.

'Baby?' said Mara. Slowly she edged herself up to look at the creature propped against her body. As she did so the afterbirth slid in a dark shining mass out onto the sheets. In that moment, as if its name had been called in a voice it recognized, the baby stirred and drew up its legs. 'Oh my Lord, the sheets,' thought Vi, and then, as the baby coughed and she knew it was going to live, she shortened it to just 'Oh my Lord.'

'What is it?' said Mara.

'A baby,' repeated Vi patiently. She couldn't help a smile on her face, a smile for all the babies in the world. Who would have thought it? Indestructible, that's what people were. Indestructible.

'I know that,' said Mara. 'Is it a boy or a girl?'

'I don't know.' Vi had been so busy she hadn't thought to look.

'Trust you not to know the difference.' Mara lifted the child's leg.

'Well, which is it?' Now, for some reason, Vi couldn't wait to know. Before it had started breathing, the baby had been all babies; now, already, it was an individual, a social being. All of its life would depend on the answer to that one question.

'It's a girl.' Slowly, Mara began to touch the child's face. 'It's a girl, like me.'

'And me.' Mara's intentness made Vi feel almost left out. If she hadn't come in time, who knows what would have happened. 'We almost lost her, you know.'

Mara appeared not to hear her. The baby lay quite still in her arms, its chest rising and falling softly. Vi had never seen a child with such pale, transparent skin. It looked as if she was going to be very fair. That was good; it was easier to place a blonde baby girl.

'Better not get too fond of her,' Vi reminded Mara.

Once again, Mara appeared not to hear.

'I shall call her Alys,' she announced suddenly. 'Because she was nearly lost.' Suddenly she turned to Vi and fixed her with her disturbing light eyes, just like the old Mara. 'Talking of lost, you'd better not have thrown away that sardine tin. There's half a guinea in it.'

8   Mysteries of Conjunction

At eleven o'clock in the morning of the eleventh day of the eleventh month of the year 1918 all London resounded to a deafening chorus of maroons and church bells. In Trafalgar Square the sky turned black as all the pigeons rose as one. Paperboys ran shouting through the streets to spread the extraordinary news. The Great War, the war to end all wars, was over.

Vi returned to Whitechapel late that afternoon, hatless, flushed and glowing. The West End had been packed with taxis, buses, staff cars full of people cheering and waving flags and blowing kisses to strangers.

'You should have seen it, Mara! It was a real party. Everybody came out, not just our sort, but everybody.'

Vi had set out that morning with Ma and the boys, but then she'd lost track of them. She hadn't minded. She couldn't help feeling that somewhere in the crowd, laughing and shouting and singing with the rest, was William. Just the thought of that had buoyed her up all day.

'Everybody?' Mara shot Vi a glance then bent her head over the baby. Vi felt a bit guilty, thinking of Mara stuck here all by herself on the kind of day that only happened once in a hundred years. But little Alys was only three months old, and the noises would have frightened her. She was a nervy, easily startled little mite, with just the faintest fluff of ash-white down on her blue-veined head. She and her mother made a strange pair, the one so fair and the other so dark. Vi contemplated them for a moment in silence. She wasn't envious exactly, but she couldn't help feeling left out.

'Have you decided yet? The war's over.'

She knew Mara would take her meaning. Soon Mr Briggs would be coming back; and Mr Briggs wouldn't be pleased to find another baby in the house at his age. He'd done his duty by six already, and one not even his.

Mara nodded.

'So what's it going to be?' There were plenty of places for pretty, healthy, female babies like Alys, it was just a question of choosing which.

Mara looked up.

'We're going to keep her.'

'What?' For a moment Vi thought Mara had gone mad. That sometimes happened to nursing mothers, she'd heard. They ran amok, overlaid their babies, took a hatchet to their husbands. But Mara seemed entirely herself.

'You and me. We can look after her.'

'What do you mean?' Vi was exasperated. There'd never been any question of Mara keeping the baby, with or without Vi's help. Neither of them had a husband, or anywhere to keep a small child. And what about money? Vi had a bit put by, but when the men came home she'd have to give up her job and go back into service – and what mistress in her right mind would take on a servant with a baby?

With a jerk of her head, Mara indicated the table. Beside the washing basket, with one of Alys's newly laundered napkins loosely thrown over it, lay a largish object.

'Go on, have a look.'

Vi felt the napkin; it was still damp.

'You really should air these, you know, Mara.'

Mara shrugged. 'She only wets them again.'

Vi shook her head as she lifted the napkin. Underneath, to her

160

consternation, she found a cerise-pink crushed velvet hat wreathed with paler chiffon roses.

'Is this yours, Mara?' She spoke sternly.

Mara nodded. 'I got it from the pawn-shop.'

'You shouldn't have, you really shouldn't.' As she studied the hat in more detail, Vi's consternation mounted. It was pretty, but the style was old-fashioned, and the fabric was sun-faded on one side, which meant it wouldn't even be worth taking back to be pawned again. Trust Mara to blow her sardine-tin money on something so useless.

'Don't worry.' Mara shifted the baby from one side to the other with a practised motion. 'I know what I'm doing. I've thought it all through and it's the only way.' She leaned over Alys, blew lightly at the thistledown tuft of hair. Then she looked up once more at Vi. 'You think the war's over, but it ain't.'

'Isn't,' she corrected herself carefully, after a short pause. 'No, it isn't over yet.'

A week later, just before nine o'clock in the evening, a carriage drew up outside 68 Regent Street. Thick November fog muffled the sound of the horse's hooves and blotted every street lamp to a greenish glow.

'The Café Royal, sir.'

The tarry smell of the fog caught at Quintin Lavery's throat as he descended. 'Wait here.'

'Yes, sir.' The coachman hunched his shoulders and pulled up his scarf across his mouth.

It was almost nine years since Quintin had last visited the Café. He was glad to see that the place had slid even further downhill in the interim; he had sworn, after that first encounter with the girl, never to enter its doors again.

But he had had his revenge for that encounter; ample and apt revenge. Quintin smiled as he remembered the stinking little room in Whitechapel. Revenge was not sweet, as legend suggested; it had

161

a salty savour. It smelled of blood and tears. He had never made love to a heavily pregnant woman before; her physical helplessness had been a novelty. He had been more violent in his attentions than he might have been, yet no more violent than she deserved.

And just as fate had led him that day to the girl, so one day it would lead him to the man he sought. His wife's letter had told him only her lover's Christian name. If Quintin had not been a gentleman he could have accused her there and then – but being a gentleman he could hardly confess to having read her personal correspondence. He had had to bide his time, while inside him burned the knowledge that he had not only been trapped into a loveless marriage, but saddled with a son he could never be sure was his.

That was the true injury, the internal bruise, invisible to anyone else, that throbbed inside him now and refused to heal.

There would be no more sons. What had been taken from him now could never be replaced. His loss was absolute, and he could not leave England till he had avenged it.

The anonymous message delivered to his club this morning had captured perfectly Quintin's state of mind. Peter, 1, chapter 5, verse 8. 'Be sober, be vigilant; because your adversary the devil, like a roaring LION, walketh about, seeking whom he may devour.' That was all, except for carefully printed details of time and place. Whoever Quintin's informant might be, he certainly understood the need for discretion.

On such a filthy night as this the Café's public rooms were practically deserted. A waiter, bowing and scraping, led Quintin through the empty chairs and tables to the private rooms at the back. It gave Quintin a curious frisson to realize that the rendezvous was to take place in the very same *cabinet* he had shared with the girl almost exactly nine years ago. As he entered he was struck by the stifling heat; in the tiny grate blazed a fire so ferocious that his eyes stung with sulphur. At first sight there seemed to be no one waiting for him; then he saw a woman reclining on the couch.

'Good evening, Mr Lavery.' Her voice was low and melodious, almost theatrical. She was wearing an old-fashioned pink velvet hat above an incongruous dark woollen dress and heavy ankle boots. Quintin stopped dead as the lanternslide of memory flashed up a brilliant, sharp-edged image. It was not possible, it could not have been predicted, but there she was, the girl, the very same, transgressing all the bounds of probability and taste. Quintin felt as if a *tableau vivant* had broken into forbidden movement before his eyes.

'Thank you for responding to my invitation.' The girl spoke calmly, intolerably at ease upon her couch. Quintin looked carefully around the room. She was alone.

'What are you doing here?'

'You have nothing to worry about, Mr Lavery.' The girl smiled at him, brazen. 'You can forget about Whitechapel. It's not blackmail I'm after.'

'What then?' Despite himself, Quintin was intrigued. She looked very different from the time he had last seen her. She was thin as a whip again, but fuller in the bosom. And apparently quite untouched by what had occurred between them on their last meeting. He was stirred to a reluctant admiration.

'I have a business proposition to put to you.'

'And what might that be?'

The girl hesitated no more than a split second. 'I want to become your mistress.'

Quintin laughed. He looked her up and down. She returned his gaze unmoved. Her eyes were the colour of diamonds.

'But I have had you already.'

She held his eyes without flinching. 'That didn't count. I wasn't at my best.'

'I can buy the best. Why should I bother with you?'

'Why not? One woman's the same as another.'

Quintin said nothing. It was as if she had read his mind.

'And I understand you.' Her tone was matter-of-fact; yes, businesslike. 'I know what you want.'

'Do you indeed.' Quintin took a moment to light up a cigar. Despite himself, he was beginning to enjoy this conversation. 'And what might that be?'

'The name of your wife's fancy man,' she answered briefly.

He eyed her carefully. 'Do you know it?'

She shrugged. 'Revenge is too easy. I want to give you something better.'

'Better than revenge?'

She nodded silently. Her eyes glittered.

Quintin waited, expecting a hackneyed answer, some prevarication. Instead the girl rose slowly to her feet and stood, one hand on each hip. 'An eye for an eye, a tooth for a tooth.' Her voice, already deep for a female, took on a harsh grating quality like a hell-fire preacher. 'Justice, Mr Lavery. That is what you deserve. Nothing more, nothing less.'

Quintin felt something cramped and wounded inside him uncoil and stretch its wings.

Justice. That was indeed exactly what he wanted.

'How?'

'There is something I know. Only I know it.'

'Really?' Quintin spoke coldly, but he felt his heartbeat quicken. 'And what is your price for this – knowledge?'

Slowly the girl removed her hat and laid it aside, turning it so that the pin glinted in the velvet.

Quintin appreciated the moment. Her skin shone like beeswax in the lamplight.

'I told you. To be your mistress.'

Quintin rubbed his thumb thoughtfully across his lips. 'And what is to prevent me, after you have told me what you know, from throwing you straight back onto the street?'

Her lips moved upwards in a faint smile.

'Nothing. Except that what I know will make me irresistible.'

'In that case it seems I cannot lose.' Quintin picked up the hat, pressed the tip of his finger meditatively against the pin's sharp point. The girl did not flinch. 'So tell me your secret, Fen Witch.'

She told him.

Quintin laughed outright.

'Not over-priced?' She regarded him with the quiet confidence of a champion ratter laying its night's kill at its master's feet.

'Not at all.' Quintin crushed the hat in one hand and pulled her roughly towards him. No fog here; just the true, icy geometry of justice. 'You have no idea how refreshing it is to meet a woman who offers real value for money.'

When Mara arrived back in Whitechapel at half past eleven that evening and told Vi about the bargain she'd made with Mr Lavery Vi was horrified.

Mara brushed aside her protests.

'It's only for a year.' She pulled off her hat, now rather the worse for wear, and threw it into Vi's lap. 'That's for your mum.'

'Don't you want it any more?'

Mara shook her head and held out her arms for Alys. As she pulled aside her bodice Vi saw that her cotton shift was wet with milk. Alys, snuffling pathetically, latched on with a little whimper that was half gratitude, half reproach. It was the first time Mara had been away from her baby for more than an hour.

'But I mean – Mr Lavery!' whispered Vi, dropping her voice as if the baby could understand her.

Mara gave her a steady look. 'I've got no complaints. He's given me generous terms.'

'But how did you manage to persuade him?'

Mara shrugged. 'I told him Leo was Alys's father.'

'You never!' Vi was appalled.

Mara nodded. 'He liked that, because of his wife. Mr Lavery is a very jealous man.'

'And he believed you?'

'Why shouldn't he? For all he knows, it's true.'

165

'But isn't that dangerous? For Mr Leo, I mean?'

Mara didn't look up. 'He won't be coming back to London, not if he's got any sense. Mrs Lavery's broken off with him.'

'He'll be back.' Vi was sure of it.

'Why?' Mara glanced up.

'Because he's in love.'

Mara shrugged.

'Love doesn't just vanish into thin air, you know.' Vi spoke with more heat than she'd intended, she wasn't sure why. It had something to do with thinking of William Gifford in the crowd. The past followed you around like a lost dog. 'I think, if Mr Leo comes back, someone should warn him about Mr Lavery.'

'Well I can't. If Mr Lavery found out he'd kill me.'

'Then I will.' Vi made up her mind on the spot. It wouldn't take much to look out for signs of life at Mr Leo's studio, just in case.

'All right.' Like a door closing, Mara turned back to the child. Vi had a sudden suspicion that Mara had just talked her into looking out for Mr Leo without so much as mentioning it. She was very good at that kind of thing.

But Mara's next words came as something of a shock.

'When I move out of here, I won't be taking Alys with me.'

Vi was nonplussed. Keeping Alys, she'd thought, had been the whole point. 'Whyever not?'

'Mr Lavery doesn't like babies.'

'Then what are you going to do with her?'

'That's easy.' Mara looked up, a swift, arrow-bright glance from her pale eyes. 'I'm going to give her to you.'

'Me?' Vi's voice rose in astonishment.

Mara nodded. 'Don't worry, I'll make it worth your while. And it's only for a year.' A little roughly, Mara sat the baby upright, so that her head wobbled on top of her comical little dumpling of a body.

'Here, take her.' Before she knew it, Vi had Alys's warm damp weight tucked in the crook of her arm. The baby beamed up at her drunkenly and then, sudden as a snuffed candle, fell asleep.

'See? She loves you already,' said Mara.

Vi sat for a moment in silence, contemplating the translucent globe of Alys's head. From beneath the pale mauve eyelids showed a line of perfect white. She smelled of damp wool and freshly churned butter.

It seemed a crime to hesitate over the future of someone who trusted her so absolutely. Slowly, Vi let her own body soften and began to rock, accommodating herself to the wool-wrapped bundle in her arms.

There was a roaring in Leo's head. It was the gun barrage, a hoarse baritone rumble enlivened by the high doleful wail of shells leaving the barrel. Each shell had its own voice; some screamed like mating cats, some howled like the souls of the damned, some squeaked like kittens.

He was cold. Bent double in the trench, he ached with the effort of waiting. At least, when the attack began, he would be able to get warm again.

'The bullet and the bayonet are brother and sister.' The phrase from officer training would not leave his head. His mind ran on, pairing dully. Bullet and bayonet. Rat and louse. Officers and men. Cold and wet. Home and dry.

Home. Dry.

He must not think of that. Nor of letters, written and unwritten. There would be no more letters. There was no place in this world for words.

The mud was rising up his body. A cold band of it now closed around his chest. He could not breathe. He heard his heart booming and shuddering like the barrage, so loud it seemed the enemy must hear it.

The enemy. He was in a train, the roar of the guns transmuted into the rattle of metal wheels on rails. It was dark still, night-time, the indivisible, endless night. He tried to remember where he was going but could not. Around him bodies pressed like corpses. He was held upright by them, borne forward irresistibly.

Fate. They said Fate was a woman. Faceless, the woman held him now, pressed up against him in the cramped confines of the corridor as close as a second skin. Her heat reached inside him to scoop out his soul, leaving him hollow, a smoking shell. Then there was nothing left of him, nothing he recognized except the infernal roaring in his head, the blackness speeding past in the night as the train rushed on like a devil in a clatter of chain-mail.

Leo surrendered himself to that pitiless onward rush at last. Let it take him, what was left of him. Let the world end.

'Wake up.' Leo heard the voice from a long way away and turned his mind against it. He wanted the war to be over. To cease upon the midnight with no pain.

With no pain. Nothing could be more beautiful.

'Wake up!' His eyes opened. Around him was dimness, not the darkness of the battlefield or the train, but a gentle blue-grey light. He had no idea where he was or how he had arrived there. For a moment, as he gazed into the dimness, the roaring in his head faded. Then, beside him, he saw a woman holding a candle. She was richly dressed. The light struck off her gown's facets like a serpent's skin.

Or chain-mail. The roaring in Leo's head returned. He recognized her now. She was the woman from the train, he had felt the searing heat of her embrace.

'Go away.' His tongue moved thick as wood in his mouth. He turned his head away towards the wall, away from the hot yellow of the candle-flame. The blue-grey dimness opened to usher him in. He would be safe there, in oblivion. He felt its coolness wash over him.

'I'm not going away till you wake up.'

Leo felt hands on his shoulders, shaking him. The movement

168

made his head ache. He coughed. The effort set blood hammering in his ears.

'Sleep.' Leo longed for it, to disappear into the wall for ever. It would be cool there, and quiet. There would be no need to breathe any more, no pain. The wall was the colour of her eyes. She was waiting for him there. He would go to her. Everything was forgiven, all the betrayals. She understood.

'Sibell.' He whispered, and for a moment, before he let himself go to her, he was purely happy, with a happiness he had never thought to feel again.

It was all right. The war was over.

Mara cursed roundly to herself as she set the candle down beside Leo's bed. She knew what she was seeing, she'd heard about it often enough. The flu – an ordinary word, but since last year thousands of people had died of it. Now, three months after the Armistice, the epidemic was at its height. They said there was nothing more you could do for sufferers once they turned their faces to the wall; that was the end. Their lungs filled with water and they drowned.

Leo was lying quite still now, his chest barely rising and falling. The noise his breathing made seemed out of all proportion. His face was grey. Cautiously, Mara touched his forehead. It was cold with sweat. He was almost unrecognizable, a paper cut-out of himself, all his vitality bleached away.

Mara wished Vi was there to advise her, but she had had to go back to Alys. Which meant there was no one to look after Leo but herself. She didn't understand illness; she herself was never ill. It was lucky Mr Lavery didn't know that, since she'd told Vi to inform him that she too had the flu. That would make sure he wouldn't come to the rooms he'd rented for her in Baker Street for at least a week.

But where would Leo be by that time? That was the way the flu worked, they said. Sufferers stopped eating first, then drinking, and in the end, in their sleep, they simply added breathing to the list of things they could no longer be bothered to do.

Looking at Leo Mara was suddenly angry. She hadn't liked the expression in his eyes before he turned his face to the wall, not one bit. Clearly he wanted nothing more to do with her, or life itself. He'd made up his mind.

Well, she'd just have to make him change it.

Extra bedding was first on the list. Vi had said he should be kept warm. In one corner Mara found a bundle of paint-stained dust-sheets, and a rolled Moroccan carpet. She shook them out and piled them onto the bed. Leo didn't stir. It was as if he were fading away before her eyes.

Purposefully now, Mara moved about the room. She lit a fire in the pot-bellied stove and washed her blackened hands with water from the ewer. Looking down at her dress, she realized that she'd have to change her clothes. Though Quintin was generous, he kept a sharp eye on the expensive outfits he bought for her, to make sure she didn't pawn them.

Shivering in front of the stove, Mara stripped down to her underthings and hung her dress and coat, draped with a dust-sheet, on the hook behind the door. Now the air of the room was icy on her bare arms and neck. Foraging amongst Leo's belongings, she found a large woollen undershirt and the blue velvet cape in which Sibell Lavery had once been painted as Britannia. She wrapped its folds around her and anchored them with Leo's belt.

The room was getting warmer now; perhaps it was her imagination, but Leo's face seemed to have a bit more colour in it. Mara went to the ewer and filled a mug of cold water. Vi had said it was important for him to drink as much as possible.

But Leo was lying too flat; she could hardly pour the water over him as if he were an aspidistra in a pot. Mara found his trenchcoat, rolled it into a bundle and stuffed it under his pillow. His head rolled, as if he was already dead. Mara felt a jolt of fear, then banished it. If he was dead, there was nothing she could do about it. All the same, as she wedged his head upright, she found her hands unsteady.

On an impulse, Mara snuffed the candle. Leo hadn't seemed to like the light before, and now the glow of the stove was enough for her to see by. She took a deep breath, gritted her teeth and held the mug to his lips. With his head raised Leo seemed to be breathing a little easier, though still with that painful scraping sound. Mara tilted the mug very carefully, and a little water ran over his lips and down his chin.

He swallowed nothing. Mara sighed with frustration. It was worse than Alys when she was learning to suckle; Mara felt her breasts prickle at the memory. Alys was five months old now, and she still liked her feed at six o'clock in the evening, when Vi brought her along to say goodnight. Mr Lavery hadn't liked Alys coming to Baker Street, even in his absence, until Mara pointed out that feeding her baby once a day kept her figure full. Mr Lavery liked a large bosom on a woman.

Mara tried again to trickle water into Leo's mouth, but again he swallowed nothing. He seemed to have forgotten how. She felt tears of frustration come to her eyes. It must be nearly six o'clock now; Alys would be missing her.

Mara looked down at Leo's remote, unreadable face. Here I am, she thought, and where is he? Somewhere else, as usual. Just like it was in the train. It's no use, my coming here. He doesn't want to go on living, he's given up. Men are babies, all of them.

It was then that the idea struck her. She looked at him, so superior in his remoteness, so determined to be dead, and she thought, why not? Maybe we can help each other.

Even as she loosened the blue velvet folds of her Britannia cloak Mara felt milk begin to spurt. As she cradled Leo's head against her breast she felt his stubble scratch her skin. The sensation sent a thrill of anticipation through her. His lips, by contrast, were soft; not so different from a baby's. The fire whispered in the stove and there was no one watching.

Live, Mara said to him silently, as his lips closed round her nipple and slowly, rhythmically, began to suckle. Any doubts in her mind eased with the tightness of her breast. The other nipple, sympathetic, oozed a perfect white pearl of milk. Mara scooped it up with her finger and put it to her lips. The fluid was warm and sweet as life itself; it tasted of vanilla and coconuts.

Lucky blighter, Mara thought, as her eyes rested on Leo's head. That's your own daughter's milk you're stealing. After this, you'd better live.

Night fell, and Leo grew worse again. Mara lost track of time as she waited, dozing occasionally then lurching awake with suspicion; she didn't trust him to keep breathing unless she had her eye on him. Once, in the small hours, he sighed, a long, peaceful exhalation, and then simply didn't breathe in again. Using all her strength, Mara pulled him up, shook him, shouted at him till the rafters rang.

'I've really pushed the boat out for you, Mr Leo de Morgan! The least you can do in return is keep on breathing!'

He coughed, and breath rattled once again in his chest. Mara let him back down onto the pillow where she'd propped him. Her arms ached with the strain. Despite herself, she found tears of relief edging into her eyes. She bent her head, pulled up a fold of the blue cape and scrubbed at her face. I'm hungry, that's all, she told herself.

It was then, for the first time since he'd turned his face to the wall, that Leo opened his eyes. For a moment he stared upwards into the dimness, vaguely, like someone exhausted from a long journey. Then, slowly, his eyes swung round towards the faint light of the fire. Mara froze, her face still half buried in the folds of the cape. She had no idea how much he could see, whether he was even truly awake. It didn't matter anyway; just so long as he kept on breathing.

Leo's eyes, still with that painful slowness, roamed over her seated figure. There was no recognition in them. Mara didn't expect there to be, silhouetted as she was against the firelight. His eyes fell on the blue cape she wore bundled round her, and his face contracted. Mara leaned forward in alarm.

Then Leo's eyes opened again, and it was as if he'd seen a vision, something so wonderful that he could hardly believe it. Mara had never seen anyone look so radiantly happy. He's dying, she thought immediately, and seized his hand, as if somehow she could pull him back. His hand closed round hers and the expression on his face intensified. Mara felt an absurd impulse to take the whole of his big body into her arms, make him part of her, share with him her own vitality. It was a feeling she had only ever experienced before with Alys; a flowing out of herself towards another human being, uncontrollable as bleeding.

Leo's lips moved. Automatically Mara leaned forward to catch whatever it was he was trying to say. Perhaps he could name what it was that was happening between them.

It took Mara only a moment to identify the whispered word. For a moment she was numb; then the flow inside her stopped as if cauterized. Leo repeated the name, this time with a hoarse, questioning note. Mara hesitated only a moment, then nodded. What did one lie more or less matter? It was what he wanted.

She watched Leo's eyes close. Already, it seemed, colour was returning to his face.

That was as it should be. She'd fed him, she'd made him breathe and live, and now she'd made him happy.

As soon as Leo's grip on her hand relaxed in sleep Mara disengaged herself, went over to the sink and downed a mug of ice-cold water. It sheared the breath from her throat; after it she felt calm and clear. He would live now, she knew, just so long as he had what he needed; something to live for.

What she had left to do was simple.

With an enormous effort Leo turned his head on the pillow. Winter daylight filled the room. Its whiteness dazzled him. By the window a woman in a dove-blue coat was hurriedly setting out small packages on the table.

Leo smiled. He felt as if he hadn't smiled in a hundred years. He was content just to watch her. Every movement she made touched him, as if she were part of himself. Every button on her blue coat filled him with joy.

Then, quite suddenly, looking was not enough. As if she sensed that, Sibell glanced over at the bed. As their eyes met, the packages she was holding fell out of her hands and she ran to him over the dusty boards. She dropped to her knees beside the bed and buried her head in his shoulder. She smelled of violets. There was snow on the fur collar of her coat.

Slowly, Leo became aware that she was crying.

'Hush.' It took Leo a moment to disinter his voice. He felt an upsurge of love so intense that he could barely breathe. Love for her, and gratitude to the world for giving him this moment. She had come back to him. They had found each other again. Nothing mattered except that.

PART THREE

Ars totem requirit hominem

9   The Gate of Blackness

As Quintin Lavery opened the door of the Baker Street rooms something dark and hairy flung itself, with a wild screech and a chatter, towards him, landing full on his face.

For a moment Quintin had the wild idea that he was grappling with Mara's soul, the indestructible, dark, wiry essence of her. The creature, whatever it was, still screeching and jabbering, leapt away, defying gravity. It hit the mantelpiece, sending a shower of small ornaments cascading to the ground. Beyond its high-pitched shrieks Quintin detected the more familiar sound of Mara laughing.

She was wearing a crimson scarf over her hair, and brass hoops as big as saucers in her ears. Beneath her full skirt her feet were bare, the toenails black with dirt. Round each ankle was a circle of little bells.

Quintin took in her appearance with an appreciative eye. In the past year of double justice, of enjoying the mother of his unknown rival's child while turning the tables on his wife, Mara had never been the same woman from one week to the next. Now a sizeable fire, despite the acute shortage of coal, blazed in the hearth, its light glinting off her earrings and golden skin. The creature, which he now recognized as a monkey, showed its teeth in a rictus grin above her left shoulder.

Mara shook out her curls and stamped her foot. The little bells jingled authoritatively. The monkey uttered a scream and launched itself elastically from the mantelpiece to the gasolier, where it clung only for a second to the hot glass before dropping to the floor.

'The last day,' Quintin said. This was their final rendezvous; their year's arrangement came to an end today.

'The Day of Judgement,' Mara replied, her eyes, outlined with kohl, glittering, and drew a knife from her belt.

For a moment Quintin felt an authentic thrill of fear. The knife-blade was extraordinarily broad. Then he realized it was merely a prop, one more element of her costume. Mara was the queen of improvisation. That was what gave her meretricious effects their impact.

'You should be on the Halls,' he observed drily.

'You dare to insult me!' Eyes flashing, Mara advanced towards him, the blade of the knife gleaming blue in the firelight. Quintin felt a flicker of excitement. In this room anything could happen; there was no audience here to censor or condemn.

'I am your master,' he answered curtly.

'No man is my master,' she rejoined, throwing back her head so that her throat was exposed and looking at him sidelong. She drew the blade lightly across the skin at the base of her neck. To Quintin's astonishment, blood sprang up along the line of the knife, dark as garnets.

'Give me that!' The blade must be razor-sharp. Quintin reached forward to take it from her, but she eluded him.

'An eye for an eye, a tooth for a tooth, a scar for a scar,' Mara intoned hypnotically. Quintin felt excitement thicken and pulse in his groin. She was once again the maddening girl he had tracked through the streets of Mayfair ten years ago. She had always been able to trigger in him thoughts and feelings he had never expressed with any other woman. Now, she had brought the wheel full circle.

He closed on her warily. Even as he concentrated on the knife in her right hand, he was aware of the perfection of her attitudes and gestures. The real Mara, if such a creature existed, was invisible. She had created around herself a sort of bubble of unreality, a crystal ball in which shadows moved and could not be identified. Tonight, she even smelled like a gypsy, of woodsmoke and spices.

He caught her arm, twisted it behind her back. The knife clattered to the boards. The monkey leapt upon it and spirited it away. Mara struggled against him, her bells jangling.

'You shall obey me. In all things.' Quintin's voice was rough. He pulled down one corner of her loose ruffled blouse over her bony shoulder, bent his head to her neck, where the blood welled. It tasted strange and sweet. He tightened his grip on her arm and she gasped. Suddenly her legs buckled beneath her. As Quintin dropped with her to the hearth he felt the heat of the flames rake against his back. The heat was such that perspiration shone across her skin. The attitude in which she had fallen, one hand behind her back, forced her small, hard breasts against the muslin of her blouse.

'In all things.' Quintin fastened his head over her breast through the thin fabric. 'Say it!' She was all the women, all the whores and angels, sirens and Medusas. 'Say it!'

Mara shook her head, mutinous. Around him Quintin heard the monkey crashing about the small room. The heat behind him made him feel crazed.

'You shall say it.' He tore at her blouse, exposing her to the flames. Instead of twisting away from him Mara arched towards him, contrary as a cat. The nipples on each breast stood up like nails. Quintin's head pounded with the heat and a raging thirst for her, a sort of madness. How could he ever have thought that she was cold? She burned, with a brilliant, inhuman fire.

As he entered her she was scalding hot, tight as a blacksmith's pincers. Everything about her seemed wet and hot, her eyes, sliding liquid under lids, her skin, slippery under his hands. Quintin felt his breath shudder inside him as if his lungs were going to explode. She moved with him, tight, inhuman, devouring. 'Say it, say it!' She shook her head. It was a race to see whether he would finish before he burned.

The ecstasy was precise, red-hot, and accompanied by the

incongruous nursery smell of scorched wool. Quintin leapt off her immediately to shed his coat. She lay looking up at him from the hearth, her eyes and teeth glistening.

'Bitch,' he said, conversationally.

'In all things,' she answered.

The monkey, chattering dementedly, dropped from the pelmet above the window, sending the knife skittering to rest between Quintin's feet. He picked it up; it still dripped blood, from, as he now saw, a cunning mechanism. No wonder the blade was so broad, to accommodate the reservoir.

'Cheap tricks,' he said contemptuously, weighing the knife in his hand. There had been no blood shed; it had all been a charade. And yet fixed in his memory for ever was the sight of her with the broad blade in her hand, as if that was the reality.

Mara smiled. 'Of course.' With quick, businesslike movements she rearranged her skirt and stood up. Instantly he desired her again.

'Come here,' he said, hefting the knife in his hand. For a moment Mara looked doubtful.

'You are still mine, for today.' Now it was Quintin's turn to smile.

After Quintin had gone, Mara checked herself carefully, then tempted the monkey down from the top of the pelmet with a water biscuit, changed out of her gypsy costume, and doused the fire. She hurt, but there was no lasting harm done. She bore Quintin no grudge. She'd known what kind of man he was before she began.

All that remained was to return monkey, clothes and room to the organ-grinder, the theatrical costumier and the landlady, in that order. How much better it is, Mara thought with satisfaction, to rent instead of purchasing outright. Possession causes nothing but trouble.

Both she and Quintin had benefited from their year's lease on each other. She'd built up a small store of capital, but that wasn't all. Being with Quintin had taught her how to read the world.

Take the present shortage of domestics, for instance. It meant that the rich couldn't entertain in Town any more on the grand scale. Take the new motor cars and aeroplanes. Why should the rich bother to rent a London house for the Season when they could reach Mayfair in a couple of hours, or Venice in three? No wonder the capital was full of houses For Sale or Rent.

Including, ever since Mrs Bailey and her mother had gone back to Paris, number 7 Derby Street.

What was more, according to Quintin, before long the American government was going to forbid the sale of alcoholic liquors. That would be perfect, the icing on the cake. All decent American citizens would have to go abroad to do their revelling, and London, suddenly on the map again after five years of war, would be their first choice.

Mara could already feel the fizz in the air, of beginnings, of rising sap. In two months' time it would be 1920, the start of a new decade. There were new names on the stamps, new hands on the money. Newness was everywhere, the buzz and glitter of change.

Now was the moment, and she was going to seize it with both hands.

Leo de Morgan, as he crossed the Charing Cross Road into Shaftesbury Avenue, was distracted for a moment by the silken flash of knees. Spring had arrived, and skirts were rising with the temperature.

He quickened his pace, aware of the interested bird-like glances that darted his way. So many girls, all different – yet every one made him think of Sibell. They might as well have been mermaids for all the use they were to him. If Sibell was in Town, he lived for brief glimpses of her, half an hour stolen here and there. If Sibell was not in Town, he hardly lived at all.

Leo was well aware, even now, that he should be working. He had already lost too much time to the war. So why, after beer and sandwiches at the Paradise off St Martin's Lane, did he find himself in Berkeley Square? And why, having discovered this fact, instead of retracing his steps, did he continue westwards down Mount Street, with his heart beating an unsteady tattoo against his ribs?

Because at the end of Mount Street lay Park Lane, and if he happened to turn right at Park Lane, after a few hundred yards he would find the high spiked wall and imposing gate behind which lay Ainsley House.

Leo halted at the junction of Rex Place with an effort that caused sweat to break out over his body, as if he were still suffering from the flu. Sibell had cured him of that, but left him nonetheless fatally afflicted.

For there was no way out of the situation in which Leo now found himself. He could persuade Sibell to leave her husband, that would be easy. He could even persuade her to leave her son. A week in Florence, and she would never go back.

But Leo could not take Sibell there, or anywhere, because he loved her. There was so much he wanted to show her, all the cities of the soul and body, but he could not. All he could do was wait – for Hugo to be older, for her husband to relent, for a miracle.

Leo forced himself to turn left, away towards Derby Street and the smaller country of the past. He would visit number 7, for old times' sake. Any distraction was worth trying.

But Lucette's little brown jug of a house, which she had kept polished and brimming with cream, was now dusty and deserted, its stucco cracked and its shutters peeling.

Damn, Leo thought, and a pulse beat in his head.

It was as if he had spoken aloud. From somewhere beneath his feet a steady stream of invective, low and monotonous but none the less intensely felt, issued into the scented springtime air.

Intrigued, Leo went down the area steps to investigate. The basement door was open. The air inside smelled of dust and old potatoes.

'Have you changed your mind?' called a sharp voice from the back of the kitchen.

Before Leo had time to reply the voice went on, irritably.

'I tell you, it has to go.'

'Why?'

There was a startled pause.

'Who is that?'

'Does it matter?' Leo advanced further into the room. 'Can't you see it's a period piece?' He had no idea what item of Lucette's furniture he was defending, but he felt as indignant as if he had discovered a thief rifling Lucette's dressing-table.

Someone stepped forward from the gloom. Faint light from the window revealed a dusty, dishevelled, but somehow workmanlike figure.

'I might have known.' Leo's mind flashed back instantly to his last encounter with Mary Mizen in the troop train on New Year's Eve. Two years ago now, but he would never forget it. He'd been out of his mind that night, after six days of passionate celibacy with Sibell. During that time, desperate to hold onto the reality of every minute with her, he'd hardly slept. He remembered standing in the crowded corridor of the troop train, reading and re-reading the letter Sibell had given him like a talisman; cold, exhausted, yet borne up by an extraordinary exhilaration. He had felt transparent, like a Chinese lantern, a weightless frame for the pure white fire that blazed inside him.

And then there had been Mary Mizen. She had touched him and all his self-control had vanished. He had discharged into her like lightning down a spire.

'Mary,' Leo said at last, and had been going to say Mizen, but caught himself in time. After the train he could hardly be so formal.

'Not any more,' she answered composedly. 'My name is Mara now. My husband's preference.' Leo observed a new edge to her voice, a cultured note.

'Really?' He was surprised, not so much at the change of name as by the possession of a husband. Mary Mizen had always seemed to him a force very much to herself. 'May I offer you my felicitations?'

'No need.' Mara's answer cracked back quick as a whip. 'He died in the war.'

'I am very sorry.'

Mara shrugged.

There followed an awkward silence which she showed no inclination to break. Leo remembered that about her; she had always had the capacity to make a man feel uneasy. It was half her power; the other half being the ability to make him feel surprisingly comfortable.

'I take it you are looking after the house for Mrs Bailey?'

'Not exactly.' Mara's teeth showed unexpectedly white in the dimness and dust as she smiled. 'I'm the new tenant.'

'I see.' Again, Leo was surprised, and a little wary. For a former kitchen maid, Mara's rise seemed meteoric.

'My husband left me a little capital. But I intend to work for my living.' Mara paused. 'You see, I have a daughter to support.'

Leo blinked. It had been hard enough to adjust to the idea of Mary Mizen as a wife, but – a mother? For some reason he felt almost disappointed. The Mary Mizen of the train, whatever she had been, demon or vision, had been a force to be reckoned with. This new Mara, prosaic, domestic, made him wonder why on earth he'd been so shaken by the episode. Perversely now, as Mary Mizen receded, he almost missed her.

'I'm glad you've come.' Mara placed her hands on her hips in a gesture that was brusque but somehow stylish. Before the war, Leo had thought her movements too quick to be graceful, the opposite of Sibell's gentleness, but now it was as if history had caught up with Mara and swung round to her fashion. Studying her objectively for the first time, Leo realized that despite her layering of dust she was no longer plain. Before the war, her sort of face had been too highly defined, too particular for prettiness. But now people needed more than mere prettiness, and Mara's looks stung the attention like neat brandy after whipped cream. Talking to her, Leo felt oddly revitalized, sharper and clearer than he had for weeks. Her directness was a sort of liberation.

'Why?'

'You can give me some advice.' Mara pointed at the massive cast-iron kitchen range built into the hearth. 'What would you do with this? The agent tells me it can't be taken away.'

'Then why not keep it?'

'This room is not to be a kitchen.'

'What, then?'

Mara looked at him for a long moment, as if trying to decide whether or not to trust him.

'A place of . . . interest,' she said eventually.

Leo was puzzled. Whatever could she be planning?

'A gallery, you mean? Or a museum?'

'Not quite. More like – a fairground. Somewhere to go after dark.'

Leo pondered for a minute. Before him lay the great iron mass of the stove. What was needed here was the philosopher's stone, he thought, to transform base metal into gold. The germ of an idea occurred to him.

'You could change it.'

'The stove?'

He nodded. 'Transform it. Convert it. Make it into something new.'

'But it is a stove.'

'Then re-interpret the idea of a stove. Ask yourself, what exactly does a stove do?'

Mara looked at him askance, as if she suspected him of making fun of her. 'It cooks,' she answered guardedly.

'By itself? Hardly.'

Mara frowned.

'Think! What is a stove, what is its essence? A stove is . . .' Leo prompted.

'Hot?' Mara ventured.

'Yes.' He waited. 'But why? Why is a stove hot?'

She looked at him as if he were mad.

'Because there is a fire inside it.'

185

'Well then. What else has a fire inside it?'

Mara fell silent for a moment. Leo had never seen anyone concentrate so hard, as if thinking was like chopping wood for winter.

And yet, when her answer came, it was not what he had expected.

'A train.' She faced him squarely.

For a moment Leo could think of nothing to say. He seemed to hear the rattle of wheels, feel the sudden heat of her as she pressed against him in the darkened corridor. She had revealed to him a part of himself he had never known existed; she had taken him beyond choice and sense.

Leo fought down the memory. It had been a trick of the war, it would never happen again.

'A train, certainly. But that was not my thought.' He shook his head. 'That was not my thought at all.'

Mara's eyes narrowed. She seemed unmoved.

'Think. Think of fire, flames, burning.' Leo waited patiently. At last he could see from her expression that she had guessed what he meant.

'The hob,' she said.

'Of hell. Precisely so.'

'Could it be done?'

'Of course.'

Mara's eyes lit up.

'A red light inside,' she said suddenly. 'Flickering.'

Leo nodded.

'And a monkey on top,' Mara added. 'Carrying a pitchfork.'

'If you insist.'

'And here . . .' She sketched the air behind the stove, taking in the wall on either side. 'A troop of sinners.'

'Why not?' Leo smiled.

She faced him.

'Would you do it?'

He shook his head. 'I don't paint murals.'

'But it has to be you,' she said.

'Why?'

'Because I won't have to pay you.'

Leo stared at her, astonished. 'What makes you think that?'

'Because you're an artist.'

'And just why should an artist work for nothing?'

'I didn't say that.' Mara gave a small smile. 'I would give you something in exchange.'

Leo eyed her cautiously. He knew what unit of exchange was Mara's natural coinage.

'Not what you're thinking,' she said equably, reading his mind.

'What then?'

'Something you need. This house is mine now, for the moment. There are lots of rooms.'

'I have no need of a room.'

'Yes you do. Listen.' Mara was intent now. 'You don't realize yet, but people are going to come here. Lots of them. Rich people, famous people. Bored people. All looking for something new to spend their money on. I have lots of rooms, lots of walls. That's what I'm offering you.'

Understanding broke in on him. 'Hanging space?'

Mara nodded. 'If you help me. You're an artist. You have ideas.'

'It could work.' Against his better judgement Leo was tempted. He wasn't quite sure exactly what kind of clientele she was planning to attract, but if she could persuade him, she could persuade anyone.

'It will work.' Mara's eyes were liquid with determination. 'This is the right area. Discreet, but right near the West End. Only a stone's throw from Park Lane,' she added, apparently inconsequentially, and those last two words sealed it for Leo. It was almost as if she knew.

Mara chose for her Grand Opening Night the second Friday of May. That evening taxis shuttled to and from Derby Street in a constant stream. Alfred the doorman, as instructed, never allowed a smile to crack his face, while Sir Boris the Great Dane, kept hungry for the occasion, devoured rice-paper invitations with terrible grindings of his heavy jaws.

From the street, if it had not been for the presence of these two, it would have been hard to tell any difference between number 7 and the houses on either side. There was nothing unusual about the narrow steps leading to the basement door, except, possibly, that primroses were a little late for May, and a stern notice warned 'Beware! These steps are slippery!' The element of doubt as guests in evening dress and furs edged cautiously down into the basement area made voices rise in anticipation. 'How odd,' they cried. 'How terribly strange.' And then, as the tiny door swung open on a pulsing red glow, 'What fun, my dears, what fun!'

Inside the Devil's Door the light was very dim. The walls were scarlet and orange, flickering with fragments of mirror shaped like flames. On the left a parade of painted figures in black silhouette progressed, heads lowered, towards the gaping maw of the central stove, from which issued at intervals a terrifying lurid jet of light and a ferocious crackling. On top of the stove a monkey with a red fez and arrow-pointed tail skittered and showed its teeth in welcome, brandishing a tiny pitchfork.

Beyond the stove were severe little tables, their glass tops inlaid with black-edged playing cards, their metal legs twisted as if in a furnace. From the red walls, at intervals, jutted the head of some horned animal – a boar, a moose, a magnificent he-goat – glass eyes catching the crimson light. The area available was small, and might have seemed claustrophobic, if it were not for the fact that from the moment guests ducked their heads to enter the low door they were channelled, guided, their coats and hats whisked away before they even thought to ask, to be suspended from lesser antlers and horns in the tiny cloakroom.

Sooner rather than later guests found themselves at the bar, where an impassive Negro, clothed in spotless white, dominated the glittering, coffin-shaped bar. It was a relief for the guests to find there familiar standbys, Gordon's gin and Bollinger champagne, for drink was too serious a matter to be meddled with. On the black and silver counter, within easy reach, lay tempting sour, spicy, salty snacks, perfect post-theatre delicacies; devils-on-horseback, impaled on sticks, roasted nuts, anchovies on toast, black caviare, all designed to enhance a thirst.

Fuelled with alcohol, guests were encouraged to penetrate further. Anyone who thought of leaving by the same door through which he had been ushered in found it impossible, for the inner surface possessed no handle. There was only one way through the Devil's Door.

But halfway into the room, just before the diminutive dancing floor, there was another door, behind a black velvet curtain. It took some time, that first night, for the guests, shrieking and laughing, to discover it and where it led. Above it a dim notice read 'No admittance – except in case of repentance.'

Behind the curtain the steep steps were stone, chilly as a tomb. Giggling in their satin slippers, guests stole up the stairs. Here the walls were papered in newspaper, banner headlines jaundiced yellow under three coats of varnish. There was a smell of incense. At the very head of the stairs loomed a huge Bible, chained to the wall, its black wings spread like a bird of prey.

The upper door was labelled, simply, Purgatory. The hallway onto which it opened was completely dark. Guests stumbled over each other as they spilled into the darkness. It took a few minutes for them to discover the rush basket full of tapers and phosphor matches, to discern by their light the black ironwork candleholders above, skeletal hands extending tall white candles, unlit. With hushed excitement girls who had never laid a parlour fire in their lives, men who had lit nothing more significant than an after-dinner cigar, queued for their moment of illumination. As one by one the candles bloomed into life their light was magically doubled by full-length mirrors lining the walls. Images from the paintings hung between them, strange beasts in human clothing, austere yet magnificent in shades of grey and clerical purple, quivered into life. At the same moment, from far above, there came a piercing cry, 'Repent!' Startled, the guests looked up to see above them, swinging on the chandelier till the glass tinkled, a lime-green parrot.

William Gifford was in Purgatory. He had passed through Hell, where he had mislaid Polly, the extraordinarily smart and terrifying young thing whom Sibell had insisted he take to this opening night, halfway on purpose, because he could not think of a thing to say to her except 'Jolly little place, this,' and the third time he had said it she had clearly suspected him of insincerity.

At least, William thought, the candles and full-length mirrors of Purgatory were preferable to the squawking brass and flashing lights below. The sight of so many people packed together had brought back unexpectedly wistful memories of HMS *Invincible* ready for action, her deadlights battened over every scuttle.

William had to confess he missed it. Not the war, but the ship, and the men, and the machinery. After less than a week of active service he'd decided that if he survived he would make his career in the Navy.

It was strange how things worked out. Cordite flash burns were a constant hazard for the gun and turret crews, but his had not been particularly severe. Invincible, that great man-made fortress of twelve-inch thick steel armour-plating, had not failed him. It was human flesh, and the gangrene that could rip through it faster than cordite, that had let him down.

Now, William wished that Gifford's Oak were more like HMS *Invincible*. In a contest between metal and Jacobean wood, metal won hands down. Ever since Mother had died, with Sibell based in Town and Hugo away at his preparatory school, the Oak hadn't been much use to anyone. It couldn't even be sold; the market for decaying country properties was dead as a doornail.

From above William's head came a stir of movement. A blonde vision wafted down the stairs on a cloud of perfume, a fold of her vaguely Grecian drapery brushing lightly against his shoulder where he sat on the lower step. He felt a tug of memory and looked around him with new eyes. No wonder he had felt happier in this ground-floor hall than downstairs in the basement. He had been here before, in the winter of 1917, just before he went to naval training camp. It was in this house, in the second-floor bedroom, that he had been honourably relieved of his virginity.

Three years ago now, and in that time a great deal had changed. Abruptly William rose to his feet, leaning slightly to the left as he had learned in the hospital to make up for his missing arm. It was astonishing, and rather interesting, how heavy a limb could be. He looked up the stairs. The blonde had come down from there, so it must be all right. Curious now to explore the place again, quite unrecognizable as the house he had visited during the war, he began to climb.

The door to the first-floor drawing-room was labelled 'Elysium', and opened easily. The room appeared, to William's surprised gaze, to be filled with flowers and half-naked women. Clothing was strewn over every available surface. His entrance was greeted with squeaks of half-pleased dismay. He shut the door again hastily. The atmosphere, if not the setting, was familiar to him from shore leave visits. But he was not looking for female company at the moment. In fact, he was not sure quite what he was looking for. A memory, perhaps; a part of himself that he had forgotten.

The second-floor landing was painted a clear gold. There was no label on the door but it was not difficult to recognize the bedroom he had visited four years ago. As he laid his hand on the porcelain handle William was surprised to find his heart beating irregularly.

But the door was locked. William could not help a slight sensation of relief. It was definitely not the action of a gentleman to go round trying the handles of ladies' bedroom doors without prior invitation. But he was glad he had come, to find that the door to the past was well and truly closed.

William turned away, poised to go back down the stairs, then caught sight on the upper half-landing of a narrow wooden gate, its lattice interwoven with small pink fabric roses. 'No entry,' it said. 'Paradise.' On the newel post sat a fine, plush-covered, long-nosed toy bear. Its eye gleamed with intelligence; taped to its paw was a silver-painted cardboard sword.

St Michael, thought William, amused, defending Paradise with his flaming fiery sword. He peered upward. Here the stairway was narrow, the treads comically tip-tilted. They reminded him of the stairs to the nursery suite at Gifford's Oak. Gazing up in the dimness he felt oddly defrauded, excluded, as if truly, up there, lay Paradise. Lucky bear, he thought, and reached out his right hand to stroke the vivid fur.

It was then that he saw the angel. It appeared quite noiselessly, a diminutive figure in a long white dress. Everything about it was pale and insubstantial. Its hair, cut with medieval straightness, was silvery-white, its skin translucent. It stared down at him from the topmost landing, behind the palisade of banisters, with true angelic impassivity. Then its eyes fell on the bear.

'Mine!' announced the angel in a voice of quite extraordinary clarity. William hurriedly removed his hand from the bear and in so doing dislodged it from its perch. It fell nose down. When he picked it up the cardboard sword was bent. Clumsily, one-handed, under the severe gaze of the angel, William attempted to repair the damage before it could be noticed.

But nothing escaped the angel's gaze. Suddenly, between one moment and the next, the pearly-white face suffused with pink. Its eyes closed, its mouth opened and it emitted a shriek of such inhuman, piercing dreadfulness that William dropped bear and sword as if he had been shot.

He heard a door above open and his heart sank. Even as he rammed the treacherous bear back on its newel post he heard the rustle of feminine draperies and a low voice.

'Hush, Alys. Whatever are you doing out of bed?'

The siren wail ceased immediately. Flushed, William looked up to see the child swept up in its mother's arms.

His smile of apology died away. Gazing down at him over the bone-white head of the child, her face pale behind its bird's-egg scattering of freckles, her beech-leaf hair tucked up above a voluminous cotton nightdress, was his very own Violet Briggs.

William's first rush of pleasure at seeing her again after all this time was followed by a shock of realization that cancelled it utterly. Here she was, his Vi, but separated from him by far more than distance and a fragile wooden gate. She was married, with a child of her own. For a full minute he could not speak.

'Wait a moment.' It was Vi who recovered her presence of mind first. Obediently, William waited. He could not have moved in any case. He felt as if his whole body had been amputated. In a daze he heard her rustle away, murmuring to the child, lovely bird-like noises which pierced his heart like so many knives. The sensation of exclusion intensified. There was no one else like Vi, there never would be. She was solid and sensible and real. You could believe what she said.

Now she was back, a solid, sensible woollen robe covering her nightdress and belted firmly at the waist.

'Hello,' she said and smiled, and William felt as if he had been hit broadside by a dreadnought. He'd spent all Armistice Day looking for her in the crowd. He'd had some good jokes lined up about farewells to arms; she was the only person he knew who would appreciate them.

But now he'd found her once again, he couldn't speak for all the things he wanted to say. In the two years since he'd last seen her he hadn't talked, not really talked, to another living soul.

It was as if she understood.

'You'd better come up to Paradise,' she said. Fumbling a little, William unlatched the wooden gate. She was there above him on the stair, still smiling. He could hardly believe she was real. He forced himself to concentrate on not making a fool of himself.

Standing beside her, she seemed smaller than he remembered. She smelled of soap and warm flesh. Looking down he saw that her feet were bare.

'You have very pretty feet,' he said, inconsequentially. Vi pulled her dressing-gown together at the throat as if that would hide them.

William noticed that there was no wedding ring on her finger. Despite himself, his mind raced into speculation. What kind of woman was she after all, his Vi? She had always seemed so proper, so respectable. And yet she had given birth to a child out of wedlock, which meant . . . He hated himself for thinking along these lines, but he could not help it. She was so near, she smelled so good. He felt that if he touched her everything would be solved, that nothing else mattered except touching her.

There, on the landing, William put his arm around her waist. Through the rough wool of her gown he could feel her warmth. She did not prevent him, did not draw away. He felt tears come to his eyes, he did not know why. The belt at her waist was easy to undo, even with one hand. The stuff of her nightdress was soft and warm against his fingers.

'Vi,' he said, and the word itself was like a sigh, as if holding her he was letting go of everything else.

'William,' she said. He kissed her hair. He had always wanted to kiss her hair. She leant her head against him. Her hair smelled of honey. He kissed her forehead, her cheeks. His whole body ached with combined pleasure and pain. Now, from the way she relaxed against him, he knew that he could have her, and yet he could never have her, not for his own.

The sailor's dilemma. There was only one way out of it.

He kissed her mouth, and every other thought left his mind.

'I don't understand.' Squeezed beside her in her narrow bed, there was no need for William to speak above a whisper.

'It's easy. Shall I tell you again?'

'Please.'

'Then try to concentrate.' William drew his fingers down the length of Vi's arm. He felt as if his whole soul were in those fingers. She had told him once already, but he had not been able to take it in. It was too much all at once, this bed, and the extraordinary fact of her body next to his.

'Promise?' Vi whispered, her breath tickling his ear.

William nodded, unable to speak.

'Alys is not my child. Do you understand?'

He nodded.

'I look after her.'

William nodded again. He could feel her heart beating, quick and irregular, like a bird's.

'I love you,' Vi said, and buried her face in his neck.

'How long?' he said.

'Since that day in the train.' She kissed him, tiny, inexperienced kisses, a child practising. His heart turned over. He pushed up her face, captured her lips. He felt as if he were floating. She had loved him enough to make him first. She was like no one else, his Vi.

'You should have told me you loved me,' he said.

'How could I?' she said. 'You weren't for me. I'm not your class.'

'Who cares about class?' he said. 'The war's changed all that. I can marry whoever I like.'

'Oh, William,' she said. 'I'm seven years older than you. I can't marry you.'

'You have to,' he said. 'We can't walk down the street like this.' It was true, they felt as if their bodies had become one entity. 'Besides, I need your arms.'

He swung her over him, placed her two warm round arms on either side of him.

'See, now I am complete,' he told her, his face inches from her own. He could see tears in her eyes.

'I can't marry you, William,' she said.

'Why not?' he said.

'There's Alys,' she said. 'I said I'd look after her. I promised.'

195

'Bring her with you,' he said. 'I like children.'

'There you are, you see.' Vi was crying in earnest now. 'You don't know anything about me. I'm a darkie. My father was an Indian off a boat. We'd have little brown babies, I just know we would. I couldn't bear it.'

'We don't have to have babies,' he said. 'Not if you don't want to. But you still have to marry me.' He pressed his face into her neck, nipping her lightly above the collarbone.

'I can't, I can't,' she said.

'Then don't,' he said, cunning at last. 'It makes no difference to me.'

'Do you love me?' she asked.

'Yes,' he said.

'Since when?'

'Since this evening,' he said, and laughed, and rolled her over onto her back, and ran his mouth down the silk of her breast. 'But I don't want you to marry me after all. I never want to leave this bed.'

At five o'clock the next morning Leo found Mara in Elysium. Her face pale but her eyes shining, she was counting money. She glanced up as he came in and handed him a thick roll of notes neatly tied up with red garter ribbon.

'The clockwork lady from halfway up the stairs,' she said briefly. 'Sold to a Mr May.'

'Not the one who clicks bones for a living?'

'The very same. Only he calls it physiological adjustment. He's rich, you know. Consulting rooms in Park Lane.'

'But why on earth . . . ?'

'He wants it for his waiting-room. As an illustration for his patients.'

Leo laughed out loud. Welcome, brave new world, he thought. The whole evening had been a masque, from the moment the first guests had stumbled into darkness to the moment Mara had appeared, at the stroke of midnight, in the guise of a pantomime cat. It was only fitting, after such a night, that his first major sale of new work should be to a mountebank.

Mara glanced up at him reprovingly. 'Take the money. You might as well.' She paused. 'Good things may come of it. One of Mr May's clients is the King of Spain.'

'I see.' Leo looked at her with renewed respect. Down her chosen tunnel Mara saw a very long way. She'd have made an excellent sniper.

He saw that she was still wearing the close-fitting black of her cat costume. There weren't many women Leo knew who could have carried off such an outfit, but even now, without the mask through which her pale eyes had glittered so effectively last night, Mara seemed stylish as a Japanese brushstroke. Her figure type, highly defined, cinder-slim, was in its own way an anatomy lesson.

Leo accepted the money, but it made no difference to his state of mind. Sibell hadn't come to the opening night. He had known that she would not, that she could not, and yet, in some part of himself, he had come alive at the thought that she might. Anticipation had emptied him. Now there was little feeling left.

'So.' He glanced up to find Mara's eyes on him. 'A success, do you think?'

She shook her head.

'Not yet.' Leo noticed that she had laid out cards on the couch beside her, labelled in clear childish print, 'Rent', 'Trades', 'Staff'. Below each card lay a roll of notes, like his own, neatly tied. 'If my credit holds. If people keep coming. Maybe.'

Mara smiled suddenly, and Leo saw that her eyes, behind the heavy black outlines, were red-rimmed with fatigue. But she quivered with energy still.

'A toast, I think.' Mara poured a glass of champagne for each of them. Leo wondered again where exactly she'd learned her social graces; when he'd first met her ten years ago she'd been raw as saltpetre. Perhaps that foreign husband of hers had wrought the transformation.

Mara rose from the couch, in one silky catlike movement. Automatically Leo's eyes took in the dip and sway of her hips as she came towards him, a brimming glass in either hand. The long wired tail of her cat costume flicked off the couch after her. She looped it carefully over one arm. Doubtless the costume, like all Mara's effects, had been hired for the occasion, and would need to be returned in good condition. Suddenly Leo had a vision of the future, a future in which possession and heritage and tradition had no more place, a future in which change and novelty, the essence of the moment, reigned.

'To the Devil's Door,' Mara said, and tipped her glass delicately against his own.

'May it thrive and prosper,' Leo replied automatically, aware of the warm place on the stem of his glass where she had held it. Despite her slimness, Mara radiated a heat which she seemed able to direct at will. Now she shot him a quick look under her brows which set him back on his heels. He sensed the triggering of certain familiar processes in himself which required swift action.

'Are you flirting with me, Mara?'

'I never flirt.' Her glance was as limpid as straight gin. 'It's a waste of time.'

There was no mistaking now the expression in her eyes.

Leo sucked in his breath. There was something about the situation, the rolls of money on the table, the sudden release of the night's tension, the oddity of her get-up, that stirred him. It promised novelty, escape, abandonment of self. Taking Mara into his arms would be like stroking a strange cat in the night; the electric crackle of fur, a mew or two, then back into the darkness.

'I don't doubt it.' Leo bent his head to drink. His fatigue was forgotten; Mara had challenged him out of it. All his senses seemed suddenly razor-sharp. Mara had a surer grip on the present than anyone he'd ever met. Now, with one flick of her pantomime tail, she'd released him from the dead space between past and future that he inhabited, made him see, for the first time in months, the moon behind the bars.

And this time it would be nothing like the train. Mara had her own brand of honesty. This time he could choose.

But before the cold champagne was more than a breath on Leo's lips the door behind them flew open. Framed in the doorway stood a man and a woman. It took Leo a moment to recognize Vi, bundled up in a red woollen dressing-gown that clashed vibrantly with her burnt sienna hair, half-embraced by a tousled-looking young man in evening dress, with one shirt-tail hanging out over his trousers.

'You may not remember me, Miss Mizen,' the young man said, and his face flushed suddenly scarlet. 'My name is William Gifford, and . . .'

'And we are to be married,' said Vi. Her tone was pugnacious. She appeared exactly what she was, a woman of virtue determined, for once, to get her own way.

'I haven't any money to speak of,' said William, his flush deepening.

'And neither have I,' said Vi.

'But that doesn't make any difference, because . . .'

'Because we love each other,' said Vi. 'Everything is settled. We are going to get married straight away. But I thought it was only fair to tell you first, because of Alys.'

There was a long pause in which no one moved or spoke a word. Leo looked at Mara and wondered with interest what on earth she was going to do about this new development. She depended utterly on Vi for the care of little Alys, who was not an easy child. Vi's defection was all the more disastrous for being unexpected. What price the Devil's Door now?

Mara hesitated only a moment.

'Of course you must be married,' she said. 'And I am going to help you. In the meantime, let me propose a toast.' She lifted her glass to William Gifford. 'To the freedom of the air!'

An odd sort of toast for a naval man, Leo thought – and he could have sworn she winked.

10   *Killing the Quick*

'I'm late.'

'Yes, you are.'

Leo rose from behind the table. He was taller than Sibell remembered, and broader, but his face was thinner. She hadn't seen him since last summer. Every change in his face hurt her.

The waiter drew back her chair for her to sit down, and for a moment it was as if she had forgotten how to move, had become once more Sibell Gifford, a schoolroom girl, with her hair in a long plait and lisle stockings wrinkled at her ankles, instead of Lady Lavery, whose husband, last year, had invested nearly twenty thousand pounds in the purchase of a knighthood.

It was a relief to find herself, somehow, seated, with the white-clothed table between them.

'I'm so sorry,' she repeated, when the waiter had retired. Her voice sounded odd to her. But then everything today seemed unfamiliar. The mirrored, red plush interior of the Embassy Club might as well have been Timbuctoo. This morning she'd spent two hours with her maid selecting her outfit, but now she had no idea what she was wearing. In the cloakroom just now, where she had left Soo Shah as usual to be cosseted by his beloved Rose and Blanche, she had glimpsed in the mirror, under her close-fitting cloche with its edging of tiny beads, the face of a complete stranger. 'Had you been waiting long?'

'Only four years,' Leo said, and Sibell's heart fell away down a dizzying slope as she felt the impact of those years in retrospect, only now daring to admit to herself the desert they had been. How had she lived through those years, how had she survived from day to day? She had told herself that she would forget him, that everything would change, and even while she was telling herself that, she had known that such a thing was impossible.

But she had had to lie to herself, every minute, every hour, in order to survive. She'd told herself that Leo would forget her, that it was for the best, that he would marry someone else and she would be happy for him, that she was lucky to have Hugo, and a position in society, and Soo Shah, and people to meet and places to go.

Now, face to face with Leo, the façade that Sibell had built around herself, with appointments and accessories and careful little half-truths, shattered, letting in the scent and sound and movement of the real world for the first time in four years. She felt a great frozen wall of unshed tears pressing behind her eyes. At any moment the wall would melt and she would drown.

Leo spoke just in time to save her.

'A very good year, 1923,' he said.

'I have fallen in love,' she said. 'I have fallen in love with the law.'

'Bottom and Titania,' he said, and his comprehension was so quick and complete that it took Sibell's breath away. The law might be an ass, but not this year, the year of the Matrimonial Causes Act, the Act which gave a wife permission, at last, to divorce her husband for adultery.

Even now, Sibell could still scarcely believe it. One stroke of a lawyer's pen meant that Quintin could no longer keep her trapped in marriage by threatening to separate her from her son. If she succeeded in divorcing him for adultery, no court in the land would deny her access to her son. And Quintin had not changed his habits in the least; there would be no difficulty in presenting evidence of infidelity. Within six months, her solicitor had assured her, Sibell would be free.

But until then, he had advised her sternly, she must be circumspect, very circumspect. Since she would be bringing the action, her behaviour must be absolutely unimpeachable.

Which meant, Sibell realized now with a shock, that until her divorce was final, she and Leo must not see each other again. She wouldn't be able to trust herself to behave sensibly if they did. At this moment it was as much as she could do not to throw herself into his arms and never leave them again.

'What will you do?' Leo asked. 'Will you stay in Town?'

Sibell shook her head. She'd always disliked Ainsley House, and now that she was to divorce Quintin she could no longer bear to stay there. William had invited her to Gifford's Oak, but with his new school for girls on the verge of opening, the last thing he needed was any breath of scandal. He'd already raised eyebrows by marrying out of his class; the presence of a soon-to-be-divorced sister in his household would be too much of a risk.

'I shall go to the coast,' Sibell said. She had planned this over long hours in bed at night, Soo Shah's comforting weight at the foot of her bed. She wanted her reunion with Leo to take place at Victoria Station, where he'd first fallen in love with her all those years ago. A romantic notion, maybe, but not many people were given the chance to start again at the beginning.

'Brighton?' he asked.

'No, somewhere small, that no one has ever heard of. I will not tell you where.'

'Thank you,' he said quietly. 'I could not bear to know.'

They looked at each other for a long while, without speaking, and already, in their silence, Sibell seemed to hear the sound of the sea. It was going to taste of salt, this last long wait.

'I have missed you terribly,' she said, having meant not to say it.

'I have missed you more,' he said.

'Not possible,' she said, and suddenly she found herself crying, tears sliding out of her eyes like a river, pouring, actually pouring onto the starched white napery before her. She watched them fall like little stones, astonished.

'Hush, my darling,' he said, and she saw the muscles of his cheek go rigid. 'We have waited so long to be happy. Nothing can stop us now.'

Mara, as she crouched on the floor of the cupboard in Hell and ruled a neat red line under a centipede column of figures, had never felt happier.

The Devil's Door was thriving. There'd been enough profit this year to finish converting Gifford's Oak. It had been her idea for William and Vi to make the old house pay its way. She doubted if the new school would ever show much profit, but it meant somewhere for Alys to stay with Vi, and that was the main thing.

Of course Leo wasn't happy, but then Mara had never met a man who was. Unhappiness kept a man useful, and busy, and attractive. But it was very unlikely now that Lady Lavery would ever leave her husband. One day Leo was going to realize that, and have to find something else to be unhappy about.

The basement door opened and Mara closed her account book at once. Not even Leo knew how much the club was making, and Mara wanted to keep it that way. He was perfectly satisfied with the proceeds from the sale of his paintings, and his unhappiness.

'Mara, where are you?' Leo sounded impatient.

Mara extracted herself carefully from the cupboard, replacing the account book under a pile of blood-red table napkins overprinted with the crossed pitchforks, each in the shape of a letter M, that made up the insignia of the Devil's Door.

'Sorting linen,' she answered as she closed the door and locked it.

'How very domestic.' There was a different note in Leo's voice, a sort of excitement quite at odds with his words. Mara studied him narrowly.

'Where have you been?' A wifely question, Mara thought suddenly. For a moment she wondered what it would be like to be married to Leo. They already spent almost every night together, though not in bed. And now that wives could keep their own earnings –

'Pussy cat, pussy cat,' said Leo absently. Even in the dimness of Hell Mara could see that his eyes had a wild sort of shine in them.

Lady Lavery, she thought instantly. The picture of herself and Leo as husband and wife, two fisherfolk trawling the night for sustenance, faded.

'And how was the Queen? Did she let you sit under her chair?'

Leo laughed. Mara recognized that laugh. It meant he wasn't going to tell her any more about it. He was striding about Hell now, picking up small objects, the bottle-opener from the bar, the soda siphon, as if he'd never seen them before.

'Why is there never anything to eat in this establishment?' he inquired rhetorically. The lack of food had been a running joke between them; in all their long acquaintance they'd never shared so much as a bloater-paste sandwich together.

This time, however, Mara wasn't to be distracted. She was being indulged, and she knew it.

'Well?' His restlessness made her impatient. It had been a long time since Leo had last seen Lady Lavery. Mara had forgotten how different he was when he came back. Sometimes it took him three days to recover.

'Very well, thank you,' came the irritating answer. 'Very well indeed. In fact, couldn't be better.'

Leo swung round to face her suddenly. He seemed to have shed years; Mara felt tired just looking at him. His physical presence, the sheer height and size of him, was enough in itself, without the addition of enthusiasm. Now he seemed to devour all the air in the room, leaving none for her to breathe. He ran both hands through his hair, staring at her as if she was some new and as yet untried sort of soda siphon.

'I'm leaving,' he announced abruptly.

Mara blinked. Suddenly the room seemed cold, too cold for summer.

'What do you mean?'

'The Devil's Door. I'm leaving.'

'Why?'

Leo shrugged. 'It's time.'

That was so exactly what she would have said in the same situation that for a moment Mara didn't know how to reply.

'What has changed?'

Leo looked at her: the answer was written all over his face.

'I don't believe it,' Mara said slowly. 'After all these years. Lady Lavery is going to leave her husband.'

'After all these years, Lady Lavery is going to divorce her husband,' Leo said steadily.

'To marry you.'

He nodded.

'But I thought you didn't believe in marriage.'

'So did I.'

They stared at each other across the room; Mara felt as if he was very far away.

'Where will you live?'

'Somewhere. Abroad. It doesn't matter where.'

The certainty in his voice convinced Mara finally. For Leo, of all people, who lived by his eyes, the look of places and people, not to care where he lived – that meant it was going to happen, it had already happened. Already, in his mind's eye, he was somewhere else; the decision had been taken.

It was only then that Mara realized she had somehow written Leo into her balance sheet. She had banked on him being there, part of the sum, for the foreseeable future, for herself and one day for Alys. There'd seemed to be so much time left to arrange it, to make the figures add up.

Now there turned out to have been no time at all.

'Aren't you going to wish me well, Mara?'

From somewhere Mara called up an answering smile; not that it mattered, because no smile of hers was going to reach him. She smiled for herself, because that was how she wanted to remember this moment; Leo leaving and herself smiling.

'Why not?' If he had looked closer he would have seen the edge of irony in her smile. 'I wish you every happiness.'

Happiness. For Sibell, a week later, as she rode on the top deck of a scarlet bus towards Victoria, the word no longer had any meaning. She had become it.

From where she sat, clutching Soo Shah's velvet collar because she had never been on a double-decker before and had not realized the ride would be so bumpy, Sibell could see right over into the Park. There was the bench where she had been used to meet Leo; brief, snatched meetings as painful as gulps of air to someone drowning. Leo was the reason she had bought Soo Shah in the first place, to give her an excuse for walks at odd hours.

But now, from the bus, with a whole future of happiness ahead of her, Sibell could see how divided, how walled and fenced and somehow sad the Park was. Its paths crisscrossed, leading nowhere. Its choices were artificial: the Round Pond, the bandstand, the Serpentine. No real lake or river, no real music.

Just a parade.

Sibell was glad that she was leaving London for good at last. She'd never felt at home here, and living at Ainsley House had spoiled the city for her. It would always remind her of a prison.

Even the thought of leaving behind England itself did not trouble her. She wouldn't see Gifford's Oak again, but then the Gifford's Oak which had been her home no longer even existed. Yesterday, when she'd said goodbye to William, it had looked unnaturally clean and smart, yet somehow dimmed. The air no longer smelled of dust and honeysuckle, but boiled potatoes and rubber-soled shoes.

Sibell should have felt sad about that, but she didn't. She felt like a traveller setting off for some unimaginable land; so taken up with her excitement that she could think of nothing else.

The rest was mere formality. Her bags were packed, her few valued possessions safe in storage, her affairs settled. Despite everything, over the years in London she had somehow managed to accumulate a whole retinue of people paid to help her keep up appearances.

Now, one by one, disguising her relief as best she could, Sibell had dismissed them all. Soo Shah's doctor, who had reluctantly surrendered the prescription for his paws; her own dentist, who had advised her darkly never to use foreign tapwater to brush her teeth; her solicitor, who had made one last attempt to persuade her to accept an allowance from her husband; her doctor, who had seized the opportunity, while Quintin was still paying his bills, to give her a full examination; her hairdresser, whom she had instructed to give her a cut that would be economical and last a long time, with the result that now her shingled neck lay bare to all the winds of fate; her dressmaker, who had wept, and then, after a decorous interval, inquired whether before Sibell went abroad she would be disposing of her last season's wardrobe.

Sibell was glad that now it was all over. She wanted to take nothing with her to her new life but those who loved her: Leo, Hugo and Soo Shah.

Fleetingly, Sibell thought of Mama and Papa and Tom. They were good memories; she wanted Hugo to have the same. Children needed families.

Leo and I will have three at least, Sibell thought, and a blush of sheer happiness rose to her cheeks. Two girls and a boy, to make up an even number. I'm only twenty-nine, there's still time.

She had no idea what it would be like to make love with Leo. If it was anything like kissing him it would be heaven. But then, just being with him was heaven.

She gave Soo Shah a cachou to stop him chewing his paws, and closed her eyes, letting the sunshine play over her eyelids till colour bloomed like a rose.

Happiness. That was what it was; an acute awareness of the present together with a radiant apprehension of the future. For the first time in years, Sibell thought, I am facing forward, not backward. If I were to die right now, I would die happy, riding in a bright red bus down Park Lane towards the rest of my life with the man I love.

Leo awoke to a fury of summer birdsong.

It was barely dawn. A month had gone by since he'd last seen Sibell, at the Embassy Club. During that month he'd kept monastic hours, not by design, but by necessity. He had no choice in the matter. He seemed to be able to hear the light outside gathering in his sleep. He'd never felt so aware of the sound and shape and scent of the world in his life, never woken so suddenly and completely. Over the past four weeks he'd come to know the note struck by an egg yolk floating in a blue bowl, the shape and texture of a dream, the colour of birdsong.

He would always remember that morning.

There was a letter for him. He recognized Sibell's handwriting on the envelope. He felt no surprise. He'd already sent her a thousand letters in his mind. They'd both agreed, for safety's sake, to commit nothing to writing, but he understood why she hadn't been able to keep to the agreement. If he'd known her address, he'd have done exactly the same.

Leo didn't hurry to open the letter. He let it lie there, chaste in its white envelope, until he'd eaten. Dry bread from yesterday, tasting like manna. Water from the jug, pure delight.

He opened the letter with steady hands. It might have been his imagination, but the paper seemed to smell of salt. He had a sudden image of Sibell writing to him, in a small low-ceilinged room, her bent head outlined by the dancing, diamond-bright mirror of the sea. White paper, white gulls, a chalk-white esplanade. He was closer to her now than he had ever been. In a few short months they would need no more letters, no more words.

My dear Leo,

I do not know how to tell you this, but I have decided not to continue with divorce proceedings against my husband.

Under the circumstances it would be better if we did not see each other again. Please do not attempt to contact me. My mind is made up.

I am very sorry. Please believe me, we could never have been happy.

Sibell

'No!' The single syllable broke from Leo in a roar as he crushed the letter and hurled it away from him. Something must have happened to change Sibell's mind. He couldn't have been wrong about what they felt for each other. Pressure must have been brought to bear on her in some way. What could it have been? Fear of scandal, her love for her son, some machination of her husband's?

Leo sprang to his feet. He would find her. If he had to search the length and breadth of the south coast, he would find her, and once he had found her, he would never let her out of his sight again.

He went straight to Gifford's Oak. William didn't know where his sister was staying, but he'd had a cheerful letter from her in which she declared that she was profiting from her seaside holiday by learning to swim. 'When I come back to Town,' she had written, 'you will find your sister a New Woman, at least in the water!'

The letter was dated three days before her letter to Leo. Fortunately, William had retained the envelope, which, unlike Leo's, bore a local postmark.

Two days later Leo drew up, the black shine of his hired car almost totally obscured by dust, outside a chalk-white house very similar to the one he'd imagined on opening Sibell's letter. It was the ninth guest-house at which he'd made inquiries locally, and as he made his way up the narrow crazy-paving path inset with the upturned ends of bottles he felt a surge of hope. This was just the kind of lodging Sibell would choose, small, quiet and off the beaten track.

The woman who opened the door to him was at first dismissive.

'Lavery, you say? There's no one here of that name.'

'Gifford, then?'

Again the landlady shook her head.

Leo persisted.

'A tall lady, fair-haired, well-dressed, perhaps with a little dog?'

'A little dog, you say?' The landlady hesitated. 'What kind of dog?'

In his state of exhaustion Leo couldn't for a moment think of the name for the snub-nosed fluffy little creature Sibell had carried into the Embassy Club a month ago.

'Long ears, pop eyes, lots of hair . . . like a small lion.'

The landlady's mouth tightened a moment, then she called over her shoulder and along the corridor, bustling with the officious waddle Leo remembered, trotted Soo Shah.

Relief flooded over Leo so suddenly that for a moment he could hardly speak.

'Where is she?'

'You mean Mrs Oak,' said the landlady grudgingly.

'Of course. Mrs Oak. Where is she?'

'She is not here now.'

'When is she coming back?'

'She doesn't lodge here any more. I don't know,' said the woman, clearly vexed. 'Tells me she wants the room for six months, and then inside three weeks she's off back to London. Can't make their minds up, these young people.'

'But the dog?'

The landlady smiled for the first time. 'Just before she left she says, Soo Shah breathes much easier here, Mrs Graves. The sea air's so good for him I hardly like to take him back to Town. So I says, what wouldn't I give for a lovely little dog like that for my very own, I'd take such good care of him. And she says, all of a sudden, he's yours, Mrs Graves, if you would like him. I says, you can't possibly, they're valuable, them Pekinese, and she says, think nothing of it, I let you down over the room. So we parted on good terms in the end, Mrs Oak and me.'

'When was that?'

The landlady thought for a minute. 'She packed up Tuesday, and she was off early Wednesday.'

Wednesday. Leo's heart ached. The day his letter had been dated.

'Thank you, Mrs Graves.'

The last sight Leo had of Soo Shah was of the dog clamped in Mrs Graves's capacious arms, its dark brown eyes half-closed in contentment.

Wearily, Leo drove back to London. The weather had changed, there was a heaviness in the air. He experienced a strange sense of unreality. He had come so close to finding Sibell, and yet she seemed somehow further away now than she had been before. He tried to make sense of what he had learned from Mrs Graves but understood nothing. The effort and emotion of the past two days had bludgeoned him, blunted his perceptions. No matter how he cast about in his mind for his inner image of Sibell, the daily awareness of her existence beside him in the world that had become as much a part of him as his own thoughts, he found nothing. As he entered the outskirts of the great city he tasted grit. It was a dry well, an empty vault, to which he was returning.

By the time Leo reached Victoria Station the newsboys were shouting the evening edition.

News.

The impersonal fury of birdsong.

Even as he heard the raucous voices, even before the meaning of the words they shouted penetrated his consciousness, Leo knew. The pattern was complete, the road ended.

*

That night was the first time that Mara had lain in her second-floor bedroom with a man and listened to him talk about another woman.

Leo arrived just as the Green Hat party was ending. When Mara saw his face she realized immediately that he'd heard the news about Lady Lavery. She had to take action at once. Though it was almost 4 a.m. the Devil's Door was still packed. Elysium was full of green-hatted Iris Storm lookalikes, while Michael Arlen himself, the suddenly famous author of the year's most popular novel, was holding forth in Hell. Paradise was occupied by Alys and Violet, who spent alternate weeks at Gifford's Oak and Derby Street. The only sensible place to put Leo had been in her own bedroom.

It had been doomed from the beginning. There were many different things that could be found by a man and woman in bed together, but they had to settle on which one they were looking for before they started. She and Leo had not made that decision, and so they had found nothing. It had been as if they were taking part in a shadow play, for the benefit of strangers. Each touch had pushed them a little further apart.

We've come closer to each other, Mara thought ruefully, discussing the design of table-linen for the Devil's Door.

But disappointment made no difference to how she felt about Leo. She never closed the book on anyone till the pages fell apart.

Now, with the effort of turning those pages over at last – it was strange how failure was always so much more tiring than success – Mara lay back against her pillows, lit a Sobranie, and listened. Behind the blind, which she kept permanently down now that she followed owl hours, daylight was breaking. Dawn, she knew from past experience, would scatter her revellers. Only children and angels could withstand that light.

'Why?' Leo was saying. 'Why?'

'An accident,' Mara repeated patiently. 'They found her body. There were no marks.'

'I don't believe it.' Leo shook his head like a wounded bull. 'It makes no sense. Why was she there at all, what was she doing?'

Mara stubbed out her cigarette carefully in the cloisonné ashtray she kept beside her bed. She knew what people were saying about Lady Lavery's death. But until Leo heard the rumours for himself, she would lie to and for him, as well as with him.

'Swimming, Leo. She went swimming out of her depth and she drowned. They found her clothes, her bag, everything.'

That letter she wrote him, Mara thought. How merciless virtue is. If she hadn't anything better to say, she should have lied. 'She's gone, Leo.'

He looked at his hands. When he spoke again his voice was quite different; calm and quiet. He seemed suddenly much older.

'Have you ever lost anyone, Mara?'

The question took Mara by surprise. She'd never thought in those terms. She'd never wanted to be possessed by anyone, or to possess, and without ownership there was no risk of loss.

But perhaps she had some idea what Leo meant. When Alys was a baby Mara had dreamed sometimes that she'd mislaid her in a pile of washing and thrown her in the copper, then woken in a sweat of anxiety with her heart pounding, only to find Alys's head hard against her shoulder.

Mara shook her head.

There was a silence. Dawn was gathering strength outside now, a bugle blast of summer light.

'It's strange,' Leo said. 'It's as if I'm the one who has died.'

Mara said nothing. The tone of his voice disturbed her. It was as if he'd left the room and gone somewhere else entirely.

'We loved each other,' he said. 'It was different. Different from anything I have ever known.'

Mara nodded again. She was beginning to get some inkling of what he meant. It was like cricket. Each team had both Gentlemen and Players, dressed alike in virginal white, but they were treated as two different species. The Players were paid, but the Gentlemen were respected. They were the ones called 'Mr' and given individual rooms to change in.

'Don't tell me I will forget her,' Leo said.

Mara shook her head. She knew better than that. Sibell Lavery would never grow old, or tired, or too familiar. 'You will love her for ever,' she said, without a trace of irony.

Their eyes met.

'Thank you,' Leo said, simply. Slowly, oblivious of his nakedness, he rose from the bed and went towards the window. He stood with his back towards her, his powerful shoulders outlined against the diffused brightness of dawn, and his hands lifted once, like a blind man's.

'Sleep,' he said quietly to himself, as if he were the only person in the room. 'If only I could sleep.'

Mara felt a new sensation, at once faint and precise, just below her breastbone. It isn't over yet, she thought. He wants to go to her.

She had no idea what to do. She had nothing left to offer which she hadn't already given him: the use of the premises, the freedom of the city.

But she must do something.

She opened the drawer of her bedside table and took out from a gaily decorated tin labelled Greville's De Luxe Sugared Almonds a sachet of white powder. Her hands shook slightly as she emptied it into a tumbler and half-filled the glass with water from the ewer.

'Drink this,' she said.

Leo drank absently, like a sleepwalker, without asking what he'd been given, without even looking at the glass. Mara knew then that her insight had been right. Truly, the father of her daughter didn't care whether he lived or died.

It was only later, after she'd finally managed to persuade Leo to return to the bed, and he lay beside her locked into a sleep so deep it was really as if he were dead, that Mara realized this was the first

215

time she'd ever lain down with a man for no other reason than to sleep.

The idea of this, a virginity that she hadn't known she possessed, pleased her. It went against the book. Gentlemen, it was well known, might stoop to become Players, but the reverse was unheard of. As she drifted in and out of sleep, and felt the shifting of Leo's body, heard his breathing intertwine with hers as smoothly as water plaiting out of a tap, Mara found herself wondering if there might be ranks and qualities of maidenhead, as layers in heaven; and dreamed of a vast, tiered wedding-cake, on top of which stood herself, a guardian angel with an only slightly tarnished sword.

There was a carillon of breaking glass and a squeal from the adjoining suite. Sir Quintin Lavery paused in the act of adjusting his bow tie and frowned. He passed through the communicating door and entered the bathroom without bothering to knock. The china basin was full of mingled face-powder and shattered mirror.

'I dropped it,' said Belinda.

A stupid name, Quintin now felt. Her nickname, Bobo, was if anything worse. Quintin disliked intensely the modern vogue for informality.

'So I see.' He surveyed with distaste the wreckage of the jade powder compact he had bought her in Manchuria. It was not surprising she had dropped it; her hands were shaking so much that she had been barely able to comb her hair, which now stood out round her head in a golliwog frizz. Belinda had a child's capacity for excess. That was what had attracted Quintin to her in the first place, her youthful appetite for life and its novelties. Having no long-term investment in the world, he relished its transient effects all the more acutely.

But now the basin was a mess, and so was Belinda's appearance. She had put on too much Crème Gypsy and rachel powder, and her pink chiffon velvet gown only emphasized the sallowness of her skin. She had lost weight too, far beyond the point of fashionable banting.

'I shall be better soon, I promise,' Belinda said, and smiled at

217

him, a smile in search of a smile. She fluttered her blackened eyelashes, sashayed up to him and ran her hands lightly over his upper body in a pretence of sensuality, using the opportunity to slip two fingers inside his jacket. 'All I need is a little help. Just to steady my nerves. You have more, don't you, darling Quintin? You're so clever, you always do.'

Quintin detached her hands. They were cold, like the paws of a marmoset.

'You have had quite enough already. I haven't the slightest intention of giving you any more.'

Belinda's eyes flashed, her lower lip trembled. 'Why are you so unkind to me?'

'Because I hate women,' Quintin said calmly. 'I told you so the day we met.'

'You're horrible,' she said. 'You're cruel and unkind and horrible.' Her voice rose in a familiar spiral. 'It's all your fault. I was never like this till I met you. I hate you!'

Quintin could have spoken the lines from this particular bad play in his sleep. 'In that case,' he rejoined smoothly, 'our parting will come as a mutual relief.'

Belinda pursued him out of the bathroom, as he had known she would. They always did. He also knew, without needing to look, that there would be crimson patches on her neck.

'You're going? But you can't, you mustn't! You can't leave me behind, not just like that! It's not fair!'

'It is perfectly obvious, to me if not to you, that you are in no fit state to be taken anywhere.' Quintin picked up his white silk scarf and gloves. 'Please make sure to be gone before I return. My man will see you out.'

As Quintin left the Grosvenor Hotel he breathed a sigh of relief. Staying in hotels, in this doubtful summer of 1929, made so many transactions easier. The knowledge that when he returned to his suite there would no more pink dust in the basin, no sharp fingers dragging on his sleeve and sharper voice tugging at his attention, lightened his step.

Only parting, nowadays, could make him feel young again. He was forty-seven years old. He had been everywhere, seen everything; now he valued only time. Now, with several hours worth of pure immortality in his inside pocket, he was the monarch of all he purveyed.

By the time Quintin reached his destination it was late, but not too late to dine. People kept different hours now, in the new electric age. Given the changes in London, Quintin could hardly now regret his decision to spend his time abroad. He had found that winter in Switzerland or New York, February in Cannes, Easter in Brazil, summer in Bavaria, autumn in the Black Forest or boar-hunting in the Pyrenees, suited him admirably. Permanence of any kind held no more interest for him. He had made the best of his available choices.

Even now, if it had not been for the urgent necessity of returning Belinda to her native shores before she deliquesced, Quintin would not have bothered to return to London. Like its air, the city was oppressive; it lacked, above all, freshness.

All the same, there had been something refreshing about tonight's invitation. It had been addressed to him, both personally and correctly, at the Grosvenor; he had found it awaiting him there after motoring up from Southampton. Clearly, someone had taken the trouble to study the shipping lists. Quintin appreciated this example of orderly thinking. 'Before the Fall,' the invitation stated. Round its bevelled edge ran, in the fashion made popular since the Exposition des Arts Décoratifs in Paris three years ago, a border of stylized, gold-embossed fig leaves.

Quintin studied with raised eyebrows the neatly painted sign which requested visitors to descend the basement area stairs. It amused him to think of the privileged classes paying good money to tread steps previously relegated to tradesmen. In the days when Lucette had occupied this house, courtesy of his own generosity, such a thing would have been unthinkable. Now, as Quintin edged slowly down, he had the curious sensation that he was breaking a taboo. Flowering jasmine was woven in and out of the railings. It breathed out scent as his gloved hand touched it.

Expecting the usual claustrophobic jazz-age chrome and neon, Quintin was surprised to find himself instead in an underground cavern. Ferns sprouted from niches in the walls, and the air was musical with water. Welling up out of the monolithic kitchen range which dominated the room was a fountain, bubbling out of the hotplate and shimmering down over the black cast iron, like a whale spouting in mid-ocean.

On a moss-covered table by the bar Quintin discovered an entire woman constructed out of fruit. Her belly was a cantaloupe, her breasts oranges, her lips pomegranate. In passing Quintin plucked out her left nipple, a glossy purple Muscat grape. As he left the table he was aware, out of the corner of his eye, of the barman discreetly replacing it with another.

Quintin smiled to himself. The world had been his spectacle now for almost a decade, but he could still appreciate perfection when he saw it.

Slowly, he mounted the narrow steps leading up from the underground cavern and found himself in a forest. All the internal doors and furniture on the ground floor had been removed, transforming the area into a succession of leafy chambers. Foliage brushed against Quintin's clothing; beneath his feet lay turf, real grass still starred with daisies. Out of the stairwell before him rose a giant fig tree, sugared fruit glistening between the grey gaberdine leaves.

On the upper landing Quintin paused. Above, there was one door that had not been removed, the door leading to what had once been Lucette's bedroom.

Instantly, Quintin wished to see what lay behind that door. He felt the irritation of a man reading a story only to find the next pages cut out by a previous reader. Even as he watched, the door opened and a man and a woman emerged together. The woman had her back to Quintin but he could see the man's face quite clearly as she turned and locked the door behind her. The man was much the taller of the two; he stood for a moment looking down at his companion with a quizzical, half-suspicious look. His deep voice carried quite audibly.

'And just what do think will happen to them?'

'They will die, of course,' replied the woman. 'But that would have happened anyway, sooner or later. I'm just giving them the opportunity to do it beautifully.' She flashed her companion a brilliant smile. 'If you don't approve, it's your own fault. I told you not to come.'

Recognition hit Quintin like ice chinking into a glass. It was nine years since he had said goodbye to Mara Mizen in the dingy Baker Street rooming house, but she was unmistakable. Yet as he stared up at her, he could scarcely believe his eyes. She had not aged at all; if anything, she looked younger than when he had last seen her. She had always had an indestructible quality, but now she seemed honed, sharpened into a definition of herself. She was deeply tanned, the colour of a Guarneri violin or a piece of fine Chippendale. Her dark hair was sculpted into a glossy jet-black cap that clung to her head like bakelite. Against her varnished coppery skin her pale eyes blazed with extraordinary light. Her lips were scarlet. She was wearing white; a low-cut white silk dress beaded and embroidered, white silk stockings, shoes with astonishingly high, slender heels. In her ears, the single, jaunty touch of the old Mara, swung earrings made of mah-jong tablets. In her hand she carried something hidden by a scarlet silk cloth.

Quintin's mouth twitched. He would not have been surprised if under that cloth had lain the head of John the Baptist. With the most delightful and recently unfamiliar sense of expectation he mounted the last few steps that separated him from the second-floor landing. The man with Mara looked up interrogatively as he approached. Quintin ignored him.

'Well, my dear. It seems you have moved on a great deal since the last time we met.'

Mara turned to him slowly. Slowly her eyes moved up and down, studying him carefully. Then her chin lifted and she delivered him the slightest of frowns.

'Have we met before?'

Quintin could have laughed out loud for sheer exhilaration. They were impeccably done, the look and the frown, but he knew now exactly who had sent him that invitation.

'Perhaps you are too young to remember,' he answered lightly. 'May I introduce myself, in that case, since you have been so kind as to include me on your list of guests? Sir Quintin Lavery, at your service.'

There was a heartbeat of silence. The man beside Mara stiffened. A look of alarm flashed across Mara's face. Instantly she disguised it, laid a hand lightly on his arm.

For Quintin, it was as if time slowed to a standstill. He relished the moment, held it close. He had waited a long time for this, more than a decade. Now, at last, someone would pay for all the wasted years. Now, at last, seeing the expression on the other man's face, he knew.

'Aren't you going to introduce us?' he inquired blandly, while his blood sang with triumph.

'Mr de Morgan,' Mara replied, after a moment's hesitation. 'The artist. He painted the pictures on these walls.'

Quintin smiled. 'Mr Leo de Morgan, I presume?'

Mr de Morgan nodded. A pulse beat in his forehead. Quintin observed it with satisfaction. The lion was trapped at last.

'I think we have acquaintances in common.'

'Had.' Mr de Morgan's voice was harsh. Sharp lines had etched themselves from his nose to his mouth.

'You were a friend of my late wife's, I believe,' Quintin continued smoothly.

'No.'

Quintin raised one eyebrow. So the lion proved a coward, after all.

'Really?'

'I loved her.' The other man's face was set. 'There is a difference.'

'So they tell me.' Quintin paused delicately. 'Not that it matters very much either way. In the end, she chose to stay with me.'

'It was not her choice! You forced her, threatened her—'

'I, my dear fellow? Whyever should I do such a thing?'

'There is no other possible explanation!'

'I beg to differ, my dear chap. I have her last letter still. She simply changed her mind. One can see why, after all. She simply decided, when it came down to it, that she would much rather live in comfort for the rest of her life than starve poetically in a garret. Who can blame her? Not I, certainly. She would not be the first woman, or the last, to sell herself to the highest bidder. It happens every day.'

'Not Sibell.' The man clenched his fists. 'Never Sibell.'

Quintin shrugged. 'Just as you please. But there are no doubts in my mind. I knew from the first precisely why Sibell Gifford married me. For money – and that makes her no better than a common whore.'

The other man moved so fast that Quintin was aware of nothing before hands fastened round his throat. It was like being set upon by a wild beast. He had the impression of great strength and heat, a sort of turbulence which was almost exhilarating. Even as he struggled for breath he felt a sense of overmastering triumph.

Then the pressure round his throat relaxed and he heard Mara's voice. 'Enough, Leo! This is my house, and I will not have it!'

Quintin's assailant released him. He was shaking and his eyes were dark with rage. Then, without saying another word, he turned away and was gone, ricocheting down the stairway as if blown by a hurricane.

The air he left behind seemed to tremble.

'Was that entirely necessary, Quintin?' Mara sent him an assessing look, her light eyes arrow-sharp.

'The Tree of Knowledge, my dear. I thought that was your speciality.' Quintin rearranged the points of his starched collar. He felt good, a deep inner satisfaction. 'We must all taste of its bitter fruit in the end. I am sure your Mr de Morgan will live to appreciate my frankness.'

'You hate him, don't you?'

'I have good reason. And I suspect the sentiment is mutual. Have you not yet learned, my dear, that men love to hate each other?'

The crowd of curious onlookers gathered on the stairs began to disperse. For a moment Quintin could not help wondering if the entire encounter had been stage-managed by Mara as a spectacle to entertain her guests.

'Talking of knowledge, what exactly prompted you to invite me here this evening?'

'One moment.' Mara walked lightly to the head of the staircase and glanced down over the banisters. Whatever she saw seemed to satisfy her. She withdrew the scarlet cloth from what she was carrying. It proved to be a gilt wire-mesh cage filled with what Quintin at first took to be multi-coloured flower petals.

Then Mara lifted the lid, upended the cage, and, tapping briskly on its base, decanted a long, fluttering kite-tail of butterflies. They eddied and gusted slowly down over the upturned heads below to a chorus of oohs and aahs.

Mara closed the cage-lid and snapped shut the fastening. One butterfly, a Scarlet Emperor, alighted on her shoulder. She let it sit there, quivering.

'I have a suggestion I would like to put to you,' she said then, and her scarlet lips curved in a butterfly-wing smile.

Quintin looked at her. He was aware as he looked of exactly how her hard, boyish buttocks, tautened by those Staten Island heels of hers, would feel inside the white silk. What precisely, he wondered, was the forbidden fruit in this case, the recipe for self-destruction, the bourne of no return? Mara returned his gaze enigmatically. Her eyes were as empty as air.

'Another of your business propositions, Mara?'

Mara inclined her head. 'You could call it that.' She lifted one foot and inspected the slender spear of her white heel, the lower inch of which was specked with soil. 'Shall we discuss it in my bedroom? The grass is a little less trodden there.'

'I admire your shoes,' he said.

'I thought you might,' she said. 'They are made of snakeskin.'

'I must confess I hardly recognized the place.'

It was an hour later. It gave Quintin great pleasure to think of what had just occurred between himself and his hostess, inside the one impenetrable room in the whole of the Devil's Door. The buzz and chatter of the other guests, all unknowing, had made an agreeable accompaniment to his private festivities.

'Oh but you did.' Mara, stark naked except for her snakeskin shoes and the mah-jong tablets in her ears, seemed quite unmoved. Quintin had forgotten her egg-like talent for seeming fully clothed when entirely nude, complementing exactly her ability to suggest nakedness even at her most clothed. 'The Bible says we were all here once.'

'Eden,' he said.

'Before the Fall,' Mara said. 'We must all speak American now.'

'Of course. But I must confess I miss the monkey.'

'The monkey's still here.' Mara straddled him, tangled her fingers in the hair on his chest. 'You are ugly, Mr Quintin Lavery. You are as ugly as sin.'

'Sir Quintin Lavery,' he reminded her. 'You have no respect. I shall have it seen to immediately.'

'Send out for it, my dear sir,' Mara answered, leaning over him so that the dark point of one nipple brushed against his face. 'Take my advice, it's the only way.'

*

225

Four months later, on a crisp November evening, Mara met Leo at the White City track. Greyhound racing, with the new electric hare, was the latest novelty. It was chic and modern, nowadays, to slum while one still could.

Mara hadn't seen Leo since the Before the Fall party. He hadn't avoided her exactly; he had simply disappeared. Mara hadn't realized at the time how much she'd miss him.

She was surprised, in a way, to see him waiting for her in the glass-walled viewing gallery overlooking the track. She hadn't really expected him to be there. He looked dishevelled and paint-spattered, but he could get away with that, because of his height. Mara knew that if she'd been dressed as carelessly as he was even the gates of the White City would have been closed to her.

'You were right,' were his first words.

'About what?' Mara asked. It was as if he were taking up a conversation left only yesterday. She didn't know whether to be pleased or annoyed.

'The Fall,' Leo answered.

'The Crash, you mean.' The disaster Mara had sensed was on its way had arrived last month, when four hundred banks had crashed on Wall Street. Vibrations from that Crash were still travelling outwards from the impact; Mara was glad that she'd taken action when she did. A few months later and she'd have had no leverage at all.

'You are looking very smart, nevertheless.' Leo eyed her up and down appreciatively. Mara felt herself relax. She was coming up to a change of role, and she couldn't be sure that the presentation which had worked in the past would still be right. This evening she was wearing Chanel's close-fitting tiers of indigo crêpe, with little flutings at hip and knee, and a rope of glistening steel beads. A little dressy for the White City, perhaps, but she would be going on later.

Leo indicated the table. 'I ordered warm beer and sandwiches,' he said. 'I know how you like to adapt yourself to your company.'

Mara ignored the reference. She'd done what she could at the Eden party; managing two men at once was impossible.

'So,' Leo continued, 'what other developments have you foreseen in your crystal ball?'

Mara hesitated. She'd hoped for more of a breathing space.

'Nothing particularly interesting, I'm afraid.' She pulled off one suede glove, turned it for a moment in her hands, then laid it aside on the table. She wasn't nervous, it was ridiculous to be nervous.

'I am engaged to be married.'

There was a moment's silence. Leo didn't seem surprised; he didn't even seem particularly interested.

'Do you want me to dissuade you?'

'Of course not.'

'Very well, then.' He lifted his glass to her. 'Then my felicitations. When is the ceremony to be?'

'Next spring.'

Silence again, but not the companionable silence which Mara was used to in his company. Beneath them on the brilliantly lit track there was the sound of a pistol-shot and the greyhounds streaked away in pursuit of the jiggling white hare.

'I cannot understand,' said Leo, his tone conversational, 'what on earth possesses those dogs to pursue something they never catch and could not eat if they did.'

'I would like to tell you who I'm going to marry,' Mara persisted, with difficulty above the roar of the crowd.

'Why?' Leo replied. 'All husbands are the same.'

'Even so, I would rather tell you myself than have you hear it from someone else.' Now Mara had come to it, her throat felt dry. She reached for the beer; it tasted of metal. 'I am to become a Lady.'

'A common illusion of the soon-to-be-married,' said Leo, with a quizzical look. 'In my experience, it doesn't last long.'

'You don't understand.' The roar died away with dizzying suddenness. The race was over; below, the dogs skittered to a halt as the hare was whisked away. 'When I am married, I shall be Lady Lavery.'

The smile died instantly from Leo's face. He placed his glass quietly down on the table.

'I don't believe you,' he said flatly.

'It's true,' Mara said. She felt a lurch of apprehension. She'd been right to choose a public place for this meeting.

'I did not say it was not true,' he said.

He looked at her for a long moment. His amber eyes were dark, his mouth compressed to a hard line. His stillness disturbed her more than violence would have done.

'Why?' he said, finally. His voice grated. His eyes seemed not to see her at all. Mara felt suddenly cold.

'I need to be married,' she said.

'Why?' he asked again.

Mara hesitated. She had a feeling there was no explanation which he would accept, but all the same she must try.

'Because of Alys,' she said finally. It sounded weak, she knew. And yet it was true. To want for her daughter something better than what she herself had had, was that such a crime? 'I have to think of her future.'

'You mean you are marrying for money,' Leo stated baldly.

'Not entirely.' For a moment Mara was on the verge of telling Leo he was Alys's father. Quintin knew – that was why he was the only man, apart from Leo himself, whom she could safely marry.

'I am marrying because I must,' she said. Her heart thudded inside her as if it had come loose from its moorings. 'Since the Crash, the Devil's Door no longer shows a profit. I have no choice.'

'That's an excuse,' Leo answered. 'I know you, Mara. You've never done anything you didn't want to do in your life.'

'How can you say that?' Mara's voice rose. She heard her accent slipping, broadening, and paused, horrified. 'How do you know what it's like to be me?'

Leo shrugged.

'I know. I know what you need, what you want. I know you.'

They stared at each other for a long moment. Mara found it almost impossible to hold his gaze. He was right; he knew her. After the many nights they'd spent together over the last five years it would be surprising if he didn't. Intensely satisfying, those nights – but always behind drawn blinds, always with something hidden.

The thought came to Mara suddenly: we have been each other's alibis.

'Are you trying to make me jealous?' he asked finally.

'What would be the point of that?' Mara said, reaching for her bag. She took out her etched steel powder compact, dusted her nose and cheeks. Seeing her own features in the mirror helped her control them. She could have asked Leo to marry her. If she'd told him about Alys, he would probably have agreed.

But the bond between herself and Leo, like that between him and his daughter, was very frail, a plant grown in semi-darkness. Leo was still in love with another woman. Since Sibell died he hadn't truly cared about anything except his work. His career was beginning to take off, particularly in America, though he took no interest in presenting his work to possible buyers. He didn't even have an agent. 'Money is of no interest to me,' he'd told her. 'I have no responsibilities, nor any intention of acquiring any.'

It wasn't enough.

Mara snapped the compact shut to find Leo watching her with narrowed eyes.

'Why are you looking at me like that?'

'You remind me of someone.'

'Not . . .'

'Heavens, no.'

'Who, then?' Mara was relieved that the conversation had reached a plateau; banter was familiar territory. Perhaps the worst was over.

'My mother.'

'Your mother?' Mara was taken aback for a moment, but she rallied. 'I didn't know you had one.'

'I don't. She died when I was thirteen.'

'Oh.' Mara risked a glance at him. He seemed calmer. 'What was she like?'

'Impossible,' he said, almost idly. 'You would have liked her. And she would have hated you.'

Absurdly, Mara felt offended.

'I see.' She lifted her chin. 'Was she beautiful?'

'Very. And elegant, and charming, and French.'

'And impossible,' said Mara with a touch of sharpness.

'That wasn't entirely her fault,' he said. 'She was always ill. And we travelled a great deal.'

'Tell me about her.' As long as a man could be kept talking, Mara knew, he could be kept out of mischief.

'She was fascinating, but she changed all the time. I never knew where I was with her.'

'What about your father?'

'He was a doctor. After she died, he went back to America to practise. I refused to go with him. It was as if, when she was gone, there was no connection left between us. He died when I was eighteen.' Leo frowned. 'She stopped me from knowing him.'

'How? How did she stop you?'

Leo shrugged. 'After I was born the doctors said she must never risk another child. Only I was allowed into her bedroom. She liked my touch.' He looked down at his hands with a meditative expression. 'I shall never forgive her for that.'

Mara was taken aback. 'You hated her.'

'On the contrary.' Leo smiled, a little bleakly. 'I adored her.'

Mara felt a presentiment brush lightly against the edge of her consciousness. Leo had never confided in her before about his background.

'Why are you telling me this?'

Leo shrugged. 'Because it doesn't matter any more.'

'What do you mean?'

'After this, you will be married. We shall not see each other again.'

'I see.' Mara made her coldness mirror his. 'You don't want me yourself, but you can't bear anyone else to have me.'

'Not anyone,' he said quietly. 'Only him.'

'Why?' Even as Mara asked the question she knew the answer. It was ironic that the strongest feelings she'd ever aroused in Leo should have nothing to do with herself at all. 'Because of Sibell.'

'He killed her.'

'No.' Suddenly Mara was angry. 'You killed her between you. She wouldn't have died if you'd left her alone!'

'That's not true!' Leo's face was white. Mara knew she was going too far, but she couldn't stop herself. She felt a sort of madness.

'Sibell Gifford was the hare, and you and Quintin were the hounds! She killed herself rather than have you tear her to pieces between you! But even if you'd caught up with her, she'd have been no good to you! Cold metal, Leo, that's all you'd have found in the end! You'd have broken your teeth on it!'

'You don't know what you're talking about. If you think that, then you have never loved anyone.'

'Do you love me?'

'No,' Leo shouted.

'Then don't you dare mention the word! You think I'm using Quintin, but you've used me too, and Sibell! That's what people do, they use each other! It's what makes the world go round!'

'Maybe.' Leo's tone was cold again. Mara could feel him retreating from her now. She couldn't reach him any more, not even to hurt him. She felt her anger drain away, leaving her empty.

'I'm sorry. I shouldn't have spoken to you as I did, about Sibell.'

Leo shrugged.

'We have no need to be polite to each other. Politeness is for husbands and wives.' Suddenly, he pushed back his seat and rose to his feet. His face was shuttered. 'I wish you every happiness. But in future you will have to go to the dogs with someone else.'

Mara watched him stride away, tasting salt. Her mouth was filled with blood. Some time in the last few minutes she'd bitten her tongue. On the track below another pistol shot rang out, another race began.

12   *Black of the Blackest*

'Perhaps he isn't coming,' said Carelia.

Alys said nothing. She was too excited to speak, but nervous too. She wished she hadn't described Cousin Hugo, who wasn't even a real cousin, in quite such glowing terms to Carelia. That was why Carelia had insisted on accompanying Aunt Violet and herself to Victoria Station, where Alys was to catch the Pullman Golden Arrow. Carelia, being the Duke of Shelburne's daughter, knew very well that she was the most important pupil at Gifford's Oak, and pulled rank accordingly, despite being only thirteen, a bare year older than Alys herself.

Now, Alys wished the station were not quite so crowded. It would be frightful if she failed to spot Hugo first. And in the February cold, muffled up in their overcoats because of the snow outside, people looked so different from their usual selves. Alys clasped her hands anxiously inside the muff which Sir Quintin Lavery, the man her mother was going to marry, had paid for, and hoped very much that her nose hadn't gone pink at the end, which would make her look even more like a white mouse than usual. Her mother said her pale colouring came from her father, the White Russian. Whenever Alys thought of him she thought of something long and thin and frosty, like an icicle.

If only there weren't so many people, and so many trains, and a truly terrifying stationmaster in silk hat and morning coat. Aunt

Violet had checked several times the number of their platform, but Alys could tell that she too was worried.

Alys had been secretly relieved when she had found out that Aunt Violet was not going to escort her all the way on this momentous journey. As Alys had grown older she had begun to notice things about the way her aunt acted and spoke that made her feel ashamed, and ashamed of feeling ashamed, because she loved Aunt Violet very much, and people couldn't help the way they had been brought up. Uncle William was very keen on that idea, that everyone was the same, but after her first term at Gifford's Oak Alys had realized it was just that, an idea; people were considerably different from each other in almost everything.

Things were bad, apparently, in the grown-up world at Gifford's Oak; that was why Aunt Violet had to stay behind in England. Uncle William declared that captains must stay with their ships whether or not they were sinking. This seemed folly to Alys; she was glad her own ship seemed not to be sinking but ploughing gaily on to brighter shores. She was looking forward very much to being rich. Her mother's marriage in two days' time would make her more equal with Carelia, whose father, being a Duke, had houses everywhere, and two ex-wives, and a Handley-Page seven-seater aeroplane, and a yacht called *White Lady*, after his favourite racehorse.

'Bless my ears and whiskers,' said a voice. 'If it isn't Alys. And how perfectly splendid you are looking.'

Alys blushed with the warmth of pure pleasure. There he was, slim, elegant, graceful, his long, vivid face alight with recognition, his thick dark hair falling sideways over his forehead. She had never felt so grateful to anyone in her life.

'I'm not late at all, am I?' Hugo inquired with a charming hint of anxiety. 'Had to stop off at my solicitor's. Dreadfully slow, these legal johnnies.'

'That's quite all right,' said Aunt Violet, and even before she said it, it was. Hugo was able to dissolve tension as suddenly as if the sun had appeared from behind a cloud. 'Carelia, this is Alys's cousin Hugo.'

'Enchanted.' Hugo smiled, smoothing back his ruffled hair with one hand. 'Always pleased to meet a friend of Alys. What a delightful name.'

Carelia stared at him, for once struck dumb. Alys almost burst with pride. Hugo looked magnificent, like a film star. He was slim as a cigarillo and beautifully dressed, right down to his Oxford bags and the lemon-yellow muffler cuffed dashingly over the shoulder of his camel coat, but it was his charm that made him look as if he were lit up from inside. He was clever, too, having gone straight from Eton to Oxford to read Modern History at Balliol.

'Thank you,' said Carelia, belatedly. Her prominent blue eyes had become quite glazed with admiration.

'Must dash, though, don't you think, Alys? Unless you've changed your mind? Are you sure it won't be a dreadful bore to keep me company?'

Alys shook her head. A dreadful bore was the last thing it would be. Her first cross-Channel voyage, with Cousin Hugo as an escort! And a night in Paris. She only hoped she would not be sick with excitement.

'No end decent of you, I must say.' Hugo possessed himself of Alys's hand luggage. Her trunk – brand-new pigskin, courtesy of Hugo's father's generosity – had already been stowed in the guard's van. He kissed Aunt Violet thoroughly on both cheeks, making her laugh, bowed to Carelia as if she had been a countess, then whisked Alys away before she had even time to feel the wrench of parting.

Hugo installed her in their reserved compartment with a flourish.

'You're cold, I can tell,' he said immediately. Alys did not know how he had guessed. She felt cold almost always. Sometimes, at night, it was as much as she could do to push her feet down to the arctic bottom of the bed. Bad circulation, Aunt Violet said. 'Have no fear,' Hugo went on. 'I have the perfect remedy.' From his

Gladstone bag he produced, of all things, a red-flannel-covered hot water bottle. Within seconds he had summoned a white-coated steward from the corridor to fill it with hot water.

'But are you sure?' Alys asked him, as he presented her with the warm bundle, only slightly damp. 'Are you sure you don't need it for yourself?'

'Absolutely and utterly.' Hugo beamed at her. 'I brought it for you, specially. I know what ladies are.' Alys felt desperately flattered to be called a lady, when she was only twelve. As Hugo smiled she noticed how long his eyelashes were. They cast quite a shadow.

'In any case,' Hugo went on. 'You and I don't need to stand on ceremony. Why, we are practically brother and sister.' This thought sent a flush of warmth through Alys even more comforting than that of the hot bottle. As she curled her gloved fingers gratefully round the damp red flannel Hugo delved once more into his Gladstone. This time he produced a glass, a bottle of port, and a lemon. Alys watched him, fascinated, as he sliced the lemon with a pocket knife that Uncle William would have envied, poured a level of port into the glass, and squinted at it knowingly. A little more port, then he seemed satisfied.

'Now for the magic ingredient.' Hugo thrust out the glass in Alys's direction. 'Just the veriest splash, the merest smidgin of hot water, if you please. Do be mother.'

A little solemnly, because she could not be quite sure he was not joking, and wished above all to seem a sophisticated traveller, Alys unstoppered the bottle and did as she was told.

Hugo tasted his port and pronounced it delicious. 'Just as I like it,' he said. 'The faintest, most inscrutable suggestion of nursery rubber.'

Alys tried hard to keep a straight face; making a business of tucking the hot water bottle inside her muff helped. Its warmth made her feel for a moment quite invincible. This was truly an adventure.

Then, on the platform outside, she caught sight of Aunt Violet and Carelia, whose existence she had for at least five minutes completely forgotten. Aunt Violet looked a little lost and out of place. Alys felt suddenly guilty for not wanting her aunt's company on this trip. The two of them had taken so many train journeys together – small, dull ones up and down to London – and now that a big, interesting one had come along, Aunt Violet, who had never been to Paris either, had to stay behind. A lump came into Alys's throat. Suddenly Paris seemed a very long way away. Did they even have hot water bottles in France?

As if he sensed her sudden distress, Hugo leaned forward. In a hushed theatrical whisper, with a sideways glance, he indicated a party of people gathered on the platform. In the centre of the group, barely visible, sat a fair-haired man placidly consuming chocolates and talking to a friend.

'You know who that is, of course.'

Alys's eyes widened. She shook her head.

'The Boy,' said Hugo.

Alys studied the man again. He was boyish-looking, and his hair was as yellow as Carelia's, but he was quite grown-up; certainly no boy.

'The Prince of Wales!' hissed Hugo.

'Really?' said Alys. She was fascinated. The lump in her throat had quite disappeared. 'Is he catching our train?'

'Of course,' said Hugo. 'Only we mustn't say so. He's travelling incog. Don't breathe a word to anyone.'

'I won't,' said Alys, delighted even to be asked. She watched as discreetly as she could as the man popped a last chocolate into his mouth and rose to his feet. He was very short, hardly taller than a boy of fourteen, but he carried himself with great distinction as he mounted the steps into the next-door carriage. Even at that distance the brilliant turquoise blue of his eyes was clearly visible. The carriage door had barely closed behind the last of his party before there was a veritable stampede of stewards down the corridor towards the Prince's carriage.

'I told you so!' said Hugo triumphantly.

'How does he get his hair to look so bright?' Alys asked, whispering, as the train gave a solemn little jerk, as if it bowed. She had the feeling, somehow, that Hugo knew the answers to all the questions that were not quite polite.

'Noblesse oblige,' said Hugo, mystifyingly, and then Alys had barely time to wave at Aunt Violet and Carelia, grown suddenly small and insignificant as the train glided out of Victoria on its way to Dover.

To Alys, the journey reminded her of nothing so much as her first science lesson at Gifford's Oak. To show the girls that science wasn't all bad smells and potential explosions, Uncle William, who felt that the subject was too important in the modern age to be taught by anyone else, had demonstrated what happened to light when it was passed through a prism. There before their astonished eyes, in the newly equipped laboratory which smelled of coal gas and ether, he had projected out of nothing but glass and thin air a perfect rainbow.

That is what is happening to me, thought Alys, as the Golden Arrow swept smoothly south to the coast through countryside rendered featureless and monochrome by its layer of snow. The Channel, which I have never crossed, is an enormous prism. How will I come out the other side? Certainly, not the same.

Already, as she and Hugo boarded the Channel packet, Alys was aware that she was changing. For the first time in her life she was with someone who had not known her since she was a child; someone who would not consider himself personally responsible for the way she behaved. That thought was extraordinarily liberating. It seemed quite all right, in Hugo's company, to scrutinize the Prince of Wales's black and silver-sealed luggage as it came aboard, to compare the appearance and behaviour of complete strangers, to discuss, in perfect liberty because of their absence, the members of one's immediate family.

'I have the most enormous admiration for your mother,' Hugo informed her.

'Everyone does,' said Alys, a little glumly.

'But she is of course quite old,' said Hugo quickly.

'That's true,' said Alys, brightening. 'Thirty at least.'

Hugo nodded wisely. 'It is frightfully important, nowadays, to be as young as possible. An absolute necessity, in fact. Even a sine qua non.'

Their gaze was drawn by the Prince of Wales, taking a turn on the slippery deck. The weather had not been kind. He looked a little ill.

'What do you think?' murmured Hugo. 'Too old?'

'I'm afraid so,' said Alys, experiencing a delicious ripple of pure treason. 'And pale green clashes with his hair.'

Hugo's eyes sparkled.

'That one deserves a toast, I think.' The deck was tipping and tilting now like the Wall of Death at a fairground. All round them people were abandoning their deck-chairs and heading below. Hugo took no notice; Alys was filled with admiration.

'Alas, no more lemon,' Hugo lamented. 'Never mind.' He poured himself a glass, quite steadily despite the canting of the deck. 'You know what they say – any port in a storm.'

Alys laughed.

'We are enjoying ourselves, aren't we,' said Hugo thoughtfully. Alys nodded.

'Two orphans ... well, demi-orphans. Shall we run away and never come back? Do let's.'

'I don't suppose we should be allowed,' said Alys, truthfully.

'That's true.' Hugo leaned back in his deck-chair. The boat shuddered as a wave hit it broadside; his open Gladstone bag fell on its side, disgorging a yellow-backed novel which proceeded to slide, in a stately, almost royal fashion, towards the scuppers. Alys rose to her feet to retrieve it, but Hugo forestalled her.

238

'Let it go,' he announced grandly. 'Words, only words! May the stream of consciousness rejoin the great ocean of oblivion!'

'But there is a letter in it,' said Alys. She could see the white envelope poking out, where he had been using it as a bookmark.

'Oh God, I had forgotten,' said Hugo. 'How dreadfully trying.' He rose a trifle unsteadily to his feet. The letter, now damp, flopped in a strange, bat-like fashion across the deck but Alys, quicker than he was, managed to pin it down before it went over the edge. Hugo took it from her reluctantly. The yellow-backed novel, taking advantage of the lull, skipped under the rail and fluttered down into the wake. Hugo watched it disappear with a trace of yearning.

'What do you think?' he said, hefting the letter lightly in his hand. 'We could still let this go too, you know. No one would ever know.'

'But you haven't even opened it!' said Alys, aghast. Correspondence was sacred.

'I know.' Hugo was unrepentant. 'And truly, I'd rather not. Solicitor's letter, don't you know, bound to be bad news. Tailor's bill, probably. Better off without it, don't you think?'

'Certainly not,' said Alys.

'Oh, very well.' Hugo gave a theatrical sigh. 'Must I open it now, then?'

'No,' said Alys. 'Just don't throw it away.' She took the letter from him and tucked it neatly at the bottom of his Gladstone, out of harm's way.

'Really, you know,' Hugo said, regarding her with admiration, 'really we are made for each other. To us,' he declared, lifting his glass out of which port flew in a red rain. 'To us! May we be brother and sister for ever and ever!'

As Quintin waited at Cannes station for the two young people to arrive he reflected that to all intents and purposes he now owned them both; Hugo by the accident of having been born in wedlock, Alys by the accident of having been born outside it.

It had not been difficult to arrange for his wife-to-be a wartime marriage in Boulogne to a Polish officer now dead, and details of her daughter's birth, in a French nursing-home whose records had been destroyed by enemy bombardment.

'Considering I have never been abroad in my life, I think I've done rather well, don't you?' Mara had responded when Quintin presented her with her new identity as an engagement gift.

'You were wise to wait,' Quintin had replied. Passports had been brought in just after the war, but if Mara had applied for one she would have had to reveal her daughter's illegitimacy. 'How does it feel to be a perfectly respectable war widow?'

'I have suffered a great loss,' Mara had said. 'But I shall try to get used to it. Just think – married, widowed and remarried, all in the same year!'

'You were always a fast worker,' replied Quintin drily.

'But I wish he had been Russian, not Polish,' Mara went on. 'Alys will be disappointed. Polish counts don't – well, count.'

'Poor Alys,' Quintin had responded with a touch of sarcasm. 'She will just have to make do.'

Alys had been lucky, he reflected. Illegitimate birth remained, in a country as preoccupied with lineage and title as old England, an indelible stain. But now Alys could progress gracefully towards her presentation at Court in five years' time.

Quintin found himself looking forward to that prospect with a bittersweet pleasure. It would be some compensation, even by proxy, to infiltrate a cuckoo's egg into the exclusive, silk-lined nest of the English upper classes.

It was not until Quintin saw Alys in the flesh that the other thought occurred to him. The sight of the young people together, Mara's daughter and his supposed son, the two cuckoo children, brought it forcibly home to him how sweet, how perfectly symmetrical, a revenge could be.

*

When Alys caught sight of her mother at the other end of the platform she was not sure whether to approach her. Her mother was not alone; the man with her must be Sir Quintin Lavery. It was kind of him to have come to the station to meet them, but for a moment Alys wished he had not. She felt sure that her clothes were crumpled from the train, and she knew her gloves were dirty. She glanced up at Hugo, and saw that he too seemed uneasy. His face had become pale; he looked much older.

'Lambs to the slaughter,' he muttered to her sidelong. 'Come on. They're only parents, after all.'

It was a stiff little meeting. Hugo shook hands with his father, who gave him a swift cold glance as if he had been a piece of luggage. Alys kissed her mother on both scented cheeks, then hesitated before the grey alpaca cliff-face of Sir Quintin. She hadn't imagined he would be so old. His neat pointed beard was grey, but the skin of his face was waxy-smooth. The thought came into her mind; he looks like someone who has died and been embalmed.

But Sir Quintin was now a relation, or nearly, and relations were sacred, like correspondence, so Alys lifted her face to kiss him, flinching a little as his beard brushed her. His skin was cold and smelled of lemon verbena.

Two porters loaded their trunks into the huge pale blue motor car that awaited them outside the station, its long highly polished bonnet reflecting the cloudless sky. Inside, to Alys's amazement, it was more like a sitting-room than a vehicle, with deep leather upholstery and a silver flower-holder on the dashboard in front of the chauffeur.

Hugo, who seemed to have lost all his sense of ease since meeting his father, began at once to enthuse.

'A Hibbard and Darrin body,' he babbled, 'on an Isotta-Franchini base, unless I am much mistaken?'

Sir Quintin eyed him up and down in silence for a moment.

'I have no idea, my dear boy,' he answered finally. 'I am not a mechanic.'

Hugo blushed a fiery red. There was an awkward moment, then Mara smiled.

'So clever, these young men, don't you agree, Quintin? I'm sure they make me feel quite out of date.' Mara leaned across Alys, her caramel-coloured summer ermine coat falling open to disclose the white silk pleats beneath. 'Do tell me more about this mechanical marriage, Hugo. Such an astonishing combination – how is it achieved? Is it left to fate or do the two motor cars have to be introduced?'

Alys could feel Hugo, tense on the leather seat beside her, beginning to recover himself.

'Not exactly, Mrs . . .' Hugo's voice tailed away.

'Oh, don't worry.' Mara dimpled at him. 'My married name is quite impossible, I can barely pronounce it myself. Just call me Mara.'

'It's quite a complicated process,' Hugo began hesitantly.

'Which means I couldn't possibly understand it!' Mara opened her eyes wide at him in mock dismay. 'Oh dear!' Then her tone brightened. 'But there is a ceremony, there must be. Every marriage deserves a ceremony, doesn't it, Quintin? I wonder now . . .' She frowned a little, delightfully. 'What would one wear for such an important occasion?'

Now both Quintin and Hugo were smiling, though they avoided each other's eyes. The bad moment was gone, and yet, for some strange reason, Alys felt worse instead of better, as if she had a splinter in her finger and all attempts to prise it out had only driven it deeper.

The rest of the ride to the Grand Hotel was spent in banter, as the two men vied to suggest more and more outlandish articles suitable for wearing to a mechanical marriage. Alys sat silent in the lordly car, her hands clasped tight in their grubby gloves. She gazed out of the window and it seemed to her that the whole of Cannes had marriage on its mind. All the women she could see were wearing white, or permutations of white; white pleats and scallops, white wool and fur, white lace and feathers. So many brides, and in the Marché des Fleurs in the crowded Rue d'Antibes enough spring flowers for a thousand weddings, a sacrificial profusion of anemones and violets, narcissi and mimosa.

Yet as she sailed along in the beautiful car, in brilliant sunlight, surrounded by her new relations-to-be, Alys sensed that something was wrong, terribly wrong. She should have been happy, but in all her life she had never felt so alone. She could give no reason for this feeling; she had no defence against it. It was only by thinking resolutely of what Carelia would say that she managed to prevent herself from bursting into tears.

Mara dressed that evening in jet-beaded chiffon over flesh-coloured bias-cut satin – her anthracite look, as Quintin called it. As she checked the silver-bound seams of her stockings and slid her feet carefully into the transparent Rhodophane slippers Quintin had bought her at Talbot's, Mara felt curiously at a loss. This was the first night for as long as she could remember that she had nothing more to do. From now on, the festivities would be the responsibility of other people, a whole host of them, hired by Quintin just for the occasion.

Mara was glad she was alone. Used to getting herself ready without help, she'd sent her new maid away to assist Lucette Bailey in her stateroom. Over the years Mrs Bailey's hair seemed to have got redder and her eyebrows blacker; now she resembled nothing so much as a fine piece of Japanese lacquerwork. But she could still appreciate an irony.

Unfortunately, without a maid to spin out the process of dressing, Mara now found herself ready for dinner far too early. Beneath her Rhodophane slippers she could feel the twenty-room cruiser that Quintin had hired for the wedding party shifting sluggishly at its moorings. Tomorrow morning at dawn, while the guests were still in their beds, the crew would furl all the bunting and *L'Aiglon Bleu* would carry them all out to the Mediterranean for three weeks' cruising down the Adriatic coast. At midday, Mary Mizen would become Lady Quintin Lavery.

It's the night before my wedding, thought Mara, and tomorrow we shall all be at sea.

She wasn't nervous. She had no doubts about her husband-to-be. She knew him too well, far better than he knew her. That was a great advantage in a marriage.

As she powdered unnecessarily and threaded a silver lamé band through her hair, Mara thought of the last time she'd seen Leo. Vi said he'd gone to America. Mara hoped so. But she couldn't help wondering exactly where Leo was now. Wherever he was, there would be women, drawn by what they sensed he offered them – no safe haven.

Mara shivered. It was still only February. Riviera warmth at this time of year was deceptive; she must make sure that Alys was wearing the light wool jacket that matched her sailor suit, even if the child was determined to do without it.

Unwilling to show herself fully dressed for dinner before time in the corridor, Mara went into the shared bathroom that separated her stateroom from Alys's cabin. Smiling, she picked up the damp towel, replaced the toothbrush, tightened the dripping tap.

Now we can get to know each other again, Mara thought. I remember when she was as much part of me as my heart. I will fill in the years between, now I have time at last.

The door between the bathroom and Alys's cabin was ajar. Mara wondered if she should speak or knock before she went in. She felt suddenly tentative. This is ridiculous, she told herself sternly. I'm more nervous about speaking to my daughter than I am about getting married tomorrow. She's only twelve, and I'm her mother. It's about time I began.

Gently, to give Alys plenty of time to register her presence, Mara pushed open the door.

*

'What a pretty dress,' said Quintin. 'Is it new?'

Alys blushed. 'Yes.' She felt rather uncomfortable under his scrutiny. 'Thank you.'

'Ah,' said Quintin. 'Presumably I bought it for you?'

Alys nodded. She felt tongue-tied. Carelia said a gentleman never mentioned money. Quintin smiled at her.

'In that case, you must show it to me properly. Come here.'

Alys looked at him uncertainly.

'Come.'

Hesitantly, Alys rose from the dressing-table stool. She felt the new dress hanging stiff on her like a cage. She stood in front of her father-to-be, unsure where to put her hands.

'That's better,' said Quintin. 'Turn around, my dear.'

Awkwardly, Alys turned. She felt a little less vulnerable with her back to him, but then she had to meet his eyes again as she completed the circle.

'You are wearing silk stockings,' said Quintin, conversationally.

Alys blushed again. Her heart was beating rapidly.

'Mother said I should,' she said. 'As it is a special occasion.'

'Yes, indeed,' said Quintin. 'And you look very nice in them, very nice indeed. Quite grown-up, in fact.'

'Thank you, sir,' Alys said. Her sense of discomfort was increasing.

'Oh, but you must not!' said Quintin. His voice had a rallying tone which disturbed Alys, she wasn't sure why.

'Thank you, you mean?' Alys was confused; both her mother and Aunt Violet had stressed that she must express suitable gratitude to Sir Quintin. Perhaps she had gone too far? It was even worse to gush than to appear ungrateful.

'Don't be nervous,' said Quintin gently. 'There is nothing to be frightened of. We are family, you and I.'

Alys was instantly reminded of what Hugo had said on the boat, about being brother and sister. Why was it that had seemed all right, while this seemed somehow shocking, as if she had put her hand down on grass in the dark and touched something cold and wet, like a slug?

'You're not frightened of me, are you?' Quintin's voice had a coaxing note. 'That wouldn't do, it wouldn't do at all. Come, tell me you're not frightened of me.'

Alys swallowed. Her heart was bumping irregularly. She had not been frightened, not till he told her there was no need.

'Go on, say it. I shall not leave this room until you say it.' Sir Quintin's voice was hoarse now, as if there was something in his throat. Alys swallowed again. Perhaps, if she said it, he would go.

'I am not frightened of you, s—'

'Papa,' he supplied.

'Papa,' Alys repeated.

'Good,' he said, smiling. 'Now it is up to you to prove it.'

As Mara opened the door she saw Quintin seated on the edge of Alys's bed. Above the snowy starched shirt front and the wing collar he still affected his face was flushed and his eyes glittered. Alys had her back to her mother, but Mara detected something stiff and strange about the way she was standing. As she watched, struck into immobility, Quintin placed his left hand on Alys's knee.

'There now,' Quintin said softly. 'That doesn't hurt, does it?'

Alys shook her head. Mara saw the ash-white cap of her shingled hair swing on the childish slimness of her neck.

'You are a good girl, Alys, a very good girl. I know that you are going to make your father very happy.' Quintin spoke in the same low tone, so ordinary that Mara couldn't believe what she was hearing. Slowly, even as she watched, he slid his hand higher under Alys's pleated skirt. 'That is what daughters are for, you see. To make their fathers very, very happy. It's so easy, you'll see.'

*

Alys could not move. She felt Sir Quintin's hand on the inside of her leg, moving relentlessly upwards like some kind of creeping creature, impossible to detach. She had no idea what to do. She fixed her eyes in desperation on the white shirt front before her, in which a diamond stick pin shone. If she concentrated on that she might be able to blot out everything else.

'This is very lovely,' said Sir Quintin in the same soft, choked voice. Alys could feel his breath on her cheek, feel his eyes crawling over her face like insects. She felt paralysed. 'But it must be our secret. No one must know. It is too lovely to share with anyone. No one else would understand.'

His fingers reached the edge of her camiknickers, slid beneath the elastic edge with a gentle probing motion like a tentacle uncoiling. Now he was touching her there, where no one else had touched her, where she did not even touch herself.

'Please don't,' Alys whispered, but she felt like screaming. His fingers moved inexorably, as if they had visited her many times before, as if they knew exactly where they were going.

'It is my right,' Sir Quintin whispered to her. Now his face seemed to have swollen; his neck was bulging over his collar. 'I am your father, remember?'

Alys began to sob, silent shuddering sobs that terrified her. Why had no one told her? If this was what being a daughter meant, she couldn't do it, she couldn't bear to. What would he think of her? What would anyone think of her?

'Hush now, none of that.' Sir Quintin's voice was rough. Through a blur of tears Alys felt him take her hand and push it down between his legs. There was something there, hot and hard, that moved as she touched it.

At that moment there came a sharp knock on the outer cabin door, followed almost immediately by a rattle.

'Alys!' It was her mother's voice, crisp and commanding. 'Unlock this door immediately!'

Sir Quintin did not move for a moment, then, slowly, he withdrew his hand from beneath Alys's skirt.

'Straighten your dress,' he commanded. His voice was curt.

Trembling, feeling somehow as if she had committed a crime, Alys obeyed. As she did so she felt as if there was something left behind under her skirt, not his hand, but something else that would never be taken away, a sort of imprint.

Frowning, Sir Quintin unlocked the door. It swung open to reveal her mother standing in the corridor outside.

'Darling!' Mara's voice was breathy, as if she had been running. 'What a pleasant surprise! Are you and Alys getting to know each other?' Without waiting for a reply, she took Alys's hand. 'Come, my dear. It's time to go down – or rather up – to dinner.'

Alys would remember that night all her life. They ate on deck, to the accompaniment of gypsy violinists and flickering torches. Every time she raised her eyes from her plate she seemed to see Sir Quintin looking back at her. Once he raised his glass to her and smiled. Alys felt sick. Their shared secret pressed down on her like a great musty-smelling blanket. She could hardly breathe.

'I'm not hungry either,' said Hugo, who had been placed beside her. He was very pale, and his eyes looked enormous. Alys was able to emerge from her own misery just long enough to realize that he too was not happy. Perhaps this is what it is like, she thought, in the grown-ups' world, all misery and secrets.

'Everything's gone wrong,' Alys said. 'I wish I'd never come.'

Hugo did not answer, just lifted his glass and drank, his eyes closed as if he could blot out the world.

The meal seemed to go on for hours, centuries. The flambeaux burned low and were replaced, course after course was cleared, conversation eddied and flowed round the table, but no end came. The white damask became soiled with wine and sauces, stretching ahead of Alys like her own life, dirty and spoiled, a mockery. Far away at the head of the table her mother glittered like a star; above, the black velvet sky seemed endless, and with every breath she took Alys wished that a great wave would arise out of the milk-calm harbour and sweep her overboard for ever.

The next morning Alys found herself, with bewildering suddenness, back in the train again, with Hugo sitting opposite, just as before, and outside the window the same Provençal countryside flying by, only this time streaming backwards, like a cinema film being played the wrong way round. Alys felt foolish. It was as if she had never really been anywhere, never really arrived. Now her journey was unravelling before her eyes.

'I am very sorry, Hugo,' she said, in a creaky voice, because she had hardly spoken to anyone since dinner on the deck last night. Everything had happened so fast this morning. In the sudden, purposeful flurry of departure she hadn't even had a moment alone with her mother.

'Sorry? What for?' said Hugo. He looked pale and preoccupied; Alys was very much afraid that he was angry with her, as he had every right to be.

'For making you miss the rest of the wedding,' Alys answered, feeling as she did so a sort of painful relief. At least this was something specific she could apologize for, not the nameless, foggy weight of guilt she felt about Sir Quintin.

'Don't worry,' said Hugo, a little grimly. 'As things were, I couldn't have borne to stay a moment longer.'

Alys looked at him questioningly. There was a note in his voice which seemed to echo her own feeling exactly.

'Were you seasick too?' Alys inquired politely. That was the reason her mother had given the other guests for her daughter's sudden departure, pointing out that Alys hadn't been able to eat a single bite of food at last night's dinner on the torch-lit deck. Mother had eyes that could see in the dark at twenty paces.

'Heavens, no.' Hugo gave a wintry smile.

'Has something dreadful happened?' Alys ventured. She could

not imagine what it could have been; they had only arrived in Cannes yesterday, and Hugo had seemed fine right up until dinnertime.

Then she remembered something.

'The letter!' she said, dismayed. 'Was it bad news, just as you said it would be?'

'I wish I'd never read it,' said Hugo, simply.

'Oh dear. It's all my fault. I persuaded you to keep it.'

'No, no.' Hugo shook his head, like someone trying to shake off a bad dream. 'It would have made no difference if I had not read it. It's just – knowing, that's all.'

'Knowing what?'

'I can't tell you.'

'I wouldn't tell anyone else, I promise.'

Hugo looked at her for a moment. For the first time, with her own misery temporarily relieved, Alys realized how genuinely ill he seemed.

'I believe you. But it's not that. There is no one in the world that I could tell.'

'That means I would be as good as anyone,' said Alys encouragingly. The corner of Hugo's mouth twitched in an almost smile.

'True.' Then his face darkened again. 'But you're too young. You wouldn't understand.'

'That's even better,' retorted Alys valiantly. 'Telling me would be like telling no one at all.'

Hugo shook his head. 'You're still too young.'

Alys sighed. 'I hate being young.'

Even as she said it, Alys remembered with a pang their light-hearted conversation on the ferryboat, when they had agreed absolutely that young was the only thing to be. Only a day had passed, but so much had changed.

'You'll grow out of it,' Hugo said with a wry smile. 'Being young, I mean. People do.'

There was a pause. Alys frowned.

'Does that mean that your letter's a secret?'

'I don't know.' Hugo frowned. 'Yes, I suppose so.'

Alys shivered. 'I don't like secrets.'

'Neither do I. But I didn't ask for this one. It just . . . arrived.'

'I have a secret too,' said Alys, suddenly. 'I wish I didn't. I wish I could get rid of it, but I can't.' She clasped her gloved hands together in her lap and stared fiercely at their hand-stitched seams. Sir Quintin had paid for her entire wardrobe; now she felt as if by doing so he had run his hands all over her. 'It makes me feel horrible.'

Hugo glanced up, surprised.

'That's just how I feel,' he said. 'Like an outcast.' They exchanged tentative smiles.

Hugo put his hand into the inner pocket of his coat and drew out the white envelope which Alys remembered from the boat. He stared at it, frowning, as if he were trying to make out in the crumpled paper, faintly marked with seawater, the face of someone he used to know.

'Who is it from?' asked Alys. 'It would be safe to tell me that.' Already she felt a strange sort of relatedness to the unknown correspondent, because if it hadn't been for her own intervention, the letter would never have been read.

'No one you know,' Hugo answered, still with that strange look on his face. 'A ghost.'

'You're teasing me.'

'Not really. It was written a very long time ago.' Hugo looked up, and the expression on his face shocked her. Disbelief, and fear, and sadness mixed up all in one twisted grimace. 'It's from my mother.'

PART FOUR

Tale quale ipsum est

13 *A Golden Humour*

Oliver, Fifth Duke of Shelburne, tipped the taxi driver with as
much goodwill as he could manage strapped into tight satin knee
breeches in midsummer. Normally he never even wore a hat in
Town; this single manoeuvre, he had calculated, saved him at least
three hundred pounds a year.

But now came the greater reckoning. The prospect of expressing
suitable gratitude to Carelia's jumped-up foreign Countess, in an atmosphere of Oriental hangings and pot-pourri, filled Nollie with gloom.

The door was opened by Carelia herself. Father and daughter
regarded each other with mutual misgiving.

'You'd better come in,' Carelia said grudgingly. Nollie stepped
into a small, spare, white-painted hall, bare of ornament except for
a bowl of lemons on the hall table. Beyond the plain sisal doormat
stretched a gratifying vista of lime-washed floorboard. For a
moment, in the middle of Mayfair, Nollie could have sworn he
heard the creak of rigging.

From around the curve of the stairs, bringing with her a faint
breeze from some open upper window, came Countess Something-
or-other. She was much younger than Nollie had expected, a slim
boyish figure with a cap of dark curls, lightly tanned, and wearing a
crisp linen dress of pale blue trimmed with white.

'Do come up,' the Countess said. 'The air is cooler in the
drawing-room. You must have found it difficult at the Palace today,
in this heat.'

255

'Damnably,' said Nollie, the frustrations of the day exploding from him before he thought even to introduce himself. Carelia's point-blank, last-minute refusal to attend her half-sister's Presentation before Their Majesties had been a shock, he had to admit it.

'Of course,' said the Countess. 'But you have made the effort, you have done your duty, and now you can relax in peace. Carelia, take your father's hat and coat, my dear, and then go upstairs to wash and change. You have half an hour. You will find fresh soap and a towel in Alys's room.'

To Nollie's astonishment Carelia did just as she was told, even humming to herself as she thundered up the stairs.

The Countess ushered Nollie into a drawing-room as white and pleasantly featureless as the hall below. More sanded boards, a plain cotton rug with a Greek key motif before the fireplace, and at the tall windows no loops and swathes of gorgeous fabric to entrap the unwary male, but simple, straightforward, blessedly mechanical holland blinds.

His hostess crossed slowly to a glass-topped table in front of the windows, on which reposed an array of bottles and one of the new ice-making machines. Nollie watched her with approval. A good action, the feet carefully placed, nothing hurried. Most women moved so fast nowadays you never knew where you were, but this one was a stayer, a potential Derby winner.

Derby winner, Derby Street, Nollie thought, pleased with himself. Rather good, that.

'It was very kind of you to take charge of my daughter at such short notice, Countess,' he said as he accepted a blessedly cool, tall glass.

'Oh, please,' said the Countess. 'Call me Mara. Everyone does.'

And then, for a long minute, as Nollie bent to his first long draught, she said nothing, absolutely nothing at all, an event so foreign to Nollie's experience of female company that he almost expected it to be marked by a fanfare of trumpets.

'We should have met before,' he said, feeling at last a tinge of guilt. The Countess, he now remembered, had written him a letter in the spring, thanking him for his hospitality to her daughter, and he had not responded as he should. Now, in this clear, cool, white room, that reluctance seemed a little shabby.

'Perhaps we have,' said the Countess, unexpectedly. 'But it makes no difference. Now we are going to be friends.'

Nollie stiffened like a gundog. In his experience friendships between men and women had a nasty knack of ending in suits for breach of promise.

'But there is one thing you must promise me,' continued the Countess equably. Nollie said nothing; he was already planning his retreat.

'Never, never ask me to marry you.' The Countess paused for a moment to place a charcoal black cigarillo in her tortoiseshell holder. 'You see, my late husband was a Catholic. I could never consider marriage to a divorced man. Friendship is all I have to offer.'

Put like that, Nollie had to admit the notion was attractive. The trouble with being unmarried was that one had no resident, reliable female to consult in times of trouble; which, when one possessed two ex-wives and two nubile daughters, were not infrequent.

And he had not felt so much at ease, so much in tune with himself in a woman's company, since the early years with his cousin Augusta.

'Carelia,' Nollie said, expelling his breath in a sigh that was both plea and lament combined.

'I know,' said Mara sympathetically. 'All of a sudden, since her mother moved to Florence, she has taken the idea into her head that she must spend her holidays with you.'

'Impossible,' Nollie declared. 'I'm never anywhere for more than three weeks at a time.'

'Quite unsuitable,' the Countess agreed. 'As I took the liberty of explaining to her.'

'And?' Despite his knowledge of his own daughter, despite having

257

walked this ground with her himself a thousand times, Nollie felt the faintest flicker of hope. After all, this extraordinarily efficient woman had managed to persuade Carelia to go upstairs and wash her hands.

'She agreed with me,' said Mara limpidly.

'What?' The idea of Carelia agreeing with anyone threw Nollie off balance. 'However did you manage that?'

Mara smiled. 'Girls are very reasonable, I find, if approached in the right way by someone who is not a relative by blood. The actual decision, of course, Carelia made for herself. I always find that's best, don't you?'

'Absolutely.' The sensation of relief that washed over Nollie at the thought that he would not be marooned at Shelburne all summer with his daughter was so exquisite that he closed his eyes. Against his lids he saw the *White Lady*, skipping over the waves, and beyond her the deliciously empty sea. The Countess, with one wave of her wand, had given him back his summer. 'But what on earth did you say to change her mind?'

'Ah.' The Countess cast her eyes down. 'I was hoping you would not ask. You may not approve, I'm afraid.'

'I shall try.'

'Well . . . You know how vain girls are at that age. I simply pointed out to her the advantages of being a young lady in Italy, where blondes are so rare, rather than in the depths of the English countryside. Carelia took my point immediately. I hope you will forgive me.'

'Forgive you?' Nollie rose to his feet and shook her vigorously by the hand. 'I shall be eternally grateful. You have saved my sanity.'

'Think nothing of it,' said Mara.

'Do you shoot?' he asked suddenly.

'Do partridges drink?' she returned, cocking her head so drolly that Nollie laughed out loud. He had lost count of the hours he had spent discussing this esoteric issue with his keepers at the Abbey. As the Countess stood there, so poised and yet light-footed, looking at him sidelong out of those bright grey eyes past her long thin nose, she reminded him very much of a smart little long-billed woodcock. Yes, that was what she was, a high, fast bird late in the season, the best sport in the world.

'You must come down to Shelburne,' he announced magisterially.

'I should be delighted,' she replied, looking preoccupied, as if it was every day that she received such invitations. 'But now, I must fly. I am due at the Blue Train Club for dinner. Let us share a taxi, and I will tell you of the time I once left a yacht in mid-ocean to avoid marrying one of the richest men in the world.'

'A frightful pile, don't you think?'

'Oh, I don't know. I expect it keeps the rain out.'

'Not entirely,' said Nollie, relieved that the Countess hadn't fallen at the first fence. It would have been too dreadful a disappointment if she had enthused. 'You should see the North Wing.'

'You must show me everything,' she said, with just the right hint of incipient boredom.

'We could take a turn around before tea,' Nollie suggested. 'But first I expect you'd like to nip upstairs for a wash and brush up?'

'Not really,' she answered, with that fascinating smile that pulled her eyes up at the corners and made her look almost Chinese. 'But I will if you want me to.'

When the Countess came down again she had changed out of her blue-grey Busvine tweeds into a simply splendid tawny-coloured dress of some silky material that floated as she walked. No flowered prints, Nollie observed with gratitude to the Deity; he preferred flowers in their rightful place, outside on the terraces.

'I don't think anyone has ever truly realized,' he informed his visitor genially, as he escorted her towards the Great Dining Hall, 'how much I detest this house.'

'Surely not?'

Peeping round the huge arched doorway which led to the dining-hall, Mara was fascinated by how different it seemed from the last time she had seen it. Then, as Lucette's maid, she had been over-awed and so determined not to show it that she'd been unable to take in more from her surroundings than a magnificent blur.

Now the shapes were clearer, re-focused by the passage of time, and Mara realized that there was something rather stagey about the mullioned windows and gold-encrusted ceiling. She was reminded suddenly of Mariana and her moated grange.

'A Gothic monstrosity,' said Nollie sadly. 'Even the guide-books have noticed. But what can one do?'

Mara rallied. She knew it would be fatal, with this man, ever to agree.

'Pull it down and start again?'

'Ah yes.' Nollie sounded wistful. 'Not on, unfortunately. Family home and all that.' He advanced into the room with an expression of resigned distaste, like someone wading into mire. 'Place has only just stopped smelling of mortar as it is.' He ran a finger down the surface of the mighty dining-table, one solid slab of dark red marble lanced with black and white veins. 'What do you think of that?'

'Very . . . substantial,' said Mara.

'Griotte,' intoned Nollie lugubriously. 'Frightfully expensive – might as well be eating off some beastly French general's tomb. A bit like raw liver, don't you think? And that—' he indicated the fireplace, large enough to park a Lincoln coupé' – Egyptian porphyry. Sausagemeat, to you and me. See this? Sicilian jasper – streaky bacon, I call it. And this one's Breccia – see, with the grey and purple blotches? Washerwoman's legs!'

The Red Drawing-room received the same treatment. 'Too much stuff,' declared Nollie mournfully, as they peered round the door.

'What might that be?' Mara asked, to distract him, pointing at a tall, multi-tiered object of mahogany inlaid with mother-of-pearl.

'You may well ask,' said Nollie. 'It's a what-not, that's what.' He gave a sudden, huge, barking laugh. 'Got plenty of those! Only thing haven't got,' he went on, 'is shelves. Imagine. All this stuff, and nowhere to put a packet of matches. Enough to drive a fellow to drink.' He paused. 'Expect you'd like to see the Green Drawing-room now,' he sighed. 'All the ladies do.'

The Green Drawing-room was no less large, but the furniture was smaller. 'Look at this.' Nollie poked the base of a delicate little chair, embroidered with green petit-point parrots, cousins of those perched in the faded tropical forest papering the walls. 'Impossible! Can't be comfortable sitting on some bloody woman's sewing!' He turned to Mara with a sudden look of alarm. 'You haven't brought your embroidery, have you?'

Mara shook her head. 'I don't sew.'

Nollie grunted with approval. 'Sensible woman.' He looked up at the ceiling, hung with gilded garlands of plaster flowers. 'Know what?' he announced, turning suddenly to face Mara with his prominent, almost owlish blue eyes. 'Can't find a single decent bedroom in this place without some great fat woman on the ceiling. 'Fraid one might fall on me in my sleep. Hellish way to go.'

'A pity you can't divorce a house,' said Mara.

The Duke rounded on her. For a moment she wondered whether she'd gone too far, then he gave his abrupt, gun-shot laugh.

'That's rather good. Damned good, in fact. Might use it myself.'

'It's yours.' Mara smiled. 'But I can't believe that there isn't one single room in the whole house that you like.'

'Not one.' The Duke shook his bull-like head with absolute finality. 'Except . . .' His face lit up suddenly.

'Yes?'

'Follow me.'

He swept her out into the Great Hall, with its panelling and heraldic glass and chessboard-tiled floor, and then, to her dismay, held open a green baize door.

Mara's heart sank as she preceded him down the stone stairs. They were heading for the servants' dining-hall, where eighteen years ago she'd sat at the long elm table and toasted the new kitchen maid in a glass of stout. Her heart sank further as she heard the Duke call out, 'Andrews? Don't mind us, we're on a sentimental pilgrimage. The Countess wants to see where I was happiest as a boy.'

'Very pleased I'm sure, Your Grace,' came an answering voice, and Mara was conscious of a battery of female eyes under pink shiny foreheads as she entered the dim vastness of the kitchen. There was a smell of baking from three sunshine-yellow Madeira cakes lined up on the scrubbed deal table, and there was Andrews, greyer-haired than Mara remembered, but otherwise as extraordinarily unchanged as one of her own pots of preserves.

A flicker of doubt passed over Cook's face. Mara couldn't be sure whether she'd been recognized or not. Feeling distinctly uncomfortable, she followed the Duke into the larder.

'Here,' he announced. 'Here I was truly happy. And to think I had forgotten! I have you to thank for my remembering.'

'Lots of shelves,' said Mara brightly. In the hush behind them in the main kitchen she could almost hear Andrews thinking.

'That's what I like,' said the Duke. 'All ship-shape and Bristol fashion.' He pointed out with simple pride the vast white enamel containers of flours and grains on their hanging shelves, the spice boxes and biscuit canisters of japanned tin, the lead-lined chests full of China and India tea. Swinging gently on its hook like a criminal on a gibbet hung a well-wrapped bundle of loaf sugar.

'I used to come down here,' the Duke whispered, 'and hack little bits off that to eat in the garden. It was very difficult not to make crumbs, I can tell you.'

'It must have been,' answered Mara. Straining to hear what might be happening in the kitchen behind them, she could hardly concentrate on what the Duke was saying. 'Where did you go when it was raining?'

'I hid under the desk in my father's study. No one was allowed in there to dust, so I was safe.'

262

'I would like to see it,' said Mara quickly. 'Perhaps the crumbs are still there.'

'Follow me,' said Nollie.

Mara was again conscious of scrutiny as she retraced her steps back up the stairs. She couldn't help remembering how Andrews had prided herself on her memory. 'Honest or dishonest, I never forget a face,' she had been used to declare with professional pride. 'No one can slip a week-old egg past me.'

As Mara followed the Duke along panelled corridors she seemed to feel the executioner's axe caressing the back of her neck. To reach the study was a relief. Clearly it had been hardly touched since the Fourth Duke's day; the desk was a mille-feuille of papers subsiding gently under layers of dust. Mara duly inspected the floor beneath it for historic crumbs, but there was barely enough light to see by. Altogether the study, though relatively simply furnished, was a sombre, unprepossessing room, its walls covered in Spanish leather as dark as stewed tea.

'Might as well be Jonah in the belly of the whale,' said Nollie gloomily. He seemed ill-at-ease on his late father's territory, and yet the study should have been one of the more attractive rooms in the house, with a clear view of the park leading down to the lake with its island pagoda. Mara saw from the window a brace of motor cars advancing down the drive and drew them to Nollie's attention.

Nollie cheered up at once. 'Tea in the Library in half an hour. I must say, I liked the look of those cakes, didn't you?'

And with that he was gone.

For a moment, without the insulation of the Duke's jovial presence, Mara felt a chill of dismay. She wondered how long she would have to wait to find out whether or not Andrews's encyclopedic memory had identified her. Not long, she suspected; rumours ran round a servants' hall quicker than a whisper round the dome of St Paul's. In the meantime there would be tea, and a room full of women who all knew each other: a sea of perils far more difficult to negotiate than a whole regiment of men.

But there was more than one kind of embroidery to bring to a shooting party. From her handbag Mara slid out a small pad of marbled paper and an ivory-mounted pencil. Sitting at the desk, overlooking the silent green view, she wrote, clearly and well-spaced, four words:

> Privacy
> Freedom
> Comfort
> Convenience

Then she smoothed over each eyebrow with a fingertip's worth of Mitsouko and set out to face the fray.

Battle was engaged almost as soon as the footman opened the tall panelled door into the Library. A freckle-faced housemaid stood aside with her silver tray to let the guest pass, but as Mara did so she received a swift gleeful glance that left her in no doubt that Andrews had indeed recognized her. Mara's heart accelerated. Ahead of her, clustered round an enormous fire piled high with logs despite the fact that summer was barely over, were the other guests for the weekend's shooting, men and women, some standing, some sitting, some draped casually over the arms of settees; all, it seemed, chattering gaily, all utterly at home.

From where Mara stood the gathering, at the other end of the long panelled room, side-lit by the declining afternoon sun, seemed very far away. I could leave now, she thought. I could plead indisposition, or a sick relative, or an urgent appointment with my bookie.

She hesitated an instant too long.

'My dear Countess!' The Duke's voice, higher than you would expect from a man of his bulk, carried down the room. Mara was conscious of a bevy of gazes, some curious, some incurious, swinging her way. The Duke swept her before him purposively.

A slight man perched bird-like on the arm of a chair rose to his feet. 'Your Royal Highness,' said Nollie jovially, without the least change in expression. 'Permit me to present to you the Countess . . .'

'Unpronounceable, I'm afraid, Sir,' supplied Mara quickly. 'Please call me Mara. Everyone does.' She saw before her with a sense of unreality the Prince of Wales, just as he appeared in the newspapers, golden-haired, smiling, casually dressed but pin-neat in flannels, soft collar and checked tie. He was deeply tanned. Mara had to concentrate hard on neither staring nor squinting. She now perceived the pattern to the gathering; the bodies of everyone, male or female, were somehow poised in attendance on this central figure, like a flock of pilot fish around a particularly slim and elegant whale.

'Quite right,' said the Prince. 'When I read your name upon the list I must confess I was intrigued. I haven't seen such a collection of consonants since I last attempted a crossword puzzle. I am delighted to meet you, Mara.' Mara realized with another shock that he spoke with a distinctly American accent. She was conscious of great charm, consciously exercised, and a deliberate effort to override status. 'Is this your first visit to the Abbey?'

It was then, as she realized that this was a man like any other, only with better manners, that Mara made her decision.

'No, Sir,' she replied. 'I was here before the War. Only then I was in disguise.'

'In disguise?' asked the Prince, and as his eyes lit up with engaging, almost child-like interest, Mara realized how tired he had looked before. 'How fascinating. May we know more?'

'Of course, Sir. In my youth,' said Mara, gravely, 'before I was old enough to know better, I wanted to become an actress. I was offered the part of a French maid, and persuaded a dear friend of mine to let me accompany her here as her personal maid, in order to learn how to play it.'

'My word,' said the Prince. 'How very enterprising. Quite like *The Barber of Seville*, in fact.'

265

'Thank you, Sir,' said Mara meekly. 'I have nothing but fond memories of the servants' hall. Mrs Andrews was very good to me.'

'And did all your researches make for success in the part?'

'I'm afraid not, Sir.'

'Why so? I am disappointed.'

'So was I, Sir.' Mara left a heartbeat's pause for effect. 'The producer decamped to California with the funds.'

The Prince laughed, the tanned skin round his very blue eyes creasing into a papery fan of wrinkles. Clearly he was a man who liked to smile.

'What a pity, after all your hard work,' he commiserated. 'And did anyone suspect you in your disguise?'

'Only the Duke,' said Mara, turning to Nollie. 'We met once, in the corridor, and you looked at me very searchingly, I remember.'

Nollie looked gratified, if a little confused.

'There you are, Nollie!' said the Prince of Wales, smiling. 'You've been caught out. Not like you to forget a woman.' He inclined his head to Mara gracefully, half ironic, half courtly. 'I certainly would not have done so.'

There was a silken rustle from beside the fire. Nollie looked questioningly at the Prince, who nodded.

'Lady Furness,' said Nollie. 'Let me present to you—'

'Oh, let's not go through all that again,' said a husky voice with a slight hint of a lisp which only added to its appeal. 'Please call me Thelma.'

Mara took in glossy centre-parted hair, tar-black, brilliantined eyebrows, china-white skin and a degree of elegance so extreme that it merited protection from frost.

'How you must have suffered,' said Lady Furness, in that whispery voice. 'Just think, David – ' she laid one of her own delicate, plump hands, with its enamelled nails, on the Prince of Wales's arm in the lightest touch of possession. 'How terribly bad it must have been for her poor hands.'

From then on, Mara did not relax her guard for a moment. The talk was of Tallulah Bankhead, who had just returned, penniless and weeping, to America, where she hoped Paramount Pictures would remake her fortune; of Augustus John, who was drying out ('Again,' said three voices simultaneously); and of young Sir Francis Laking, who died three months ago of a surfeit of yellow Chartreuse, leaving all his motor cars to Tallulah.

'Only he didn't have any to leave,' said the Duke. 'Shall we any of us have anything to leave Tallulah, I wonder?' he added gloomily, and pointed out to no one in particular that with taxation quadrupled and domestic servants' wages doubled, the average landowner could hope to see only five hundred pounds a year from an income of twenty-five thousand.

'Where do you live?' a red-headed girl in lemon chiffon asked Mara out of the blue, her aristocratic long-nosed face suddenly disturbingly acute.

'I have a house in Town,' answered Mara. She knew that to mention Mayfair would be underbred; in these circles, Mayfair was assumed.

'And you actually live there? All the year round?'

Mara nodded.

'How quaint. I thought one kept a house in Town just for changing for the theatre.'

'I am quite out of touch,' answered Mara sweetly. 'You must come and visit me some day. On your way to the theatre.'

The redhead blushed. 'Actually,' she said, 'I've been out of the country myself for some time. The Amazon, you know.'

Which brought the conversation more safely to women's new freedoms, and Amy Johnson's solo flight to Australia earlier in the year, and *Vile Bodies*, the shocking new novel by that amoral young man, Evelyn Waugh, which everyone had heard of and would soon get round to reading, and Gandhi's Salt March, which showed that brute force did not have to rule the world. A young man in the Foreign Office muttered something about some new German party which had just won six million votes by promising war and conquest, but all agreed that the shape of Marlene Dietrich's eyebrows in *The Blue Angel* would have a far wider-reaching effect on the man and woman in the street.

At that the Prince of Wales smiled his Pied Piper smile and there was a perceptible drift to follow him as he made his way gracefully to the door. 'You won't insist that I shoot anything tomorrow, will you, Nollie? I would far rather catch up on my petit-point.' He caught Mara's eye and smiled once more. Again she was conscious of his charm. 'My secret vice, I'm afraid. Nollie hates me to mention it; I only do it to bait him.' Nollie grunted, and with that the company dispersed before dinner.

Mara closed her bedroom door behind her with relief. She'd refused the Duke's offer of a maid to help her lay out her things and dress. She had decisions to make which could only be made alone.

Ever since she'd returned to Derby Street six months ago with a suitcase full of clothes slashed in ribbons Mara had known what she must do. Alys's future was at stake. Her first meeting with the Duke, on her own territory, in a number 7 newly decorated to his taste, had gone just as planned.

But this all-important second meeting was spinning beyond her control. She'd planned to wear for dinner her dressmaker's copy of a Lucien Lelong, but now she realized that the close-fitting black crêpe with its trimmings of white fur and matching elbow-length cape would never do. She hadn't expected such a battery of rich and beautiful women.

Slowly, Mara took off her afternoon dress and hung it from the tall brass bedstead. Her room, despite its enormous size, held nothing so ordinary as a wardrobe. Obviously aristocrats never hung up their own clothes. Fortunately, aristocrats were not above the need to relieve themselves; underneath the bed, gloriously bedecked with coronets and initials and, for some reason, bees, Mara found the biggest chamberpot she'd ever seen.

The room held no dressing-table, however; that would have been bourgeois. Mara studied herself in the large gilt-framed mirror above the fireplace. Her satin slip shone with an oystery radiance; for a moment she thought of wearing it as a dress. It matched the necklace of twiggy baroque pearls Quintin had chosen for her bridal outfit, and if she appeared in it she'd certainly attract attention. But though amusing, that would be vulgar; and after the amusement had worn off she'd be just another woman in her underwear.

Mara held up the black dress against herself. Here, in the brighter light of the countryside, the rabbit fur looked what it was, a cheap alternative to ermine. Quickly, because time was passing, Mara took hold of the witty little fur-trimmed panniers on each hip and ripped them off.

Fur flew and she sneezed.

The black dress was now servant plain. Even the pearls couldn't enliven it. What was she to do?

Mara held the fur-trimmed panniers to her head and tried to twist them into a witty little cap. It didn't work. She almost despaired.

Then the idea came to her. It was a risk, but perfect in its simplicity. Mara's eyes sparkled as she reached up to the bell above the mantelpiece and pulled it hard.

Forty-nine people sat down to dinner in the Great Dining-Hall; men in their evening dress, women in shimmering pastel satins and jewels like Jubilee fireworks. Nollie, entering last, felt at first a feeling of old-fashioned feudal satisfaction at having such a company, headed by the Prince of Wales, at his table; and then, as he noticed an empty chair halfway down the right-hand side, a flicker of irritation. There was always one woman reluctant to leave her mirror, or determined to make a grand entrance.

A quick mental calculation told him that the missing guest was the little Mayfair Countess. He had forgotten about her momentarily. What had happened to her? Perhaps she had not heard the gong, perhaps she was unwell, perhaps she was merely unused to country promptness? His irritation deepened. He was hungry; and one expected a certain cooperation from one's guests. Why the devil hadn't one of the servants seen to it that she was called?

Nollie summoned a footman and instructed him to send a maid up to the Countess's bedroom to inquire. Then, there being more important matters to consider, he signalled for the first course to be brought in. It was a challenge to persuade the Prince of Wales to eat more than a mouthful here and there, but this evening, Nollie felt, he had come up with something irresistible. Instead of resigning himself to the vagaries of his kitchen staff, he had ordered from Jackson's of Piccadilly everything required; terrapin soup, Rhode Island turkey, canvas-back duck, Virginia ham, waffles, sugar corn and sweet potatoes, to be followed by brandy peaches for the gentlemen, popcorn and candy for the ladies, and whisky and soda in the library for both. In other words, the complete, quick, reliable, modern American meal, to be eaten with the stainless steel cutlery which he had been the first man in England to import from the United States twelve years ago, and served up by the best-trained footmen in Britain; the ideal combination, in fact, of American convenience and British tradition.

Which made it even more insufferable, since he had made this evening's menu his special province, for the Countess to be late. She was behaving like a damned foreigner. She could hardly still be in the bath. There were only three bathrooms at Shelburne, and the blood-red water from their rusty geysers hardly encouraged lingering.

Nollie became aware out of the corner of his eye that the maid had returned. She had entered so quietly, as befitted a well-trained servant, that he had not noticed the opening of the door. She stood beside him now, waiting unobtrusively for him to finish his spoonful of soup, and dry his lips with his napkin before inclining his head to hear what she had to say. As he did so he noticed with approval the glossy starched ruffles of her apron. He remembered such aprons from his childhood; maids then had been enormously decorative, with their little bird caps and perky white ribbon tails. Why had they ceased to be so after the Great War? Problems with laundering, perhaps. Nollie was all for modernity, but he had forgotten the biscuity attractions of a starched ruffle.

'Yes?'

'The Countess has asked me to give you her apologies and says she will be down in a moment, Your Grace.'

'Very well.'

The maid, eyes demurely lowered, glided away with the faintest rustle, like a ground bird through undergrowth. He caught a glimpse as she retreated of a trim little waist – these modern dresses, dashing though they were, did not make the most of a woman's figure – and a matching pair of ankles. Nollie bent his head to take another mouthful of soup to fortify himself before conversing with his neighbour on his right. He was surprised to find on her face when he looked up the most extraordinary expression. Her eyes, wide open and glazed, were fixed on a spot away to his right, as if she had just seen a murder committed, or at least another woman wearing the same gown.

Following her eyes, Nollie realized with astonishment that the maid, her eyes still lowered, had settled herself into the place allotted to the Countess.

There was a moment of absolute silence, when not a spoon tinkled on a plate and not a breath was taken. Composedly, the maid nodded to the footman behind her; impassively, he ladled soup into her bowl. Delicately, the slender nape of her neck showing beneath her upswept hair, the maid bent her head to taste it. Then she laid her spoon aside, and dabbed her lips.

'Quite delicious,' she pronounced. 'I'm sure we could do with some of this in the servants' hall.'

It was the sharp-eyed Prince of Wales who laughed first, a laughter taken up by the other guests in a ragged ripple, first doubtful, then, as realization spread, delighted. The little maid remained composed.

When at last the laughter died she turned to Nollie with a mock-tragic look.

'Oh, Nollie. I felt so sure you would remember.'

'Mara! Well I never.'

'I'm afraid so.' She smiled at him, a wicked smile in which her teeth, dazzling white as the maid's cap which sat so pertly on her dark hair, caught the light. 'Are you disappointed?'

Nollie paused for a moment. Then, lifting his glass of sherry – cocktails might be all the rage, but nothing could divorce a good soup and a good sherry – he returned her smile, feeling as he did so the little spurt of exhilaration that he would feel tomorrow morning at dawn when he set out with his bearer and his two best dogs to set the feathers flying. In her crisp black and white, without a single jewel, only the wink of some crooked little pearls at her throat, Mara outshone every other woman in the room. Nollie's throat thickened. He had been brought up by maids, goddammit, a succession of them. The twin smells of starch and cooking had been the best memories of his childhood.

'Disappointed? Not in the least,' he rejoined. 'Now eat up your soup before it gets cold.'

'There's something more I need from you, Nollie.'

'More?' Nollie opened one eye. He was exhausted. 'What more could there possibly be?'

'A room,' said Mara.

'A room?' Nollie's eyes widened. He had been confronted by many requests in his time, but never one quite like this. The Countess had a perfectly good house of her own, she could hardly be asking for him to maintain her. 'A room where?'

'Here, at Shelburne.'

There was a short silence.

'But . . .' Nollie was hard put to it to phrase his next question tactfully. 'Surely you are not meaning to live here?' It just wouldn't do, it wouldn't do at all.

'No, no, I wouldn't dream of it.' Mara laughed out loud at his expression of relief. 'All I want is a room, just one. In fact, one in particular.'

Nollie's mind raced. Which could it be – the Ballroom, the Dining-Hall, the Blue Room? Each alone was as big as most people's private residences. 'Which one?'

'Your father's study.' Mara smiled at his surprise. 'And not for long. A month would do, I think. Just while you're away.'

Nollie was lost for words.

'Oh, and half one week's income.' Mara smiled angelically. 'In cash, in advance.'

'A thousand pounds?' Nollie's voice rose in disbelief. 'Whatever for?'

'I know it doesn't seem much,' said Mara sweetly, 'but believe me, in the right hands, a thousand pounds can go a long way.'

'I believe you,' said Nollie with feeling. 'And what, precisely, are you planning to do with my father's study and a thousand pounds?'

'Make you happy,' said Mara. 'That is my speciality. Do you trust me?'

'Not an inch,' said Nollie.

'Good,' said Mara. 'That will make things easier.'

By the time Nollie returned to Shelburne after a month in New York he had almost forgotten about his bargain with the little Countess. He had arranged before he left for his estate manager to supply her with the sum she had requested, though now he could not quite remember why. She had a certain charm, the Countess, a mesmeric quality, like the best kind of fortune-teller.

But now, late on a cold, wet, windy October night, the sort of weather that was good for female complexions but very bad indeed for male temperaments, Nollie could not help hoping that the Countess had flown the coop with his money. He was in no mood for complications after his journey. What he wanted most in the world was a piping hot plateful of bacon and eggs, something he

273

could have had served up to him at any halfway decent hotel in the civilized world – but at Shelburne? He knew better than to torment his staff with the asking. No electricity, you see. Might as well be living in a mud hut.

Nollie dismissed his chauffeur, thanked Williams the butler for waiting up for him, and declared himself capable of getting himself to bed without the assistance of Parker, who valeted him whenever he returned to the Abbey. He also declined to remove his coat; after the blissful central heating of New York apartments, the hall felt as chilly as a cellar.

'There are sandwiches made ready in the library, Your Grace,' said Williams, with that touch of bullying hauteur which distinguished the really good butler. 'And the Countess asked me to tell you, if you returned before eleven, that she would be in the study.'

'The Countess?' Nollie was momentarily taken aback. 'Is she still here?'

'I believe so, Your Grace.' Not for the first time Nollie felt sorely tempted to ask Williams some pertinent questions, but as always he suppressed them. It did not do to consult one's butler; to do so was to put the fellow in a difficult position.

Ceremonially, Williams handed over one of the two oil-lamps he was carrying. Nollie received it reluctantly.

'Mutton, I suppose?'

'Indeed, Your Grace.' Nollie sighed. In no other country in the civilized world was cold mutton considered a suitable restorative for the returning traveller. Still, there would be brandy in the library, and, provided he didn't stray further than two feet away from the fireguard, a modicum of warmth.

But first, because she would undoubtedly have heard his car arrive, he must attend the Countess.

'Goodnight, Williams.'

'Goodnight, Your Grace.'

Williams and his lamp receded towards the lower quarters. Nollie, coated and hatted as if instead of arriving from a journey he was beginning one, plodded reluctantly towards his father's study, holding the lamp carefully away from his suiting. The hall always reminded him of St Pancras Station; the corridors that led from it, of school. Both institutions were of course very well in their place, but not what a man wanted of his home.

As he approached the study Nollie became aware of a very slight humming noise. It reminded him of the *White Lady*'s engines idling at dock just before a voyage. In his imagination he even smelled diesel oil, that faint, bracing, masculine tang which lady passengers so often found nauseating.

The door of the study was closed, but beneath it showed a fan of brilliant golden light. The door had no handle. Perplexed for a moment, Nollie pushed. The door swung noiselessly open at his touch, admitted him, and then, gently, closed itself behind him, the whole operation so easy in execution that it had something dream-like about it.

The room Nollie saw before him was quite different from the one he had left behind a month ago, and yet he recognized it instantly. His throat filled and his eyes burned with an emotion as unexpected as it was irresistible. For almost a minute he was unable to speak. He simply looked, while something inside him that he had almost forgotten, a pleasure so simple, so unique that he could find no words to identify it, radiated out from his heart to fill every cell of his body. It had something of childhood in it, something of revelation, something of pure, down-to-earth practicality. Satisfaction, that's what it was. The satisfaction, so rarely attained in adulthood, of feeling for once completely, perfectly, understood.

'How did you know?'

The woman curled up in the deep curved chair before the wide sweep of oak desk uncoiled herself slowly. She had waited, in silence, for him to enjoy this moment; he would never forget that. Only dogs, in his experience, were capable of such tact.

'You told me,' the Countess replied. 'I had nothing whatever to do with it.'

Nollie nodded. No other reply would have satisfied him. This was a room that he had created; it had been built round him, like the mounds of sand his elder daughter Olivia had covered him with at the beach in Scotland when she was a child. Without him, there would have been no room like this; it was the fullest, most natural expression of his personality that he would ever see.

Silently, reflectively, like a man running his hand over his own chin after shaving, he touched his room. The desk, solid, simple, curved light oak. The walls, simply panelled in the same scrubbed wood, and on them, against them, a glory, a luxury, a necessity of shelves. Deep ones and broad ones, tall ones and small ones, shelves as welcoming and accommodating as the branches of a tree. More to the point – empty.

Already, in his mind's eye, Nollie raced ahead. Here he would keep his treasures; here he would marshal his thoughts. With these shelves he could keep his desk clear as the open sea, but reach out at a hand's length to find whatever he needed. No more etchings of ladies with double chins, just two portraits; one of Jimmy Donaghue the jockey, the other of a schooner in full sail. Beneath them no open hearth, requiring constant tending and interruptions from the staff, but a glowing five-bar fire.

'Electric,' Nollie said, swinging round.

'Of course,' said the Countess. 'I felt you would prefer it. In this day and age.'

Hence the humming noise he had heard earlier, Nollie thought; a generator. Not a trace of that sound was audible within the study itself, because of the panelling. He smiled in delight. It had never occurred to him to electrify just one room, to see his study as a yacht in the middle of a cold, lightless ocean. Now he saw that it made enormous sense. Why, he could retire in here and be amply catered for without bothering to heat up the rest of the house just for himself; why, he could save money!

276

'Let me show you something else.' The Countess drew the floor-length curtains that covered the window. Nollie heard the click of a latch. A curl of cool night air scented with wet leaf tumbled into the room. There was nothing like a warm room indoors for the appreciation of the pleasures of an English autumn.

'French windows,' said the Countess. 'In case you wanted to escape.' She shut the double doors again; the oily click of them was music to Nollie's ears. Nothing in this great damp house ever shut properly any more. 'And here,' the Countess continued, 'is another door.'

Located in the panelling, as if it were part of the continuous wall, was indeed a door. It opened onto a small, severely elegant, almost monkish bathroom. No geyser, no blood-red ring round the bath's white enamel. Stainless steel taps. Above the basin, the single note of fancy, a mirror set inside the radiating spokes of a ship's wheel.

And, glory of glories, a proper, sit-down, wash-down, plumbed-in closet, Officers, Gentlemen and Convicts for the Use of.

'For your convenience,' said the Countess.

'Lord,' said Nollie reverently. 'What a convenience.' When one reached a certain age, there were some things one appreciated out of all proportion.

Nollie barely took in the rest of the guided tour – the couch, placed across the inner wall for warmth, which once stripped of its cushions instantly became a serviceable bed; the innocent-looking right-hand cupboard beneath the desk which opened to reveal a refrigerating unit and well-stocked shelves of drinks; the telephone, swinging on its own platform at just the right height; the strategically placed tins of biscuits from the kitchen, each lid flap-up, not lift-off; the extra space beneath the desk to accommodate a gundog or two.

It was as he gazed, half-mesmerized, half-disbelieving, at his metropolis, his airport landing strip, his Scottish moorland of a desk – my, how much work he could do at that desk! – that Nollie noticed something. Just above the drawer holding the refrigerator, motionless, presumably dazed by the approach of winter, clung a late-season bee. Nollie brushed the insect away with the edge of his coatsleeve, but it remained. Looking closer, he realized that it was not a real bee but a facsimile, so cleverly painted, including its own blurred bee shadow, that it seemed alive.

'What is this?' he asked.

'My trademark,' said the Countess. Nollie stared at it, racking his brains.

'I've seen it before somewhere. Damned if I can think where.'

'I know,' said the Countess. For the first time since he had entered the transformed study she smiled.

'Where?'

'Under the bed in the Bird Room.'

'Of course!' Nollie remembered it now, the Napoleonic chamber-pot, allegedly used by the great man himself, a suitably imperial vessel festooned with crests and bees. Slowly, while he considered this surprising piece of information, he took off his coat and hat. In the overwhelming surprise of discovering his study – already it was his, as if it had always been so – he had forgotten every social nicety. He had plunged straight into conversation without sparing the Countess anything more than a passing glance.

Now, with a considerable sense of relief, Nollie perceived that she looked much the same. Women nowadays were quite capable of turning up in broad daylight with green eyelids and bald eyebrows, but it seemed the Countess had her own appearance and was going to stick to it.

'So why, my dear Countess, have you taken a bee out of my chamberpot and stuck it on my desk?'

'I knew you had a passion for plumbing,' said the Countess demurely. 'But that is not all. Can you keep a secret?'

'I think so.' Nollie propped himself on the desk. It gave not an inch under his considerable weight. Solid timber, solid construction; his heart creaked with delight. Just the right height for sitting on, too. This room was as made to measure as a suit from Savile Row.

'One might have thought the bee stood for Bonaparte,' said the Countess, seemingly at random.

'I suppose so – though, come to think of it, the fellow was a Frog. What's the French for bee?'

'Abeille,' said the Countess.

'Ah.' Nollie was beginning to enjoy himself. This had the makings of a good story; he could see himself showing people round his study, making them guess the function and meaning of the mysterious little bee. So little in life, nowadays, had the capacity to intrigue. And what a mine of information she was, his little Countess. 'It can't be that, then. So what is it? Why the bee?'

'Well . . .' The Countess hesitated deliciously. 'I may be wrong, but I rather hope I'm right. Are you sure you can keep a secret?'

'Of course. If you ask me once more I shall be offended.'

'I was in the library – rather a good library you have here, actually.'

'Thank you.'

'I found a book on *Flora and Fauna of the British Isles.*'

'I always wanted to meet Fauna,' said Nollie. 'She sounded a lot more fun than Flora.'

'And in the book, in the section on bees, I couldn't help noticing . . .' said the Countess.

'Yes?'

'I never did any Latin at school, but as I say I couldn't help noticing that the Latin for bee is "apis".'

'Yes?' Nollie was puzzled.

'And that seemed to me to make an admirable connection with the chamberpot,' said the Countess, smiling seraphically. 'If you see what I mean.'

'Hah!' Nollie laughed explosively. 'Damn good!'

'I know,' said the Countess. 'But you see why I would like it to remain our little secret.'

'Yes I do,' said Nollie. 'What beats me is why you have chosen it as a trademark.'

'Privacy, freedom, comfort, convenience.' The Countess recited the words like a sort of litany. They fell like music on Nollie's ears. 'Some people might call these luxuries, but they are not. They are necessities. I want to be your bee. I want to render your life, as the French put it – *plus commode*. I want you to be as relieved to find me in the middle of the night as Napoleon must have been to locate his chamberpot. *Voilà*.'

Nollie beckoned her to him. He had never heard such a simple statement of intent from any human being, let alone a woman. It rendered him quite speechless. The Countess stood neatly within his arms; he felt her solidity, the wiry strength of her body, the power and energy of the thoughts that buzzed in that mind of hers.

'My dear chamberpot,' he said, and at the thought of it a tremor of mirth rose inside him. She was an extraordinary woman, that was for sure. How had she guessed that on certain nights, when the brandy had flowed freely and the conversation had been too riveting to leave, a man would sell a night with Argive Helen for five minutes alone with his back turned? 'Whenever I see that bee, I promise, I shall think of you. But now—' he pushed her back a little so that he could see her eyes. 'Now you must tell me, truthfully, what you are after.'

'I thought you might ask that,' said the Countess a little ruefully. 'I'm afraid my reasons, though perfectly legal, are not entirely respectable.'

'Good,' said Nollie. 'Come on then, spill the beans, as they say over the water.'

'As you know, I am a single woman,' said the Countess. 'Well, a widow with no intention of remarrying, which amounts to very much the same in practice. And practice is what we are concerned with here. I have very little income, no capital, and my daughter's future to consider.'

Nollie opened his mouth to speak but she forestalled him.

'But I have no intention of asking you or anyone else for money. You have helped me quite enough in that area by permitting me to

280

design you a Dream Room. When people see it, with a little encouragement from you, they will want me to do the same for them. You are a Duke, after all. So I shall be perfectly well able to earn my own living. I would not want it any other way. But—'

'But?'

'I want to see my daughter presented at Court.'

'How old is she?'

'Just thirteen.'

Nollie smiled. 'Five years?'

The Countess nodded in agreement. 'And in return, I shall find you a wife.'

'But I thought—'

'Oh, not me. I have no intention of marrying you or anyone else. But you will need a wife eventually, and finding one is too hard for a man on his own, especially one in your position. The choice is too wide. But I shall have five years to study your likes and dislikes, in fact everything about you. At the end of that time I shall find you the perfect wife, don't worry.'

'I believe you could at that.' Nollie was intrigued. After all, he employed experts to make his clothes and prick out bedding plants in the park; there was no obvious reason why choosing a wife should be any different. 'And in the interim?'

'In the interim,' the Countess answered calmly, 'I will make you very, very comfortable. I shall accompany you wherever you wish to go, and make sure you don't fall prey to every harpy between Menton and St Moritz. You know very well that if you are on your own you will drink too much, get fat and worry about money. But if you are with me you will not be bored for so much as a minute. I am very good company, you see.'

'You have thought all this out, haven't you?'

She nodded again. 'Like this room – it takes planning.'

'And I am to be part of your plan?'

'As I shall be part of yours. Think what a team we will make.'

'Laurel and Hardy? Abbott and Costello?'

'Boiled chicken and onions,' she said.

Nollie shook his head in amazement. She had even taken the trouble to find out his favourite dish. What could a man do?

The Countess reached up, flicked a switch, and with exquisite, effortless immediacy – no trimming of wicks, no smoke, no smell of burnt oil – all the lights in the room went off, leaving only the dramatic crimson glow of the electric bars.

'I think we should inaugurate the room, don't you?' she whispered. 'Unless, that is, you are too tired after your journey?'

'Not any more,' Nollie answered.

Slowly, before the vivid red slashes of the glowing elements, they sank to the floor. It was blissfully, unexpectedly warm.

'Underfloor heating,' whispered the Countess.

'Convenient,' Nollie answered, a little breathlessly.

'Efficient,' she rejoined, indistinctly.

'Like you, my little bee,' Nollie continued hoarsely. 'Tell me, what else do bees do, in their busy, busy lives?'

The Countess laughed, a long, liquid chuckle that set every hair on Nollie's body quivering. 'They make honey,' she said.

14　*The Peacock's Tail*

'You can't possibly not,' said Carelia. 'Not now. Not after I've gone to all this trouble. If you weren't going to go ahead you shouldn't have agreed in the first place.'

'I know,' answered Alys. 'It's just that now it seems . . . wrong, somehow.' She knew it sounded lame.

'What are you worried about? Your mother finding out? How can she, when she's out with Father? The Eve of Parliament Reception goes on for ages.'

'Yes, but – what will I say to her tomorrow?'

'Nothing. Why should you? If you ask her lots of questions about Lady Londonderry she'll forget all about you.'

'You make it sound so easy.'

'It is easy. I do it all the time.'

But you're different. Alys wanted to say. You're always so sure about everything.

'Anyway,' Carelia continued undeterred. She'd been born in the year of the invention of the tank, and what she lacked in flexibility she made up in momentum. 'Bet your mother would have done it without a second thought, when she was your age.'

Alys had to admit that Carelia was probably right. She tried to imagine her mother at fourteen and failed. But Carelia was clever about people, she could sum them up in a glance.

'Come on, it's only one night. No one will ever know.'

Alys had the hazy impression that that wasn't the point – surely whether people knew shouldn't make any difference? – but she couldn't have explained exactly why, even if Carelia would have listened, which she would not.

'And you want to, you know you do.'

Alys nodded. Of that at least she could be sure. She just didn't have Carelia's automatic confidence that wanting to do something was the best justification for doing it. Sometimes Carelia could seem almost American.

'That's settled, then. Now, this is the plan.'

If it had been the first night of *Cavalcade*, Noel Coward's runaway musical success, then the two girls who entered the auditorium of the Drury Lane Theatre just after the interval would have attracted more notice than they did. But the play was well into its third week, and though tickets were still hard to obtain they were not impossible. The long queues for the gallery had diminished, and no one noticed that the two girls' clothes, though expensive, were not entirely suitable for evening, and their lipstick a little amateurishly applied.

'I wish we were down there,' said Carelia, as she craned over the heads of the people in the row in front to inspect the lower part of the auditorium, filled with couples in evening dress and the sparkle of jewellery.

'I like it up here,' said Alys. 'We've got a better view.' Even though Carelia, at fifteen, had the height and confidence to pass for at least seventeen, Alys still felt nervous that someone would spot them and make them leave. It was the first time she'd ever been to the theatre, though Carelia had attended thousands of times all over the world. Alys was taken aback by the hum and rustle of the audience; it was like being inside an enormous beehive. Not like school assembly at all.

She and Carelia were barely settled in their places before the houselights dimmed and the orchestra struck up. After the curtain rose it took a few minutes to work out what was happening, because they'd missed the first half. They'd had to wait for Olivia to go to bed before they could leave Derby Street; it was lucky that Carelia's half-sister kept country hours.

Carelia was the first to orientate herself in history.

'Victoria's funeral,' she whispered in a not so *sotto voce*. Alys hardly paid attention. The stage was crowded with extras, all in gloomy black, and she searched their faces eagerly. But it was impossible to make out individuals behind the heavy beards and moustaches. Alys leaned back in her plush seat with a sense of anticlimax so acute that it surprised her. For a moment her eyes were quite blurred; suitable sentiments, she supposed, for a funeral, but Queen Victoria's death meant very little to her. 1901 seemed as far away to her as the beginning of the world.

The next scene was better, featuring the noise and bustle of Victoria Station during the Great War. The make-believe platform was crowded with Red Cross workers distributing tea and sandwiches to the embarking and disembarking soldiers, who could be told apart by the colour of their complexions, either bright pink or livid grey. More of the men were clean-shaven now and it was easier to see their faces.

But everyone on the stage would keep moving; it was terribly hard to fix on one face long enough to identify it, and the uniform caps got in the way.

Then, just at the end of the scene, with a jump of the heart which almost brought Alys out of her seat, she spotted an embarking soldier, one of the pink-complexioned variety, halfway to the back of the stage. He was propped up against his kitbag and smoking a cigarette; just another khaki figure, but something about the elegance of his movement and the turn of his head was tormentingly familiar. Then the crowd shifted to hide him, and before Alys could look again train doors opened and slammed and he was gone. She felt a flash of panic, as if he had caught a real train to a real war and might never come back.

The next scene, after the drama of the station, was something of

285

a disappointment, at least to Alys. It portrayed a peaceful sunny day at the English seaside, complete with striped swimsuits, buckets and spades. It was so brilliantly lit, so poster perfect, that even Alys, who loved the seaside dearly, found it hard to believe.

But no one else in the audience seemed to object. The seaside scene was received as rapturously as the rest, with fusillades of applause and shouts and whistles from the gallery.

'It's not right,' whispered Alys uneasily to Carelia, who was applauding and cheering like the rest. 'The seaside isn't really like that.'

'Of course not,' hissed Carelia. 'It's only a play.'

Alys sank back into her seat, conscious once more of the gap that existed between herself and the person she wanted to be. She wasn't always conscious of this gap. Sometimes it disappeared altogether, but at other times, like now, she felt it open up inside her as if it would swallow her up. Now, she could clap and cheer as much as she liked, but inside her a small, steely sort of voice, a poisonous, dripping sort of voice that only she could hear, whispered, 'I know you. You don't fool me. You are only pretending to be like other people. I know.'

The gap. It was there when she played the piano too. No matter how hard she practised, no matter how hard she tried, between what she heard in her head and what she heard with her ears there was always the gap.

Then, mercifully, the last scene arrived, an epilogue, set in a nightclub on New Year's Eve, 1930, only two years ago. On a darkening stage dancing couples revolved like automata to the insistent rhythms of the blues. The women were garishly made-up, the men pale and haggard. One of the male dancers moved with a particular haunting grace; Alys fixed her eyes upon him, all her despondency forgotten. What a privilege it was, she realized suddenly, to watch someone you knew dancing. It was somehow personal, a sort of sharing.

And then, with shattering pomp, a huge Union Jack rose out of the darkness, to the surge of the National Anthem. Like a huge flower opening, the stage lightened to reveal the massed cast singing 'God Save the King'.

Whistling, cheering, applauding, the theatre audience rose to match them, singing at the tops of their voices as the burly echoes flung themselves around the auditorium. Alys rose too, her own voice indistinguishable in the hubbub, but it was not the King she saluted, only the slender figure two rows back on the right, with his glossy brilliantined head and dark eyes catching the light. It seemed to her that he was looking straight out at her, that she could feel every movement of his body as he bowed to take the applause. She experienced a dizzying combination of pride and humility.

Then it was over, and Carelia, before the applause had even faded, picked up her coat and began to thrust her way past the row of still cheering people towards the aisle.

'Come on,' she called to Alys over her shoulder. Her face had its tank look. 'We've eaten our greens, and now it's time for pudding!'

Bundling her coat up into her arms, Alys tried as best she could to keep up with Carelia as her friend bobbed resolutely down the aisle towards the exit. The applause from the final scene was still echoing round the auditorium; no one apart from themselves had so much as thought of leaving. Even as Carelia sped down the steps towards the lower levels the curtain was still swishing to and fro as the assembled four-hundred strong cast took call after call. Alys felt like a traitor; she should have been standing applauding like the rest of the audience. But she wasn't at all sure she would be able to find her way back to Derby Street without Carelia.

It turned out that Carelia had no intention of returning to Derby Street. Between one hurried heartbeat and the next, as if she had followed the White Rabbit down a hole, Alys found that she had crossed an invisible frontier. No more red plush and soft lights and packed auditorium, but a maze of corridors with peeling paint and battered doors opening off in all directions. They were backstage.

It was like being inside a packing-case, or rummaging past the neatly folded garments at the front of her dressing-table drawer to the jumble of odds and ends at the back. As Carelia strode swiftly and purposively onwards, as if she truly knew where she was going, Alys felt a pang of alarm. She would not have wanted to expose the back of her dressing-table drawers to public view, and probably the Drury Lane actors felt much the same about their dressing-rooms. Surely members of the audience needed permission, a platform ticket or something, to penetrate backstage?

Carelia, however, had no such qualms. 'Look as if you belong, for heaven's sake!' she hissed over her shoulder as Alys shrank into a doorway to avoid two men carrying what appeared to be half a brick wall.

Alys did her best. She was relieved when Carelia ducked abruptly into an open doorway. 'Seen Hugo?' she called, so loudly that half the theatre must have heard her, but the crowd inside the tiny room seemed to find that perfectly normal. 'Next door!' they chorused, and before Alys could catch her breath she found herself in a narrow low-ceilinged room filled with more people than it had ever been meant to hold. The light was blinding, the heat intense, the air a thick soup of perfume and powder and perspiration, and the level of noise enough to shatter glass.

'Hugo?' bellowed Carelia.

'Over there,' came the jovial response, accompanied by a waving bottle. Through the haze of cigarette smoke Alys caught a glimpse of what might have been the top of Hugo's dark head. She would have turned back at that point – after all, anything resembling conversation was clearly out of the question – but Carelia forged on.

Hugo, or what they could see of him, was sitting down surrounded by what seemed a complete circle of semi-naked female backs, a sort of Hadrian's Wall of velvety wriggling shoulders and jewelled napes. Carelia grabbed Alys as if she were some sort of talisman and pushed her in front of her. 'Make way!' she shouted. 'Make way for Hugo's cousin, all the way up from the country!'

Before Alys could protest – she was no relation to Hugo at all, really, and Derby Street was hardly the back of beyond – a gap opened up magically in front of her and she found herself precipitated practically into Hugo's lap. His arms went up to catch her and for a moment his face, inches from her own, looked completely unrecognizable behind its thick layer of greasepaint. How strange, thought Alys, in a curious, detached part of her mind. He looked much more like himself on stage.

And then, to her relief, Hugo's face broke into the most delighted of smiles. 'Alys!' he announced. 'I thought you weren't coming! What a wonderful surprise.' He so clearly meant what he said that Alys found herself smiling foolishly in return, all her nervousness draining away as if it had never been. He really was pleased to see her. He really was.

Now, Hugo pivoted her round like the ballerina on Uncle William's cigar box and presented her with a flourish to the circle of floury doe-eyed faces before them. 'Girls,' he went on, his musical voice dipping instantly into drama. 'Allow me to present to you my very own cousin Alys. She and I – well, we have barely a mother and a father between us. We are alone in the world, aren't we, Alys? Babes in the wood.'

'Aaah,' said the girls, like a chorus in a pantomime, and their vivid faces expressed so much instant emotion that Alys felt quite overwhelmed.

'But we have each other, and that is very much, isn't it, Alys?' Hugo's eyes were alight now. 'We have been to Paris together, and the Riviera. We have dined on yachts by torchlight, we have travelled on the Blue Train!'

'The Blue Train?' sighed the girls, eyes round.

'The very same,' said Hugo. 'And we had the best time, the best time in the world. Isn't that true, Alys?' He seemed to beseech her with his eyes to agree with him; Alys felt at once confused and disbelieving and immensely flattered. Could it possibly have been the same for him as it had for her? Belatedly she nodded.

'There you are,' said Hugo to the assembled faces. 'We agree about everything, Alys and I.'

Alys blushed. It amazed her that she should be linked in any way with Hugo, this glamorous, extraordinary, popular creature. She could see mirrored on the other girls' faces her own fascination. Hugo was wearing, whether for the purposes of his part or not, she could not tell, a small Ronald Colman-type moustache, which lent his features maturity without disguising them. His face was so mobile that Alys felt she could have watched it for ever; his skin, revealed down to his chest where he had torn off his collar and studs, was made up the milky brown colour of butter toffee. He seemed like some other race of being, newly invented; even his curls, sprung loose from the brilliantine, now fell in perfectly symmetrical spirals. Hugo is a work of art, Alys thought, suddenly. I wonder if he knows?

'Are you going to go on the stage too?' asked one of the girls. 'Like our Hugo?'

Alys looked alarmed. Hugo interceded for her.

'Alys is far too clever to waste her life in such a frivolous manner,' he said. 'But she is an artiste, of course. One can tell just by looking at her. *Ça se voit, n'est-ce pas?* He ran his hand lightly over her hair, and as he did so Alys caught sight of her own reflection in the mirror, and truly, next to Hugo, she did look rather remarkable, her monochrome, ash-pale colouring contrasting dramatically with his darkness. For a moment, through Hugo's eyes, in this motley gathering, the thought that she might possess some secret talent, something that might one day astound the world, seemed almost possible.

'She can play the piano,' said Carelia, with what sounded like a touch of malice.

'Really?' came the chorus. 'How fearfully clever!'

Alys's heart sank. She had wanted very much to play the piano, but that was before she had actually tried to do so. Now, or so it seemed to her, the keys themselves had got in the way of that ambition. There was such an army of them, all cold and hard and shiny and uniformly unforgiving. Thank goodness this dressing-

290

room was far too small ever to accommodate a piano, or Alys might have found herself propelled towards the keyboard to show off her non-existent repertoire.

'Is your mother waiting for you outside?' asked Hugo, and Alys was once more struck dumb. She turned in appeal to Carelia; having had no idea of Carelia's intention to visit behind the stage after the performance she had made no plans for this eventuality.

'Alys's mother couldn't come,' explained Carelia airily. 'Another engagement. So a taxi brought us.'

'Then you will be needing an escort home,' declared Hugo instantly. He stood up and his admirers fell from him in a shower of pink and white like blossom off a cherry tree. He picked up his coat and just as he was, greasepaint, costume and all, extended an arm to each of the girls. 'You will excuse us, I know,' Hugo explained. 'But family is family.'

The three of them swept out on a tide of goodwill.

'Now tell me, Alys,' said Hugo, as they progressed through the corridor maze with none of the furtive speed with which they had arrived. 'Tell me every single thing that has happened to you since the Blue Train.'

'Nothing important,' said Alys, and then, surprising herself, 'Nothing till now.'

'Do you mean that?' Hugo looked down at her with his eyes alight. 'Do you really, really mean it?' Alys nodded. His face was so bright she could scarcely bear to look at it. 'I think that is perfectly splendid.' He tucked her arm more firmly into his, then turned to Carelia. 'Please forgive us, won't you? We have so much history to catch up, Alys and I.'

Outside the theatre Hugo whistled up a taxi. To Alys as she climbed in it seemed as if everything she saw, the floodlit façade of the theatre, the streams of traffic, even the street pedlars, had changed in a flash from hostile to friendly, just because she was in Hugo's company. Now, the Drury Lane theatre was floodlit for her, not against her; the cabbie at the wheel of the taxi was there to take her wherever she wanted to go, not whisk her back home in disgrace. I belong here, with Hugo, she thought. It is just as he says, and there is no explaining it; it is a fact.

Hugo took them to the famous coffee-stall at Hyde Park Corner where late-night revellers assembled with their taxis to stock up for the small hours. He bought them both hot sausages and mustard, and Alys had never felt so hungry in her life. Hugo's presence redressed the balance between herself and Carelia; she no longer felt overwhelmed and ill-at-ease. They both told him how wonderful he had been in his various roles, and he was becomingly modest.

'I think, you know, I am an actor,' he said solemnly. 'I think that is what I must be.'

'There must have been a lot of competition for those parts,' said Carelia knowledgeably. 'How did you manage to get them?'

'Oh, the usual thing,' replied Hugo airily. 'I had to know someone who knew someone. And smile a great deal.' Then, in the same breath, as if questions bored him, he went on, 'I have left Oxford, you know. My father was not at all pleased, but there you are. I knew, I just knew, that Modern History was not for me. There is no end to Modern History, you see, more of it is being made all the time. How could I possibly keep up? In any case – ' Hugo threw his arms wide in a gesture that embraced the world and nearly knocked Alys's sausage to the floor of the cab ' – look at me! I am Modern History in person! One cannot study history as well as be it!'

Much of what Hugo said was beyond Alys's comprehension, but she didn't feel out of her depth. Hugo's incomprehensibility was somehow reassuring, a sort of magic cloak of words and ideas in whose folds she felt quite safe. He didn't seem to expect her to understand, or even to contribute, only to accept. So she nodded, and chewed, and nodded again, as he told her that he would miss the Hypocrites' Club, and drinking to excess in full evening dress on the Penzance to Aberdeen express, and riotous dinners at the Spreadeagle at Thame, and soaring back through the inky night in his racing Vauxhall to be back in college by midnight.

'You do think I'm right, don't you, to give it all up?' he inquired.

'I think so,' answered Alys after reflection. 'I don't see how you would have time to fit in everything.' The dreaded black and white of the piano keys flashed up before her mind's eye, and she felt somehow that in releasing Hugo from the burden of Modern History she was also releasing herself.

Apparently, she and Carelia were the first guests apart from university friends to have seen Hugo in his new guise as an actor. His father had said he had no interest in watching Hugo make a fool of himself in public, while Uncle William and Aunt Violet, though they had sent their good wishes, had not been able to bring themselves, deep down, to enjoy something so basically frivolous as the theatre. It made Alys feel important to have been Hugo's first and only family guest.

At last it was time to go back to Derby Street. Hugo deposited the two girls outside number 7 a few minutes before midnight, and while Carelia was unlocking the front door he and Alys were left alone for a few moments. Looking up into his face Alys saw it shadowed and strange in the lamplight, as if he was reluctant to say goodbye. He seemed for the first time hesitant, as if there was something he wanted to tell her, and he was trying to make up his mind how to say it. Alys found herself wondering suddenly what he would do after he left; return to the empty theatre or go back to his rooms alone?

'I wish I had something to give you,' Hugo said at last. 'Apart from a sausage and mustard.'

'That's all right,' said Alys, with absolute sincerity. 'This has been the best evening of my whole life.'

'That's what I mean,' Hugo said. 'That's why I want to give you something, something special. To remind you.'

'I won't forget,' she assured him.

'People always forget,' he answered. 'I know. I've read Modern History.' He ran his hands down his costume under his light overcoat, patting pockets. 'But I haven't anything except cigarettes.

293

And I hardly think your mother would approve of that. She's not exactly fond of me as it is.'

'Not?' said Alys, astonished. She could not imagine anyone not being fond of Hugo. 'Why?'

'See?' said Hugo. 'You've forgotten already, and it was only last year. Your mother was going to marry my father, remember? Then she called it off at the last minute. Now she won't have anything more to do with either of us.'

'Oh,' said Alys, and at the back of her mind something stirred, but she suppressed it. She could hardly remember anything about her time on the yacht, only the journey, and being with Hugo. The rest was a blur; too much excitement, she supposed.

Suddenly Alys felt a stab of panic. If Hugo was right, if people did forget, then what was left? She searched his face, willing herself to imprint every line of it on her memory, but in the dimness it dissolved every time she tried to focus on it.

'Your mother's letter,' she said in sudden desperation. 'Tell me about that. I would remember that.'

Hugo hesitated, then shook his head. 'I wish I could,' he said. 'Maybe I will one day, when you're older.'

'When?' Alys felt a sort of hunger for a plan, a future. Something with a number on it. 'When will I be old enough?'

'I don't know. Eighteen, maybe.'

'Do you promise?'

'It means that much to you?'

Alys nodded. Her knowing what was in the letter would be a bond between them, something concrete they could share. Somehow, obscurely, she felt it might help him to tell her. It seemed as if he had no one else to tell.

'Then I promise.' Hugo smiled at her, his complex, fascinating smile, never the same twice, as if he was constantly experimenting with it.

'Swear,' she said.

His eyebrows rose. 'On what? Cross my heart and hope to die?'

Inspiration came to her. 'Outcasts' honour!'

Hugo studied her for a moment. 'Very well,' he said quietly. 'Outcasts' honour it shall be.'

'Swear too that you will never ask me to play the piano!'

Hugo had the instinctive good sense not to ask her why. 'Consider it sworn.' His lips quirked up at the corners. 'Satisfied?'

'I suppose so.' Alys sighed.

'I know,' Hugo said. His face looked sad. 'That's why I wanted to give you something.' There was a pause. Alys was aware, behind her, of Carelia ostentatiously half-closing the door. Her friend was waiting to lock up again, so that in the morning Olivia would never suspect their illicit outing. Time was running out, faster and faster towards the end, just like the sand in an hourglass.

'Wait! I have it, the very thing!' Suddenly the laughter and certainty returned to Hugo's voice. 'As plain as the nose on your face – or as pretty, in your case.' With a quick movement he reached up to his face and, wincing melodramatically, whisked off his pencil-line moustache. This, with graceful precision, he proceeded to fix on Alys's upper lip. He stood back to admire his handiwork, and smiled. 'There,' he said finally. 'That is truly unforgettable.' Then, unexpectedly, with his newly naked, familiar yet unfamiliar mouth, he bent and kissed her.

His lips were warm and strong and alive. They were very gentle but Alys felt as if all the breath in her body had been knocked out in one blow. She stood, dazed, as Hugo leapt into the waiting taxi and sped away into the darkness without a backward glance. She watched him go, the moustache on her upper lip a delicate, alien pressure, as if he were still kissing her.

Then, very carefully, she peeled it off. The little strip of hair smelled very faintly of greasepaint, and spirit glue, and Hugo. Gently, as if it were a skeleton leaf or the corpse of some tiny hedgerow animal, Alys laid it between the folds of her handkerchief, and went in.

15 *Seed of Two Dragons*

'So, what do you do all day now that you are grown-up?'

Alys lowered the brim of her coolie hat and did her best to look sophisticated. It was only three weeks till her eighteenth birthday, but she felt no older inside than she had at fourteen. She had debated for hours over what to wear for this all-important luncheon. Fashion this year was all wit and dash and Schiaparelli, but she hated to attract too much attention.

So this morning, knowing herself a coward, Alys had chosen last year's simple white Vionnet afternoon dress with white sleeves, long narrow cuffs and twenty-one pearl buttons down the front, one for each step of the staircase at the Café de Paris. It was a little young for luncheon at the Ritz with a Hollywood film star, but the hat, she hoped, lent her a touch of maturity. She knew its unusual shape suited her, made her narrow, triangular face seem intriguing rather than childish.

'Oh, what we all do. Go to balls, and theatre parties, and supper parties, and photo sittings. And bazaars.'

'And do you feel very different, now you have Come Out?'

Alys hesitated a moment. Being presented at Court had involved mostly standing, waiting and looking decorative – trivial female accomplishments, but difficult all the same.

'Just a little.' The ability to evade direct questions was another of the accomplishments a débutante needed to acquire.

'Don't change, Alys. You are perfect as you are.'

Despite herself, Alys blushed. She had been cited as one of the season's beauties in Lady Lygon's column, she had received her quota of pleas from society photographers and compliments from elderly men at after-theatre receptions. But it was only now, with Hugo, that she found herself longing, suddenly and impossibly, not for beauty itself but for something else, a sort of certainty, an inner conviction that someone, somewhere, saw her for what she was and found that good.

Could that, possibly, be what Hugo had meant? Alys stared at his face, trying to read his expression.

If anyone was locked into the prison of his own good looks it was Hugo. Now, at the age of twenty-five, he was beautiful enough to make her eyes blur. This afternoon he was wearing informal clothes, a loosely-cut pearl grey lounge suit and soft white piqué shirt, and against the dove grey and pearl white his skin glowed as if it had been polished. Without needing to look around the restaurant, Alys knew that at least half of the diners would be at this moment glancing furtively in Hugo's direction. He had that effect.

'What is it like, acting in moving pictures? Is it very glamorous?'

'Not in the least,' said Hugo. 'It is mostly fittings, and standing for hours under very hot lights, and waiting to be told what to do.'

'Really?' The parallel struck Alys almost instantly. That was just how she spent most of her waking hours too.

'I'm afraid so. I hope I have not disappointed you?'

'Not at all.' Alys laid down her silver fork. It was only now that she realized how tightly she'd been holding it.

'You're not hungry?'

'It's not that.'

'What is it, then?'

Alys took a deep breath. Seeing Hugo again for the first time since he had left for Hollywood three years ago had made her anxious enough to forget all about what was to happen this afternoon, but now, as she found her true self again in his company, apprehension rushed in afresh.

'Come on, what is it? You can tell Uncle Hugo.'

Alys almost smiled; no one, looking at Hugo, extraordinarily youthful despite his elegance, would ever have taken him for an uncle.

'I'm nervous.' It was strange; just to say those words to Hugo eased her anxiety a little. The rapport between them was intact, as if they had seen each other only yesterday.

'What about? Surely not me?' The expression in Hugo's eyes was so comical that Alys could not bring herself to tell him that she had in fact been nervous about this luncheon, all the way through this morning and half of yesterday too; in fact, right up to this moment.

'No. It's this afternoon. I have an appointment.'

'With a white slaver?' Hugo sighed in mock regret. 'I'm sorry I can't compete. I know those pashas find blondes irresistible.'

'No.' Alys's lips twitched into a reluctant smile. 'That would be easy by comparison.'

'Where, then?'

'A charity matinée.'

'How frightful.' Hugo's tone was suitably sympathetic. 'Sitting through one of those is enough to give anyone a migraine. Perhaps you should succumb to one a little in advance?'

Alys twisted the napkin in her lap. 'I don't think that would do. You see, I'm not just going to it, the matinée I mean, I'm in it. I'm supposed to entertain the audience during the interval.'

'Not...' Hugo mouthed the word across the table as if it had been the name of some dreadful disease, hushing the first half and stressing the last – 'not the p-i-a-n-o-forte?'

Alys nodded. 'I'm afraid so.'

'Oh dear.' Once again, Alys was relieved that Hugo understood immediately. 'What happened?'

'I'm not quite sure. All the other girls were doing something, and I was on the Committee, and...' Alys's voice tailed away.

'You couldn't say no?'

Alys nodded dumbly.

Hugo thought for a moment.

'Would it help at all if I were there? The ultimate sacrifice, and all that?'

Alys laughed, then shook her head once more. 'That would be lovely, but it wouldn't make any difference. If you see what I mean.'

'How long have you got?'

'Till four o'clock. Maybe a bit longer, if I miss the first half.'

'And you've practised – no, silly question. Of course you've practised.'

'There's such a difference, you see, between practising . . .'

'And performing.' Hugo frowned. 'Believe me, I know.'

'A gap.' Alys felt she was closer to explaining the gap than she had ever been even to herself.

'Into which one can fall and never be seen again,' said Hugo, with instant, miraculous understanding. 'But we must not let that happen to you. Here.' He pushed aside his plate and rose, extending his hand. 'Take me to the nearest piano. This is an emergency.'

As Alys let herself and Hugo into the hall of number 7 half an hour later she felt rather like a criminal. Her mother wouldn't approve of her seeing Hugo, because he was a Lavery, but that wasn't the whole reason. Alys didn't want a name given to what she felt about Hugo. Their relationship was different; no one else would understand that difference, least of all her supremely practical mother. Hugo was the only person Alys had ever met who demanded of her nothing but that she be herself.

It almost seemed possible to Alys now, as they went up the stairs together, treading quietly even though Mara would be out till six o'clock and there was no one else in the house, that one day she might actually be able to play for Hugo, not just the music she practised, those stilted, tinny sounds with which she was only too familiar, but the music she heard in her head.

299

'So this is the famous house,' said Hugo. He seemed excited; his eyes were alight.

'Famous?' Alys was perplexed.

'Of course – the Devil's Door,' said Hugo. 'All the Eton boys talked of nothing else. I expect you were too young to notice, but those parties were a legend. Your mother too.'

'Oh.' Alys hadn't thought of her mother in that light before. Perpetually fascinating as Mara was to her, she hadn't realized she might have the same effect on people who'd never even met her. Now, she saw her mother suddenly as Diana, goddess of the moon, or an Ancient Greek priestess, or one of those strange birds with metal feathers that dined off shipwrecked sailors. It was true, there was something legendary about Mara, as if she came from a much older world, where people were less polite.

Alys opened the door to her room on the top floor rather dreading that Hugo might be disappointed. The room was on the small side, and crowded with furniture – wardrobe, washstand, dresser, bed – plus, of course, the piano, but all the same it seemed somehow bare. The effort of ferrying her favourite toys from Gifford's Oak and back again had prevented Alys from acquiring as many as she might have done. Somewhere along the line she'd grown out of the habit of possessions. Now, as she perceived the room through Hugo's eyes, she was a little ashamed of its bareness, as if he'd looked inside her soul and found it empty.

'You're like me,' said Hugo suddenly. 'You have no history.' It was very quiet up here at the top of the house, and in the early summer afternoon even the pigeons which usually rattled across the rooftiles outside had fallen into silence. Hugo's voice sounded loud, even though he spoke hardly above an undertone. Carefully, Alys removed her coolie hat and laid it on the dresser. The pin crackled as she re-inserted it in the straw.

'You're so neat,' Hugo said, in a soft, surprised tone. 'It's astonishing how neat you are. Most girls are so – messy.'

'Are they?' Returning his gaze, Alys felt a pang of envy for all the

300

girls he must know, while simultaneously resolving that she would be neat for ever. 'My piano teacher says neatness is my problem. She says I should forget myself, that my playing will never come right until I stop trying so hard.'

'Counsels of perfection,' said Hugo. 'I like you neat.' He turned to survey the piano. 'It looks like an instrument of torture to me,' he said. 'Big enough for a rack, fiddly enough for a thumbscrew.'

He lifted the lid, ran his finger idly across the keys. At the sound Alys felt the familiar mixture of dread and longing. 'Black and white,' said Hugo musingly. 'A bit fierce, that. No room for compromise.' He bent his head, and a lock of dark hair fell over his forehead. 'What do you say, Alys – shall we invent a grey piano?' He glanced up sidelong and Alys had a sudden vision of them both in the room, the gentle, abstract tinkle of music linking them, he so dark, she so light, like the piano keys.

The thought clearly occurred to Hugo in the same moment. 'Alys,' he said, pressing the ivory. 'Hugo,' as he ran his fingers over the ebony, a haunting, Celtic-sounding scale. Then, in a great crashing discord he brought both hands down forcefully at once. 'The world!' he shouted, above the booming, pulsing cacophony. Alys jumped with shock; never in her room had there ever been such a loud noise; never would she have dared to treat the piano with such exuberance.

'Come on!' shouted Hugo. He was thumping away now with a vengeance; every piece of furniture in the room seemed to vibrate. Alys began to laugh, but there was so much noise that she could not hear herself. 'You take the bass,' shouted Hugo, 'and I'll take the treble!'

Alys obeyed, and the sound of four hands on the keyboard, with no concern for harmony or rhythm, was like the Last Trump. Out of the corner of her eye Alys could see Hugo's hands flashing over the keys beside hers. He played with his whole body, like a child or a lunatic, hair tossing, head thrown back. Alys felt herself caught up in his frenzy, borne along in a tide of pure racket.

'Torture the torture machine!' cried Hugo. 'Slay the mechanical zebra!'

Alys, dizzied, deafened, threw herself at the keys with relish. How often had she suffered up here in her room, hour after hour, her own will pitted against the monstrous, mechanical implacability of the piano. It was time for revenge – no, revenge was too petty a word. It was time for vengeance. She thumped and banged and crashed and thundered like the wrath of God, and all around her she heard the walls of Jericho tumbling down.

At last Alys could do no more. Breathless and giddy, she was hardly aware of Hugo taking her hand and turning her away. Silence boomed like a thunderclap. Hugo's face was smooth and urbane as slowly, gracefully, he bowed to an imaginary audience.

'Thank you, thank you.' Hugo smiled to left and right, shaking his head modestly at imagined applause. 'You are too kind.' Then he turned again, stepped back, presenting Alys to the invisible spectators with a splendid gesture that conveyed deference and condescension at once. Alys, flushed, her heart drumming, found herself bowing as if pulled by strings. Hugo advanced once more. He embraced her, kissed her upon both cheeks, stepped back to admire her, shook his head, kissed her once more, presented her with an imaginary bunch of flowers. Then, taking her hand once more, head up to gather in the last of the applause, he led her off-stage.

The bed, invisible at knee-level, cut Hugo off abruptly. Together, laughing, breathless, he and Alys collapsed onto it one after the other.

'No harm done,' said Hugo, when he had recovered his breath. 'We're off-stage now. No one cares what happens in the wings.'

Alys had fallen across him, half in and half out of his arms. He adjusted her position gently. She was struck by how carefully he handled her, quite unlike the piano. It was lucky that he did so, because one of her twenty-one Café de Paris buttons had become entangled in the buttons of his jacket.

'Careful,' said Hugo.

'Let me,' said Alys, feeling responsible. It was quite unnecessary to possess so many buttons, just asking for trouble.

'I'd rather you didn't,' said Hugo quietly. There was a sort of sadness in his voice which took Alys aback. 'I'd rather stay here with you, like this. Just for a bit. If that's all right with you.'

Something happened inside Alys at that moment, a sort of unclenching, as if something she had been holding very tight in her fist to prevent it being lost or stolen had been quietly released. She lay very still, half in and half out of Hugo's arms, and became aware of the movement of his chest as he breathed in and out, the clean soft smell of his jacket, the faint tang of soap and warm skin. His chin was against her head and she could feel his breath ruffling her hair. He did not move or speak, and for a long, timeless moment Alys felt as if she were floating, as if all the world beneath her and above her had disappeared.

'Tell me,' she said, and it was as if someone else's voice had spoken. 'Tell me now about the letter.'

'You're not old enough,' Hugo replied automatically, and even though his lips touched her hair as he spoke he sounded a thousand miles away. Alys's heart contracted with a new sort of pain. The gap yawned wide, but she fought it.

'I shall be eighteen in August,' she said. 'I am quite grown-up, I promise. I must be. I have Come Out.'

'That's true,' Hugo said, with a hint of surprise. Alys was so close to him she felt she could almost hear him thinking. He wanted to tell her, she could sense it. He wanted to have it told.

'Tell me,' Alys said. And then, with a cleverness she hadn't known she possessed: 'It will be neater.'

Hugo sighed. 'Very well,' he said at last. 'But you must promise to lie quite still. I shall not tell you if you wriggle.'

'I shall lie still,' Alys answered, though deep inside her a tremor began. She fastened her fingers round the two buttons which entwined their clothes. If she concentrated on the two buttons perhaps the tremor would go away.

'As you know, the letter was from my mother.'

'Even though she is dead,' whispered Alys, still awed by this communication beyond the grave.

'Yes.' There was something dead in Hugo's voice as he spoke. 'She died thirteen years ago. But two days before she died, she wrote me a letter and arranged with a solicitor to forward it to me when I was eighteen.' There was a long pause, and Alys felt Hugo's arm tighten almost imperceptibly round her, then slacken again.

'Why not before?'

'She wanted me to be old enough to understand.'

'Oh. Like me.'

Hugo nodded. Now Alys felt a tremor of fear. Perhaps she didn't want to know what the letter had to say after all, perhaps it would be better never to know.

But it was too late now. She must eat up what she herself had placed upon her plate, like a good girl.

'In the letter,' Hugo said carefully, 'my mother told me that she loved me very much. That she would never have left me if she hadn't been ill, very ill. She had to write to me, she said, because there was a chance I might have inherited her illness.'

Fear lanced through Alys.

'I don't understand.' Hugo seemed so well, so full of life. 'Are you ill?'

He shook his head. 'No. But I might have been.'

Relief washed over Alys. 'Then everything's all right.'

'Yes.' But Hugo didn't sound as if that was so.

'What's the matter?'

'She died, you see.'

'I know. She drowned. Uncle William told me all about it. It was very sad, but it wasn't her fault. She'd only just learned how to swim, it was an accident.'

Slowly, like the beat of a drum, Hugo shook his head.

'That's what she wanted people to think. But it wasn't an accident at all. She drowned herself, because of the illness. She didn't say so, but I knew as soon as I read the letter. It's obvious. She'd already decided what she was going to do. Otherwise she wouldn't have written to me in the first place.'

'Oh.' Alys shivered. Her first thought was that her own mother would never have drowned herself, not for anyone or anything. And then, for a moment, floating above them in the summer light she seemed to see Hugo's mother, her hair streaming out behind her. Supposing, just supposing, at the very last minute, when she felt the cold water rushing into her lungs, Lady Lavery had decided she wanted to live after all, and called for help – only there was no one to hear.

Alys shivered. Poor Lady Lavery. Poor Hugo.

'What are you thinking?' Hugo asked her, his voice barely above a whisper.

'I am thinking,' answered Alys slowly, 'that maybe it would have been better if she hadn't told you.'

'I know. But I might have needed to know. She couldn't be sure.'

'Then she must have loved you very much.'

'I would rather she had stayed alive,' Hugo said. 'I was away at school, I didn't know what was going on, just that one day she was there and the next she was gone. All this time I knew she was dead, but I never really felt it. Until I read that letter. That was when she died for me. Do you understand?'

Alys nodded without words.

'I love you, Hugo,' she said.

After Alys had spoken there was such a long silence that she wondered if perhaps she had said the words only in her mind. It did not matter. She felt quite peaceful having said them to herself; it did not make them any less true.

Hugo sighed. 'And I love you.' He sounded almost sad. He turned round sideways, edged down until his face was opposite hers. Gently he cupped her face in his hands, one either side. It was not like being touched by anyone else. His eyes, the brown of them so

305

dark it was almost purple, were inches from her own. Lying down, he looked even younger.

'Never grow up, Alys,' he said softly. 'Stay as you are.'

'I'll try,' she answered. 'I'm so glad you love me back.'

'How could I not?' he whispered. 'It's like the *Jungle Book*. "We are of one blood, you and I."'

Alys recognized the moment as the one to which her entire life had been leading. She closed her eyes for a second, perfectly happy.

Then she remembered the piano.

'Oh Hugo!' It was already half past three, and even Hugo couldn't come up with something that would change her from one kind of person into another in under an hour. 'What on earth am I going to do?'

'There has been a slight change in the programme for the interval,' announced the girl in spangles in a high and rather nervous voice to the overheated audience. 'Instead of the billed piano recitation of J.S. Bach's well-known air from Cantata 68, "My Heart Ever Faithful", there will be a double act featuring a new theatrical partnership – um – Halys 'n' 'Ugo.'

From behind the curtain, to a random spattering of applause, appeared two figures dressed like New York down-and-outs, one a girl, tall, slender and very fair, the other a man well-grimed about the face and much padded out round the waist. He came out haranguing his partner in an accent straight from the Lower East Side, and carrying a battered box which he set down centre stage. Together the two pushed the waiting piano and stool away into the wings, the man keeping up a running commentary all the while. 'Modern music, that's what we want. Modern music!' He cupped a hand round his ear and leaned suggestively towards the audience. 'What do we want?'

Someone tittered.

'Modern music!' bellowed the man. 'Am I right, or am I right?'

With a flourish, a dramatic shooting back of non-existent cuffs which sent the first ripple of genuine laughter round the audience, the man opened the mysterious box to reveal a gramophone. He took out a phonograph record from inside his tattered coat and placed it reverently on the turntable. His partner stood by meanwhile, drooping like wet stockinette on a line.

The first strains of Irving Berlin's 'He Ain't Got Rhythm' galvanized the man into immediate movement. Leaping and twirling, he took hold of his partner as if she had been a large doll and spun her round into the music. He whirled her, he swung her, he danced behind and before and over her; throughout she remained docile but unmoved. The contrast between the two shabby figures was hilarious – he portly and perspiring, she limp and lank; he the demon puppetmaster, she his marionette, floppy as rag. When, after a particularly violent manoeuvre, the girl's hat fell off, she made no effort to retrieve it but simply reached forward lackadaisically to help herself to his instead.

By the end of the record the audience were clapping and cheering in time. As 'Ugo and Halys took their bows the loudest cheers were for Halys, still gloomily unmoved. She sidled off in mid-curtain call and had to be retrieved by 'Ugo, with voluble apologies. 'Never says a word, does Halys,' he explained. 'But that girl swings like a gate!' They exited, hand-in-hand, to a chorus of encores.

Alys found herself backstage, dazed, dazzled, amazed and most of all relieved. It was over, and there had been no piano. The torture machine had been for once outwitted. No one had seemed even to miss it.

And she, Alys, had succeeded in making complete strangers laugh. She, who had always dreaded making a fool of herself, had never dreamed how good that could feel. And to accomplish this miracle she had not had to take lessons beforehand; she had not had to study for years; she had simply followed Hugo onto the stage, and he had decided that the audience should laugh, and they had laughed.

'How can I ever thank you enough, Hugo?' she whispered to him as they stood side by side in the dusty wings, trying to catch their breath, unwilling to turn their backs on the brightly lit scene of their impromptu triumph.

'Just don't tell my agent I was ever here,' he answered, still laughing, the Hugo she knew bizarrely visible through the disguise which had made him unrecognizable to her on stage. How had he managed to transform himself, instantly, into what people wanted him to be, something they would like?

'And one other thing.' Hugo's grasp tightened on her hand. To Alys's surprise she felt him trembling. He had seemed nerveless on stage, but perhaps it was afterwards he suffered. 'Would you like to marry me? One day, when you are old enough? With your mother's permission, if we can persuade her?'

'Marry you?' Alys felt a smile lift inside her, wide and bright, as if her face had turned into that of another person altogether, the one she had wanted to be. 'You mean we could be together all the time? Not just an afternoon?'

'Oh yes,' Hugo said. 'That's what married people do. Day and night.'

'Day and night,' Alys echoed. She could hardly believe it, and yet it was so simple. An end to loneliness.

'Night and day.' Hugo lifted his other hand, grimed with Leichner's No.12, and lightly touched her cheek. 'Black and white.'

'Hugo and Alys,' she said, remembering the piano.

'Halys 'n' 'Ugo,' he corrected her. 'I can see it in lights.'

'Do you promise?' she asked, suddenly fearful, as cast for the next item on the programme bundled past them, pushing her back into the shadows. It would be so easy for him, with so many people to meet and places to go, to forget a single afternoon. 'You won't marry someone else while I'm waiting?'

'Lovely Alys . . .' His voice was soft, only for her. 'I shall never marry anyone else, I promise. Outcasts' honour.'

16 *Red Poppy of the Rock*

The doorbell rang, and Alys froze, her heart in her mouth. She was supposed to be in Florence, with Carelia.

The ring came again, peremptory, and Alys remembered the drawing-room windows. She'd opened them just a crack, because of the heat. It had seemed safe, with her mother and the Duke abroad. But perhaps her mother had sent someone to check the house, just in case? Now that betraying gap would give away the fact that the house was occupied.

And Alys had only a few hours before her train left King's Cross for a quite different destination.

She opened the door with excuses at the ready. On the step stood a tall man who was clearly as surprised to see her as she was to see him.

For a long time they stared at each other. The man seemed quite old to Alys; his face was set, his golden-brown eyes guarded, as if he had travelled a long way and seen too much to remember. Everything about him, his height, his clothes, his way of standing, was larger than life. He was not, as Hugo would have it, at all neat. He looked somehow as if he should have been wearing a cloak.

'You must be Alys,' the man said at last, and at the sound of his voice, a golden-brown, larger than life voice, Alys felt a stir of recognition.

'Why, Mr de Morgan,' she said, and relief poured through her as she realized she hadn't been found out after all. This was no minion of her mother's sent to check up on her; Mr de Morgan lived in America. She remembered him vaguely from her childhood.

'I'm afraid my mother is not in at the moment,' Alys said. 'She has gone to Berlin. As a special guest of the German government,' she added, because it sounded rather grand, and there was no need to let on that the invitation had really been for the Duke, who would go anywhere as long as someone else paid the bill.

It was only a moment before Alys realized her mistake.

'Surely your mother has not left you here alone?' Mr de Morgan's lips tightened in disapproval. Alys felt momentarily disloyal to her mother, but there was no helping it.

'My mother and I understand each other,' she answered airily. 'I'm quite capable of looking after myself.'

And then, having trapped herself into this proclamation of independence, Alys had to invite him in. The last thing she wanted was for Mr de Morgan to raise the alarm, or, even worse, elect himself her protector, which he looked at the moment only too inclined to do.

'In any case, I shan't be staying in Town,' Alys improvised hastily. 'I've been invited to the country for the rest of August.'

That would explain her cases waiting on the first-floor landing; she felt quite proud of her quick thinking.

In the drawing-room, stripped down in preparation for the arrival of the South American widow who had rented number 7 for the whole of August, Alys did her best to behave as if entertaining a man alone at home was part of her normal routine. Fortunately Mr de Morgan refused a drink, for her mother had locked up the contents of the cocktail cabinet and to have ferreted about with keys would have looked very suspicious.

'What brings you to London, Mr de Morgan?' she asked. He looked even bigger in the drawing-room than he had in the doorway; she wished he would not stare so much. He was an artist, she recalled; perhaps that was why he stared.

'London is not my destination,' he replied. 'I am on my way to Spain.'

'For a holiday?'

'No, not exactly.'

Alys flushed with embarrassment. Of course, the Spanish War. If she hadn't been so preoccupied herself these past few days she would have remembered. It had broken out only a few weeks ago, a mad sort of war between Communists and Fascists.

'Isn't that rather dangerous?' Alys had already learned, from hours of sitting amongst the smilax and wired roses of her first London season, that men of all ages loved to talk about dangers, past and future. It made them feel important.

But Mr de Morgan didn't answer her question directly, only smiled.

'Possibly. But then it can be dangerous anywhere.' He was looking round the room now as if he was reliving something, or attempting to memorize it so that he could paint it at a later date. 'Sometimes it is more dangerous to stay away.'

Thinking of Hugo, as she always did now, ever since that day two months ago which had changed her whole life, Alys had a flash of insight. Perhaps, she thought, Mr de Morgan has come to say goodbye to my mother, in case he is killed in Spain. Suddenly she warmed to him, even though he was so old, maybe even forty.

'Would you like to leave my mother a message? You could write something. I'm sure she would be glad to hear from you.'

'I don't think so,' Mr de Morgan replied, and Alys could not be sure which part of her question he was answering. 'Perhaps you would simply tell her that I called.'

'Of course.' Alys stood up. She had left her mother a letter in any case; it would be a simple matter to add a few words about Mr de Morgan.

'I knew you when you were a little girl,' Mr de Morgan said abruptly. 'You have changed a great deal since then.'

'Have I?' Alys smiled a social smile. 'For the better, I hope?'

'I hope so too,' answered Mr de Morgan gravely, and Alys, after warming to him, felt a stab of annoyance. His going off to die for some other country's cause, whatever that was, didn't entitle him to be rude.

And yet there was something about Mr de Morgan, his size maybe, or his way of looking at her as if he really saw her, as if it mattered to him that he should see her truly, that made Alys suddenly, ridiculously, want to fling herself on his broad chest and confess to him her plans. It would be such a comfort to know that someone understood; that there would be someone, if it all went terribly wrong, to whom she could return without having to explain.

But there was no one like that, and Alys knew that if she told Mr de Morgan he would feel either obligated or embarrassed. He was a friend of her mother's after all, or had been, even though, Alys recalled, he had always seemed a little apart, as if there was some place inside him that her mother hadn't been able to make her own. So, in a way, she and Mr de Morgan were in the same boat; rebels against her mother's empire.

'Goodbye then,' Alys said, and extended her hand. He took it, and seemed about to say something, frowning, but then changed his mind. His hand was very warm. Alys tried to assume an adult tone. 'I hope you will return safely from Spain.'

'It does not matter,' he said. 'As one gets older ...' He didn't complete the sentence. 'But you, you are at the beginning.' Then, as he released her hand, leaving her feeling oddly bereft, he said a curious thing. 'Begin well.'

It was only as the front door closed behind her visitor that Alys realized she hadn't asked him on which side of the war in Spain he intended to fight. It would have been polite, she supposed, to have inquired, but then she wouldn't have understood the answer.

And there was no time left to worry about the missed opportunity. On the landing, draped carefully over her travelling cases,

312

lay the silver lamé trenchcoat, only eight and a half guineas at Fenwicks, which represented the beginning of her new life.

'You'll be for Glencurry, Miss.' Softly spoken, it was a statement, not a question. Alys barely had time to nod in surprised assent before the porter picked up her bags and began to escort her out of the station.

Alys felt a mixture of relief, guilt and nervousness as the porter loaded her baggage into the boot of a pale grey Daimler. The uniformed chauffeur behind the wheel gave her no more than a single discreet glance, taking in her silver trenchcoat as if it were completely usual for a Scottish August; as if she was indeed an expected guest.

But Alys knew that was impossible. No one except Carelia had been forewarned of her plans, and Carelia was sworn to secrecy. Perhaps, then, Alys had been mistaken for someone else? In which case it would hardly be fair to take advantage of this heaven-sent transport, even though no one else had got out of the train. She leaned forward a little hesitantly. 'It is very kind of you to collect me . . .'

'Tomkins, Miss,' supplied the chauffeur obligingly as he swung the purring car smoothly down the narrow road leading away from the station. 'It's no trouble. Sir Quintin has us meet every London train. Just in case.'

'Every train?' Alys was impressed.

A faint smile glimmered momentarily behind the chauffeur's moustache. 'There's only two a week, Miss. Wednesdays and Fridays. The rest of the trains go straight through to Inverness.'

'Oh.' Alys felt she should have known that, but she wasn't used to planning journeys on her own.

'Is it a big party?' she asked. It was Carelia who had found out all the details – such as they were, for staying in the country was no longer the formal business it used to be. Apparently, the annual Lavery house party was very much a spontaneous, casual affair. Sir

Quintin simply laid on a house, a different one each year, staff, an ample supply of Gin Fizz and, as Alys now realized, transport from the station.

'But how did you know,' asked Alys, emboldened by the chauffeur's friendliness, 'How did you know that I was one of the guests?'

'I always know the young ladies from London, Miss, by what they're wearing,' said Tomkins, and again his lips twitched. 'The young men, too. Though it's sometimes hard to tell t'other from which, nowadays.'

That was true, Alys reflected. Garbo had inspired modern women to wear trousers and trenchcoats and berets, while young men peacocked in silk pyjamas. It was only the fashion, but out here it must look a bit outlandish. She could have wished, herself, that her silver coat didn't look quite so bright. She'd forgotten how much more light there was in the country.

The drive was long and winding, and after half an hour, during which the road ahead narrowed more and more, Alys felt herself becoming disorientated. Her wristwatch stated one time, the scene outside another. She'd never travelled so far north before, never seen light fade so slowly from an evening sky. The whole landscape took on tones of pearly blue, and yet the sky kept its brightness, clear as a mirror. Perhaps, she thought, it never becomes quite dark here at this time of year.

The persistent daylight was unnerving. During the past week of planning and dreaming, Alys had always pictured herself arriving in comfortable darkness, not this strange, glowing twilight, luminous as radium.

But as soon as she saw Hugo she would feel all right, she knew that. Everything would be all right just as soon as she saw Hugo.

Quintin tapped the pipe, then inhaled deeply. Such a soft, sweet, intelligent smell. Always faithful, always the same.

He felt laughter balloon slowly inside him, silent and invisible. If they only knew, the lads and lasses, if they only realized the size of the parody they presently inhabited, the enormous, empty metaphor which he had invented for their delectation, a fisherman floating out his most elegantly beaded lure.

Here, in August of 1936, he had recreated an Edwardian summer retreat. In those far-off days before the First War no gentleman would ever have dreamed of renting someone else's country house for the summer, any more than he would have worn another man's shoes. But no one, now, sneered at new money. It was enough every year for Quintin to hire an Italian chef, supply a tennis court and despatch a few dozen return railway tickets in order to fill his summer with gilded youth.

He inhaled again from the narrow pipe. Shimmering up from the past came Eton days; all the boys in their golden down, sweet as Victoria plums upon the tree. Heroes, hoisted shoulder-high to their Houses; Bloods and semi-Bloods at evening Parade, arm-in-arm to the strains of the barrel-organ; big boys in tails and buttoned boots; little ones, the Ducks and P.B.s, pert and pink in knitted ties and silk socks.

How Quintin remembered it; the secret trading of Jobies; the splendid vision of the Castle from the train; the endless lushing of top hats; the panelling in the Upper School, with its famous family names carved out like claims in a goldfield.

Not that there had been much gold in Quintin's House, sited between the Old Cemetery and Wise's horseyard. Against his will Quintin recalled the stink of gas on the leadened stairs, the stained baths stacked on the tables at night, the pallid girls from the Clewer home for fallen damsels who scrubbed the steps.

His memory prospected further. Once more he crouched in the cold and dark under the fagmaster's bed so that he could answer for him when the housemaster made his round; marched to the Old Queen at Windsor, for even Her Majesty bowed to Eton men; dived for freshwater mussels off Athens, while a hundred naked boys drowsed among the cockchafers. The rhythms of that time had stayed with him: Long Leave, Short Leave, Lords Leave, Bisley Leave, Henley Leave; only once, at the beginning of the Boer War, an aberration in the mighty systole and diastole – special War Leave, for boys to say goodbye to their fathers.

Fathers and sons. A coil of bitterness that no smoke could sweeten unleashed itself deep in Quintin's mind. Over the years he and his heir had achieved, not an armistice exactly, but an armed truce. They had become useful to each other. Hugo had soon realized that it was better for him to sow his wild oats in England, away from the anxious eye of his studio. Every summer Quintin provided a suitable setting, and each year young men responded in droves to the siren song of money, while Hugo – even the mere mention of his name, it seemed nowadays – brought girls, in quantity and variety, a cavalcade of girls hungry for experience and glamour and contact with that Holy Grail, that modern unicorn, the movie star. Hugo, even if he had so desired, could not possibly have satisfied them all.

Ah, the girls. They prided themselves so on being hard-boiled, apparently unaware how much easier it was to peel an egg of its shell in that condition.

Quintin glanced at his watch. Tomkins would have delivered the next consignment by now. He smiled to himself, pushed aside the spirit lamp and rose.

The house before which the car drew up at last wasn't quite what Alys had expected. Clearly designed more to keep out bad weather than for appearances, it looked like nothing so much as a large granite box. Alys chided herself for her secret disappointment; if she had wanted palaces, she should have gone with Carelia to Florence.

At second glance the house revealed more subtle assets; a stretch of well-maintained woodland sheltering it to north and east, newly painted white windows and doors, covered garaging for half a dozen cars, a green baize croquet lawn in front and a tennis court adjoining. The steps to the front door were freshly swept, the drive newly gravelled, the stone urns on either side of the front door frilled with geraniums.

Even so, Alys felt a tremor of unease as Tomkins, after depositing her and her case at the front door, eased the Daimler silently away to the garage. It was getting late, and there was no other human habitation within miles. A stiff little evening breeze pressed the collar of Alys's silver trenchcoat against her neck.

She shivered. The house seemed much bigger than it had done from the road. It was set on a slight elevation, and now, as she looked up, hoping that no one had observed her solitary, unannounced arrival, each gleaming window reflected back the evening sky with perfect blankness, as if behind lay nothing but air. Alys was relieved when the door opened to her ring on a perfectly ordinary, sensible maid, the kind that everybody looked for nowadays but very rarely found.

The hall into which Alys was ushered was warm and quiet and comfortable, rather like the lobby of a very good hotel. There were no old-house creakings or whistlings to be heard, no rebellious currents of air coiling round the ankles, just the smell of flowers, beeswax and newly laid carpet.

'I'm looking for Mr Lavery,' said Alys.

'Would that be Mr Hugo Lavery, Miss?' asked the maid politely and Alys felt herself blush.

'Yes, please.'

'There's a party of young people in the drawing-room, Miss, and some young gentlemen playing billiards. I'm not sure about Mr Hugo, but I saw him come in from tennis only a moment ago, and he hasn't yet gone up to change.'

'Thank you.' Now she had come so close at last Alys felt her heart beating irregularly. It felt odd to hear Hugo's name on someone else's lips; at home, she had had to train herself never to mention him. Somehow, that had made her feel that Hugo was her secret, that only she knew of his existence. Of course she'd known with her mind that he had his separate life, but now the thought of him playing tennis, simply passing the time away, gave her an odd feeling almost of bereavement.

'Shall I send someone to fetch him for you, miss?' offered the maid, and Alys shook her head immediately. She didn't want to meet Hugo again through a third party; she had so much to tell him, so much that only he should hear. She would find him herself.

'Your luggage will be in the Blue Room, miss,' said the maid, but Alys hardly heard her. It did not matter what happened to her cases; nothing mattered except making her way as quickly as she could towards Hugo.

The house was larger even than it had seemed from the outside, stretching back far deeper than it was wide. But unlike the other country houses Alys had known, the degree of luxury did not diminish the further back one went from the front door. As Alys advanced, she was amazed by a continuing glory of fresh paintwork, discreet lighting, trimly fitting doors, carpet so thick and soft that her footsteps made no sound.

From the open door of the drawing-room came a murmur of desultory voices, but none of them was Hugo's. Further on, as the maid had promised, lay the billiard-room, thick with cigarette smoke and laughter, where a mixed party was engaged in a raucous game. None of the players was Hugo, and Alys was glad. She didn't want her reunion with Hugo to take place in a billiard-room.

She stole further down the passage. From somewhere ahead came the faint sound of a piano.

Alys halted, every nerve in her body plucked into attention. She had never heard the instrument played more beautifully, with such a sweet, autumnal edge of melancholy. There was no tension, no bravura technique in the playing; the notes slipped by seamlessly one after the other, melting one into the other like globules of mercury. This is how the piano should be heard, Alys thought instantly; from afar, out of sight, the sound of silence singing to itself.

Even as she listened, Alys knew that she had found Hugo.

Turn after turn through the maze of corridors she followed the delicate thread of sound, willing it not to stop before she reached him. Gradually the sound become louder, clearer, a trickle of notes building into a melodious flow. At last, right at the back of the house, Alys reached the fountainhead, welling from behind a door of glossy green leather studded with brass. As she touched the door it opened silently as a flower and music flooded out to embrace her.

Alys halted, momentarily transfixed with pleasure.

Ahead of her the room was dim. None of the many lamps had been turned on, rendering the interior monochrome, but in the light from the uncurtained sky Alys could see two figures dressed in white. One was seated at the piano, the other standing leaning against its side. Her heart recognized the standing figure long before her eyes made out his face. His cheeks were flushed, his dampened hair spilled over his forehead. He was smiling. Even as he smiled, the music ceased, as if it had performed its duty by guiding Alys home, to the warm, dim centre of the maze.

The pianist, as if recognizing the importance of the moment, remained quite silent, head bent, as the last reverberations pulsed away. A pang of jealousy gripped Alys ferociously around the heart and then, laughing at herself, she realized that it was not, as she'd first thought, a slender, golden-haired girl whom she'd just heard play so enchantingly, but a young man. Now, without speaking, Hugo laid one hand on the shoulder of his friend and slid gracefully into place beside him on the piano bench.

They are going to play a duet, Alys thought. How lovely.

As she watched, the two heads, gold and black, turned in perfect synchrony to face each other. Hugo moved, a slow, deliberate movement, using the hand still resting on his friend's shoulder to pull him closer. With the other hand he cupped the young man's face. For a confused moment Alys wondered what Hugo was going to do, and then, as the two heads moved together, gold melting into black, there was no room left in her mind for confusion.

Shock exploded silently, turning the borders of Alys's vision black. She heard nothing, saw nothing, and yet she felt the burning pressure of Hugo's hand as if it were her own cheek that he was turning towards his mouth, felt his mouth on hers, felt herself split under that pressure into a thousand screaming, voiceless pieces. They are kissing each other, she thought. They are kissing, and it is I who am ashamed.

For it was beautiful, the kissing. Even as pain sheared through her Alys could recognize the beauty of the two strong male throats intertwining in rapturous equality, thrust to thrust, pulsing back and forth like drowned men in a tide; so sure, so knowing, so alive. It's like a game of tennis, she thought wildly. Or the piano played by ear. Never, she realized immediately, with a throb of mourning that was like dying, never would she be able to kiss anyone like that.

Not even Hugo.

Deep inside her yawned the gap, shadowy, triumphant.

For beside that kiss, everything else faded. It turned all her plans to nothing, a paper castle blown into the fire by the first opened door. Love. What was love? It meant nothing, beside the reality of that kiss. Beside that kiss she herself was nothing – pale, insignificant, a child frozen in the doorway of an adult's room.

A sigh came from somewhere, the rustle of clothing. The two white figures on the narrow bench struggled and wrestled against each other, as if they were trying to give birth to something, or kill something, or both. They had blended now into a single mass from which Alys could no longer disentangle Hugo.

Hugo, Alys cried out one last time in her mind, as if it were not too late, as if he might hear her. But already she knew that Hugo was gone. There would be no answer. The keys were mute, and there was no music left in all the world.

Mara entered the hall of number 7 to a violently ringing telephone. She ignored it, picking up instead the letters that had collected while she was away. After Berlin she and Nollie had spent the rest of their last trip together in an Austrian schloss belonging to one of

Nollie's many German relatives. Nollie had been bored and difficult; Mara felt she deserved a rest.

But the telephone thought otherwise. On the fifteenth ring Mara gave in. It was just possible it might be Alys calling from Italy, to see if she'd got home safely.

'Hello? Mara? Thank God.' It was Vi, her voice unusually high and breathless. 'I'm coming round. I shall be there in ten minutes.'

Vi rang off immediately. Mara stared at the receiver in her hand in puzzlement. What could be the matter? Hardly trouble at the school, since it was the holidays. Perhaps William had had an accident?

But if anything had happened to William Vi would never have left him. She and William were the most unfashionably devoted couple Mara had ever met.

Fortunately Alys couldn't be the cause of Vi's present anxiety. Mara had had one of Alys's skimpy but regular Florentine postcards only this morning.

Mara checked the letters in her hand. One from the South American widow; a quantity of bills; an invitation or two – and one, unstamped, in her daughter's writing. It must have been written a month ago, before Alys left for Florence.

Dear Mother,
   I am going away, to be with Hugo. We belong together.
Please don't try and make me come back.
   Best of love,
   Alys.
P.S. Mr de Morgan visited today on his way to Spain.

The letter was dated the 4th of August, the day Mara and Nollie had left for Berlin. Mara couldn't make sense of it. Hugo, Leo . . . What did it mean? And more important, where was Alys? The other side of the world? Upstairs in her room?

'Alys?' Mara called, lifted by a sudden hope – perhaps Alys had changed her mind about Florence, decided to spend a daring month in London by herself? – but there was no reply.

So where, in this convenient modern world that could whisk people thousands of miles away in a matter of hours, was Alys? Possible destinations flashed up in Mara's mind like probabilities on the White City totalisator. Italy, Spain, Hollywood? South America? Berlin?

Mara took a firm grip on her spiralling imagination. For a start, Alys wouldn't be in Spain. Neither Hugo nor Leo would have been so foolish as to take her there, in the middle of a ferocious civil war. And surely Carelia couldn't have been so irresponsible as to post those postcards in Alys's absence?

Mara opened the door to Vi in a daze. The two women stared at each other with blank faces, like strangers.

'You did this,' said Vi.

Mara shook her head. 'I had no idea.'

'That's what I mean. Look.' Vi thrust another letter at her. 'It's from Alys. I received it this morning.'

Dearest Aunt Vi,

I am writing this to say thank you for always looking after me. I shall not be coming back for a long time. Would you please tell my mother? I don't want to write to her. She has lied to me about something very important and I will never forgive her.

You are not to worry about me because I am being looked after by someone else now and I have everything I need. I have lots of clothes and everything I want and I don't mind in the least about anything.

I must go now because some people have come.

Love from

Alys.

P.S. Please tell Uncle William that I am keeping my promise not to smoke cigarettes.

The envelope bore a French stamp and postmark; the letter was undated. There was no return address.

'How could you? How could you let this happen?' Vi's eyes were full of tears. 'Why has Alys run away?'

'Eloped,' Mara corrected. She felt numb.

'But she's only eighteen!'

'True.' Mara felt as if her mind had turned to stone. She knew, but she couldn't accept what she knew.

'Who is this man she has run away with? Not Hugo, I know it can't be Hugo. I saw him in June, he would have told me, I know.'

'No, it isn't Hugo.' Now, too late, Mara wished it had been.

'Who then?'

Mara couldn't think how to begin. There was no gloss possible on this fact, no lie strong enough to change it. Her mind scrabbled for a toe-hold like a rat in a steel trap.

'Hugo's father.' She couldn't bring herself to say his name.

'Sir Quintin?' Vi looked almost relieved. 'That's not possible.'

Mara said nothing. She was thinking of *L'Aiglon Bleu*. Something in her face must have shown Vi she was telling the truth. Vi's face paled.

'Are you sure?'

Mara nodded. Her throat felt dry. She pointed wordlessly at the letter. There was only one lie she'd ever told her daughter, and that was about the identity of her father.

Only Quintin had known the truth. Only Quintin could have told Alys.

'But why? Alys hardly knew Sir Quintin! She didn't even like him!'

'I don't know.' Mara felt as if she'd seen Alys poised to jump off the top of a high building and had been unable to stop her. 'It makes no difference why.'

'Not to you, maybe,' Vi retorted. Her face suddenly flushed with anger. 'But then you've never cared about anyone but yourself!'

The words rang out in the small hallway. Mara was vaguely

aware of what Nollie called 'the aroma of burning bridges', but she didn't bother to defend herself. There was no point. Proving Vi wrong wouldn't change anything. Alys was gone.

Vi paused, out of breath. There was a brief, electric silence. Then Vi gathered herself almost visibly. 'I'm not going to stand for it. It's not too late. I'm going to bring her back.'

'Are you,' said Mara, without expression.

'Of course!' Vi stared at Mara in exasperation. 'What's wrong with you? You can't just leave her to trail back of her own accord, like a lost lamb! Why, he'll – he'll ruin her reputation!'

'Oh Vi.' The old-fashioned phrase, for some reason, brought tears to Mara's eyes.

If only it were so simple.

The burden of explanation weighed on her like a tombstone. She knew Quintin and his passion for ownership. How he had persuaded Alys she didn't know, might never know, but somehow he had managed it; the perfect revenge.

Mara waited an instant, as if life itself, forgiving, would intervene to put an end to this nightmare.

But nothing happened.

'Don't you see, Vi?' She spoke quietly. 'He's married her.'

Two months later, in Lucette's tiny Parisian sitting-room, Mara accepted a soot-black demi-tasse and prepared herself for the most important piece of diplomacy she'd ever attempted in her life. Mrs Bailey was Quintin's friend and ally; Mara must tread very, very carefully. Alys's whole future was at stake.

'Lucette, you look twenty years younger.' It was the simple truth, as well as the right thing to say. In the six years since Mara had last seen her former mistress on *L'Aiglon Bleu*, Lucette seemed to have shrunk but intensified, like a pressed flower.

'Thank you, my dear.' Lucette dealt her a glittering smile. 'If you promise to be discreet, I shall tell you all about it.' She caressed the large oatmeal-coloured cat draped across her lap. '*Mon petit lion*,' she explained, lifting the creature's sack-like body by his front legs so that his eyes squeezed up to slits. '*Il est beau, n'est-ce pas?*' Her face shone with pride.

Mara's heart sank. The Lucette she'd known had taken no interest in anything with four legs. If her former employer was subsiding gently into senility then the telegram she'd sent her could be meaningless.

But the pink, powdery face under the candy-floss hair shone with intelligence, and more, a sort of exhilaration. Lucette leaned forward conspiratorially.

'You must promise not to be shocked.'

'I promise.' Mara felt her teeth grate with tension on the gold rim of her cup; she set it down, afraid she might break it. Any sign of impatience would make Lucette suspicious.

'Very well then.' Lucette drew herself up in her chair with queenly dignity. 'I found out quite recently that I have a touch, just a touch, the smallest *soupçon*, of syphilis.'

Dregs caught in Mara's throat and she almost choked.

Lucette continued undeterred. 'In fact, I feel better than I've ever felt in my life. It's wonderful, Mara, like being twenty-two again. I cannot recommend it too highly. It has given me back my *joie de vivre*.' She stroked the cat on her lap and electricity crackled up the filmy sleeve of her négligé. 'When I saw Quintin last week he told me he'd had it too. He had himself cured in Buenos Aires, during the war. But I don't want to be cured.' She smiled. 'Now, I wouldn't be without it for the world.'

'Where is Quintin now?' Mara asked casually. Her nerves were strung so tight that she could almost hear them humming. 'You said you'd seen him.'

'Why, at the Ritz, of course.'

'Is he alone?'

Lucette smiled coquettishly, idly twirling the cat's tail.

'He is when he comes to visit me.' Then she relented. 'He and

Alys are married, isn't that extraordinary? And I wasn't even invited to the wedding. But then I have my own life to lead.'

Something in Lucette's tone made Mara look around her with new eyes. She'd thought when she arrived that there was something both familiar and odd about Lucette's Paris establishment. The deep pink velvet on the walls, the dim lights, closed doors, shuttered windows and, most particularly, the noiseless stairs.

Now it was suddenly, blindingly, clear. Her former mistress was running a brothel.

Mara studied the older woman in her powder and pigment, at once superbly disguised and superbly herself. Lucette had always glided along the fine line between gaiety and decay as imperturbably as a cat along a roof-ridge. Mara couldn't help but admire her for that. She'd stayed true to herself.

'Thank you, Lucette.' Mara meant it. There'd been no need for Lucette to help her, no inducement. It had been a kind of generosity.

'That's all right, my dear.' Lucette shot her a swift glance from under turquoise wrinkled lids. 'By the way, you owe me three months' rent.'

An hour later Mara entered the single revolving door of number 15 Place Vendôme. The plain bulbs picking out the words 'Hotel-Ritz-Restaurant' were not illuminated. The Ritz was a city that kept its secret gold very much to itself.

Fortunately, because there were no signs, Mara knew the way. She'd always chosen to enter the Ritz by the Vendôme side, because of the vitrines that lined the eighty-yard corridor leading to the bar, where Nollie had liked to wait for her. Perhaps Alys was there now, sitting over a Frank's Special, swinging her foot in that idle way she had. The possibility made Mara feel faint. She'd never in her life come closer to praying.

'*Madame?*' The reception clerk looked up inquiringly.

'I have come to see Lady Lavery. She is expecting me.'

Impossible, at the Ritz, to show the slightest sign of doubt. The hotel actively discouraged what it called disparagingly '*les gens extérieurs*'.

'*Je regrette, madame.* Lady Lavery left us some weeks ago.'

Mara's heart plummeted.

'And her husband?'

'Sir Quintin Lavery is still in residence, *madame*.'

'Then I shall see him instead.'

'*Je regrette, madame*, but he has left instructions that he is not under any circumstances to be disturbed.'

Mara took a deep breath. 'I am sure he will want to see me. All you have to do is ask him.'

The clerk hesitated, inspecting discreetly her travel-creased clothes and minimum of luggage. Mara realized she was in danger of being labelled a '*présence indésirable*'. She must act before doubt crystallized.

'And how are *Monsieur* Auzello's feet this year?' she inquired with the brightness of desperation. It was a gamble. Nollie had told her about the celebrated *Monsieur* Auzello, manager and undeclared monarch of the Ritz. A veteran of the Great War, his frost-bitten feet made it difficult for him to climb the Ritz's many stairs, but even so nothing that happened inside the hotel escaped him. 'Do give him my regards when you next see him.'

To Mara's relief the clerk's face cleared immediately.

'Who shall I say, *madame*?'

Mara told him, and he reached for the telephone. Within minutes Mara was ushered into the hall of the first-floor Vendôme suite, the most expensive accommodation in the whole of the hotel. Even with Nollie she'd never risen to these heights.

'*Madame la comtesse*,' the pageboy announced discreetly. As the perfectly-synchronized double doors closed behind her Mara tried not to think of a crocodile's jaws snapping seamlessly shut.

From the salon ahead of her came a rustling sound.

Cautiously Mara approached the open door. The room was dim,

and despite its vastness, very hot. Firelight caught the staring eyes of gilt sphinxes on the fireplace and furniture, summoned the stucco bas-reliefs of scenes from Napoleon's Egyptian campaign into flickering life. The effect was magnificent and somehow sinister; a Dream Room for an emperor.

There was a strange smell in the room, sweetish, like a sickroom. *'Ma chère comtesse.'*

Mara flinched. The hoarse whisper rasped like a knife on bone. In the dimness she couldn't at first make out where it had come from. Then she saw outlined against the fire a large white blur. Quintin was sitting in a high-backed chair. He didn't get up to greet her. As her vision adjusted to the dimness Mara realized why.

In the six years since she'd last seen him, Quintin had grown and multiplied beyond recognition. Now he was enormously, impossibly fat. Surplus flesh spilled over the edges of the chair, strained at the seams of his jacket, rolled over his collar. The knot of his tie was invisible beneath a waterfall of chins. Perched on his high chair he had the air of a grossly swollen, malevolent baby. The rustling sound she'd heard was his softly stertorous breathing.

But Quintin's eyes were the same: dark, opaque, with no apparent centre.

'Welcome to my sanctum, my dear Countess.' He wheezed a little but his diction was implacably clear. 'That is, if you are still a Countess?'

There was the lightest, most velvety suggestion of threat in his tone. Quintin had supplied her with her false identity six years ago. He could have no idea how little that mattered to her now.

'And to what do I owe the pleasure of this visit? Have you come to Paris to do a little shopping?'

Mara felt her smile stiffen on her face.

'Not this time.'

'To see me, then?'

The innuendo in Quintin's tone grated on Mara's nerves like the grit inside her travelling costume. If only it were possible to change the past like a suit of clothes.

'Partly.' She kept her tone light. 'I came to look for my daughter.'

'Alys?' Quintin spoke the name musingly, as if he barely remembered it. Mara felt a flash flood of anger that receded to leave her drained. She was grateful for the dimness of the room.

'And have you found her?' Quintin inquired.

'No.' Mara forced herself to speak in a level tone. 'I was hoping you might be able to tell me where she is.'

'Why?' Quintin's mouth, seeming even smaller and redder than Mara remembered, lapped round as it was with extra flesh, framed the word precisely.

'Because you are her husband,' said Mara quietly.

Quintin laughed then, a silent, close-lipped tremor which made the high chair creak.

'What difference does that make? Ask anyone. The husband is always the last to know.' He gazed vengefully into the fire. 'When Alys left, she didn't tell me where she was going. I know now, but I shan't tell you. Why should I? She's your daughter. You can find her on your own.'

Mara felt perspiration break out all over her body. No sound came from beyond the heavily curtained windows. It was as if they were a hundred miles underground.

When Quintin spoke again his tone was conversational.

'This is like old times, Mara.'

'Old times?' Mara had to force herself into speech. 'Hardly.'

'That's one of the things I always liked about you,' said Quintin. He leaned forward slightly in his upright chair, like an inquisitor. Mara was suddenly struck by the difference between Quintin and Nollie. They were both big men, but Nollie's bulk seemed comfortable, almost jolly, an expression of his enjoyment of life, while Quintin's was unsettling, a grotesque disguise. To be liked by Quintin, to be complimented by him, was somehow soiling.

'What do you mean?'

Quintin smiled. 'You never agreed with me just to keep the peace.'

'And Alys?' If she could just keep him on the subject of her daughter there was a chance he would let something slip.

Quintin pursed his lips. Meditatively he stroked the scar on the back of his left hand, then looked up at her with his lightless eyes.

'I have to tell you that your daughter has been a great disappointment to me. A great disappointment.'

The sudden fury in his tone took Mara aback. She played for time.

'She is very young.'

'Dull.' Quintin spat out the word like a curse. 'Dull, and always complaining. It was a mistake to marry her.'

Mara gritted her teeth. 'Then why did you? To revenge yourself on me?'

'Perhaps.' Quintin moved restlessly. 'I can no longer remember. She wanted to be married. It doesn't matter now.'

Disbelief coursed through Mara like liquid fire. 'She wanted it?'

'Of course.' Bitterness rang in Quintin's voice. 'All women want is marriage and children, children and marriage. Except you, Mara.' Suddenly his voice was fretful. 'You. You never disappointed me, not once, even at the end.' Mara watched in astonishment as his head dropped forward onto his chest as if it had suddenly become too heavy for him to carry. 'I thought if I had Alys it would be the same as having you. But it wasn't.'

Quintin's head rolled. Now his gaze was unfocused, his voice a barely audible mumble. 'No one has ever understood me, no one has ever let me be what I want. Except you, Mara. You never judged me. With you I never had to pretend.' His hands twitched on his wide lap, swollen hands, beautifully manicured still, but the hands of an ageing baby. 'I had my dreams, Mara. You knew what they were, you helped me. No one else has ever helped me. No one else has ever let me be myself.'

Suddenly Quintin's whole body began to quiver, and with a

shock Mara saw that he was crying, tears rolling away over the smooth globes of his cheeks to disappear in the rolls beneath his chin. 'I have been plundered, Mara!' Quintin's voice issued high and small from his huge bulk. 'Look how I have been used and plundered! Everything I wanted has been taken from me! Oh, my children!'

Mara's eyes widened in amazement. 'Children, Quintin? What do you mean?'

Words came spilling out of him between the blubber of his cheeks, half whisper, half wail. 'The Regent Street women, they ruined me, and then the doctors cured me, but after the mercury I could have no more children, so now I have no children, not a single one. More money than I could ever spend, but no children. You'll never know what that's like, Mara, it's worse than anything in the world.'

Mara groped to make sense of what she was hearing. Quintin, locked in his misery, seemed scarcely aware of her presence. The muscles of his face jerked and twitched as if he was in a nightmare.

'But you do have a child, Quintin. You have Hugo.'

Quintin's heavy head lifted for a second; his eyes glared. 'Don't you understand, Hugo isn't my child! I was deceived, Mara, deceived! Sibell cheated me! I should have guessed from the beginning, she was so quick to marry me, but I wanted so much to do the right thing, to be accepted, oh Mara, I have suffered so long. All these years, I told no one, there was no one who would understand, only you, Mara, and you went away, and then there was Alys, and I thought she could be mine, that I could make her mine, but it was no good Mara, no good at all, and when I told her there would be no children she left me too, and now they've all gone, all the pretty little things, they won't stay with an old man, a fat old man who's eaten all his children.' Quintin buried his face in his hands and rocked to and fro.

Mara took a step towards him. Suddenly he reminded her

overwhelmingly of Alys as a baby, riven by nameless grief, the torment of living.

Quintin rocked faster, keening. 'I deserved better, Mara, I know I did. I have always tried to do the proper thing. I have always paid my way. I have never cheated any one. But I have not even a child, a child of my own. I would have given everything for that, everything. Do you believe me, Mara?' He lifted a hopeful tear-stained face, bleared with grief like a melting candle.

'I believe you.'

Mara turned away. She felt as if a great weight was pressing on her chest. Looking back she could no longer be sure what it was exactly that Quintin had done that was so terrible. To be unlikeable, to be unlucky, those weren't crimes. People had feared Quintin because of his temperament, sensing in him the darkness they most feared in themselves. That had been Quintin's fate all his life, to be a dark mirror from which people turned away in horror.

Suddenly an image of Quintin on *L'Aiglon Bleu* after she'd broken off their engagement swam into Mara's mind. She saw the razor flash in his hand as he rifled through her clothes repeatedly, examining their labels, hurling them away, picking them up again with a crazed, fanatical thoroughness. She'd wondered then what he could be looking for; evidence, perhaps, of betrayal.

But now, at last, Mara realized what he'd been doing. He'd been trying to make absolutely sure that he slashed into ribbons only those clothes which he himself had paid for.

Now, in the huge mirror above the fire, Mara could see her own face reflected and beyond it the pale crumpled mass of Quintin, slumped in his chair. She saw the two of them together in the vast empty room, and somehow, held in the mirror's impersonal embrace, what separated them seemed less than what they held in common. In the end, it was only the past that remained, and a large part of that, good and bad, they had shared. In the dim light of the Napoleon suite, if she half closed her eyes, Mara could choose to remember Quintin as she'd known him fifteen years ago, before the Devil's Door, when somehow she'd felt responsible for him, like the keeper of a particularly unpredictable savage dog.

Everyone must have a place, Mara thought suddenly. Everyone must have somewhere to belong. Quintin has tried to build his own, a monstrous cathedral of flesh.

For another long moment she hesitated, and then the clock on the mantelpiece before her began to strike into the darkness, long, melodious, fluting tones.

Midnight, the great eraser.

There must be no more enemies, Mara thought. The whole tangle we have made, Quintin and Leo and Sibell and I, we made between us. Sibell should never have married him; that was the beginning. Because of that, Leo lost Sibell, and I lost Leo, and maybe Alys too.

But Quintin can still have Hugo. If I decide. If I decide.

And then it seemed as if Sibell Lavery herself, who once was Sibell Gifford, slipped silently into the room. Mara saw her in the mirror of her mind's eye, wearing her cream gown and blue cloak. She raised her hand once, in acknowledgement or benediction, and then, like a shadow, she was gone.

Mara leaned forward towards the mirror, pulled into the swell of the figure's passing like a dream. But there was nothing there but the dim glass and her own reflection.

Embers popped in the grate. The fire was dying down.

'I have something to tell you, Quintin,' Mara said, and her breath pearled on the cool glass.

The Brûleur des Loups, a small café in the seedy Opera quarter of Marseilles, had only one distinction, apart from its unusual name: it had two doors, one leading into the square outside, one into a side street.

At five o'clock on an October afternoon the interior of the café was almost empty, apart from a small group of shabbily dressed men hunched over their glasses at a corner table. They glanced up as Mara sat down, and one, a young man with red-rimmed eyes and a wispy moustache, rose to his feet and approached her.

'Did you find your daughter, *madame?*' he asked politely, in the Marseillaise twang, made more nasal by the beginnings of a head cold.

Mara nodded. She placed the crocodile-skin valise carefully on the chair beside her.

'That is a fine valise, *madame,*' the young man volunteered.

Mara nodded again. 'It belonged to my daughter.'

The young man smiled. 'And she has given it to you. *C'est gentil, ça.*'

Very steadily, Mara lifted her cup. The dark liquid in it seemed to have no heat or taste. She felt as if she would never be warm again.

'But she was only eighteen!' Mara heard again her own voice, laying logic before the French doctor as if somehow it could reverse history. It should not have happened, therefore it could not have happened.

'It happens. Her resistance was very low. When your daughter arrived here at the hospital, *madame*, she was already severely weakened.'

'What do you mean?'

'*Vous ne saviez pas?*' He shrugged. '*La morphine, madame. Elle en avait l'habitude.*'

All Alys had had left by the time she'd been admitted to hospital suffering from pneumonia had been the clothes she was wearing and a crocodile-skin valise, the unofficial badge of the Riviera *fille de joie*.

At first Mara had refused to believe that the nameless girl the authorities had buried on a hillside just outside Marseilles could have been her daughter. The city was full of people without documents: refugees from the war just over the border in Spain, *contrebandiers*, petty criminals on the run. The girl under the dry yellow mound of earth couldn't possibly be Alys. Mara had the address of the Brûleur des Loups to prove it.

Quintin had given it to her after she'd finally convinced him that Hugo was really his son. He'd found the address on a piece of paper crumpled up in the waste basket in Alys's dressing-room. 'Justice,' he'd mumbled as he handed over the precious piece of paper, moments before lapsing back into a drowsy stupor. 'An eye for an eye. A daughter for a son.'

Mara had found no one at the café who had seen or heard from Alys, but she'd taken that as a hopeful sign. Only two weeks had gone by since her daughter had left Paris for Marseilles. Mara was sure that sooner or later Alys would be bound to come to the café to contact whoever she'd arranged to meet there. Alys had no money of her own, no other friends. She was bound to come.

Mara had sat at the same table every day, sure that at any moment Alys would walk in through the door.

Then, this morning at the hospital, they'd shown her the crocodile-skin valise, and inside it, grimy round the neckline but folded with loving care, had been Alys's peony-pink wrapper with the swansdown trimming, the one she'd been wearing at breakfast the morning Mara left for Berlin.

'Such a beautiful girl, in her photograph,' the young man went on wistfully, wiping his eyes with a dingy handkerchief, and suppressing a sneeze.

For some reason, at the sight of his watering eyes, Mara felt tears prick treacherously at the back of her own. She hadn't cried at the hospital, when they'd shown her the swansdown wrapper; she hadn't cried beside the mound of yellow earth, cracked and dusty under the mignonette and white roses she'd brought from Marseilles. Those had been occasions too terrible for tears. But now she felt her self-control falter. She shouldn't have come back to the café, she knew that now.

335

'*Vous aussi, vous souffrez, hein?*' said the young man nasally through his handkerchief, and nodded with understanding.

His unexpected sympathy, misplaced though it was, melted the last of Mara's self-control. Her eyes spilled over, and she found herself crying for Alys, and the muddy coffee, and the young man's pitiful effort at an adult moustache, all at once. She dug out a handkerchief from the pocket of her costume and she and the young man, strangely companionable, mopped and sniffed together.

'Thank you, *monsieur*.' He blushed with pleasure as Mara held out her hand to him. Their fingers had barely touched when the street behind them outside erupted into noise as suddenly as if someone had dropped a giant accordion. Engines roared, brakes squealed, doors slammed in a fusillade, followed by a clatter of boots, shouts, and then, instantly recognizable to Mara from shooting weekends with Nollie, the crack and spit of gunfire.

Instinctively, she ducked her head. Between one volley and the next her companion melted away through the side door.

Before Mara could follow him the main entrance door hurtled open. A man dressed in workman's overalls and a faded cap plunged across the room and out through the side door. Seconds after his disappearance the café filled with armed police.

Mara hesitated no more. If ever there was a moment to scream, this was it. She opened her mouth wide. Into that scream she put all her grief and frustration, all her scorn for uniforms and guns and regulations, all her longing for Alys, and the noise she made stopped all thought.

The *carabiniers* skidded to a halt. The barman dropped the glass he was polishing with a crash. The men at the corner table hurled back their chairs with oaths.

All eyes swung round to Mara.

'Thank God!' she gasped, thinking fast. 'That man, oh, that man!' She pressed her handkerchief to her mouth. 'I was so frightened, *messieurs*! My poor little valise, he would have stolen it,

I know it!' She clutched the crocodile-skin to her bosom. 'Thank God you came in time!'

'Which way did he go?'

Mara looked dismayed. '*Oh monsieur! Je suis navrée!* I was so frightened that I closed my eyes! Such a man, *un vrai monstre*, you have no idea—'

The *carabinier* cut her short. 'You! Out of the way!'

The barman, who'd been standing in front of the side exit, obliged with a shrug. The police wrenched open the door and poured through. Mara heard their boots pounding into the street outside.

She snatched up the valise and fled. Her hired Renault was parked in the side street. As she started the engine she could hear other police vehicles arriving in the square; a whole cowardly army of authority mustered against one man. How many minutes had she gained for the fugitive, one, two? She'd acted out of pure instinct. All her sympathy had been with the man who ran. One way or another, she'd been running all her life. But the last thing she wanted was to be held for questioning in a Marseilles gaol.

Three hundred yards from the Hotel Colbert Mara heard a rustle of movement from the back of the car. Before she could turn her head a hand fastened round her throat from behind and cold metal pressed against her temple.

'Keep driving,' said a guttural Marseillais voice in her ear. 'That is, if you want to live.'

An electric shock of pure terror shot through Mara's body. She'd thought, until this moment, that with Alys dead she didn't care whether she lived or died. Now, with a jolt of intense physical certainty, she realized that despite everything she still cared very much indeed.

The hard hand round her neck was making her head pound and her vision spin. 'If you want me to drive,' she coughed out with difficulty, 'you'll have to let me breathe.'

The noose round her neck slackened. Mara gasped for air.

'Don't look round,' ordered the voice harshly. 'Drive on.'

Now, after the first shock, Mara felt a surge of desperate exhilaration. One against one. Those odds had always suited her.

'Where to?'

'The station.'

As she neared the station Mara found herself driving slower and slower, aware that these might be the last streets, the last human faces she would ever see. How could she ever have thought she hated Marseilles? Now it looked like Paradise.

But the approach road to the station was blocked by *paniers de salade*, the forecourt swarming with uniformed *gendarmes*.

'Goddamn!'

The expletive nearly rocketed Mara from her seat. Her hands slipped on the wheel and the car swerved madly, nearly unseating a cyclist. Mara straightened up with an effort. For the first time since she'd discovered an armed man in the back of the car she risked a glance into the rearview mirror. Her passenger had wedged himself well back against the padded far corner of the back seat, and because of the cap he was wearing she could only make out the lower half of his face – but even under a layer of grime there was no mistaking that long chin, that familiar mouth. Mara's heart thundered with a Wagnerian mixture of elation and pure relief.

'Leo!' She'd never been so glad to see anyone in her life.

There was a pause, then she saw Leo's mouth tighten. He glanced down and Mara heard, oddly distinct against the hum of the engine, a small, silken click that chilled her. She knew enough to recognize the sound of a safety catch being applied. Leo, even though he must have known who she was as soon as she entered the car, had been prepared to shoot her in cold blood.

'Yes.' It was a flat statement. Leo's voice sounded quite different from her memory of it; hard and dismissive. Mara's relief faded.

'Why were you running away?'

Leo laughed out loud, a short, hard sound.

'Let's say – a small difference of opinion.'

'With the police?'

Leo shrugged. 'The police are only an instrument.'

'Don't tell me any more,' Mara said suddenly. She couldn't explain the sudden sense of dread she felt. How well did she know Leo, after all? She hadn't seen him for six years. A man could change a great deal in that time.

Mara felt suddenly alone, more alone than she'd felt before she went into the Brûleur des Loups. She gripped the wheel tight.

'That's a terrible cap you're wearing.'

Her attempt at lightness fell on deaf ears. Leo's expression didn't change; his face wore the uniform of preoccupation.

'Petrol. How much have you?'

Mara glanced down. She considered lying, but decided against it. 'Half a tank.'

Leo thought for a moment.

'Outside Marseilles, head for the Spanish border.'

Mara felt a shiver of dismay.

'Won't the police be watching for you?'

'Not where we're going,' answered Leo cryptically.

Mara felt suddenly exasperated. If she was going to take her life in her hands she wanted to know the reason.

'What on earth have you done, Leo?'

Another laugh, ghostly this time. 'A bit of this, a bit of that. You know how it is.' The finality in his voice told her he wouldn't say any more.

From that moment Mara drove in silence, and as fast as she could without drawing attention to the car and its occupants. She followed the winding coast road towards the Spanish frontier, and then, just before they reached Cerbère, Leo directed her to turn due west, into the blood-red remains of the setting sun and the foothills of the Pyrenees.

It was almost dark now, and cold, and Mara realized she was very hungry. She hadn't eaten since yesterday. Preoccupied with her hunger, she forgot to keep an eye on the petrol indicator.

Somewhere along the ribbed, rutted track leading up into the mountains the Renault began to cough and splutter and Mara felt an explosion of panic. Half a shuddering kilometre later the engine cut out completely.

The silence after the car stopped seemed endless. There was no birdsong, no stir of wind. The darkness was profound.

'Leo?' Mara whispered. No answer came from the back of the car. Perhaps he'd fallen asleep. Perhaps, Mara thought suddenly, disorientated by fatigue and hunger, perhaps both of them were asleep and dreaming, and none of this was real. Any moment now she'd wake up at Derby Street.

But the darkness was real, a pulse of blackness beyond the glass.

'Turn off the lights,' came a harsh command from the back of the car.

Mara did so. With the lights off the darkness seemed to edge a pace nearer, like a large animal emboldened. Mara pulled her jacket closer round herself. Her teeth were chattering with cold.

'Get in here,' ordered Leo from the back seat.

Silently, Mara obeyed. In the darkness she could barely see Leo's face, only the glitter of his eyes. She was aware of a strong smell of cheap brandy. She tried hard to make out where he'd put the gun but failed.

'Here. Drink.' Leo passed her a metal flask. Mara took a swig, the cold edge clattering against her teeth, then gasped as molten heat ran down her throat.

'So. No more driving tonight.' Leo slid across the seat towards her. The smell of brandy intensified: he must have spilled it on his clothes. Mara's heart lurched. What did he mean, no more driving? He made it seem so – final.

She reached for words to put between herself and that finality.

'What are you going to do?'

Leo paused. Mara heard rather than saw him frowning.

'Wait till dawn, then cross the border. I know the way.'

'What about me?' Mara asked. Her mouth was dry; the brandy lay in her empty stomach like a pool of fire.

'You.' Leo paused. Mara was aware of his breathing, harsh, rapid, completely at odds with the calmness of his tone.

'You could leave me here,' she suggested brightly.

Leo nodded. 'I could do that.' The leather upholstery creaked as he reached forward with his right hand and grasped the collar of her jacket. He seemed suddenly very large in the cramped confines of the back seat. Into Mara's mind's eye flashed a sudden image of her favourite jacket, with its leopardskin facings, sodden and matted with blood. She felt a ridiculous impulse to ask if she could take it off first.

Then Leo was too close for her to ask him anything. He pulled her towards him and before she knew it his tongue, hot and hard and tasting of brandy, was in her mouth. She gave an involuntary gasp of protest and then, quite simply, every other thought left her mind. There was no room for fear or death or danger; the only reality was the warmth of her mouth filled with his mouth, her breath taken by his breath.

Leo pulled away from her at last and wiped his mouth with the back of his hand. Mara felt herself drop from his grasp like a rag doll.

'And now, Mara Mizen,' he said, and his voice was like a pistol-shot. 'Tell me what the hell you were doing in the Brûleur des Loups.'

'I take it you don't trust me.' Mara felt a flare of anger at the injustice of it. She'd practically saved his life back there in the café, and not for the first time either.

'Why should I?' he answered curtly. 'The last time I heard, you were an official guest of the German government in Berlin. We're on opposite sides, you and I, Mara. Perhaps we always have been.'

In that moment the memory of the last twenty-four hours swept over Mara with the suddenness of an avalanche. The small warmth

341

of her anger faded away and she was left cold and empty. There were no more sides worth taking, no more roles to play.

'I'll tell you why I was there,' she said at last into the darkness. 'I was there because of Alys.'

Leo listened in silence as Mara told him about the crocodile-skin valise and the swansdown wrapper and the little yellow grave.

When she'd finished he said nothing. He appeared to be waiting for something else. Mara couldn't imagine what it could possibly be. Her imagination was as exhausted as the rest of her. It didn't matter anyway. Alys was dead.

When Leo spoke at last it seemed to be at a tangent.

'You're a strange woman, Mara.'

In any other circumstances Mara would have taken it for a flirtatious remark; now she couldn't follow his thinking at all.

'Am I?' she said wearily, her mind fogged by loss.

'I don't understand you. I never have.'

'There's nothing to understand,' said Mara. She'd always been too busy to think much about herself. Now she wondered if it might have made a difference. Perhaps she could have made something, with thinking, to protect herself against this pain.

'I don't know.' Leo seemed to be debating something in his mind. 'I still don't know.'

He turned to her suddenly. 'Did you love your daughter?'

It seemed suddenly then as if he was offering Mara something, and yet she couldn't accept it. She was too raw, it would hurt too much. Instinctively, she evaded.

'What kind of question is that?'

'The Spanish call death the moment of truth,' Leo answered levelly.

'You want the truth?' Mara felt herself shudder on the brink of a terrible temptation. Like a hurt dog, she wanted to bite the first person who came too near, just to share the pain.

'Of course.' Leo's voice was stern.

Mara's head began to throb. She felt a sudden overpowering urge to burn up everything, all the lies and half-truths. She seemed to see Alys, peering wide-eyed at her through the third-floor banisters, waiting for her to appear in her latest costume, as a jockey, a clown, the Pied Piper, Nefertiti. The time was past for masks and disguises. Alys would have the truth now, with all honour, no matter what the cost. It was the only thing Mara could still give her; a Viking funeral, with fire.

'She was your daughter.'

There was a long silence. Mara heard Leo expel his breath in a sigh that seemed to come from the bottom of the earth. Then he reached out with one long arm and pulled her towards him. With her head buried against his cotton jacket Mara could hear his heart racing, strong and wild as a drum.

'You're never going to forgive me for this, Mara,' he said.

'But I don't understand. What about the swansdown wrapper?' Mara didn't know whether minutes had gone by or hours. She was drunk, dazed, remade. She felt as if she were flying.

'Alys sold most of her clothes in the first week. She needed money to live on till I came. She wrote to me a month ago, in San Sebastian, asking me for help. I had no idea then she was my daughter, but I came anyway, just as soon as I could get across the border.'

'Why?'

Leo pulled her closer. Mara leaned into his arms. It was like stepping into the heart of the sun.

'You shouldn't have to ask that. She was your daughter. Anyway, I had business to attend to.'

'What kind of business?'

'Come on, Mara. There's a war on. The French government is against us; someone has to beat the blockade. That's why I gave Alys the address of the Brûleur des Loups, in case she needed to contact me in a hurry. It's one of our rendezvous points.'

'But where is Alys now?'

'In hiding in a little village in the Ardèche. She was worried Quintin might try to find her before the baby's born.'

'Baby?' Mara sat up in shock. 'What baby?' She half expected Leo to produce an infant from under his jacket, like the statue of Hermes rescuing the infant Dionysus that Quintin had taken her to see in the British Museum.

'Quintin's, I assumed. She's four months' pregnant. Isn't that why she married him?'

'But it can't be Quintin's. He's not able to father children, he told me so himself.'

They stared at each other in the darkness of the car; never had two parents felt more in the dark.

'No wonder Alys had to leave Quintin,' Mara said at last. 'He'd have been furious once he found out. But if Quintin isn't the father, then who is?'

'She was in love with Hugo,' Leo volunteered helpfully. 'That's partly why she married Quintin, she told me. Some disappointment over Hugo.'

'Hugo!' Mara breathed. 'Of course! He was in London in June, Vi told me.'

Suddenly Leo began to laugh. 'No wonder Alys wanted the baby to be such a secret!'

'What do you mean? If she'd told me Hugo was the father I would have welcomed it! Anyone would have been better than Quintin!'

Leo laughed and laughed till his eyes watered and the Renault rocked on its suspension.

'But don't you see? An illegitimate baby – after making such a fuss about her own parentage, Alys could hardly come straight home and admit to an illegitimate baby of her own! She's very proud, our daughter. I can't imagine where she gets it from.'

'And she never told you you were her father?'

Leo shook his head, his voice still brimming with merriment. 'I think – I think she wanted to interview me first!'

'Oh my,' Mara said. Such effrontery. She was beginning to feel more than a little in awe of her daughter.

'Or maybe she found out I was Jewish.'

'Are you?'

'Of course. Quintin knew. He hated me on sight, do you remember?'

'Of course, the pieces of silver! Is Alys Jewish, then?'

'Only if she wants to be.'

'And she's not a drug-taker? Even after being with Quintin?'

Leo shook his head. 'She told me she tried it once, but it made her feel sick. And she didn't want to end up looking like Quintin.'

Mara held on tight to his jacket. Her mind was reeling but there was something that needed saying.

'Do you realize what this means?'

'It means you're a grandmother,' said Leo wickedly. 'And so young too!' He seized her face in both hands and planted an unshaven kiss first on one cheek then on the other. They were both trembling like children, with shock and cold and excitement. But Mara knew she mustn't let herself be carried away.

'Yes, I'm a grandmother.' She took her courage in both hands. 'And so is Sibell.'

Leo released her. 'Sibell.' Suddenly his voice sounded very young. 'I hadn't thought of it like that.'

Mara felt her throat constrict. After all this time, Sibell still mattered to him. It was almost as if she were still alive.

'I wasn't going to tell you this,' Leo went on, 'but when Alys was at her lowest ebb, trapped in the Ritz with Quintin and missing Hugo, she thought of doing away with herself. Thinking of Sibell stopped her. It was after that that she wrote to me for help. And come to think of it,' Leo went on, running a hand through his hair and sounding bemused, 'if it hadn't been for Sibell, Alys would probably never have been born in the first place.'

'Are you suggesting that Sibell is the mother of our daughter?' said Mara, incensed.

'Of course not.' Leo began to laugh again and pulled her back towards him. 'I'm just saying that neither of us was exactly ready for parenthood at the time.'

'I'm glad,' said Mara, with as much goodwill as she could muster. She'd had enough of Sibell as the heroine of the piece. Now, having thought of telling Leo about her vision of Sibell in the mirror in the Napoleon suite, she decided against it. She'd tell him one day.

Maybe.

But there was one more thing Leo must be told about Sibell.

'I think I know why she died, Leo.'

Leo's tone changed, became almost curt. The laughter faded like mist.

'So do I. I've had plenty of time over the last six years to think about what you said at the White City. You were right. Sibell killed herself because she couldn't choose between me and Quintin. If it hadn't been for me, she'd still be alive.'

'No.' Mara knew she had to tell him while confession was in the air, before better judgement took over. 'It wasn't your fault at all.'

Bluntly, because she hadn't had much practice with the plain truth recently, she told Leo about the disease Sibell must have caught from Quintin before the Great War.

'It's the only explanation that makes sense. When Sibell found out what she had, she couldn't bear to bring that to you as her dowry. She loved you too much. Don't you see? That letter she sent you was meant to set you free.'

There was a long pause. When Leo spoke again there was a note in his voice that Mara hadn't heard for a long time. It was as if he'd just set down the receiver after a long-distance call and was back in the same room with her again.

Mara felt a ragamuffin leap of the heart. She'd done right to tell him. The dice had fallen her way at last.

'You wouldn't have done that, Mara.'

She shook her head.

'You'd have made do.'

'That's true.'

'So where does that leave us, Mara?'

'In a situation of some discomfort,' Mara answered gamely. She had no idea even what time it was; certainly it was getting colder and colder. She and Leo had to hold each other just to stop themselves shaking.

'We may have to get married,' said Leo into the top of her head.

'Why, are you pregnant?' Mara asked into the warm folds of his shirt, and was rewarded by a tremor of silent laughter.

'We're grandparents, for God's sake, we have to set an example!'

Marriage, the great thresher and shredder of souls, Mara thought. But with Leo marriage was hardly the issue. By this time, it was too late for them ever to be free of each other; they were each other's hundred-year-eggs.

'Do you think, if we do, Alys will marry Hugo?' Mara hazarded. 'I'm sure he loves her. I'm afraid he rather likes men too, but perhaps he'll grow out of it?'

'Always the optimist.'

Now a cool grey light, so faint it was hardly worthy of the name, was beginning to dilute the blackness outside the car. Perhaps there's going to be a marvellous dawn, Mara thought, with picture palace peaks and glorious colours, and Leo and I will remember this as the most romantic episode of our lives. She waited, pressed against him as if they were one person, for the sun to discover them and make its declaration.

But it wasn't to be. Instead, between one minute and the next, Leo sat up and said abruptly, 'I must go. I have to get back across the border before first light.'

Mara, with his warmth scissored away, felt suddenly bereft.

Leo looked at her, trying for the last time to see her as other people saw her. In the bleak half-light her vivid face was dulled, but her eyes were bright as a knife-blade seen through water. She seemed at once new and familiar, like an image in a dream. He'd never been able to fix her in his mind; young and old, urchin and witch, empress and beggar, she refused to be distilled.

Every artist has to be a good whore, he thought suddenly. That's what art is: the ability to choose the moment, pick its pockets, force it to yield up every last grain of gold. What he'd recognized in Mara from the beginning was his own vision, the force of creation, naked and ruthless: life climbing up the ladder of itself. Loving Sibell had been easy; loving Mara was like stumbling barefoot across a rocky plain. He had never come to the end of her, and now, he realized, he never would, because if that moment came, if the circle was broken, if the burning dragon lost his grip on his own tail and fell wailing into chaos then the world itself would end.

Hats in the fire, then, Mara, he toasted her silently. To the freedom of the fire.

'You realize I may be killed,' said Leo.

Mara nodded. 'I'd rather you stayed alive,' she said.

'That's the most I'm going to get from you, isn't it?'

'That's all there is,' she said. 'It's the secret.'

Leo shook his head slowly, half-smiling, and the look in his eyes was all for her. 'Still no food in the house, Mara? Better stock up before I come home.'

Then he was gone, with a rattle of stones, and she was alone.

Mara had no idea how long she waited, numb, for sunrise to turn the rocky peaks to golden spires and minarets, but it didn't happen. The day simply began, grey and matter-of-fact. Clearly, Mara thought, she wasn't going to have anything made up to her.

In which case she would make it up to herself. She fished in her handbag for her scarlet lipstick. She hadn't worn it since she'd learned about Alys's death; now it seemed like an old friend. In fact, almost good enough to eat.

Mara restrained herself from devouring it wholesale and applied a careful layer, feeling for her lips in the dim light as she'd learned over the years, familiar with the geography of her body in a way no man could ever be. Men had so much else on their minds, ideals, and theories, and women. She'd always liked them for that.

Slowly then, stiff with cold and missing Leo very much, Mara clambered out of the Renault. The air was sharp as spirits of salts. Steely sky, a rocky path. Up which, she saw now, teetering on ballerina legs in the grey light, came a very small donkey and a boy.

Quickly Mara reached into the front of the car and took out the crocodile-skin valise. She waited till the boy, open-mouthed, his breath misting the chilly air, drew level with the Renault. He was wearing a large flat black beret and, despite the cold, open-toed sandals.

'*Pour vous*,' Mara said, with a beguiling scarlet smile, holding out the valise and hoping she was still in France. The boy's face broke into delight.

Five minutes later Mara, astride the donkey, observed that the crushed velvet of the back of its ears was softer even than the fabric of the ostrich feather hat which had begun her ascent up a different kind of mountain more than twenty-five years ago.

I would die for a cup of coffee, she thought, as the path began to wend downwards. Coffee, croissants, and Alys, in that order. One needed to be at one's best to confront a pregnant daughter newly returned from the grave.

No wonder I found her difficult, Mara thought, and smiled. She's just like me.

And then it came to her. Something to live for, something to die for. A city of dreams. Everybody had one, a longed-for destination, a spire on the horizon. Love, or freedom, or children, or fame. But mine, Mara realized with a shock of recognition, is the world, no more, no less. The literal, rocky, fiery, icy world.

Yes. She hoped with all her heart that Leo would come back safe from Spain. But if the worst came to the worst, she knew she would survive it. She was made for the world, it was her material. She'd always been able to see it as it was and find it good.

So it had been there all along, her golden city, not in the distance, but in the palm of her hand. She didn't have to own it. She simply had to let it be. In fact it wasn't possible to own it. Everything came out of the fire and went back into the fire. But in between, what a peacock's tail of colour to wonder at, all shades from dark to light.

Mara thought of Hugo, the other side of the world, ignorant of the drama that had played itself out around him; of Alys, realizing for the first time how practical pregnancy could make a woman; of Quintin, locked in his opium dream; of Vi and William, who would be astonished by a child begun, like a phoenix, out of ashes; of Lucette and her secret of eternal youth; of Leo, with one ideal restored to him, ready to risk everything in the battle for another; of Alys's unborn baby, with more grandparents than any mortal child could possibly expect; and finally of Sibell, who had died long ago but whose presence seemed to reach out across the years with the fragrance of violets. This is what Sibell would have wanted, Mara thought with faint surprise. She would have wanted a happy ending. As if we've all been figures in her dream.

But this was no ending. This was a beginning.

Stones crunched under the donkey's diminutive hooves and the boy began to sing.